Mr. Penrose

William Williams: *Self-Portrait*
  (Henry Francis DuPont Winterthur Museum)

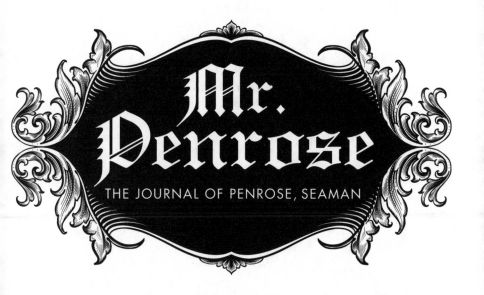

Mr. Penrose

THE JOURNAL OF PENROSE, SEAMAN

William Williams

INTRODUCTION AND NOTES BY
DAVID HOWARD DICKASON

AFTERWORD BY SARAH WADSWORTH

INDIANA UNIVERSITY PRESS

Bloomington & Indianapolis

This book is a publication of

Indiana University Press
Office of Scholarly Publishing
Herman B Wells Library 350
1320 East 10th Street
Bloomington, Indiana
47405 USA

iupress.indiana.edu

Telephone orders   800-842-6796
Fax orders   812-855-7931

First paperback edition 2013
© 1969 by Indiana University Press
All rights reserved

Manufactured in the United States of America

The Library of Congress has assigned the hardcover edition
the following LC control no.: 69016004

ISBN 978–0–253–01047–6 (pb)
ISBN 978–0–253–01052–0 (eb)

2   3   4   5   6   18   17   16   15   14   13

For
MARJORIE *and* CINDY
who shared my most pleasant
and rewarding year in England
in pursuit of the elusive
WILLIAM WILLIAMS
alias
Penrose

Contents

8 CONTENTS

Editor's Original Acknowledgments

The discovery of Williams' original manuscript and the preparation of this volume were made possible by a senior Fulbright Research Fellowship to England, and a concurrent sabbatical leave granted me by the Trustees of Indiana University. I should also like to thank both the Indiana University Foundation and the Office for Advanced Studies and Research for financial assistance.

I am obviously very grateful to Mr. David Randall, Director of the Lilly Library, for the acquisition of the manuscript from its English owner, and to the late Professor William Riley Parker, Chairman of the English Department of Indiana University, for vital support in the project.

Many persons in England contributed essential data, but I should like to acknowledge here the special kindness of Miss Elizabeth Ralph, City Archivist of Bristol; Frank Simpson, Esq., of London; Dr. and Mrs. John Eagles of Corsham; and Major and Mrs. Philip Graham-Clarke of Abergavenny, Wales, who directed me to key documents and ultimately to the manuscript of *Penrose*. Colonel John F. Williams of San Diego, genealogist of the Williams family in his *Fifty-Six Generations*, has been most generous in sharing information.

Illustrations

INTRODUCTION

I

A colonial American painter of portraits, conversation pieces, and symbolic landscapes who flourished in Philadelphia and New York—William Williams (1727–1791)—may now be identified as the author of one of our earliest novels, *Mr. Penrose,* or, as he subtitled it, *The Journal of Penrose, Seaman.* This narrative in point of composition is very probably America's first novel—that much argued and ever elusive phenomenon. It was first published in England in 1815, anonymously, posthumously, and in a completely restyled and bowdlerized form,[1] and has never been listed in any bibliographies of American fiction. Although Williams was born and died in Britain he may be counted an American by virtue of his thirty years of adult residence in this country; and his novel evidently was written during that period. A signal addition to our early national literature, *Mr. Penrose* is here printed from the original manuscript for the first time.

The saga of a Caribbean castaway in the Crusoe tradition (but varying widely from that prototype), *Mr. Penrose* is an absorbing tale of crisis and adventure against an exotic background, and of a man's efforts to formulate a viable personal philosophy, a *modus vivendi,* under adverse circumstances. A laconic first-person narrative, it employs the realistic mode in the meticulous reportage of scene and event, yet it is suffused with the spirit of high romanticism.

These qualities are evidenced in the account of a young Welsh lad,

Llewellin Penrose, who leaves an unhappy home for the lure of a privateer's life; and after imprisonment by the Spaniards at "the Havannah" is deserted by his shipmates on the Moskito Coast of Central America. Here he not only survives, but establishes amicable relations with the local Indians (evidently of the Rama tribe), and finds a shapely maiden of seventeen as his bed-partner (Luta, a "Green Grove," suggestive of an early Fayaway or Rima in her *Green Mansions*). With her he enjoys a tropical idyll, albeit in primitive circumstances, which is terminated by her death as she bears their second son. Her successor adds twins to Penrose's menage, of whom the girl is christened America.

Through the years his little community grows by accretion of Indian relatives and friends, shipwrecked Dutch and Scottish sailors, and an old Negro, the escaped slave Quammino. A child drowns, an Indian girl is killed in the jungle, and two violent deaths occur in a sailors' brawl. But Penrose and his people withstand the rigors of earthquake, hurricane, and fire, the depredations by *tigres* (wildcats), snakes, and other natural enemies, the threat of apprehension by the Spanish military, and the stringent limitations of a tiny self-contained society. After twenty-seven years on shore as the benevolent but firm-handed paterfamilias and regent of his little utopia, Penrose, having refused all opportunities to return to the pressures and self-seeking materialism of white civilization, dies among his adopted clan. His final request to his son is to dispatch his cherished Journal to safe hands in the English-speaking world.

II

There are, indubitably, some autobiographical echoes in this narrative. Born in Bristol, England, in 1727, no doubt the son of the "William Williams Mariner" entered in the *Bristol Burgess Book* of 1734,[2] young Williams attended the local Grammar School, but found that "his greatest delight was to go & see an elderly artist who painted heads in oil, as well as small landscapes"; and, as the eminent Benjamin West later recalled concerning the man who became his first

THE

JOURNAL

OF

LLEWELLIN PENROSE,

A

SEAMAN.

A NEW EDITION.

LONDON:

PRINTED FOR TAYLOR AND HESSEY,

93, FLEET-STREET,

AND 13, WATERLOO-PLACE, PALL-MALL.

MDCCCXXV.

Title Page of Second English Edition
(Vignette by Edward Bird, R.A.)

art teacher, "his greatest wish was to be a Painter; but in that he was disappointed."[3] No great scholar, he became an early drop-out; and as was the case with many boys from the school he was "put to the sea" by his parents. In the great tradition of Captain Woodes Rogers of Bristol, who brought Alexander Selkirk back from his Crusoe island, it would be pleasant to envisage the young adventurer voluntarily setting out to see the world, but this was not the case.

He signed on as an apprentice seaman in the Virginia trade under a Captain Hunter, who recalled many years later:

"When he was on board my ship I often remarked him engaged in drawing, & soon distinguished him to be a Boy of no common capacity, and it was my intention had he remained with me to place him in my Counting house at Norfolk, to better his situation in life."

But two decades later Williams himself admitted to his former master:

"After going the second voyage . . . when in Norfolk in Virginia—to tell you the truth—I left the ship & sailed for the West Indies, where I hoped to be unknown, that I might work my way to some places—& accomplish my wishes as a Painter:—and after some years had elapsed I was able to come to this city [Philadelphia]."

While Williams himself lived for two or three years at most in the Caribbean, his hero Penrose spent twenty-seven years in voluntary exile (Defoe similarly extended Selkirk's four years on Juan Fernández to Crusoe's twenty-eight). There is no categorical proof that Williams actually passed his castaway days with the Rama Indians of coastal Nicaragua (though he does declare elsewhere that he was "shipwreck'd"), for dozens of synthetic accounts were whipped up by resourceful eighteenth-century "Travel-liars." But as a contemporary reviewer argued:

The internal evidence is, on the whole, favourable we think to the authenticity of the story. Some of the traits of character are so *naive*, some of the impressions so natural, the whole course of the story so matter-of-fact, so utterly unlike a *made* tale, that, if it be a fabrication, it is to say the least, an uncommonly skilful one.[4]

Benjamin West, for one, was persuaded that the setting was authentic, and many of the earlier episodes autobiographical. But since the work is indeed a novel it is a moot point.

Benjamin West first met Williams in 1747, when Williams, then aged twenty but looking older than his years, had recently arrived in Philadelphia from the tropics. West, a precocious lad of nine, was visiting prosperous relatives in the city. Much impressed by the boy's promise, Williams lent him two books on art and took him on as pupil and protégé. Fifteen years after Williams' death, West wrote:

From the year 1747 to 1760, my attention was directed to every point necessary to accomplish me for the profession of painting. This often brought me to the house of Williams; and as he was an excellent actor in taking off character, he often, to amuse me, repeated his adventures among the Carribs and Negro tribes, many of which adventures were strictly the same as related in your manuscript of Penrose. . . . He spoke the Negro and Carrib tongue, and appeared to me to have lived among them some years.

And as recognition of his formative influence on his career West added: "Most undoubtedly, had Williams not been settled in Philadelphia I shd. not have embraced painting as a profession."

Under the sign of Hogarth's Head in Loxley's Court in Philadelphia Williams in the 1750's carried on his "Business viz. Painting in General," and since income was uncertain he likewise advertised "an Evening School for the Instruction of Polite Youth, in the different branches of Drawing, and to sound the Hautboy, German and common Flutes."[5] Both his versatility and economic necessity were demonstrated by his further role as America's first professional theatrical scene painter, for David Douglass as manager of the Hallam Company in the Southwark Theatre in 1759, and very probably in its successor in 1766.

In search of portrait commissions among the prosperous planters in "the West-Indies"—an area which revived memories of his vagabond days—Williams made an extended trip in 1760-61, as his intriguingly brief note indicates: "Pictures painted in Jamaica 54—." Shortly thereafter he became involved in another practical art in a situation that doubtless provided him with his pseudonym. Wrote West:

It has often occurred to me that Williams must have given the name of Penrose to his manuscript in compliment to a very great friend of his in Philadelphia of that name. Mr. Penrose was one of the most elegant ship builders in all America, or I believe to be found in Europe—And it was the painting, & ornamenting of his ships that was Williams' best employment. . . .

The Penrose family, from Bristol-born Bartholomew to Thomas and his son James, were indeed famous Philadelphia shipbuilders. Williams certainly knew both Thomas and James (who died at the age of thirty-three in 1771), and felt for them both a personal friendship and appreciation as employers and patrons in a successful enterprise.

Meanwhile, Williams (who perhaps had deserted an Indian mistress and half-caste son) had married "a respectable townswoman of our City," as his Captain (later Colonel) Hunter described her. Hunter also noted that he visited Williams "in his family" in 1755. Certain ambiguities remain, but since Williams in his will referred to "portraits of my two wives,"[6] it is probable that he was soon left a widower with two small sons, and that he promptly remarried. His second wife was the young Mary Mare, born about 1740, the sister of a New York artist, who bore him a son on November 17, 1759, appropriately christened William.[7] A newly discovered checklist of Williams' works does, in fact, contain the entry, "a small whole length of William Williams Junr Painter,"[8] and this boy grew up to be known as William Joseph Williams, the artist of the hard-jawed, unflattering *Masonic Washington* and many other portraits. Two sons by Williams' first marriage (but not the above William Joseph) died in the Revolution, for as West stated: "His sons being born in Philadelphia, they soon became attached to America & took up arms with thousands of other youths to join her Armies, & were killed in some of the battles."

By 1769 or before, Williams moved to New York City, where, under the sign of Rembrandt's Head in Batteaux Street, he again undertook "painting in general, viz. History, Portraiture, landskip, sign painting, lettering, gilding, and strewing smalt. N.B. He cleans, repairs, and varnishes any old picture of value, and teaches the art of drawing."[9]

Though his *Imaginary Landscape* and several portraits are extant from that period,[10] the stringencies of the approaching war years lessened the demand for even these varied artistic services. His wife Mary Mare had died after only four years of marriage, so Williams, once more alone and discouraged, made the crucial decision to leave New York. As West recorded it:

Mr. Williams finding himself advancing in years—& much dejected at the loss of his sons, & the revolution of families and things . . . availed himself of a friendly proposition made to him by an English gentleman returning from America, to embark with him for England—to reside under his roof in Bedfordshire, & to paint there for his amusement for the remainder of his life.

On their arrival in London in 1776 Williams sought out West, his now prominent ex-pupil (soon to be President of the Royal Academy), introduced his sponsor, then retired into the country in what would seem an ideal situation. But only eighteen months later his patron died, and Williams returned to his one friend in the metropolis—"He was frequently at my house," West recalled—and to his studio, where the first version of *The Battle of La Hogue* (1778) was in progress. Too proud to accept financial succor, Williams happily served as a model in that large marine composition: "I introduced a likeness of Williams in one of the Boats, next in the rear of Sir George Rook[e]."

The old artist diverted himself by collecting engraved portraits of painters; but after a year or two he drifted back to Bristol, where he attempted once more to set himself up in business, as attested by a professional card (now in the City Archives): "Williams, Portrait & Landscape Painter, No. 29 Clare Street, Bristol." With a resurgence of energy perhaps inspired by a monumental religious triptych by his much admired Hogarth in the St. Mary Redcliffe church, Williams produced and advertised for public exhibition at "the Mulberry Tree in Broad-Street" three large pictures "Representing the Birth, Death, and Burial of Our Saviour Jesus Christ," together with a "Variety of high-finished Pictures and Drawings in History, Landscape, &c. many of which are to be dispos'd of."[11] His local riverscape *Hotwells and Rownham Ferry* also dates from this period. His strong *Self-Portrait* was painted after he entered the Almshouse.[12]

During this time the lonely old man apparently married again, for his first will makes a bequest to "my Daughter in Law [i.e., step-daughter] Mrs Mary Byrchmore, the only Daughter of my Late Deceas'd wife Esther Williams," who evidently was a widow with a grown daughter when he married her. Documentary proof is lacking, but it seems probable that this marriage was contracted in England and that Esther died not long afterward, for Williams was solitary and defeated when he sought shelter through the aid of Thomas Eagles, an eminent Bristolian. On his request to obtain for him "a pass to St. Peter's Hospital" Eagles protested that it was "a wretched place . . . for the lowest paupers." Instead, Eagles provided tactful financial assistance and genuine personal hospitality to the old artist until in 1786 a place became available in the very comfortable Merchants' and Sailors' Almshouse in King Street, Bristol, sponsored by the august (and still active) Merchant Venturers' Society. In this safe haven the old mariner-painter-storyteller lived out his few remaining years.

III

Internal evidence strongly suggests that Williams worked on his long manuscript over many years, and carried with him from New York the essentially completed tale. A letter of transmittal at the conclusion (sent to an unnamed recipient by a Paul Taylor, mate of a brig at "the Havannah" to whom the Journal had allegedly been handed by two English-speaking Indians in 1776) is clearly a post-script to the main tale. Its final date-line is "New York May 2, 1783." This may, in fact, be considered the signature date as Williams, in Bristol, was about to hand over his manuscript to his benefactor Thomas Eagles for a twofold reason:

During the time I was out of employ at Charlestown, I took it into My head to Coppy it all out and send it You, as you live at this Time in London. I think it may be of some Service to you, and if So shall be proud of the little kindness I can render for the former services you have shewn me. If you do not get it soon Published I shall dispose of the Original at Philadelphia or New York. . . .

This seems to be a personal statement by Williams to his patron under a very thin fictional disguise. The indirectness is consistent with the subtlety of the writer's character; and without such an interpretation the device would be superfluous. In any case the Journal was complete when Thomas Eagles saw it shortly after the beginning of their friendship in the early 1780's.

As the chief friend of the indigent author, Eagles was so intrigued by the manuscript of *Penrose* that after Williams' death he presumed to recast it throughout (with numerous additions and deletions) in a syntactically correct, polite and conventional form, with the intention of making it more literary, more printable—but thereby destroyed much of its original vigor, color, and directness. A brief sampling will indicate typical editorial treatment. The situation is Penrose's proposal of marriage to his Indian sweetheart, with Luta's brother Ayasharre (Harry, for convenience) as chorus:

WILLIAMS	EAGLES
Harry . . . leaped at once on his feet, and taking Luta by the hand put it into mine, then he fell to Shouting, hollowing, Whooping, dancing and making his Obedience to us, after the manner I had learnt him—Crying, Eat it, Drink it, Eat it, drink it, catch it, have it, catch, get Luta, and thus he went on like one frantick with joy. All this time the Girl stood looking silently on the ground. I then gave Harry to know that I understood him well, shewing by my look, that I was pleased with his proposal, It being	Harry . . . leaped up at once on his feet, and taking Luta's hand, put it into mine; then fell to shouting, hallooing, whooping, dancing, and making his obedience to us, after the manner I had learnt him; and thus he went on like one frantic with joy. All this while the girl stood looking silently on the ground. I then made signs to Harry that I understood him well, and was pleased with his proposal.

| a matter I could by no means be against as She was a young Creture of so charming a disposition and so ready to administer her kind services on all necessary occasions.—I then asked Luta if she was willing to sleep with me, as having no other address wherby to convey my intimations of making her my Wife. . . . | Indeed, it was impossible to have any objection, as she was a young creature of so charming a disposition, and so ready on all occasions to administer every kind office in her power. I then asked Luta if she was willing to be my wife, explaining by signs what I meant. . . . |

Eagles then submitted his revised form to several London publishers, who were interested only in a true, documentary journal, not in "a work of mere imagination." Meanwhile, he had recorded in memo form some salient facts of Williams' career.

The Reverend John Eagles in due course inherited his father's library and papers, including both the original Penrose MS and its edited but still unpublished version. He then expanded Thomas Eagles' memoranda to serve as an "Advertisement" or preface to the rewritten *Journal* (appropriately dedicated to Benjamin West), and in 1815 placed it with John Murray in London as publisher for £200.[13] Walter Scott as editorial reader for Murray approved the narrative and found it a tale well and vividly told, with its theme and philosophical stance sympathetic to his own richly romantic tastes. Even Lord Byron reputedly had difficulty in restraining his enthusiasm:

I have never read so much of a book at one sitting in my life. He kept me up half the night, and made me dream of him the other half. . . . It has all the air of truth, and is most entertaining and interesting in every point of view.[14]

Following the London publication of Eagles' edition of *The Journal of Llewellin Penrose, a Seaman* in four volumes, a pirated German translation appeared two years later as *Der Neue Robinson, oder, Tagebuch Llewellin Penroses, eines Matrosen. Aus dem Englischen.*[15] Meticulous footnotes in German and Latin were added to provide the scientific names of all of Penrose's tropical plants and animals (another indication of Williams' accuracy in factual description). And in 1825 a further "refined" English edition in a shortened form, intended particularly "for the amusement and instruction of Youth," appeared in one volume.[16]

IV

Mr. Penrose in its narrative form and basic subject was not, of course, a newly invented genre. In the eighteenth-century British novel the pseudo- or semi-autobiographical travel narrative employing allegedly realistic details was a familiar and popular form. After the dramatization of Selkirk's career in *Robinson Crusoe* in 1719 numerous sequels soon appeared. These included Longueville's *The English Hermit, or the Unparalell'd and Surprizing Adventures of Philip Quarll* in 1727; *A Narrative of the Life and Astonishing Adventures of John Daniel,* presumably by Ralph Morris, in 1751; Paltock's *The Life and Adventures of Peter Wilkins,* in the same year; the pseudonymous *Travels of Mr. Drake Morris,* in 1755; Dibdin's *Hannah Hewit; Or, The Female Crusoe,* at the end of the century; and many other similar but less known works. Fielding and Smollett in particular were purveyors of novels of picaresque adventure, in the broad definition of that term; and the sentimentality of Richardson and his followers had widespread appeal and impact. A spate of presumably true travel accounts had appeared by such worthy adventurers as Captains Woodes Rogers, Edward Cooke, George Shelvocke, Lord Anson, the earlier William Dampier, and others, which offered copious notes on the New World. But except for a few very minor echoes or possible coincidences in descriptive detail, William Williams' story shows no signs of any eclectic influence of either British or American sources.

By contrast with the other early so-called novels found in this country, which are primarily religious or political allegories (Joseph Morgan's *History of the Kingdom of Basaruah,* 1713, or Hopkinson's *A Pretty Story,* 1774, for example), *Mr. Penrose* strikes one as a "genuine" fictional narrative rather than as a theological tract or patriotic propaganda. And spurning the saccharine and sentiment of such tenuous domestic tales and pseudo-biographies as Charlotte Lennox's *Life* the Journal of Penrose, Seaman.

If ever the following lines should reach my dear country,
the Reader is not to expect to meet with any persuasive
Arguments to enforce belief, or language to adorn
the Story, as the Author never received more learning
than what a common country School affords.
In the first place, I shall give the reader a faithful
Narrative of every occurrence within my memory,
form the day of my birth, unto the time I first left
my native shore, to cross the Atlantic.

Lewellin Penrose is my name. I was born near
Caerphilly in Glamorgan shire, in the month of
May, anno dom 1725. My father who was a Sailor,
was cast away in a Ship belonging to the city of Bristol,
called the Union Frigate commanded by a certain
Cap.t Williams, who was his own countryman, in the
great January storm, at the Texel in Holland,
where every soul perished of a fleet consisting of near
60 Sail of Vessels, only one Dutch Dogger which
lay without, riding it safe the whole time.
My Mother being left a Widow, with two children, (One
my self and a Sister five year younger, after a time,
married a School-master, and removed with him into
Worcestershire, thence into Monmouth shire and after
that into Wales. This man, I may justly remark, at
least in my own opinion, proved the innocent or rather
obstinate cause of many hardships I have since had to
undergone, as I shall ...

First Page of Williams' Manuscript
(Lilly Library)

of Harriot Stuart (1751), Edward Bancroft's *History of Charles Wentworth* (1770), Thomas Atwood Digges' *The Adventures of Alonso* (1775), Ann Eliza Bleecker's *History of Maria Kittle* (1781), and the anonymous *Amelia, or the Faithless Briton*—generally disclaimed as "American" because of the transient residence of their authors and typical use of European materials—*Mr. Penrose* stands out as uniquely engaging, direct, and full of the vigor of sea and shore; and it is peopled with individuals who arouse our interest and concern.

Throughout, the author's urge for verisimilitude is indeed as pervasive as that of Defoe; and this novel makes a signal contribution to realism in early American fiction in its presentation of setting, character, and event—but in an inherently romantic situation. Thus it differs sharply from the more familiar domestic-sentimental *The Power of Sympathy*, the satiric *Modern Chivalry*, and the Gothic *Wieland* of the years immediately following. The hitherto unrecognized "New Robinson," William Williams' *Mr. Penrose*, thus merits an eminent place in this seminal group of the earliest American novels.

Within the framework of his fictional *Journal* William Williams shows himself to be far ahead of his times in his themes, attitudes, and even certain basic episodes which would reappear in American letters, the later writers unaware that they had been thus anticipated, for no lines of direct influence can be discovered or claimed. From his untutored origins Williams ranged widely in his intellectual and social interests.

One such fundamental focus is on the romantic ideal of the "natural man," the virtues of the unspoiled, uncorrupted folk culture and *mores*, and therewith the concept of the escape of a white protagonist to a pastoral utopia. When a sardonic Irish sea-captain asked Penrose how it was possible for him to live so many years "among these dung-coloured Savages," the castaway curtly retorted that they had indeed proved themselves to be his "true and experienced friends"; he was so well content with his situation that he "would not of a choice change it"; and the "happy state of Innocency" in which they lived more than compensated for the lack of worldly, sophisticated contacts. Here

Williams (perhaps in Rousseau's train, though no evidence is extant that he had read him) antedates Freneau and Cooper in their stress on the virtues of their wilderness figures, and Melville's portrayal of his Polynesian natives before their corruption by European influence.

Williams likewise appears to be the first of our men of letters, with the exception of some of the historians of the early settlements, to deal sympathetically with the Indians of the western hemisphere, as Freneau in his poetry and Robert Rogers in his drama *Ponteach* would do shortly after the composition of *Penrose*, and Bryant, Cooper, and Simms at a later date.

In the *Journal* there is also a very vivid and empathic recreation of the old Negro Quammino's sad story of blood, the first antislavery propaganda in our book-length fiction. Beaten and branded by his white masters, with his two wives also victims of their brutality, he goes from his slave-ship to Cuba, Barbados, and Jamaica, then escapes to the safe haven of Penrose's little colony. The author's stance is clear. On querying the Negro if he had ever been Christianized, Penrose ponders his reply.

"What good would that have done me? . . . Would it have made the White men love me the better? No, no! Dont they Curse and Dam each other, fight, cheat and kill one the other? Black men cannot do anything Worse than what White men do. They go to Churches and Tell God they will never do harm to any people, and the same day they come out and Kill, Cheat and say Lies again. . . ."

Penrose silently puffs his pipe, for indeed, said he, "I had little to answer in behalf of my own colour, but I told him I believed him a much better man than many Thousands who call'd themselves Christians." A contemporary of John Woolman with his *Considerations on the Keeping of Negroes* (1754 and 1762), Williams here was many decades ahead of Uncle Tom.

On a more mundane level he offers a buried treasure sequence which Poe might indeed have known. While pursuing an iguana into a thicket not far from the beach an Indian boy finds a stoppered bottle. Penrose deciphers the enclosed piratical round robin and cryptogram (reproduced in the text), and succeeds in uncovering not only the bones of the unfortunate guardian of the treasure but a vast quantity of silver plates, candlesticks, cob dollars, and perhaps most memorably some solid silver chamber pots.

Also by coincidence one finds in *Penrose* a climactic scene that recalls the death of Captain Ahab through his challenge of the power and malevolence of Moby Dick and all that he symbolized. A late joiner of Penrose's community, the Scotsman Norman Bell, dares to pursue a school of killer whales, equipped only with his fragile *canoa* and hand harpoons and accompanied by two Indian youths. Penrose counsels against such pride and foolhardiness: "I thought it one of the most Presumptive undertakings Bell ever took in hand"—and feared "what dire effects the cursed undertaking Would work in the end." His prescience was tragically borne out, for on the return of the Indians they dolefully recounted Bell's frenetic excitement as he hurled the harpoon, then pursued his quarry until with one stroke of its tail the whale crushed the canoe and beat them all into the sea. Bell, though a fine swimmer, vanished in the melee, and they were certain that he had been killed as the canoe was split. Here Penrose's relationship to Bell obviously suggests that of Starbuck to Ahab; and the young Indians reporting the action parallel Ishmael as narrator of Ahab's demise. The overlay of symbolic significance may be less complex, but in the complete context the episode is both real and moving for the Scot, like the Yankee, dares to challenge egotistically a superior, ruthless, and impersonal force and dies for it.

It is of historical importance, too, to recognize Williams' early use in long fiction of speech peculiarities, dialects, and verbal mannerisms to distinguish and to characterize many of his persons—devices which were already current in brief newspaper pieces and which would become the stock in trade of nineteenth-century local colorists and humorists in both prose and verse. Williams' assorted Dutch, Spanish, Irish, and Scottish sailors and adventurers speak each in his unique tongue; the author also aptly phrases the broken English of his newly bilingual Indian friends. A careful reader will discover certain lapses, especially in long speeches which begin in the colloquial but taper off

An 18th Century Map of the Moskito Coast
(The British Museum)

into conventional forms. But the novel as a whole is enriched and enlivened by Williams' sensitivity to linguistic variations and his ability in echoing them.

His contributions to humor in the early American novel, abetted by this same technique in manipulating language, are also considerable. A frequent device is the employment of highly colored metaphoric phrases, as when Penrose in an early episode was trying to rescue a naked lady in distress in a Bristol boardinghouse. He went below to the fore-parlor to rouse some of the snoring tars, but might as well have spared himself the trouble: "They were all so snugly moored in Sot's Bay that it was out of my power to trip one of their anchors." Occasionally Williams rings an unexpected change on a familiar turn of words—as the source of his imposing treasure Penrose (said Captain Horgan) was a very fortunate man "to find Turtles that laid Silver Eggs." More specific devices are also incorporated, such as the deliberately exaggerated episode or tall tale. The "Royal Salute" by exploding Mexican jumping-beans which leaped quite out of their box, or the happy globe-fish allowing dolphins to toss him back and forth in a game of ball are cases in point.

This latter passage suggests another of Williams' experimental efforts in the domain of fiction. A pioneer nature writer with an observant and appreciative eye for both the flora and the fauna of his tropical habitat, he was as gifted a reporter as Melville would show himself to be in *Typee* and *Omoo*. The mangrove swamps, parasitic jungle figs, "cashoo" and cotton trees, wild limes, prickly pears, candlefruit, the "alloes" or century plant all vivify the landscape. Biological forms attract fuller description, from the reptilian "Guano's" (iguanas) and a vast variety of snakes, "centipeeds," and scorpions, to wild tapirs and "warees," *tigres* or "Wood cats," anteaters, turtles—a moonlight frolic on the beach is a charming scene as they ride the huge carapace of a sea-turtle into the surf—together with "barrow-cooters" or barracudas, rasp- and sting-rays, land crabs, flamingoes, iridescent tropical butterflies, and a hundred other creatures. As a contemporary reader of the restyled manuscript (before publication) asserted: "This narrative of *Penrose* . . . is fully equal in point of interest, and superior in point of information respecting some parts of Natural history, to the celebrated volumes of *Robinson Crusoe*."[17]

A stronger emotional—and at times sentimental—appeal is evident in the accounts of his domesticated zoo, which at first cheered Penrose in his loneliness and later diverted his domesticity. Among these early "animal stories" the most notable is the tale of a wild fawn reared as "Miss Doe" and trained to hunt iguanas by trampling them with her forefeet. When she is mortally clawed by a *tigre* Penrose reluctantly puts her out of her misery; and his wife can barely swallow a venison dinner which he insists on serving. A tamed fish-hawk named Yellow-bill becomes a presumptuous household figure. Luta, not fond of her husband's luxurious un-Indian beard, teaches a parrot to reiterate endlessly, "Cut it off, cut it off, cut it off!" But perhaps most touching is the sad saga of "Jockko," the pet monkey of Penrose's young son Owen. The boy had taught him to ride on the dog's back equipped with a miniature jockey-cap and whip. But one day when "His Imp-ship," as Penrose called him, mischievously upset a *yabba* of boiling water on the child, Penrose ordered the appealing little creature thrown into the lagoon with a stone tied to his neck.

Two other aspects of the *Journal* must be noticed briefly. Throughout the work, interwoven among the themes and moods already suggested, a reader finds expressed an attitude of calm acceptance of life's offerings, and a firm but gentle piety. With leisure for meditation on the sins of his youth (his friend Somer suggests that if they had had their pirate hoard as a privateer's prize in old England "it would all have been shared among Whores, Fidlers, Pipers and Publick Houses"), Penrose asserts that they must now "learn to live so that we may never be in dread of the day when God shall call us off." Henceforth he will rely on "leaving all to the divine will of God and making ourselves as cheerful every day as we could. . . ." Or in the more elevated mood of a biblical patriarch, inspired by the multiplicity and brilliance of tropical jungle life, Penrose ponders:

How manyfold are the Wonders of our Divine Creator when our Eyes behold these things. Should we not say: "In the Majesty of Thy Wisdom, O Lord, hast Thou created them to the improvement of our understanding and to lead us step by step to a proper Idea of Thy Omnipotence"? . . . Step by step may they bring me and all mankind to a proper sense of my own state and their own, so that in the End we may all become worthy members of that divine abode through the Merits of Him who descended from whence Eternal happiness flows.

That this attitude was Williams' own as well as that of his *persona* Penrose is shown in a telling phrase from his last will: "Previous to that day [of death] & on that day I beseech my Glorious Redeemer's intercession to his Divine Father for the Remission of all my Sins."

Finally, one may find passages of a deeply sensitive and natural poetic expression. Williams/Penrose may have been only an "illiterate Sailor," as he himself asserted, but he was indeed a perceptive and evocative *poietes*, a maker and shaper of the language. At the time of the death of the Dutchman Somer, who had married a native girl, her relatives come not only to mourn but also to urge a rapid remarriage in the custom of their people:

"You far water stranger, Your Skin is whiter than ours, White like the Moon shining in the night. Can you expect our actions to be whiter than your own? What is the things I know, I hear and see? Has not the Wind of voices gone through the trees and by the side of the shore That my Brothers and Sisters have given their Flesh and their Blood for a mixture with yours? Show me more friendship than this as we shall then own it is whiter than ours. Now we hear the voice of the wind saying, 'Oh, the blackness is coming of the Bird which devours the dead.' Must we not all go to sleep? Are you not picking off the flesh from the bones? Our Sister here must return without a covering of love because her love is gone to sleep. Could she keep him awake any longer? Or tell us, did she put him to sleep? You will say, 'No, no!' Awaken his Spirit again, as it is in your power, that she may find joy and laughing hours, Least the Winds carry the sound of Black sorrow among our People and they should forget the way to this place."

In spite of the apparent simplicity of its unassuming style and straight-line or chronological first-person account, which is broken only by two major flashback sections, considerable subtlety and suspense are evident in the story's total development. Williams not only employs a carefully patterned alternation of descriptive scenes, action, and philosophical commentary, as illustrated by the foregoing passages, but he also uses the modern "dramatic" technique in characterization. Instead of offering descriptions and analyses of his characters, as was so frequently done in the novel of the eighteenth century, the author presents them directly through speech and deed, with minimal explication of his own, thus allowing each reader to formulate his own impressions.

Even the minor personages such as the voluble Captain Horgan, old Quammino, or the ancient Spaniard "Daddy Nunez" emerge three-dimensionally in the author's persuasive accounts (although he is less successful with the characters of the Indian girls.) Penrose's beloved companions, the Dutchman Somer and the Scottish adventurer and mountebank Norman Bell, in particular assume a solid reality as the events unroll. Most memorably of all, Penrose after a picaresque and unrestrained youth (he was, he says, "accustom'd to all Vice except Murder and Theft") discloses himself in maturity to be a perceptive, gentle soul altruistically concerned with the welfare of his little com-

Edward Bird, R.A.: *Penrose's First Sight of the Indians*
(From Second English Edition)

munity. But he also responds hedonistically to his lush tropical environment, which he describes with color and penetrating insight, showing himself to be at the same time a romantic adventurer and idealistic new-world philosopher as well as a practical man of affairs.

Williams was his own man, a self-taught, self-sufficient individual with talent in both art and literature. As a painter he produced over two hundred canvases; but *Mr. Penrose* is his one novel, uniquely based on his own real and imagined experience.

v

With Williams' holograph manuscript as his source the present editor has retained the author's exact terminology (with some annotation of archaic or technical forms), his spellings (and misspellings), and his random capitalization, as evidenced in the several preceding quotations. Since Williams' pages were innocent of paragraph units and quotation marks it has seemed desirable to employ these convenient devices, and to supply normal punctuation to eliminate the author's typical terminal commas and run-on constructions of incredible length. Since Williams divided his narration only by the numbered years of his residence, further chapter headings have been inserted. But for the first time *Mr. Penrose* is here made available in the author's own style and idiom, a much more muscular and dynamic tale than the "doctored" version of 1815.[18]

NOTES

1. *The Journal of Llewellin Penrose, a Seaman* [edited by John Eagles], 4 vols., London: John Murray, and Edinburgh: William Blackwood, 1815.

2. St. Augustine Parish Records, Bristol City Archives, by courtesy of the Reverend Canon Gay.

3. Thomas Eagles' copy of a letter to him from Benjamin West, dated October 10, 1810, now in the Lilly Library, Indiana University. This twenty-page letter is the source of the several following quotations.

4. *Electic Review*, New Series V: 395–98 (April, 1816).

5. Quoted in Alfred Coxe Prime, *The Arts and Crafts in Philadelphia, Maryland, and South Carolina, 1721–1785*, Walpole Society, 1929, p. 13.

6. Quotations from Williams' two wills by courtesy of Major Philip Graham-Clarke of Abergavenny, Wales.

7. Marriage Records of the First Presbyterian Church, New York, by courtesy of Colonel John F. Williams, San Diego, California, who supplied a photostat. See also his *William Joseph Williams, Portrait Painter and His Descendants,* Buffalo, N.Y., 1933.

8. This was inserted as a starred note in West's letter of 1810 under the comment: "X in the Vol of his copying of the Lives of the Painters—at the end is a list of his Paintings—".

9. Quoted in Rita Susswein Gottesman, *The Arts and Crafts in New York 1727-1776,* New York, 1938, p. 7.

10. The Newark Museum owns the *Imaginary Landscape;* the Brooklyn Museum, *Deborah Hall;* the Winterthur Museum, *William Hall, David Hall, Jr., Portrait of a Gentleman and His Wife,* and Williams' *Self-Portrait,* recently acquired from a descendant of John Eagles. Colonial Williamsburg holds *Jacob Fox;* and various dealers and private owners share some half dozen other works among those thus far identified as by Williams.

11. *Felix Farley's Bristol Journal,* November 13, 1784, by courtesy of the Bristol Reference Library.

12. *Hotwells and Rownham Ferry,* a scene on the local Avon River, is in the City Art Gallery, Bristol. John Eagles discussed the *Self-Portrait* among other data on Williams in his "The Beggar's Legacy," *Blackwood's Edinburgh Magazine,* 77:251-72 (March, 1855).

13. Letter from John Eagles to John Murray, Esq., August 18, 1814, and other correspondence, by courtesy of John Murray, Publishers.

14. Stanley Hutton, *Bristol and Its Famous Associations,* Bristol and London, 1907, p. 190.

15. A. Schmidt und Co., Jena, 1817. Copy in New York Public Library.

16. Edited by John Eagles, London. Illustrations by Edward Bird, R.A.

17. James Stanier Clarke, *Naufragia, or Historical Memoirs of Shipwrecks and of the Providential Deliverance of Vessels,* 2 vols., London, 1805-1806, preface, n.p.

18. A fuller study of Williams' career and contributions is currently in press and will shortly appear: David Howard Dickason, *William Williams, Novelist and Painter of Colonial America, 1727-1791,* Indiana University Press (Humanities Series), Bloomington. Mr. James Thomas Flexner's several books and articles on early American art first set me on the trail of William Williams as a novelist. To Mr. Flexner I am therefore greatly beholden, although he may not agree with all my conclusions.

Mr. Penrose
The Journal of
Penrose, Seaman

Chapter I

If ever the following lines should reach my dear country the Reader is not to expect to meet with any persuasive Arguments to enforce belief or language to adorn the story, as the Author never recived more learning than what a common country school affords. In the first place I shall give the reader a faithful Narrative of every occurrence within my memory, from the day of my birth unto the time I first left my native shore to cross the Atlantic.

Lewellin Penrose is my name. I was born near Caerphilly in Glamorganshire,[1] in the month of May *anno dom.* 1725. My father, who was a Sailor, was cast away in a Ship belonging to the city of Bristol called the *Union* Frigate,[2] commanded by a certain Capt. Williams (who was his own countryman), in the great January storm at the Texel in Holland, where every soul perished of a fleet consisting of near 60 sail of Vessels, only one Dutch Dogger which lay without riding it safe the whole time.[3]

My mother, being left a Widow with two children, (Viz) myself and a sister five years younger, after a time married a Schoolmaster and removed with him into Worcestershire, thence into Monmouth-

---

1. In south Wales.
2. A ship by this name is listed in Commander J. W. Damer Powell, *Bristol Privateers and Ships of War*, Bristol, 1930, p. 102.
3. This was the "Great Storm" which occurred in 1734/35 rather than the more famous one of November, 1703, which was described by Defoe and others. A dogger is a two-masted ship with a blunt bow.

shire, and after that into Wales. This man, I may justly remark at least in my own opinion, proved the innocent or rather obstinate cause of many hardships I have since his days undergone, as I learnt a few years after of his death.

And pity it is that parents take such notice of their own Children's budding genius, speaking of them with such Adulation in their infancy; yet when a Youth becomes of an age capable of recieving an Education suitable to the talent the Almighty has bestowed upon him, Every delight shall be snatch'd from him at once, Because perhaps an Uncle, Cousin, or neighbour has acquired some little welth by this, that, or other calling. Now Jack must be placed under such a Master at once; as to the natural bent of the boy, such a thing becomes intirely out of the question as being by no means a competent judge of the matter.

This was truly my case. In short, nothing would suit but that I must be placed with a Lawyer, and that without the least inclination on my side.

My poor Mother always sided with her Husband, and thinking his advice the best gave me so many lectures day after day that I grew quite wearied out as I detested the Profession. And now I determined to follow the seas.

When they found me so averse they took another method with me, as thus. They came to a conscent that I should go a voyage, but this as I found afterward was only in view of weaning me. Now when I had been three or four small trips they again renewed their dissuasions. This only aggravated my mind, and as it was now War-time[4] I entered into a new Scheem with a companion of mine. This young lad's name was Howell Gwynn, and to run away we were resolved. We conducted our affair so artfully that no soul knew or had the least dream of our elopement.

And here let me beg the kind Reader's permission to let fall a few tears, as it brings to remembrance a kind and tenderhearted Mother.

4. The so-called War of Jenkins' Ear or Spanish War was declared in 1739, the War of the Austrian Succession in 1741, ending with the Peace of Aix-la-Chapelle in 1748.

Alas! to think now on the Wickedness of that act chills my blood. Notwithstanding it may be reasonably judged, the Ocean seldom softens the passions. I observe this here as a caution to any young Fellow who, if God so please, may come to read my singular story.

I say, then, having found means to convey our cloaths and other trifles away, with no more than four shillings in money, we very erly in the morning in the month of September in the year 1744 quitted the houses of our parents without the least remorse of conscience, to make the best of our way for Bristol. We took care to evade all enquiries, sleept in Barns and Stables, now and then asking for a piece of Bread and Cheese on the road saying that we had been cast away and to make our money hold out the longer. I shall observe one thing here. As we went through a Village called Pile[5] a young fellow met us who was then returning from a Cruise, and advised us by all means to return back to our parents, he having been unsuccessful. But the reflections we thought to meet with should we so do determined us to proceed untill we got the whole length of the journey with three half-pence in store.

The first thing we did was to march to the Quay, where by chance we met with a young Fellow who was a kind of relation to me, and a Sailor also. He no doubt was pleased to find I had taken such a turn, and undertook to get us births. The City then swarmed with numbers of Privateers' men. My cousin took us to a Rendezvous on the Quay, the Sign of the White Lion and Horseshoe. We had not been long in the house before my companion Howell was persuaded to Enter,[6] but as I had a greater mind to become a good Seaman than to commence Hero all at once I evaded all their temptations. This I was advised to by my kinsman, who observed that it would be better for me to take a trip with him to Ireland. Now as I was in a strange place without money I took my friend's advice. My companion Gwynn took his leave of me to go down to Hungroad,[7] and from that day to this hour

5. Downriver from Bristol, on the Avon River in the "West Country" of England.
6. That is, as a privateersman.
7. An anchorage near the mouth of the Avon below Bristol.

we never met more. I remain'd all the evening with my cousine, who I found to be a hearty cock and never flinched the Can of Grogg. Now I being in no way inclined to liquor left him in company and went upstairs to sleep on a rush-bottomed couch in the foreroom.

In the midst of my sleep I was roused with a most sad outcry of a boy, as I thought, under severe disciplin. This alarmed me much, as it was accompanied with most horrid imprecations from some man. Being but a Stranger in the house, and finding the man went downstairs I determined to make my best way down also in order to find out my relation. There was a small light gleem'd into my room. On I pushed, but as I went along the passage I heard a soft voice call to me, beging me to come into a room on my right hand. No sooner did I enter than I saw a charming creture standing stark naked before me. I was for passing on, but she laid hold on me and made me sit on the Bedside with her. She began to tell me that her husband the landlord had beat her most cruelly through a fit of drunken jealousy. No mortal was ever much more alarmed than me in that Scituation, as dreading her husband's return.

She shewed me the goosberry bush he had beaten her with, and indeed he had curried her to some purpose. Now it happened the candlestick fell down. This was a luckey stroke for me. I directly offered to go down and light it. To this she consented; but [I] took care not to go back with it. And well for me, perhaps, for shortly after the husband went up the stairs again and gave her the second part of the foregoing tune, and plaid it as well. I groped my way into the fore-parlour in order to rouse some of the snoring tars, but I might as well have spared the trouble; they were all so snugly moored in Sot's Bay that it was out of my power to trip one of their anchors. At last I ran foul of a man in the Entry, standing in his shirt. "Who are you, messmate?" said I.

"Oh, cousin," he cried, "is it you?"

"For God's sake, let us get out of this house," said I, "at any rate."

Shortly after this we heard the Watchman pass, when we took courage and hailed him. "Go to sleep if you are all drunk," he said.

We then called through the keyhole and said: "Murder! Knock at the door, man!" He then called two more and they thundered at the street door. We then drew back into Sot's Bay when down came Mr. Bean, the furious Landlord, with the candle and opened the door. No sooner did he do it than out we pushed and insisted on their taking us off with them, as we greatly feared the fellow would murder his wife before morning light. This was about three o'clock. After this we marched the streets untill six, when we entered another house call'd the Champion of Wales. There we got breakfast and proceeded down to the Gibb where his boat lay. He took me down to Pill [Pile] next tide, where he purchased me a few articles.

The wind coming round to East, we stood down channel the next day and took in a load of coal at Neath,[8] from whence we proceeded to Cork. On the passage I learnt that It was my cousin Bean had recieved the cause of his jealousy from, and that he had given him a fine basting before I awoke.

Now it happened as I was standing on the Quay on a day before the bow of the Vessell, a Man Siezed me by the hand, and clapping my thumb between his teeth threw me over his Shoulder and in this posture carried me into the next publick house, where he called for a quart of Ale on my head as a new Import. I was greatly amazed at the first, but some of our people following and laughing told me it was the custome among the porters. This man's name I well can remember was Billy Vane.

One Evening after this my cousin would need have me go on shore with him to look out for a Brute, as he used to call the ladies of pleasure. He was then in liquor; and remembring the Bristol adventure, Upon the whole I refused. He then began to upbraid me with what he had done for me, but as I dreaded the consiquences I persisted to remain on board. He then told me I might march on shore and shift for myself. He had not been gone above two hours when I left the Vessell and repaired on board a Snow[9] bound for London. There I begged my passage for my work.

8. Near Swansea in Wales, on the Neath River but with its own port on the Avon called Briton Ferry.
9. Snow, a small sailing vessel resembling a brig.

After my coming to London I directly entered on board A Privateer, having not one Shilling in the world. I followed it up, playing the same game as other Sailors do when on shore with prize money. After this time I was pressed[10] and shifted from one to another untill I found means to make my escape, going under different names as it best suited my purpose. Thus I spent my time untill the year 1746.

I then ship'd myself on board an old Indiaman calld the *Harrington*,[11] bound for Jamaica and at that time laying at the Red House, Deptford,[12] one Hunter commander. With what little cash I had left I purchased some few Shirts and trowsers, a Jackket, Scotch Bonnet and a pair of Shoes, and a small seaman's Chest. After this the Ship fell down to Gravesend, from thence to the Downs, and there I experienced the first Thunder-Storm I had ever been in on the Salt water. The rain and wind was so violent off the shore that she was soon on her beem ends, as we were then getting under way. The flashes of lightning were so quick that I could scarcely keep my Eyes open, but it was of short continuance. After this we proceeded to Spithead, there to wait for the Convoy.

In three or four days we put to sea, being about a hundred Sail bound to different ports. Our Convoy was a Ship called the Old *Chatham*[13] of 50 guns. Our Ship mounted 20 guns. With a letter of Marque we parted company in the Bay of Biscay and proceeded alone. Nothing of note happened on our passage except some of our main-topmen who, during the time we were at Exersize with the great guns, chanced to set the mizzen topmast staysail on fire as they were busy in the main top; but it was soon happily extinguished. Nevertheless it put all hands in a great hurry, as no misery can equal that of a Ship on fire in the main ocean.

10. Impressed into the navy.
11. The records of the East India Company include the logs of four voyages of the *Harrington* to India and the East Indies before the ship was "retired" to private service in the Caribbean.
12. Near Greenwich, on the Thames below London.
13. This ship was built at Chatham in 1691 with 48 guns, rebuilt at Deptford in 1721, and sunk as a breakwater at Sheerness in 1749. A new *Chatham* with 50 guns was built at Portsmouth in 1758.

After this we made the Islands of Antigua, Mountserrat, Nevis and St. Christopher's [St. Kitts], and passed between them. Here we spoke a French flag of truce. A few nights after, we ran in with the Isle of Vash[14] on St. Domingo in a very dark night indeed, but saw it time enough so as to recieve no damage. The next day we came abrest of the White Horses[15] on the Jamaica south shore. Here the Pilot came on bord, and we got safe into Port Royal. And here I shall observe that our first Captain did not go the Voyage with the ship, and a Certain Mr. William James, then chief mate, took the command at Spithead.

During our stay here Admiral Davers[16] died; and as all the Ships in the harbour were firing minute guns on that occasion, when it came to our turn one of the guns on the larboard side discharged before its due time. I happened then to be standing on the gangway and saw a young fellow of the name of Palmer sinking. The blood flew from his head and arms like a spout, and a piece of his Scull I found in the main chains. This unhappy young man had been sponging the gun and left some of the old Cartridge on fire within, which on his ramming home another, it took fire and blew him to pieces, at the same time blasting the fingers of ye boatswain who at that time held them on the touch hole.

About the latter end of November, having our full lading in, we set sail for London; but the Almighty was pleased to frustrate our intentions and to disperse us in a wonderful manner. We beat to windward for several days to little purpose. At length we carried away our foretopmast, top and all; two of our hands went overboard with it but saved their lives.

Our Commander then proposed to bear away for Blewfields[17] to repair our damages. After we had got up a new top and topmast we

14. The Isle de Vache, near the southwest tip of Haiti.
15. The White Horse Cliffs, a few miles east of Port Royal.
16. Thomas Davers, after serving under Admiral Vernon, became commander-in-chief of the squadron at Jamaica in 1745. He died there on September 16, 1747.
17. A small settlement on the southwestern tip of Jamaica, not the Bluefields in Nicaragua.

put to sea and bore away for the Gulph of Florida.[18] Some time after this on a blustery night we had like to have ran on shore on the Isle of Pines; however, we wore her and stood off again. From this time the weather proved very hazy with small rains, and in this sort it continued untill Christmas Eve. Every Mess was now busy in making Puddings, but alas, now began the prelude to our future troubles.

A Sqall arose about the second watch, and all hands were call'd out. It blew for about half an hour; after this we jog'd on under an easy sail untill break of day. Little did I think at the time that would prove so fatal a Christmas day to me.

Our chief mate, Mr. Ramage, shortly after he came on deck spied a Sail right ahead of us. Directly all hands were call'd to quarters as she was laying too not two miles from us. Just as this happened we discovered the Moro Castle quite plain under our lee. Now as the Enemy was stern too we could not judge of her force; nor did she seem to take the least notice of us, and as we were in no kind of fear about her we stood on. Shortly after this as we came abreast of her we plainly percieved her to be a Ship of force. She then bore down into our wake, hoisted Spanish Colours, and began to fire several random shott at us. Directly we ran out two stern chases, and crouded all the Sail we could; but in a short time after away went our Maintop Gallant mast, and as she then gained on us fast our Captain ordered the Ensigne to be haled down.

The Ship we struck to was a Spanish Man of War, and called *El Fuerto*, mounting 50 guns commanded by One Capt. Mahony, a good-natur'd old Irishman. We were carried into the Havannah, and there our Crew was divided on board of two Men of War (Viz) *The Dragon* and *Conquistador*.[19] So that I well remember my Christmas dinner was changed from plumb pudding to Horse beans and poor Jerked beef.

In this place we remain'd prisoners and had the grief and mortifica-

18. The Gulf of Mexico.
19. Originally built in Bristol and christened the *Gloucester*, this ship was captured by the French and then sold to the Spanish, who renamed it the *Conquistador*.

tion to see Flags of truce come in and go out every day, it being a practice in those times For Flags to visit the Spaniards from N. America Laden with flour and other articles; and this was supported through the sneeking contrivance of their bringing and taking away one or two prisoners at a time that by this low cunning the game might last the longer, while hundreds of His Majesties loyall Subjects were detained to labour at the Moro Castle in the abject condition of carrying Stones to repair their enemies fortifications against their will.

Our Employment on board of those two ships was picking of Ochum, pumping ship, hoisting in their water, and the like. We had our Birth alotted between two great guns on the lower deck. It was then proposed by the elders of our brotherhood in Captivity to form a set of Laws among ourselves, as well for our better keeping peace as not to anoy the Enemy. We in the first place concluded never to mention the word Spaniard but to substitute that of Hoopstick in its stead. By this means we could talk freely about them at all times as none of them understood English. Another law was strictly to observe the hours of 10 in the morning and 4 in the Evening for the ridding of the Vermin with which we greatly abounded. This law was so strictly observed that if any one was found to transgress he was directly brought to the gun where he recieved a good copping, alias ten and a puss on his posteriours with a Barrel Stave.

The Spaniards took much pleasure in hearing us sing or play at Cards. But there was one thing which I never thought commendable in our English, which was deciding their foolish quarrels on shore in a boxing bout, to the great derision of our Enemies and their own shame; the Spaniards never failing on such occasions to call them Peros Engleses, English Dogs.

We were served every day with fresh beef from ye town, but as poor as carrion; yet we had bread enough so that we used to sell a part to the Marines on board. They took our money on shore and bought Roots or green for us, so that we did not fare miserable.

Divine service was duely observed by them every day, after the Catholick manner. In the meantime our Jacks, far from thinking of the like, were used for to Assemble below and fall to singing, for which they were often reproved. But there was one refractory Chap who was every now and then laid in the stocks. N.B. Their way is to lay the person on his back with his neck in the hole and a block under the head.

It happened while we were there News came in of the Accession of Ferdinand to the throne of Spain.[20] There was great rejoycings on the occasion for several days. Medals were struck and thrown to the populace. Bells jangled the whole time. A Castle was erected in order to be attaqued by an English Ship drawn through the Streets on a carriage. On her quarter deck was placed the figure of Admiral Vernon.[21] Her rigging was hung with all sorts of fireworks so that when she came to engage the Castle she soon became on fire, when poor Vernon fell a sacrifice to their rancour. But, by the bye, this was a farcical pantomime of their own.

Every evening all the churches, Castles, and batteries were finely illuminated, but our curiosity to see those curious Sights had liked to have cost some of our people dear. Now as we were never suffered to go on shore on the town side, in the Evenings we used to get up in the Ship's tops to behold the sights on shore. One night as we were innocently aloft and the Hoopsticks under us at prayers on the forecastle, no sooner had they done than up they ran on each side of the Shrouds and fell to paying the poor English as fast as they could come at them. Some ran down the stay, others fought their way down the shrouds the best they could. None could understand the meaning of this treatment or what it meant. As many as could got between decks. At last we found out the Story to be thus. In the foretop was a small Hurricane house for the Captain of the Top to sleep in. In this place was a small Model of a Ship, in which some of our people had through laziness watered. Unfortunately for us she had a small hole in her bottom, and the urine ran down on the Hoopsticks as they were at prayers. But the

20. Ferdinand VI succeeded to the throne in July, 1746.

21. Vernon at this time had left the Caribbean for service in the North Sea; but his earlier attacks on Jamaica, Portobello in Panama, and Cartagena had made him a prime villain in Spanish eyes.

whole thing blew over next day as we all declared none intended it as an insult.

We had been there about six weeks when they thought best to send us all away in an old leakey Sloop. The appointed day came, and she came along side to take us all on board to proceed for Jamaica as a flag of truce. There were on board this Vessell some 5 or 6 Spaniards with an Irish Captain Who knew no more of the Sea than a Parson, and to the best of my memory about 70 of us.

We proceeded to beat through the old Streights of Bahama under a ships nurse.[22] The sloop worked so well that she had her wake ever on the weather crutch, the pump continually going. This, added to our Pilot's ignorance, made them at last give her into the charge of our Mate, Mr. Rammage, to navigate her to the island of New Providence.[23]

We met with two sail who took out a few of our people. Now the rest by some means or other found out some cash hidden in water casks and the like. This discovery was Imparted to but a few; and to defend the booty they made Bludgeons as to guard against the press they pretended. This the Spaniards found out, but I cannot say whither Rammage was to be rewarded for his labour by the Spaniards or not. But just as we came abreast of Rose Island near to New Providence he broke the matter to them to return the money, but they peremptory and boldly denied it. At this time the wind was died away, and the monyed heroes insisted on having the boat hoisted out to go on shore, thinking that it was Providence itself. Away they went by force and left us to sink or swim; but providentially the wind sprang up or we had certainly all foundered. This breeze brought us into the port just as the heroes were crossing over from Hog Island to the town.[24]

The Captain immediately laid his complaint before Tinker,[25] who

22. Apparently an auxiliary sail.
23. A small island in the approximate center of the Bahamas.
24. Hog Island lies across a narrow channel from Nassau, the capital.
25. John Tinker was Governor of the Bahamas from 1740 until his death in 1758.

was at that time Govourner and as great a trickster as those the captain laid his charge against, as the report then went. Some of them were taken up and examined before his Excellency, but they had all found means to secreet the cash one way or other except a Certain Frank Harris, with whom some of the dollars was found. This Poor young fellow was by the Governors order clapt into the fort and compassionately forced to become a Grenadier, after he had obliged him to ride on the Wooden horse repeatedly.

In this place we rambled up and down half naked and all friendless, without the means of any present support.—And here I shall give the reader a rough draught of my Garb as I then appear'd. (Viz) a long pair of ragged and narrow Spanish trowsers, a fragment of an old blue Shirt not enough to pass under my waistband, a remnant of an old Red Handkerchif round my head, without either shoe or stocking to my feet. I had yet my old blue bonnet. Now this place being full of Privateering, we all enter'd one way or other; as for my part I was full in for it by way of retalliation on our Enemies.

Chapter 2

And now, in serious mood, let me acquaint the Reader that not being as yet convinced of my folly by the hard sufferings I had hithertoo fellt, On a fatal hour I enter'd on board a Schooner called the *Recovery*[1] of which James Strike was the Commander, Anno 1747, on a Cruise—against whom? Alas, against my poor self. Having obtained

---

1. A schooner *Recovery* is listed among the Royal Navy vessels of the period; but this is probably an anachronistic use of the name of a famous Bristol privateer first mentioned in 1758.

a few dudds, as the Sailors term Cloaths, from the Skipper which were to be all paid for out of our prize money, now as I was going with a People who act with some difference from the Europians I conducted myself according, and got me hooks and lines for my profit as well as pleasure on the Cruise.

We sailed out at the East end,[2] as they termed it, and after a short time came too at an island called Andross. Here we staid but a short time, then stood away for an island called the Bimmeny,[3] above 100 miles west of Providence. Here the batteaux or canoa was hoisted out, and all hands became full of Spirits. Some of our officers went on shore with fowling pieces; in the meantime some of the crew fell to fishing. This new mode of life agreed well with my mind. In the evening our People came down on the shore and the boat went and brought them off, but not in so good a condition as they left us. For it happened that one of them rambling about by himself, and not being percieved by another who was then taking sight at a bird, recieved part of the shott in his posteriors as he was discharging a point of necessity. The smart drove him mad for a time; but where there were a people round him who have little feeling of the tender passions it turned all to ridicule and diversion. However, when he was brought on board, the doctor restored him in a few days.

From hence we crossed the Gulph for the Florida Keys, and on one of them our people Shott three Birds such as I had never seen the like of in my life before. They were when erect near six feet high and Red as Vermillion, the neck and leggs being extreamly long but the body no bigger than a fat hen. We had plenty of Rum on board, but I observed that there was not the least oeconomy among them; and indeed I had learnt to relish the thing very well my Self by this time.

I shall here give the reader a specimen of our frugality. At Key West where there is plenty of Water we got into a notion of Spending a few hours at the Sign of the Fountain, as we termed it. In order to this, some of our most Potvaliant hero's took on shore flasks of Rum and

2. Of the channel between Hog Island and Nassau.
3. The North and South Bimini Islands lie directly east of Miami, Florida.

Sugar, and seating themselves round the Well discharged the rum and sugar into it. Of this bole I pertook. When our mighty bole grew weaker we replenished, untill the greater part what by hooping and singing fell asleep. N.B. These wells are Casks sunk in the sand with holes bored through them.

In the mean time while several lay snoring on the grass the man at mast head cried, "A sail, ho!" We all hurried on board, and what was very extraordinary, in a few minutes every man appear'd to be got quite Sober again, so great an effect this fresh alarm had on their spirits. The Sail appeared to the Southward and we gave chace under all the Sail we could croud right large. We chaced her the whole evening without gaining the least upon her; the next morning saw no more of her, she having altered her course. We then haled our wind and stood in shore again. Shortly after this we discovered some of the Savages on the shore, but as they proved too shy to come on board we ran in closer, where some of our most Valiant Gents took the whim of fireing on them. This I thought cruelty indeed, to take a few naked poor Cretures as a mark out of mere sport to shoot at.

While they were at ye game the Schooner got aground. Now the Skipper begant to rave, and ordered all the tallest overboard to shove her off again. And I could soon see their mighty courage began to ebb, fearing to be wreck'd on that inhospitable shore; but they shoon [soon] hove her off again.

The next day we saw two sail in the offing, and gave chace; these we came up with in the evening. They proved to be two small Sloops of no value. These we took the hands out of, and sat them on fire. The wind fell and it became a dead calm, so that it was amazing to see what towering columns of smoak asended from them. After this we stood away for the west end of Cuba and there landed our Prisoners.

In this lattitud we cruised for some time, when one day the man cried, "A sail on the weather bow!" We directly gave chase, but as she was going large we soon got the wind of her. The Chase then began to croud all the sail she could make, but we overhaled and got within cannon shott of her about five in the Evening. She proved to be a Spanish Ship of fourteen guns, and engaged us for about two glasses. This ship killed us three men and wounded seven. When she shott away our jibb stay and two of our Shrouds this affair nonplussed us for the present, and during the time it took up in getting stoppers on them she haled her wind and ran for it. We soon made after, but lost her in the night. On the morrow she could not be seen from masthead. This day we were in the Lattitude of Seventeen north.

We had now been out a full month and had taken nothing of value, so that our crew began to murmer greatly and begged of the Captain to cruise on the Spanish Main. He objected that our provision would soon run short. Nevertheless, I could find a general discontent to reign among the people. I now wished heartily that I had never came among them, and as we had some of the true descendants of the old Buckkaneers among us did not know what they might intend. At last they privatly drew up a Round Robbin; the major part of the Crew signed it but I declined putting my hand to the paper. The Officers, finding this, were obliged to comply and away we shaped our course for the Main shore.

A few days after this the wind came to blow fresh at North, and increased so that we were forced often to lay too. At length it became more moderate. We were now in the lattitude of 15, and in the night one of our hands cried out, "Breakers ahead!" We tacked immediatly but had only time enough and that was all. As the wind died away we let go the anchor in 8 fathom, and thus waited for day. When the morning came, a morning I never longed more for in my life, we found the vessel surrounded with rocks and Shoals. Not above two of our hands knew where we were, and those not determined in the same opinion. At last they agreed it to be those dangerous shoals called Quita Suenno or Prevent Sleep.[4] A concern new fell upon my mind as thus— what a pitiful state we were really in, a small Vessel full of people and

4. The low-lying Quita Sueño group stretches from about 14° to 14° 30′ N., some 150 miles off the coast of Nicaragua.

no more than one poor Canoa to help us in case of extreamity. One of these quandom Pilots advised us to stand away for Santa Catarina,[5] where we arrived two days after, took on shore water casks, and boot-top't[6] the Vessel. Here the sons of noise took it into their heads that they should have no luck untill they finished all the remainder of the Rum on board. And after the water was all on board, the play began; and matters were carried to such a height that it became one round of Gunning, Fishing, drinking, fighting, and uproar. And I now began to think I truly experienced a tast of Piracy, saving that we had a good Commission on board.

The next day we stood away to the Southward, and on the next a Sail hove in sight. We chased her the whole day long, gaining but little upon her. On the morrow we saw her right on the lee bow; we had the wind then Northerly. The chase was now renewed and we seemed to come up with her hand over hand, when she altered her course right before it and left us like the wind. About sunset we saw land and took it for the Main, so kept under an easy sail all that night. On the morrow we found she had given us the slip and that We had nighed the Shore greatly by a Current. We stood in for a few hours, and then ran along ranging the shore at the distance of about 4 leagues untill the evening when we fell in with the soundings in thirty fathom. Shortly after, it shoaled to 16 with patches of Rocks. Here we hove too, and all hands fell to fishing with good success. While we were All busy at this sport a Tortoise swam alongside. They called for the Grainge,[7] and three of us jumped into the Canoa then alongside and pushed after it, but without success, As it was now almost dark. When we came back they vered her astern and I remain'd in her, where being much the worse for liquor as that very day we had finished the last drop on board the vessel [*sic*].

5. Santa Catalina, called Providence Island by its English Puritan settlers, lies directly south of the Quita Sueño group, halfway down the Nicaraguan coast.
6. Cleaned and daubed over with resin, etc., the upper part of the ship's hull, by rolling or heeling it from side to side.
7. Properly spelled grains, a fish spear or harpoon with two or more "grains" or prongs.

Chapter 3

How long I slept I knew not untill the great motion of the boat awoke me; and as I was rubbing my Eyes to my great wonder I missed the Schooner. The consternation soon sobered me, and what to do or how to act I knew not in the least. Horrible was now my condition as the wind freshed up more and more. At last I saw a flash and heard a gun go off, but a great way out. But for me to pretend to gain the Vessel again was impossible, so I at once gave over the thought. Thus I drove and baled as I drove in a Sort of despair untill the dawn of the day.

I was now close inshore and put into a small beach where I ran the Canoa on shore, jumped out, and haled her up. I could just discern the Privateer in the offing a great way out. Now while I was standing thus eagerly gazing about I saw a large brigg streatching out as in quest of our Vessel. She was near enough for me to see that she was a Cruiser. Thus I marched about, sometimes seating myself on the gunwale of the Canoa. It is impossible for me to give a just idea of the state of my mind, but thus I remain'd untill I lost sight of both the Vessels. I now looked round me and could see nothing but a wild country of Palmetto trees and Shrubs, but if inhabited or not—as being an utter stranger in this part of the world—I knew not.

Now as I thus sat musing what was next to be done—having no more than a Sailor's frock over my shirt, a pair of petticoat trowsers, my knife in one pockket, and my fishing tackling with a few hooks in the other, and my Bonnet on my head; these with the Canoa, Paddles, and Grainge were all my store in this my state of desolation—the first thing

I went upon was getting a stone for a killick[1] to my boat. This thought naturally made me cast an Eye on the Painter,[2] and I found that it had slipt the belaying.[3] Thus I spent the day in dolefull dumps.

At the end of the bay where I landed ran out a Reef of Rocks. Now while I was gazing every way round me, to my great surprise I beheld a Man standing on the shore and could discern him to be naked, holding a kind of Oar in his hand. I directly concluded he was a Savage, he being not above two hundred yards from me. I directly laid myself flat on the rocks and sand to observe his motions undiscovered. Shortly after this he began to walk towards me, looking out now and then. My heart now beat in my breast, and whither to speak him or not was the case. The prospect before me was now become dreadful, (Viz) Either to starve for hunger or to fall into the hands of merciless Savages who perhaps would soon rid me of all my troubles. However, committing myself into the hands of Providence, I determin'd to make my self visible as he was now within 60 yards of me. Up I got and stept down on the beach. When he first saw me he halted. I then hail'd him and made signs for him to come on. The first salutation was he clapped his hands over his Eyes, leaning forward, and then spread them abroad. I then did the same. Upon this he stept up to me and held out his hand. I recieved it, then he looked me full in ye face and said, "Christianos?" I answered, "Se, Señor" or "Signior." He then stooped down and made a cross with his finger in the sand, then laid his hand on my shoulder and made as for me to follow him. I did so, and we walked along the shore. He talked to me the whole time but I could make out nothing.

At last we came to a small inlet. Here was his Canoa, and in it sat a Woman stark naked and had a little boy about three years of age with her in the same state of nature with herself. She seem'd to be greatly alarmed at the sight of me. I found the man, who seem'd to be about 50 years of age, to use all manner of menes to clear her of her doubts. Upon this I went to the side of the canoa and patted the child on his

1. Anchor.
2. Rope.
3. A wooden peg or pin on which ropes are fastened.

head; this pleased the man much, I found. He then gave me a piece of half roasted turtle out of his boat. I was quite ravenous, having not had one morsel from the time I went adrift.

Now the man gave a sort of cry as to a person at a distance. I looked and saw a boy run among the high grass. The Indian then gave me a sign to stay by the Canoa, and away he went after him. Upon this the woman sat up her pipes and began to bawl to some purpose, the child bearing his part. This brought the Indian back again and he took me along with him. He went in among the grass and by much adoe brought out the other Boy, but the poor lad was so much frighted that I should have imagined he had never seen a white man before. When we came back the Woman began afresh. I observed they had several articles in the boat such as turtle, Eggs, guano's,[4] and the like. Their boat was not above two feet wide altho she was above 16 feet long. After this ye man and boy got into her and I naturally thought they woud give me a seat with them. Now as the wife still went on with her clamour the Man he handed me out a large Calabash by a string, and pointing to a place said, "Agua, agua." I understood he meant Water, and ran off to fetch it but after serching a time could find none. Now the reader will be surprised when on my going to return I saw the Indians paddling off as fast as they could, and were got above 50 yards from shore. I stood like a man thunderstruck for a time, but they soon got round a point of rocks and left me to shife [shift] as I could.

The Sun was now set and I had to ramble back to the Canoa. Now as I was on my return it came into my head that my late new friend had certainly handed me out the Calabash as a stratagem in order that he might gaine time to escape, As I supposed by the woman's behaviour, She would not consent to my going with them through some fear of my ill behaviour to her or hers. At last I got back to the Canoa and seated myself in the sternsheets. I then haled up the boat as high as I could and pulled off my frock, then laying at my length in her covered my breast with it to ward of the dew which falls so heavy in

4. Iguanas or large lizards.

these parts, and then fell to reflecting within my mind, but in hope I should see the schooner next day. But, alas, never did I see the *Recovery* more in my life.

When I fell asleep I knew not, nor did I waken untill the Sun was high. Directly I turn'd out to look in the offing, but to no purpose. I was forced to cut a bit of lead off my poor Sinker to chew, as I was almost choaking with thirst. After this I marched along shore to hunt food, and found plenty of Wilks (a shell fish).[5] These I broke against the rock stones, took them to my boat where I sat down and ate four raw as they were, with the tears of true Sorrow trickling down my cheeks. And now, had I had my hat full of dollars, they should all have gone for one stick of fire.

The next thing was to go in serch of Water. I wandered about for above an hour and return'd without finding any. In this ramble I found that I was on an Island as I conjectured by its position, or else a long point. After this I began a new rout and in this march came very near the end of my tether on a point terminating with rocks and a small reefe. I then came back and took out a paddle, went away toward the point, and finding a clear place of sand fell to digging. This work cost me an hours hard labour, but still no success. I then threw down my paddle and then myself on my face, not caring whither I lived or died; but after a time I got up thinking to return, launch my boat, And put along shore the other way. But as I stooped to take up my paddle, to my unspeakable joy water had sprang up in my well. Instantly I stooped down and tasted it with my hand; it was brackish but tollerable. This was a great relief, and on all fours I drank my fill. After this I return'd to the Canoa. Thus kind Providence in so short a time provided me both meat and drink, such as it was.

Now I became easier in my mind, being out of dread of immediatly starving. I then went back to fetch my Calabash full, brought it, and fixed it in the boat. After this I took a walk along shore westward. In this march I found a Conch, and with a stone returned, sate down on the bow of the boat, and worked round the crown of the shell untill I

5. Whelks, edible shellfish with a spiral shell.

drew out the fish; and as it is of a sweet taste found it very pleasing to my palate. In the evening I prepared to compose myself to rest and slept sound the whole night, arose next morning by daylight, and walked away along shore as far as the little creek[6] where the Indians forsook me.

Here I finished the remains of my Conch (or Conck), then tramp'd on through the creek about 2 miles farther. Here I could plainly see the full extent of it and that it was an Island. Upon this I mounted an old dead tree to look out, and to my great sorrow found it to be not above half a mile over. I presently took the alarm as judging it no place of any great Succour for me. Now as I thus explored the places around, I saw at about the distanct of five miles or so a more promising shore as of a much bigger Island or perhaps the Main itself. Down I hurried and made back for my boat as fast as I could, being determined if the weather Proved moderate the next day to take leve of this place. The rest of the day I spent in preparing for my departure.

I never failed to keep a sharp look out for the Schooner as I was far from giving her quite up; but finding she did not appear again came to this opinion, that the Brigg I had seen stretch out for her had either sunk or taken her. If not so, they had concluded to shape their course some other way, not caring to risk the seeking of me and the boat again. At other times I would Imagine they had returned to those Maroon Islands[7] again, and had either bilged on them or foundered at sea. Thus agitated betwixt hope and despair I passed my lonely hours. I could not sleep for the great hurry of my mind.

About midnight it began to rain hard and lasted so that I was drench'd and much water in the Canoa. At last it began to hold up, and the day came on as still as a clock. I then got out, took my frock and wrung it out, then threw it on the grass. I did the same with my shirt and trowsers, then put on my frock that it might dry on my back, and in this trim I fell to bale out my boat. I then took the Calabash to

6. In the sense of inlet, not a fresh-water stream.
7. Modern gazetteers do not identify any specific Maroon Islands. The word (possibly a corruption of Spanish *cimarón*, wild) referred to fugitive slaves living in the West Indies.

drink and found the rain had so freshen'd it that it quite rais'd my spirits. After this I clapt on board my killick, and when I had got her afloat I replaced my calabash. I then took a walk along shore, gather'd about 20 Wilks, and threw them into her. By this time my shirt and trowsers were tolerably dry and I put them on and then prepared for my departure.

I paddled away along shore, passed the place where my well was, and then ventured out to double ye reef of rocks. I then stood away north on new discoveries. The deepest water I had seemed to be about 3 fathom and often not one. After I had been on my voyage for about three quarters of an hour I observed on a small key some odd white spots. Thither I turned, but as I drew nigh an incredible number of Birds of many kinds arose like clouds. Their noise almost made me deaf. Here I landed and found those white things to be King Conks. These shell are so large some of them will contain three quarts of Water. I put five of them in my boat and then began to gather Eggs. While I was at this work the Pelicans would brush by my head so as almost to knock off my bonnet.

After this I put off for my new shore, and in about an hour got close in under the land. Here I found it bluff too, then a beach, the land overgrown with trees. Now as I paddled along I Espied a kind of Creek about a pistol shott over; in I put and found the water to Shoal to about 4 feet. I was so delighted with these new scenes that fear never once entered my noddle. I found the land on both sides about the height of a boats mast; but as I advanced in farther I found it to be a Lagoon or Lake. Here the Mangrove trees hung over my head laden with Oysters like traces of Onions. It abounded with fish of diverse kinds in great abundance. The Spoonbills, Galldings, Cranes, sat on the trees without taking much notice of me as being seldom used to the sight of men. At length I came to an opening. Fortune directed me that I should take to the left; this brought me to another branch where it opened wide all at once. Here I found a small sandy shore. I then threw out my killick and jumped on shore.

It was now about meridian as I judged by the Sun. Here I walked up the bank and found the soil bare with rocks for about an hundred yards round; and as I stood viewing I saw a kind of gap at some distance among the trees. Thither I walked and when I came to examine the place I found to my surprise another branch, and that I was got on a small precipice with a pretty sandy beach beneath me. I then looked out for some way to get below. Now as I was doing this I saw plainly over the trees the Island I had left in the morning. At last I got down on the sands below. Here I found a Cavern running into the Rock; into this place I went and found it to be about 15 feet deep. There I halted to look round. The mouth was as I judged about 10 feet in height and 18 feet wide with a gravel bottom. Here I seated myself and found a piece of wood cut in the form of a masque. Now, I thought to myself, I am not the first of Mankind who have visited this place.

After this I returned to my boat, being resolved to find out a way by water to this place if possible. When I came with the canoa to the point of the opening I there cut a branch of the mangrove and hung it up perpendicular by way of knowing the place again. I then took to the other arm of the Lagoon and in a short time after found it to bring me round to the Cave, and there I resolved to take up my abode for the present. Then I carried on shore all my little matters—my whole furniture consisted of my lines, three spare hooks, the Calabash, and the 5 shells.[8] After this was done I seated myself on the ground, fell too on my raw wilks, and took a draught of Water, then laid me down and fell fast asleep.

About 5 I awoke, when the dread of my wants in future took such impression of my mind that I got into my Canoa and away I went round to the place where hung my new Signal branch, and from thence paddled out to the mouth of the creek. After this I ran her on shore and threw out ye killick and went along shore in qust of food, but found only three wilks. This threw me into a heavy quandary. Now as I thus moved on with my face to the ground my ears were struck with a soft murmer as of water. I directly followed it; when going up to a small opening between the trees, to my unspeakable joy

---

8. The author apparently forgot his previous reference to his "grainge" or fish-spear.

I beheld a pretty little linn[9] of water falling over a shelve. This was an Estate to me worth more than the whole Bank of England. I ran back to my boat, paddled away as fast as I could for my Calabash, and returned forthwith, with two of my largest Shells also. These I fill'd and then chocked them up with stones and returned to my Cave with them, intending to go no more out untill morning. At the close of Night the Moskeetoes and sand flies begant to anoy me much, which took off many hours repose, but I had no remedy for it as wanting fire. I then crawl'd into the back part of the cave and covered my face and hands with my frock, and rested midlingly well untill day.

The first I went upon in the morning was to get a few Penama shells as they are called, and with these I concluded to keep my Reckoning, so concluded to put them into one of the conck shells and lay it in the back part of the Cave. This done, I went in quest of Conck bait with a view of fishing, then return'd into the lagoon and there came too. I saw fish in great plenty, but in such dread was I of loosing a hook that if any fish larger than ordinary drew near the bait instantly I drew up my line. Here I caught 7 or 8 Grunts and with them went to the cave and eate part of them raw. This was my dayly practice. At length I found my strength to deminish daily in a gradual manner owing to my way of diet, as I thought. I grew lean, and judged if my body became no better used than at times I found myself to such a course of living, my days would be short in this land of desolation. This made me spend many a day in black melancholy, thinking that this Cave or some more exposed place would soon become by Death Couch.

After I had been here about a month I began to give the Schooner quite over for lost to me; nor had I seen one thing since the Indian Canoa in the form of a Vessell. One evening the clouds began to gather very thick, and came on to rain very hard with terrible Thunder and lightning. I was just at that time return'd to the Cave from the Shore with a few concks. This Gust lasted above two hours, and I had just and great reason to be thankfull that I had a dry house over my

9. A cascade or torrent.

head, and it brought to my mind a saying of my poor Mother when she would see me runing to play in wet weather.

Erly the next day as I was walking by the sea shore all at once I observed a smoke rising out of the bushes. Directly I concluded there must be Indians nigh the place. How to act I could not tell at first, but judging that inevitably I should not escape them long, and as the man I had met already had treated me well, I went resolutely up the beach and peeped among the trees. But what joy took possession of my Soul when I discovered it to be an old tree on fire. For a few moments I stood to observe this old dead trunk, then concluded it had been done by the lightning. Off I ran to my boat and placed a quantity of sand amidships; after this I gathered a parcel of drift wood and filled the bow of the Canoa. Away I then flew and got some of that precious Element and laid it on the sand and placed a few sticks over it. The joy I felt on this most happy occasion almost turn'd my brain. With an air of satisfaction I seated me in the canoa and paddled off with my prize for my cave, and became so proud that I seem'd to want no more for the present. N.B. I never once returned my thanks to that compassionate God who had kindled it.

Directly on my going on shore I transferred my Fire under a shelving projection of the rocks to preserve it from the rain when it might fall; and now having got me a good fire I directly fell to cooking some fish. It was now a month since I had tasted a morsel of any food except raw. So grateful was this to my palate that I cleared all I had at that time caught. Now after my meal a thought poped into my head in regard to the manner of continually keeping my fire burning. I knew the Poppanack wood would keep fire to the last bit; therfore where ever I found any I never failed to bring it home. I had often tried the rubbing of two sticks togather, but to non effect.

Seven weeks did I live thus, each day alike, keeping my account very regular by Shells, when I took a fancy to explore the shore for some distance by way of recreation. Now as I was marching along the strand I observed something at a distance from me. As I came near I soon found it to be the work of art, and then ran up to it. It proved to be a small square chest, Spanish make. I turned it over and found it yet locked and not very heavy. At a small distance lay a wooden bole. I clapped the Box on my shoulder and taking the other in my hand return'd to my boat and put them both in and return'd with them up ye lagoon. There I landed my little freight and then ran to my fire, found it in good order, renewed it, and fell to examine the contents of my prize. After I had got it open I found in it 2 blue striped shirts and one red and white striped, one pair of long striped trowsers and 3 pair of canvas, 4 red silk handkerchiefs, a pair of shoes with silver buckkles in them, two fishing lines and a small bag of hooks and sail-needles, a roll of tobacco for chewing, a small Spying glass in a Woodden case, two clasp knives, and a palm[10] with a ball of twine. These things I could see were not English by their make.

As for the tobacco it was of no worth, but if it had it was not of use to me as I had never practised that custome. And the shoes I feared to ware least they should bring my feet tender again, having gone so long barefoot. How those things came there without my seeing part of the wreck I could not judge at that time. All these things I placed away with great delight and then renewed my fire, when I turned in for that night.

The next day I went out in serch of bait, and returned in order to go a fishing. I never failed to catch of diverse kinds, and my new mode of Eating soon recruited my strength and restored me to health.

Some time after this as I rambled along shore I found a small yard, a boats rudder, and an empty cask of little use. These proved to me the box had belonged to some small sloop or Schooner wrecked on that Shore some while past. While thus I explored this beach I observed a tract [track] here and there of Tortoises. No sooner did I espie this than I followed one of them up the beach; here I found one of them had been at work. Directly I fell on my knees and began to turn up the Sand, but soon found it a false place as they are apt to do this to avoid a serch or as not liking the spot. I then began on another and found myself right, but shortly after I was surprised to see a parcell

10. A sailmaker's instrument made of leather and metal, serving as a large thimble and fitting the palm of the hand.

of young gentery[11] about the size of an half crown daddling over my fingers all in perfect Turtle shape. I must confess it alarmed me at first. Directly I left them to shift for themselves and proceeded to another place. In this I got about 75 Eggs in good condition, went back to my boat and laid them in at two trips with my calabash, and returned home. N.B. I always took home with me the driftwood which lay in my way, but this was not my only office in that way for I, before that, used to gather all the small brush I could find.

After this sort I lived untill the wet season came on, never seeing a living soul but myself. It was my way to were but few cloaths, that those Providence had bestowed on me might last the longer. Often I went without anything but trowsers, but now I was forced to ware them as it was rather cold at times. I used to make my fire within my Cave least the continual rains should deprive me of that blessing, which would have been a loss indeed to a man in my forlorn condition. I daily laid up some small dry wood, as it rained more or less for above a month according to the best reckoning I could make. In all this time I went no farther from home than to fetch palmetto leaves for to make my bed, go a fishing in the lagoon, and get water.

After this the weather began to clear up again, and nature appear'd in a short time dressed anew to me. Now I concluded in my mind to take a small trip abroad in my boat. I made every thing ready and, leaving a good fire, I put out of the lagune in the morning. I stood over for the small Bird Key, wher when I arriv'd I found Concks and Wilks in plenty. After I had thrown above a hundred of them into my boat I went on shore and got a few Eggs with three young birds, then put off. On my return a very large Shark followed me; as he swam with part of his tail and coblers knife above water I judged him to measure 14 feet in length. He followed the canoa for a good while, but on my throwing over a conck he left me and went down after it.

On my arrival at the cave I went to roasting a Conck. Now as I was doing this I observed a bit of Spongey stuff which grew on a part

11. Gentry, folks.

of my fewel to kindle and burn very quickly. I directly broke it off
and put it out, then touched it at the fire and soon found it to answer
the purpose of tinder. I well knew there were plenty of a bastard kind
of white flint pebbles along the shore; those I concluded with my knife
would set me up. After I had eaten I put it in practice. They were not
so free as those of the dark kind in Europe, yet answer'd my purpose
very well. I then went on the hunt for more of the punck and found I
could master that matter well enough, there being enough about the
dead stumps of trees. After this I prepared a shell as a tinder box and
was never without it wherever I went, either afoot or in my Canoa.

By my account I had been on this shore about 9 months now, and a
most solitary life I lead. Sometimes the tears would burst out as I
walked along. Such preturbations would take place at times that I most
wickedly wished myself dead. Never did I once concieve it to be no
more than my own desert. My grief sprang from this—my being seperated from those dear companions I had lost; and if they were fortunate how much prize money might have fell to my share, to have
squandered away in madness and folly. Alas, little did I then think the
kind hand of Providence was so carefully watching over me, rescueing
me as I might say from the power of the Devil, to place me here in a
state of innoscence if I could but conform to the will of God. But I
was young and full of the vanities attending a life of dissipation.

But to proceed. One morning I resolved to go along shore Eastward,
and here I found the land to fall low with much Palmetto trees growing in a sandy soil. At last I came to a small kind of inlet. Here I went
on shore, and after going about 20 yards up a sand bank I found a fine
Salina or Salt pond. Here I found a large company of Soldiers all
ranged in their regimentals, enough to have struck any single unarmed
man with dismay had I not been well acquainted with their peacfull
disposition, they being nothing more than a large flock of Flamingos.
And here I had an opportunity of observing the way these Birds breed.
They raise up a piramid of sand in the pond; in the top of it they
make a pit; over this they Sit to lay and hatch with their long leggs
hanging down on each side. N.B. Altho those Birds are as red as
Scarlet when old, yet their young are for a time of an Ash colour grow-

ing red by age. This bird is of a Very stupid nature. It will not move for the noise of a Gun, so that if a person can keep concealed he may load and fire often eere they will take flight.

Not long after this I counted over the number of my shells and found to the number of 315; and from that time untill I had compleated my whole year I remained in Solitude seeing nothing to disturbe my peace or give me hope in the least.

Chapter 4:
Second Year of My Lonely Condition

About a month after I had began my second year I had a very odd adventure, as thus. One evening as I was sitting on the shore, and at that time about two miles from my Cave, all at once I heard a great snort as I thought among the bushes. I jumped up and ran down to the boat as fast as my leggs could convey me. After my first alarm was a little over I began to reflect within myself what this could possibly be; and in this mood I paddled along shore toward my home, keeping a proper distance off shore fearing a second alarm. But just as I passed a short bay to my great astonishment I thought I beheld a troop of Indians marching along shore right abreast of me. Now I was terrified indeed. The first thing I did was to lay along in the canoa least they should espy me, and thus observe their motions—but I was soon undecieved by discovering them to be a train of twenty odd Deer. Now as I lay with my head raised up a little my foot happened to tumble a shell. This caused the foremost to halt and stare directly at the Canoa. On this he gave two strong snorts, when they all scampered up the beach into the woods. Now all my fears vanished, and I put away for home as fast as I could. Nothing but the Deer ran in my head for several days together. As I had no Gun or ammunition I could not expect to succeed as a Hunter so gave all thoughts of a Venison repast quite over for that time.

There were here two sorts of Lizzards with which I was often amused at times. One of these frequented the rocks above high water mark and, contrary to all others I ever saw, had their tails in a curl on their backs, were of a yellow brown, beautifully mottled with dark spots, and carried their heads quite erect like little Dogs. They were seldome above 5 inches in length. Hundreds of times have I seated myself, as knowing their way, when three or four of them would come round me, look me in the face, and if I began to whistle they would first turn their heads to one side and then to the other and listen very attentive; yet so alert were they that if I offered to stir they were gone in a moment, so that I never could catch one of them alive by all my cunning.

The other sort is what they call in Jamaica the Woodslave. These are larger than the other sort, and I remember the first I saw of them surprised me much. It was on the limb of a low tree and of a Verdigrease green, but during the time I had my Eyes on it it began to change its colour, turning to a fine gold yellow, from that to a dead leafe colour with brown stripes down the side from head to tail; from this it changed to a deep brown, and lastly to a profound black. Some of these I caught now and then by means of a small noose round the neck, and tying them afterward round the loins with a small bit of twine kept them about my place for a week or more at a time. I could never see that they took any kind of food except they caught a flie now and then.

I went on in the same way for several months. In this interval of time I made me a Table and a stool; this I perform'd as follows. I cut twigs and wattled them after the manner I had seen the country folks do at home, then fixed them on four uprights; and I cannot boast they were so strong as I desired for I never ventured to cut anything very large with my knives, fearing to break one of them, the preserving of which was of the utmost consiquence to me so scituated.

I shall digress here to observe a singular circumstance altho of no great moment; yet as It was attended with drollery and a means whereby I got me a Companion I shall recite it. One day as I had been catching some Land crabbs, and having tied three of them togather, I left them on the beach while I gathered a few of those kind of Shells our silversmiths at home turn into Snuff boxes, as thinking should I ever get home again they might turn to some account. Now as I was busy at this amusement I heard a noise over my head, and looking up I saw a Fish Hawk bearing off my bunch of Crabbs. But it turned out otherwise for him, for he could not raise with them but came soon down to the beach, Crabbs and all. Altho I could not be expected to be in any merry mood yet the thing drew a smile from me; and of a trutch [truth] it was the first time since my landing here. When I first came up to him I found that two of those amphibious Gentlemen had fastened on his legg. He soon began hostilities against me, fighting with his wings and beak. But to put the contest to an end I took an opportunity and got him round the neck, knowing full well my other myrmidons would not quit their holds. In this sort I bore the whole bunch to the boat and there bound up his beak, then his legg, and thus brought home the whole body of disputants.

The first thing was to disengage them by putting fire to the Crabbs, which soon made them quit their hold. I then cut one of my new Comrades wings; after this I provided him a small log to one of his legs. When this was finished I cut the string from his beak to enlarge him. During the whole business he endevoured to do his best against me. I then gave him over to his future fortune. This Bird was of a most beautiful plumage of a mix'd White, yellow, brown, and black, yellow leggs and bill, the long tallons black. He was about the size of our Engish Kite and his cry much like that bird.

I soon found my care for his running away needless, his leggs being so short that he could make but poor way on the ground, those birds always devouring their prey on the limbs of old dead trees from whence they sit and behold the fish with a keen eye. Add to this the Crabbs had hurt his legg not a little, so that he was lame. After this I offered him some broiled fish which he refus'd with disdain, nor would he taste one bit for two days. But on the third I observed when I returned from my fishing that his Stomach began to crave. The fresh fish drew on an appetite as I judged by his crying, and I threw him some garbage. He eyed it for a while and then fell on greedily and gorged the whole in a short space. This so pleased me that my mouth opened incontinently and I cried out to him, in the Welsh tongue: "Much good may it do you, Mr. Yellowbill!" And in fact they were the loudest words I had uttered from the time ye Indians left me to that hour.

In the course of a month we became very intimate, so far that when I came home he would salute me very kindly and I used to return the compliment, being proud of having any one to speak to. After this wee became almost too intimate—he would hale the fish away without my leave or license. At length this poor fowl became so docil that I could do any thing with him. In an evening as it grew dark he would come in to roost of him self, so that I began to pitty his dragging the log about and I took it off. He knew his name and would come when called (Yellowbill). When ever I seated my self he would come and place himself by me and remain, picking his feathers the whole time. This caused me to amuse my self often with talking to him, or her as I knew not its Sex.

Now one day as I sat fishing I took a resolution for a small journey on the discovery, and for this purpose concluded on my return to fix all things in order and leave meat for my bird least the night should overtake me. Accordingly the next day I got some roasted fish and water into my boat least I might not find any soon, and put away out with my tinder tacklin also towards the Salina. There I left the canoa and marched away over a barren soil producing nothing but Palmettoes and Prickly Pears. Then I walked away for a kind of Grove at about a miles distance. On my arrival I found the shore grew rockey and incline more to the left; here it ended in a reefe. Over these Rocks I took my way. Here the land trended yet more to the left and I saw before me a great bay of sand, the country full of large Woods. Shortly after I came to a kind of inlet and here I espied a large Guano. This pleased me highly as I now hoped to find out their haunts as they are good Eating.

Up the side of the Creek I went for near a mile, saw thousands of Fish in it; here I found the trees hanging over the water in many places. It now became difficult for me to pass on that way; therfore I took more into the wood, keeping the creek still in view. Here I saw many lime trees full of fruit. These were most pleasing objects to my sight. I pluck'd one of them and cut it, and altho they are the most sharp acid the taste was most gratfull to me and exceeding refreshing. Now I found the creek to change its course. Therfore I began to suspect that I might loose my self as I could no longer see the Coast, so concluded to seat myself and take a short repast. Not far from this on a small rising ground I sat down and saw at its foot a small ripple of fresh water, with multitudes of Land crabbs about it. Down I seated myself and began to relieve hunger, amidst numbers of birds of various kinds some of which warbled most delightful.

In this place I observed a singular kind of bird call'd the Old Man from its having the feathers of its crop of such a length that when it perches it resembles the Grey beard of an ancient person. After this I arose and pondered whither to proceed or return, but at length curiosity gained the better and I went up a small height where it became very level and full of brush excep here and there. But I now fell upon a sight that really was uncouth enough. At a small distance grew Several Manchiniel Trees whose fruit is deadly poison to Man. The very juice of its leaves will raise terrible blisters so as to deprive a person of his sight.—Now from beneath those trees, to my no small amusement, I beheld armies of Land Crabs marching off on my coming, with each an Apple in his claw and many of them had two. The sight was truly drool, the more so as they carried them upright.

After this I walked on for the distance of 100 yards, keeping a good observation of the Sun. Here an odd appearance catched my sight. On a plain place stood a huge Rock stone almost upright, about the magnitude of a small Church tower and as I judged 40 feet in height and almost a square. When I came up to it I found many scratches on it made by some instrument or other, in the form of Ovals, Triangles, rude immitations of heads and the like. These I judged to be the work of Indians. As I walked round it I found many letters cut as with knives. These I judged to have been done by Spaniars and others, perhaps Pirates. Some few of them I took down after-

wards for my own curiosity, and I shall give them a place here.—
M+A. P+V. JL. E+S. L$^+$O. V$_+$M. R   +C &ccc. I also observed
four dates in different places added to names as thus, I+E 1589. Bat
S.^{s} 1605. A+A 1582, and W^m R 1673. In another place was to be seen
the following characters,   N.B. Those letters
having crosses between them I attributed to the Spaniards. The others
were the marks of Buckaneers or Pirates who had rambled over these
parts in former times.

I now thought of returning home and arrived at my small cove
where the boat lay towards Evening, then put away along shore for
home and got in just in the dusk, well pleased with my cruise. I found
all safe as I left it and was kindly recieved by my new Comrade who
expressed great joy, raising his large Wings, Stretching forth his neck,
making a soft and murmering noise, and rubbing his head and beak
against my bare leggs.

The following night I had a very troublesome dream occasioned
without doubt from my Excursion the day before. In my sleep I
thought that I was then sitting by the aforesaid huge Stone I have
mentioned, when all at once as from behind me I heard diverse voices
approaching. Casting my eyes back I beheld several men advancing
toward me. The uncouth garb they were dressed in caused me to jump
directly. They came on and hail'd me thus: "Buenos dia, Signior."
These men had all of them whiskers and were in armour. Then an old
man asked me if I had seen any thing of Manuel Guiterez that way. I
answered that I had not seen any Mortal man since my first landing on
this shore except three or four Indians. They then asked me how long
and by what means I came there, to all of which I answered in good
Spanish as I then thought. Upon this they all began upon me and said
I was the King of Spain's prisoner, and laying hands upon me said
I must go with them to the Mines for a Slave.

This, as I suppose, gave my whole frame such a shock that I awoke,
Hollowing in a most fearful way. It so frighted the poor Hawk that
he flew into ye water and would most certainly have been drown'd had
not the sight of its distress brought me to my senses again. I ran away
to its relief, and then seated my self before the Cave, where while poor

Yellowbill was endevouring to replace his plumage I fell into a deep revery as thinking perhaps this Vision might be veryfied on me one day or other, and perhaps that day not far off. Now I had good grounds for this fear, as I had learnt it to be the practice with the Spaniards in this part of the world upon English men who should be caught on their coast through misfortune; and most certain it is that many a poor Woman has lamented the loss of a husband, Son or Sweetheart as supposing them dead when perhaps they were at the same time in a far worse condition. I became so greatly troubled by these ruminations that it caused a fever which lasted three days. After this I got better again and threw it off as a mere dream. And now I determined in my mind sincierly to resign myself up to Gods disposal, concluding for the future to be as placid under all my sufferings as the nature of the thing would admit of.

Soon after this I went to my reckoning and found by the number of my shells that I had been here above one year and four months. I never omitted casting in a Shell every morning of my life directly after I had turned out, having some provided near for that End. And in this place I must observe one thing, as thus. I cannot be expected to give a just record of time and things at this distance, as then I was not posses'd of materials for the purpose; so that the reader must be content with circumstances as they come to my Remembrance.

After some time I came to the resolution of making a Voyage westward as I had nothing to hinder me spending my time in one round of Fishing, Eating, Drinking, and Sleep. So, fixing all in order at home with provision for Yellowbill, I put out on a fine morning expecting to return the next day. I kept along shore for the Space of two hours untill I began to explore new scenes, the land running here high, there low, indented with fine sandy bays. At length I opened a fine Lagoon. Into this place I put and proceeded up it for a good distance. Every thing appeared most inviting when, as I turned round a low rocky point, I was struck with the sight of several human Sculls as I then took them to be. They were white as snow. To shore I put and went up to them. I now judged my opinion right, and that they had belonged to a Gigantick race of people nigh this place. I saw there had been fire in time past by some remains of ashes and burnt ends of sticks. Now, thinks I, this proves beyond all doubt that this place is, or has been, frequented by a Wretched crew of Cannibals. I then took up two or three of the heads and put them in the Canoa, and determined to get out of that place as soon as possible. Away I went, needing no driver, and put along shore.

After this I spent so much time in viewing places that night came on and I put on shore. Not long after this the clouds began to gather thick all round, the ran came on with thunder and lightning. Here I haled up my boat high and dry. Here I walked up to get under shelter, but to little purpose. The flashes were so frequent and the Thunder so terrible that I thought one of the claps had seperated the whole mass of Nature. I was so stunned by it that I stood motionless for some time, and as soon as I could well recover myself I ran down and flang the Sculls out on the beach through a foolish and Idle Superstition. After this I marched about the shore untill day began to peep, when it all dispirsed and the sun arose fair and clear.

Now I had not a dry thread about me. My fire tackling and food was all afloat in the boat. There was no help for it and I fell to spreading out my dudds and baleing out the Canoa, and thus I remain'd untill the sun was about two hours high. Curiosity made me take up one of the Sculls, and as I turned it round in my hand I observed that it had no signes where the teeth should be. I then examined another and found it the same, when it came into my head that they could not be human but that they were the Sculls of Loggerhead Tortoises. After I was thus convinced I got into my boat and like a poor convicted fool paddled away homewards and arrived safe, but should have been miserably at a loss for fire had I not been master of spare tinder in ye Cave as all the other fire was totally out.

After this frolick I staid a long time at or near home and employ'd my thoughts as much to make my life easy as I possibly could. And, indeed, to make honest Confession, untill now I had never felt a gleem of that true contrition a Man in my condition ought to feel in his heart. But from this time I frequently called myself to account when my thoughts earned [yearned] for the onions and garlick of my native shore. After a time I so reasoned with my own heart that I became quite resigned and easy.

Shortly after this it came into my head why did I not Endevour to penetrate into the Woods nigher home. Now this put my wits to work how to accomplish that End. I had neither Ax or any other cutting instrument wherby I could expect to gain my point, and to venture the use of my knives would be a sort of cutting against my own interest. Nevertheless I took it upon me to put it in force but with the greatest oeconomy possible, and to this end looked out for the most convenient place to begin my incursion. I chose a place about half a mile west of my dwelling, and a few days after made a beginning. In the first place I cut me a large Pole, which took up some time as it was both hard and heavy. With this, after I had cut away with my knife, I beat down the bushes so as to get about twenty yards into ye Woods. At last I came athwart a huge yellow Snake and killed him with my pole. This animal measured as I judged full six feet, and ten inches round. This made me begin to grow a little timid and I began also to find I had given myself a large task and could not tell to what great end, so had a mind to decline it when a thought popt into my scull, that suppose I try fire. Accordingly, waiting a favourable wind least it should draw toward my dwelling, I went to the place one morning, and with a load of dry brush sat fire to it. It soon began to work with great force. N.B. I simply thought it would burn only the low bushes, but to my great surprise in the space of an hour Even large trees were on fire.

I retired down to the shore, and now I began seriously to repent of the deed as the fire became dreadful, such amazing crackings I heard at times that were wonderful. After this sort it burnt for the whole day, but when night came it was awful indeed. I slept not a winck that night, as a thought struck me—what if the wind should shift, it would then come directly toward my Cave perhaps. But toward morning it became quite a calm, yet the fire continued to burn more or less for seven or Eight days. At last a glutt of Rain came and subdued it; nevertheless, a huge smoke ascended for above a week longer.

In time when I thought the fire must needs be all out I took a march

over a part of this desert of ashes. The scene was truly odd. Every here
and there stood the trunk and limbs of a Cedar or Cotton tree, with
other sorts I knew not. At last I came to a stump which gave me great
vexation—it was of the true Plantain tree of which the Creoles use the
fruit as a substitute for bread. Now how did I grieve that there was no
getting at them but by their destruction, a means flatly against my interest, and answered only this end to inform me that they did grow
in the neighbourhood.

I now began to turn my mind to making of fishing lines. This I
was informed how to do by an old Negro on board of our Schooner,
which to soak the leaves of the Corritoo or the Aloe and work it into
fibrers. And I found it to answer my purpose well so that I never
wanted on occasion after. And in this sort I spent the day by day, being
seldom idle. Had it been otherwise I should have lead the life of a
mope. But here let me note I had one kind of attendant who generally
whetted my memory every two or three days, (Viz) a small insect
called a Chigua which, getting into the feet, there nestle and breed.
These must be got out with a needle or the point of a knife. But after
I had gotten callous footed they seldom gave me much trouble.

Chapter 5: Third Year of My Residence

By my account I found I had exceeded two years by some few days,
for I cared not to reckon too often as it generally gave me a melancholy
fit after ward. About this time as I was on my walk Eastward I had
the curiosity to taste of the Prickley Pear fruit, and Eate three of them.
I was then going in quest of Guano's. Now when I arrived on the spot
nigh to where the Stone Tower stood I had a call of nature, when to

my great terrour I saw my urine Red as Claret. The reader may judge my consternation before I recollected the true cause, as that it must proceed from eating those Pears. Yet I was not quite reconciled all that day, but on the morrow all my fears vanished as I did not find any ill consequences follow.

I shall observe that during the time of the wet seasons I stir'd little abroad excep to catch fish, and I could not dispence well without them. In all this long series of Solitude I never had the sight of one vessel moving on the face of the Ocean, nor did I open my lips to a fellow of my own form from the time I left the Long Key; yet I had learnt by this time not to repine at this my desolate scituation.

I shall remark in this place a circumstance which always happened whenever any light shower of rain fell, which was this. Immediately a noise as of multitudes of chicken began, nor could I with all my industry learn what it might proceed from altho it would be frequently close by me—unless it were done by the Lizzards, yet I have kept my Eye fixed on one of those animals without percieving any cause to proceed from them. N.B. This never happened but in the Woods. I could never learn the true cause as yet.[1]

I shall now give the reader an account how my houshold affairs Stood in regard to provision and the various methods I used at times. In the first place I never wanted the three grand articles, Fire, Water, and Fewel. Fish never fail'd—I had that kind of food in plenty and of great Variety Such as Groupars, Hinds, Porgies, Black and Red Snappers, Grunts, Rainbows, Parrot fish, Coneys, Gillambours, Doctor fish, Yellowtails, Pork fish, Marget fish, Cuckold fish, Schoolmasters, Tango, Squirril fish, Sucking fish, and Cray fish. As for Sharks and Barrowcooters [barracudas] I industriously avoided them least they should rob me of too many hooks, as I valued them above pearls. Yet at times I would run the venture with my lines made of Corritoo. I then went out into about three fathom water perhaps a mile distant by

---

1. Inserted in the MS at this point, apparently by a different hand, is the phrase: A kind of land crab called by the sailors and West India fishermen fiddlers.

way of novelty. There I caught an Old wife, Hogfish or a Small Jew fish. Nevertheless a Shark would get the better of me at times and carry away a hook.

And here it may not be amiss to relate an odd adventure I had as I was at this amusement. The day was very still and flat calm. Now as I sat very composed at my line hanging over the side of the Canoa, all at once I heard the violent rushing as of a Cannonshott through the Air. Down I dropt into the boats bottom, and so lay for about a minute. But when I raised my head I saw a large Bird called a Man of War rising up from the surface of the water with the garbage of a fish I had lately caught in its tallons. I having caught a Groupar who gorged my hook, I had opened it to recover it and had thrown the gutts overboard, and it had drifted away to some distance. Altho this affair may seem trifling to many, yet to me—a poor lonely creture—it was truly alarming, being never disturbed with any noise louder than the cry of a poor bird.

As to fruit and vegetables I never touched those I was a stranger to. Sappodillo's, Guavas, Limes, Mammees, cocoplumbs, Cassia fistula and Sea-Grapes, Colliloo &ccc I made use of as I found them. Flesh, except that of Guanos and a few birds out of nests, were what I seldom tasted. I found out a way to catch the Ground Doves, as thus. I took notice that after my great Fire in the wood numbers came thither to bask in the ashes. I took the hint and now and then made fires in bare places, among the ashes of which I laid snares and by this means caught many of them from time to time, which I roasted.

Now I well remember, as I happened to be after this game Chance brought me to the spot where lay a Young Faun about two or three days old. I was eagerly going to take it up in my arms to take it home when a thought came into my head, in what way I should feed it. This made me conclude to leave it where I found it, and thither I repair'd every day to scrape its feet. Thus it remained for three weeks or more. I then got some corritoo twine and belay'd it to a stump. The old one came always in the night to suckle it as I suppose, for I coud never get one sight of her in the day time. When it was about 5 weeks old I brought it home to my place, and there made it fast among the low trees hard by. It soon became the tamest of cretures, and if at times I cast it loose it still attended me. It was a female and I gave it the name of Miss Doe. It now fed any where round my dwelling and at last became so familiar that she followed as a Dog.

One day I took a notion to have a trial with her so made her fast, then got the boat round to the beach. I then returned and cast her loose. She followed me to the seaside. I then got into the boat and she jumpt in also, gazing round her wildly; but no sooner did I put off and she felt the motion than out she sprang in an instant to a good distance, and there fell to capering like a mad thing. After this I put along shore and she stood with her head erect gazing after me, but on my whistling she began to frisk it along the sands after me. Now as I could not coax her into the Canoa I put too and got out. She then ran to me, reared up her forefeet on my shoulders, and then fell to licking my face. And here I must needs observe that this was a scene of real pleasure to me, reflecting in my mind how the Divine Providence should thus throw in my path this poor inoffensive animal as an inno-cent amuser of my disconsolate hours. Some time after, she became so used to the boat that she would jump in the moment I took my seat, and went with me any where.

About this time appear'd on the coast numbers of Whales. I saw them first in the morning as I was then sauntering along shore. They remained in sight blowing and playing the whole day, and on the morrow they were still in View. As I was every now and then casting my Eye that way I saw one of them raise its body above half out of ye water. At other times their tails came out seemingly very high. Thus they kept blowing and sporting in sight for three days and then went away to the southward.

But to return to my household matters. In the turtle season which was generally about June, July, and August as I judged, I then feasted sumptuously but found my body to break out in large blotches after eating of them long togather. But it had this effect, that I became always more healthy afterward. At times I cut the lean parts of them into narrow strips and laid them in brine, then hung them up in the Sunshine where they became hard and dry. These strips I boiled at times with some Colliloo in a large shell. My fish I cooked either Boiled, Roasted, or Stewed, and this last was my general way. But I must observe I had one way, especially when in haste, which was to cover up a fish just out of the water under the hot embers, where it remain'd about ten minutes. After it was done I then took off the skin intire, opened the belly and took out the internals. Thus I obtained the true flavour of a fish, as the sooner they can be cooked the better.

I must not omit to observe that by frequent boilings my shells grew crazy,[2] which obliged me to look out for more. I took the utmost care of all my Europian articles. Now my head became full of making baskets, and I resolved to make a trial. I sought out the most favourable twigs, but to my great disappoint few that would answer my end. This put me on my old work of wattling again. I first made the bottom, then fixed uprights at the four corners, and then wattled up between them, and thus I formed an ordinary kind of basket which would hold about half a bushell.

Some time afterward as I happened to be out in my boat nigh to the Bird Key and going over a very shoal place, I saw a large fish close along side the canoa. It was the first I had ever seen of the kind. I struck it on the head with my paddle, when it began to flounce at a most high rate. The water was so shallow that it had not depth enough to swim. At last, as it was endevouring to get round, it got its long saw over the gunwale of my boat and plaid away at no small rate. At last I jumped out on the off side with my paddle and began to pay away at it; but it soon got out of my sight. This fish seemed to be about ten feet in length. Had I at that time my grange with a line I could have caught it with Ease.

I shall in this place take notice of an affair which often gave me much uneasiness, I being not altogether free from that wretched prejudice imbibed by the generality of children concerning Apparitions. This they suck in with their Nurses milk, and often from their own simple mothers tales. I say this had never left me and it gained as I travelled, having it renewed by the constant repetition of Sailors, a set

2. Warped or twisted.

of men by no means clear of such imaginations. N.B. My present uneasiness proceeded from a noise I often heard late on moon-light nights. This was a hollow treble tone, as thus: Yaoho, Yaoho, repeated perhaps three or four times togather. This was answered at a distance by some other like sound; this was always to the westward of me in the high land and at a great distance. Now the chief cause of my terror Originated thus. While I remain'd in Providence[3] I had frequent converse with an Old Negro Man, a native of the Island of Jamaica, who in his younger days had been well acquainted with many of the Buckneers, sail'd with them, and knew many of their haunts, but had come in by the Queens Act of Grace and then followed Piloting or went out to hunt after wrecks about the coast. This White headed old fellow, altho he could write and read and was well versed in the Scriptures, had been in England, France, Spain, and all over the coast of the Spanish Main, was yet full of superstition. Now this old man, whose name was William Bass, among other stories related to me concerning a sort of Nocturnal Animal who walked upright as a Man and the same size, that they were black and wonderful swift of foot, that they sucked the blood of all animals they caught, and left them dead. He observed also that by the track of their feet one would think their heels were placed foremost, and that their Cry was as above related. He observed likewise that nothing but a bullet made of silver could kill one of those cretures, such credit did he give to those romantick notions.

Now altho I did not care to credit him to far, yet when my own Ears became charged with the like sounds I verily thought I should see them, and perhaps too soon. But as I was not visited by them I became the less concerned unless when the sound seemed to be nigher than ordinary.

Thus time went on with me untill the wet season was coming on, and I prepared to lay up a Store of Wood, brush, Concks, &c. The latter I could keep by me for a long time togather by making a small fence round them in the water, and by this means had my bait gener-

3. In the Bahamas.

ally near at hand. About this time I had a most dreadful dream indeed. Methought it was the wet season and that the whole country was overflow'd, and that I was obliged to quit my cave in my Canoa. Like a Second Noah I wandered about for land, but could see only one small hummock at a distance for which I paddled with all my force. This dream so wrought on my spirits that my striving awoke me, and glad was I to find it no more than a dream. Little I thought then that it would be verified so soon after, as it was in some degree.

The Rains came on, and so great was the fall of the Water day by day that it overflowed the lagoon quite up to the enterance of my dwelling. And now I was forced to bestir myself with all dilligence, hurrying away with all my poor articles to high water mark and covering them the best I could. Here I was forced to remain quite exposed to the weather for two days, when it abated. In this my great hurry I had forgot my poor bird; as for Miss Doe, she stuck by me. After this I ventured to visit my Cave where I found that the Water had fell a good deal, and that had I but retired into the back part with my things they would have been all safe. I then began to look around for poor Yellowbill. At last I found him up in a low bush stone dead, as he had had no food for three days or more.

Now I began to call a council within my self, as thus. Fire and Water are no friends to Man unless under a strict limitation; therfore resolved with dispatch to erect me a Hurricane house to which I might remove on the shortest notice. Soon after I had removed my things back to the Cave I began this work and made it in the form of an Awning close at one end and a door at the other, thatching it well with Palmetto leaves. After I became a little settled again I began to think on my poor bird; and had not the Faun supplied its loss in some measure I should have found myself more solitary than ever, so great a consolation is any companion in any place recluse from the rest of the busy world.

One day as I happen'd to be out in deep water fishing I espied a sail in the NorthEast quarter. She came away large, and I in about an hour could percieve her to be a small sloop; but she kept a great offing and stood away in the Southward. Yet I kept my Eyes on her as long as I could percieve her untill she ran the horizon down, this sight being so great a novelty to me it brought back a kind of retrospect. I longed, and that earnestly, for to be once again removed among men. But when I reflected that she was certainly a Spaniard with whome I had no desire to associate, in a few days my craving began to vanish. Nothing from this time worth remembrance came on til by my reckoning I had began another year.

Chapter 6: Fourth Year of My Residence

Fourth Year commenced, And as far from any expectation of relief as ever but I endevoured to make my mind as easy as possible. Now I frequently used to make a party at Hunting at this period, and the Reader may be surprized how I brought this to pass. It was thus. Of a morning I used to prepare things ready in my boat and then with my mate Miss Doe, for whom I had made two small baggs to carry on her back any trifle of a load—thus Equip'd, away we went along Shore for the East Lagoon wher I landed and walked over land to Towers Field, as I termed it in my mind. At this spot I used to unrigg my companion and then light a fire. From thence we proceeded to a sandy plain, a great resort of the Guanos. Those cretures have burrows in the ground like our rabbits and can run very swift. Yet now and then I proved too hard for them, knocking them down with a short stick. But if they got so far the start as to gain their holes, In that case I made fire over their burrows. This seldom failed to fetch them out, when I was sure of them. Now having been often out on this business I shall observe a drool piece of Entertainment Miss Doe gave at times, as thus. When she would percieve me in full chase of a Guano off she would fly and be up with it in a trice, where she soon beat the creture dead with her fore feet. Such a sight as this could not fail to divert many of our English sportsmen, to see a man hunt with a Deer instead of a Dog.

I now began to think the cause of my never seeing above one Vessel in all the time of my abiding here must proceed from their knowing the coast to be dangerous, full of Shoals, Banks and Reefs, and that possibly it might be long eere I should see another, conjecturing that those who chanced to fall in with the land in the day time knew it their best way to keep a good offing if possible. But in a few days after I had been thus forming my cojectures a large Ship hove in Sight standing to the Northward. She was about four leagues out, and this threw me into a fresh relaps again; and when I parted sight with her I could have laid me down and given up ye Ghost. But time works strangly on the Mind of Man. After a few week had Elapsed I again returned to my usual tranquility and then resolved, that go fate how it would with me, I would repine no more. But as the most sagacious men are but as Idiots in the Eye of God, how then should such poor worms be able to forecast what shall be most fitting for them? Yet we must arrogate to ourselves a judgment as we list; and if the thing meditated fall as we desire, then is our God forgotten and we claim the applause. Now I lay all this to my own charge, as thus—what an Eager desire had I to be off in that Ship which passed by the other day. If so, perhaps we had never gained any port, but all have perished in the vast Ocean. Oh! The ways of the Omnipotent, are they not hid, and all things come to pass as He wills them to be? This I have all the reason on Earth to believe by what followed soon after.

According to my account I had been on this shore about Three years and two months, and I had not been abroad for many days as the Wind had been very fresh at south with frequent rain and thunder storms. Now after it had settled for a day or so I concluded to make a trip over to the Bird Island after Concks and Wilks. Accordingly off I put the next morning very erly, but I had not got far out before I espied a Canoa about a mile to the westward of my dwelling, with two people on the Shore. Directly I put back, thinking they had not seen me, and haled up my canoa. Then I ran along shore and got to a convenient place behind some trees. There appear'd no more than two persons, one standing, the other sitting nigh the canoa. I then saw them retire up to the bushes; after this they came down again and both looked into their Canoa. After this they both began to run about the strand making many odd motions, then threw themselves on the ground and acted like people beside their reason. At length I determined to get nearer to them as I knew there could not be above three or four of them by the size of their boat. At length I approched them so near that I could plainly percieve one of them to be a Woman. I could see them now and [then] Caress each other most lovingly, then in a moment they would fall into most extravagant franticks, throwing the sand over their heads and crying in the oddest way immaginable. What all this could mean I knew not. At last I resolved to shew myself. I had nothing on at that time but my bonnet, a ragg round my waist, and my Paddle in my hand, and thus I sallied down on ye beach. They were at this time not 60 yards from me. No sooner did they get sight of me than away they ran among the bushes. I hollowed to them but they never once cast an Eye back.

I then marched up to the Canoa where I beheld a very aged man in her bottom, seemingly at the very point of Death. I took him by the hand but he never opened his Eyes. I then spoke loud, wherupon he lifted up his Eyelids and seemed to look on me. I then began to call after them. At length the lad came out; I beckoned him but he stood stock still at first, then came on again, and continued to do the like untill very near me. At last he threw himself at my feet, taking one of them and placing it on his head returned it and did the like with the other. Upon this I lifted him up, clap't him on his back, and shook him by ye hand. He now stood before me like one under conviction. I then smiled in his face; this gave him some courage and he went to the Canoa side, spake to the old man, but soon he closed his Eyes and died away. I then made signs for him to call the Woman, which he did. She then advanced, but in a manner that plainly indicated her great fear of me—but by my repeating my civilities she came and did the very same tokens as the other had done. Now while these things were transacting, the old man gave one deep groan and Expired.

Now when I found the Old Man was absolutly dead I made signs for them to get into their Canoa and paddle along shore as I directed them. They readily obeyed, and the lad guided her along shore abreast of me as I went. Thus we went on untill we came to the spot where lay my boat. I then launched mine and made signs for them to follow me. This they did in profound silence untill we arrived at my own Cave. When I landed I Invited them on shore in the most friendly manner. They now began to cast their eyes round them seemingly with much concern, now and then gave a sorrowful glance at each other. I then produced fish and placed it before them, but they shook their heads and declined it, seemingly very melancholy.

I had now abundance of business on my hands, to have new tenants and a corps to bury all in one day. And now the Reader may be curious to learn what kind of company I had got, and their characters. I shall therfore describe them in the most intellegent way possible. The Girl seemed to be about the age of 17 perhaps, about the height of 5 feet 3 inches, her complexion that of the Nut brown or rather lighter, her Eyes black and the whites of them a China cast inclining to a blue, a small nose and mouth, her teeth even as dies, her Neck, shoulders, arms and leggs most finely turn'd, her hair like jett parted before and curiously tied behind, hanging down in plattings united togather with strings of beads of many colours to a great length. Round her Neck, arms and leggs she wore three rows of teeth belonging to the Tiger[1] or some such animal. Round her hips ran a narrow piece of wove cotton answering the Fig leaves of our firs parent Eve.

The lad seemed to be about a year younger but stronger built. As to his head of hair, it hung over his forehead and shoulders after the order nature had disposed it, in which she had by no means been Sparing. As to dress he was compleatly to be seen in his birthday suit without any manner of a disguise by art. Sometimes I thought them to be Twins as they were both of a height and so much resembled each other in features that it seem'd impossible for it to be more so.

The rest of the day was spent in endevouring to gain them over to

1. The Central American *tigre* is a wildcat, not a tiger. The author later refers to "Tigers and Wood Cats."

a good opinion of me after the best manner I was master of. Now as they both continued to behave in a melancholy strain I attributed it to proceed from a twofold cause, first the death of that aged person who I took to be a Grandfather, and the other their being so unexpectedly discovered by me. The tears constantly flowed over the Girls breast when ever she cast her Eye toward their Canoa. The lads trouble seemed to be of a more manly kind.

But as there was at this time much to do I could not spare the time for condolence, as I had lodging to provide in the first place and then the funeral to be ordered. Therfore without loss of time I took part of my own couch and carried it to my tent and spread it the best I could. I then shewed them where to turn in for the night. They both obey'd in a condesending way, shewing at the same time their gratitude. I slept little the whole night. Into my canoa I got by the peep of day and went out a fishing, then returned in about two hours, where I found them both sitting in their own Canoa weeping. I call'd them out and cheer'd them the best I could, and began to kindle my fire. When this was done I fell to cooking as fast as possible. After this I made signs for them to come and Eat with me. The lad came directly but the Girl declined it. I then went to her, took her by the hand and brought her to the table and bade her sit down. I then gave each of them a roasted fish. Hunger now gained the day over grief and they both eat heartily, which pleased me much.

After breakfast I made signs for them to wait on me to the Canoa and I then took the Corps up by the head and shoulders, pointing for them to take up the legs. They did so, and we carried it to a distant place and laid it down. I then began with a paddle and dug a sort of Grave, then made them help to lift it in. I then went and sat down to rest myself, watching their behaviour, but they seemed only to be waiting my motions, so then I got up and began to cover in the Sand as fast as I could. Now the lad began to assist me and the poor Girl threw herself flat on the sand, weeping exceedingly. When we had made up the grave I then took them back with me.

I must observe in this place immediately on the appearance of my new guests Miss Doe abscented as being frighted at strangers for the first day, but the next morning she thought proper to follow the Corps at a distance.

In a day or two my new friends became a little more free in their behaviour. This gave me reason to thing [think] my conduct had made them entertain a good opinion of me. They began to converse a little togather. Nothing could be softer than their Speech, yet it seemed to me very difficult to attain as they drew their words in with the breath and then uttered them as from the throat. I found the Girl extreamly modest and bashful, especially when ever I looked on her, she never failing at such times as not to see me; yet with the glance of an Eye I could every now and then catch her at viewing me as she found opportunity. In about 7 or 8 days we became more sociable togather, but I could observe when ever we were on the shore they would be pointing to the Southward and the sighs would escape the Girls breast frequently. The lad would point that way with his finger and say a great deal to me.

Now I had one great difficulty to master, as this. I could by no means what ever learn their names, for when ever they spake to each other there would be some kind of change in the words so that I could not fix on any as appelatives. The method I took was this. On a day as the Girl was washing some fish out of the Canoa, and knowing the Lad to be out of Sight, I made signs for her to call him. But here I was decieved again, for standing up she began to cry in a small shrill voice, "Hoo, oo, oo, ahee!" He soon came up and I was quite nonplus'd. I put him to stir up the fire as a pretext for her Calling him. But as we were sitting at victuals I pointed to my own breast and said, "Penrose." Directly the lad understood me and nodding his head looked at his sister; then pointing to his own breast said, "Ayasharre, Ayasharre," then directing his finger to the girl said, "Yalut-ta, Yalut-ta." Now, thinks I, it may not yet be what I would be at; therfore some time after I took an opportunity to call "Ayasharre." He came running and smiling to me directly. After this I took occasion to go into the cave and called the Girl the best I could. She came at once and I gave her a shell to bring me some water as a sham. Now, thinks I, this is enough; but I repeated the lads name so often that at length I had brought it to Aharry, so resolved thence forward to call him Harry; and the same method I took for the Girl, calling her Luta for shortness. Hithertoo I had not once meddled with any thing I saw in their Canoa altho I saw there was much trumpery in her. Now Harry, as I call'd him, and I went into her and among the things he grabbed out a Yam and ran Eagerly to the fire to roast it for me, as I judged. This sight made me run and snatch it out as soon as I could, it being a most precious jewel to me. This caused them both to wonder but I soon made them understand that I would plant it in the ground. With that he ran down to the Canoa and brought up 3 more. I felt such joy on the occasion that I became transported. After this I went with them and examined their freight, and this is the invoice of the cargo: Two very neat paddles bladed at each end, two small harpoons fixed with lines and staves, a bow with several arrows headed with sharp stones and Sting Rays bones, a Small Silver Bell, half roasted turtle, eggs, and part of a Dead Dog or some other animal resembling it. The two latter articles I made them throw into the lagoon as they Stank like carrion. Several sorts of Fruits and roots—these we used and planted a part of them. But what transended the whole Cargo in value to me was a clever small Hatchet, good as new. On this Hatchet was stamped the Makers name, as follows: "Pedro Munoz, Cadiz." By this I knew they had a traffick with the Spaniards.

It was with the greatest difficulty that I could keep my legs in this canoa, yet they had a small mast and a matt sail which they could ship and unship as they had occasion. Yet I many times afterward saw four tall Indians stand and paddle one of them with great dexterity, when I am certain the most Expert of our Seamen could not have kept his balance in her.

I now began to learn them a few words at times, and the first Word in English Harry caught was "Come" as he heard it so often repeated by me. As for the Girl she betrayed a very great reserve when ever I aim'd to instruct her. But one day as we were sitting togather, the Deer coming up to her, She said "Miss Doe" as plain as I could speak it myself. The method I took with them was this. Every morning I shewed them two or three objects and named them, they aiming to say the like. By this method they soon came on. At last Harry would ask me the name of a thing he had forgot, when the Girl would never fail to set him right. By this I found that altho she did not speak so often as her brother, yet she retain'd it much better in her memory. These poor innocent young cretures became every day more and more the delight of my mind, being always eager to obey me in all I desired or directed them to do, and I Industriously strove to gain their regard by every means I could study. Nevertheless I carried my self so as that they should regard me as a kind of superior to them.

Harry was so delighted with my method of Striking fire that he would ask me for my knife every now and then to be at it and would even put the fire out for the purpose of lighting it again, so that I was forced to refuse him often.

Now it happened that I took Harry with me one day to take a view of the burnt ruin I had made. The Girl Perceiving it began to weep; this moved me to know the cause. Upon this she threw her arms round her brothers shoulders and whispered some words. Upon my wanting to know the meaning of it he was put to it for an explanation but began thus: "You go, me go, Yalut-ta go not, never come, dead, sick, die." Upon this I took her by the hand and made her go with us, as I could not think of giving her the cause to complain. So off we went togather, Miss Doe in company, but when we came to the spot I was much surprized to see what a great change appear'd. Multitudes of thing had sprang out afresh, and even blossoms were on many shrubs to be seen. This made me determine to plant my Yams here at all events. Now as I had never seen one Deer for the space of the whole time after my burning the Woods, I concluded they had forsaken the parts. Here Miss Doe, percieving the great space before her, would set off and race away to a great distance, yet immediately on my whistling she would bound back to us as swift as an Arrow. The next day I made them take the Yams to the same place and made them plant them, and from those we obtain'd sufficient for our use ever after.

Some months passed on thus in perfect harmony when an accident happened of great moment to me, as thus. As I went on a time to my

Reckoning I found that I had more shells than I ought to have, or that I was much decieved. I pondered it in my mind but said nothing as I knew my reckoning was totally marred, and it gave me a great deal of uneasiness as I suspected in what way it had happened. The affair proved according to my conjecture. Some two or three days after, I observed Mr. Harry to bring in a few shells and throw in to the basket before my face, and out of pure good will as to oblige me certainly. Now how to return him thanks for this great service I knew not, but burst into a fit of laughter and so turned it off as it was a folly to pretend giving my reasons for what the shells were intended, so told him he had enough of them.

Now I became obliged to invent some new plan wherby to keep my time, and for this purpose determined on the following, (Viz) To cut it on the trees with my knife 50 days at a time; and for that purpose I looked out a large Cedar tree or rather Fig tree Whose bark resembles in texture those of our Beach bark, and on one of those trees I cut the date of my full time as nigh the mark as I could possibly conjecture. It was just 3 years and 2 Months when I first found them on my shore, and they had at that time been with me perhaps 4 months, so that I fixed the period at 3 years and 6 months. From this period I continued to add by fifties, giving Harry a strict charge never to touch the marks on pain of my anger. Now as those characters appear'd to him a kind of conjuration he studiously avoided even touching the tree.

Having mentioned this Fig tree I shall give the reader some account of its singular qualities. N.B. This tree does by no means resemble that of our tree of the same name in Europe. The manner of its first acting when in its infant state is thus. It grows perhaps to the height of 9 or 10 feet, at which time It becomes so weak that it stands in need of a succour. Its to be observed it seldom fails of springing up some 2, 3 or four feet from a stately Cedar. At this height seemingly as from instinct it parts into two arms tending toward the Cedar tree, where it clasps it as with two arms, being so weak in its own nature that it must needs fall to the ground unless thus supported. After it has thus attain'd succour It begins to grasp and climb, growing daily stouter and higher; and I have observed frequently that altho other trees would at times interveen, yet it shun'd them in order the better to come at the Cedar tree. And thus it proceeded to gaine strength and magnitude untill it attained the very top branch of the highest tree in the forest. At the same time its body, having the same kind of adhesive quality, extended itself in such a manner round the bark of the Cedar that it totally envelop'd its kind benefactor, unless in some few places the Cedar could be percieved through. And thus in the process of time the whole External appearance became an ample Fig tree or a Grand counterfeit. This the reader may rely on as a matter of fact as I have been an eye witness of it above a thousand times.

N.B. I frequently called them in my mind Ingrates, comparing them to such kind of Men who in adversity will abjectly fawn and whedle themselves into the favour of any, the very meanest of Company, so as to obtain relief in adversity. Yet if fortune but once smile on them they prodigally reject and shun their very benefactors. This I may with the strictest propriety charge my own soul with, as thus. Did I not, and that without any absolute provocation on her part, slight that tender Parental-hearted Cedar tree, My own Mother, whose arm had so kind and tenderly supported my infant fig tree State untill I attain'd to that strength so as to stand erect? I say, did I not then suffer her to wither and dry away as the Sap from the Cedar in weeping for my folly, While I plumed myself in all the extravagancies of a mad headed Fig tree among the thorns and thistles of this World? But let me hope that I have made some atonement for that great act of ingratitude by the dire Contrition I have since felt, and the mortifications I have since that day undergone.

One evening as Harry and I were walking on the shore I chanc'd to hear the Yoho's cry. Upon this I bade him to listen and asked him what he knew concerning it, expecting some odd account or other. But to my no small confusion he laughed as said, "That Birry."

"What is Birry?" said I.

"Bird," said he. "Go all nights, bite bird little." Then clapping his hand to his mouth made exactly the same noise. That was enough for me. I at once concluded it to be but an Owl or some such nocturnal bird, and called my self an Owl or an Ass for implicitly swallowing down such Idle tales recited by credulous fools. N.B. These Anecdotes are not to be supposed to have fell out exactly to the very time as I recite them, but in or neare as best I can remember, I having no use of Pen, Ink or Paper as then untill the time the Dutch Ship was lost.

In order to divert the time I used to play at Quoits now and then with my Messmate Harry, and this he learnt to such perfection that he soon became my match. And often when we were at this sport which was always on the beach, Luta—as I called her by way of an Abreviation—would seem much Elevated when ever I won the game. This I found never fail'd to cause much sniggering in my friend Harry, but as it always passed in their own language they thought I disregarded it. But sometime after this as they were with me in the Cave Harry Came and stood before me and said, "Where you come?" This I knew meant whence came I. It put me to a great stand as I knew they had not English enough to comprehend my full information, so I pointed to the Sea, made as though I slept often on my journey in a Canoa, and then arrived on their shore. This I found made them very thoughtful and the Girl wept much, but to pass it of as well as I could I began to instruct them in words. Now as Harry observed me to be much pleased with his Sisters pronunciation [he] leaped at once on his feet and taking Luta by the hand put it into mine. Then he fell to Shouting, hollowing, Whooping, dancing and making his Obedience to us after the manner I had learnt him, crying, "Eat it, Drink it. Eat it, Drink it. Catch it, have it. Catch, get Luta!" And thus he went on like one frantick with joy. All this time the Girl stood looking silently on the ground. I then gave Harry to know that I understood him very well, shewing by my look that I was pleased with his proposal, It being a matter I could by no means be against as She was a young Creture of so charming a disposition and so ready to administer in her kind services on all necessary occasions.

I then asked Luta if she was willing to sleep with me, as having no other address wherby to convey my intimation of making her my Wife. It is natural to suppose the Ladies, if ever these lines should reach their hands, may be curious to learn what kind of answer this fair one made me. It was this: "Penoly"—as that was the nearest they

could sound my name at first—"Penoly not go out," pointing to the
sea. "Me make fire all days," directing her finger to the embers. This
I concieved as a figure of conjugal love. I then told her she and I
would make up a new fire every morning. At this speech she fell on
her knees and kissed my feet. I then lifted her up. When her Brother
saw this he ran and clasped us both round and fell to dance, sing, and
whoop louder than before, uttering all the English he was master of
in the most confused way; yet I could plainly understand the true
meaning that it was the joy of his very Soul, and I must Confess by no
means against my own inclination as I imagined a thing of that nature
would infallibly unite us as one. But I kept all such thoughts aloof,
leaving it all to time least I should perhaps disgust them.

Here was a Wedding indeed, but without a Parson. Yet trust me
when I aver there never came a young couple togather on more Equal
terms. Our Love, interest, fortune, desires, and intentions were one,
(Viz) that of becoming an help mate to each other; and that kind
Providence had given us the power to perform even in this Wilderness. This happened just 3 years and 7 months after my first landing
on the Spanish shore or main coast (as I learnt it afterward to be, altho
at that time I thought it an Island). I now proposed to Harry that he
should go to sleep in my bower. This he readily gave into with and
slept there afterward; telling him that when he could find out a Wife
for himself I should be very glad.

Sometime after this great affair was settled my new Brother and I
went over to the Bird Island after concks and Eggs. When we came
on the shoal and haled up our boat nigh a clump of bushes there
seem'd to be a great stir beneath them, and, observing, we found a
multitude of Shell fish or rather amphibious gentry call'd Soliers or
Soldiers from their red colour. And as the nature of those beings Is
altogather singular I shall give the description according to my own
knowledge. (Viz) They are always to be found inhabiting Small
Shells of various kinds, but the Wilk is largest they seem to dwell in.
The fore part of this small animal resembles the Lobster when boil'd;
the after part within the shell is of so delicate a nature that it can not
suffer the least injury. They come out of the sea most certain, or go

thither for the shells. But what is most remarkable, Soldier-like they frequently commence hostilities and joyn in combat; and in these warm contests they beat each other out of their tents, never failing to take advantage of an empty house. Immediately on the others leaving it as they grow larger, they shift from one shell to another yet larger. They are good eating roasted on the coals, leaving the Shell directly as the fire touches them. They begin to bite as soon as caught, and that sharply with their claws.

After we had gathered about half a peck of those Soldiers I took a walk toward a point where were many Pelicans, and some so young that they could not fly. But I had not been long on the Spot before the old ones, taking a circuite round, gliding on the Wing, would return with such slaps on my head that I was forced to defend myself with a paddle as I retreated. After I had gathered a few Eggs I returned to the Canoa where Harry shew'd me a large fish call'd a Ten-pounder he had Struck with his dart. These fish are shaped like a Mullet, Exceeding swift of finn but very boney; but it served to shew me the great dexterity of my new brother, he having struck it on its full career as a good Shottsman would a Swallow on the wing. After this we hunted out for a few large Shells and between us found 5 whole. Now as we were at this work Harry took up a trace of an odd kind of stuff, the like of wich I had kicked before me often on the Shore. This he shewed me was young Concks and on his breaking one of the parts it proved to be so, there being above 40 young ones in the Cell, all compleatly formed. This trace of stuff was at least two yards long, and must contain thousands as the joynts were close together, in form like to the plant House leek and of an odd texture, in colour resembling sandy yellow.

Now this leads me to a remark seldom taken notice of by the most of Seafaring men, (Viz) that Shellfish, as they increase in age and magnitude, retire still into deeper water and this is the reason why we so seldom find shells with the fish in it of a great size when such numbers of the small are frequent, they never coming into shole water but when worked up by tempestious storms. And this I think I am clear in—as I once sat fishing in about ten fathom water there came up with my hook a monstrous Shell with the fish in it alive, of the Helmet species. Now I had seen thousands of them along shore but not one of them quarter the size of that I found, it weighing at least 10 or 12 pounds.

After we had got about 50 yards from the shore I espied a small Chicken Turtle on the top of the water. I shew'd it to Harry who, snatching up his dart, bade me to paddle slowly for it. I did so, and he struck it in the back. The staff drop'd out and away she towed us, he tending the line which was fastened to the dart till she grew tired and we got her in, being about 20 pounds. We then returned home and had a feast with it.

This adventure determined me to set about and make me a strong line for the very purpose, and accordingly I ordered Harry to prepare stuff for that end. After this we often got a Turtle; and this put my brain to work afresh, which was to endevour by the help of my brother Harry to contrive to make a small Turtle Crawl to confine a few of them as we caught them, and by dint of labour we accomplish'd it to our satisfaction.

Now finding they understood English so as to comprehend me, I sounded them about their Country. I asked Luta how far off their place was where she came from. She shook her head and said, "About 3 Sleep and 3 Walks," meaning about three days journey; but Harry tartly said it was long more than 4 Sleep, he was certain. I asked her then who the old Man was who died in their Canoa. She said he was her Mother Father called Coduuno, that their own Mother was dead, and their father put dead by the fighting men, and that she and Harry lived with the Old man, having two Brothers and two Sisters who were married to men and women like she and I were. I then asked them if ever any white men came among them. They said not every day, but once in many sleeps; that she had never seen but three old men of them long ago once when she was but so high. I asked her what they did when they came. They brought Crooked sticks with them, she said, and made the Women tell everything. I asked her then if they did not exchange things with them. "Some small, all for good," she said—but that her people did not like to walk with them. "Why?"

I replied. Because, she said, they used to kill all her old people when the very old trees were but small, as she heard the old folks say. But as they were now every where her people had no way to get out from them, and they could not push them into the Sea. I then asked Harry if their people did not Eate Men when they killed them in fight. He gave me a sneer and spit on the ground, saying, "No, no, no, never not!"—but that the Old Men said the oldest Men heard that such things had been done when the Moon was a little Star.

After this I asked Harry how they happened to come to my place. To this he made answer that they came out to fish and catch turtle but after they had been out two days the Old man fell into a fit, as I understood him then, which he was much subject to; and that the wind came off the shore so strong that they could never regain it; and finding the Old man to grow still worse they had at length gained my shore after being out 9 days, drifting away with the current quite out of their knowledge, having never been so far from home before. "Should you be willing to go back?" said I. On this they both Eagerly cried, "Go, yes, go! You go, you go!" I told them I would go when I could find the way thither, and drop't it.

Thus things went on untill my fourth year ran out.

Chapter 7: Fifth Year of My Residence

Fifth year commenced. One evening as we were all three sitting togather I reasumed the Subject of their going back again. On this they both caressed me fondly and said, "Yes, go, one, two, three!"

"No," said I, "if I should go your folks dont know me and so would have nothing to say to me. But there is your Canoa—go when you please, and I can remain as you found me."

Upon this a kind of Sullen Silence ensued, and I observed the tears to fall from the Girls eyes. Upon this I took her in my arms, and told Harry to observe his Sister. He then fell to blubbering and said, "I never go, Penoly, out you and Luta."

In the midst of this affecting scene all at once I felt a thing sting me on my thigh sharply. I got up and found a huge Centipeed under me. In a short time it becam almost Intolerable and gave them so suddain an alarm that it quite dissipated the other passion. Harry ran and killed the inseect and pounding it with some wet dirt laid it on my thigh, and Luta bound it up after the best way she could. I then retired to lay down, was in a feaver for above an hour with my head on the Girls lap, weeping over me in the most tender manner; and thus I fell asleep. How long I lay I know not, but when I awoke I was almost choaked with thirst. They gave me some fish soup, and by the morning I felt not the least uneasiness. But when I began to shew myself as was usual, Luta said to me softly, "I never go, Penoly, no go. But Penoly go, and Harry too."

I now began to reflect within myself that there can be no true pleasure proceed from giving pain to others; and as it was but a wanton kind of trial in me of their affection, I was but fitly served and had met a very just cheque for my wanton inquisition.

I began now to consider Harry as my chief mate in all undertakings; and one day as he returned from gathering Wood he brought a large Yellow Snake with him. I had seen of them before, also a small Green sort with another like a Barbers pole, one sort Black and long, another Yellow as Safron. I asked him what he woud do with it. "Eate it," he said.

"Do so," said I, "if you can stand Poison." He then cut off the head and skin'd it, after this gutted it and laid it on the coals, and when it was done he brought it to me to taste it but I declined it. Then I asked Luta if she liked it. She said yes, that "it very good." So when I found them fall too I tast'd it and must confess it to be tender as a chick and of a fine relish.

Another time he brought home a prodigious large Callabash on his head. I was then in the cave and Luta called me out to see it, and

I must confess it was the largest production of any Fruit kind I ever beheld. To speak within reason, it could not weigh less than ¼ of a hundred. Harry cut it in two and then seated himself to scoop it out, and certainly when it was made hollow each part would contain above a Gallon of water. This monstrous pair of Shells he laid by in the Shade to harden, and when so it became of very material use to us standing always in the cave full of Water for our use by way of Buckkets.

Shortly after this, as being now become better able, I determined to revisit the new lagoon where I found those Turtle Sculls I have mentioned. Therfore I bade Harry to get ready both the Canoas, and the next day we dressed a few fish and filled one of the large shells with water and left the câve, Luta and myself in my Canoa, Harry and Miss Doe in the other. We had no interruption on our passage but arrived at the place of the Sculls with ease, then proceeded up untill we came to a place full of Mangroves. Here we saw a great multitude of Mullets and other fish, with plenty of Whistling Ducks, Cranes, Galldings and other fowl of those kinds. The Bald Eagles, Fish hawks, &cc were in greater numbers than I had seen before, which was a sure signe of much fish in the lagoon. There was a channel about four or five feet deep all the way to the mouth of it, but at the enterance the water deepened to two fathom in most places untill we came up it the distance of halfe a mile, where it became shoaler by degrees. The whole length of this Lagoon Is about 1 mile or perhaps more, with its Enterance so shut in by a point that at the distance of 100 yards it is not perceptible. Now when we had got to the head of it we discovered a large and spacious place with a beautiful fall of water coming down from a Clift seemingly about forty feet high, with fine Trees overhanging the clifts. This water had its course to the Lagoon head down a fine lawn mixed with patches of gravel. This lawn gently ascended to the fall for about the distance of 100 yards. Nothing could exceed the beauty of this fine View. It form'd a kind of halfe Circle measuring by computation about a mile, Every where environed by groves and thickets except on the right as you advance, where you may walk up among the trees untill you gain the summit where you may have a

View of the whole Area, the lagoon and all, seeing out to sea for a vast distance.

I now told Harry to make fast our Canoas and then we all proceeded up the lawn for the Waterfall; and as we advanced a large flock of Parrots flew over our heads making a most confus'd Outcry. This made me halt a little, it being the first time I had Ever seen any of those birds wild. As I was thus gazing round me I percieved a kind of vacancy at a distance among the rocks. Thither we bent our course, and on a nearer view we opened a kind of passage between them. Here we discovered a fair Cavern with its enterance oblique to the Lagoon and, as it were, facing the run of water which came from the fall. It is difficult for me to give any exact discription of its form unless I say that the enterance resembled a kind of high Arch resembling some of our Cathedral doors, about 20 feet perpendicular but irregular and about thirty feet wide, all of a ragged kind of Rock and the floor fine gravel and small stones. I then told them to follow me, being determined to explore the whole place.

As we advanced the Eccho was so great that our common words sounded very loud. When we were got in to the distance of 5 yards I found the roof more lofty by much than at the enterance. At this place I thought it proper to return, and bade Harry gather some sticks and kindle a fire. This he did, and after it had burnt for a time I concluded to go in farther with fire brands in our hands. Now while this work was doing I discovered many marks and letters cut on the Rock on both sides the enterance in like manner with those I found cut in the Tower Stone as before mentioned. By this time I knew full well many had been at the place before my time. It is needless to give any discription of them as they are similar to what I have given a sample of already, Except that I remark that Two of the marks contained the names at length of perhaps two very great villains, and are as follows: Martin Fletcher and George Needham 1670.

We now took each of us a brand in our hands and advanced forward. When we got in about the length of 8 yards it then Contracted on all sides to about halfe the magnitude and inclined much to the left, so that a total darkness would have ensued had it not been for our lights. Soon after this we heard a strange bustle within, which put us all to our heels in a moment; but we were soon followed by such a Posse of Harpies that we were out into the blessed light of day in a trice with numbers of fluttering fiends at our Van. These were huge Batts, whose ancesters had inhabited that old mansion for many ages for ought I know.

After this alarm was a little over I told Harry to get fresh light and make another search. This he did boldly, contrary to my way of thinking. All the time he was gone I could not refrain from Laughter, as expecting him to return again after the same sort. At last he came running and Whooping out with a whole legion of those nocturnal gentry before him, crying, "Poo, poo, poo, poo!" and laughing at no small rate, whisking the fire brand over his head like a crazy fellow.

"Well, what now," said I, "Harry? Have you found the end?"

"Yes, yes," he said. "I hand me put there, too."

"And how is it?" I said.

"Very dark, very little short," he replied. By this I knew he had been to the end of it.

Soon after this Harry pointed and shewed me a very fine Plantain tree, and I directly espied two more. This so charmed me that I turn'd short round to Luta and asked her if she should like to live there. She said yes, if I liked to come live too. Upon this I came to a full resolution of moving without farther delay, being so taken with the place that I never once reflected on those necessary obstacles which then stood in the way such as retiring so far from our Yam patch, and becoming quite land locked from the sea. But when I once reflected on that it put me to a sort of stand. Yet when I came to weigh the great gain on the other hand such as that we should be quite safe from storms and inundations, together with many more advantages, and that we could by the help of the hatchet clear a way up to the clift and there have a more grand view of the Sea than from the simple beach below, I gave wholly into it at all events.

Here we spent the remainder of the day and then went into the great enterance and prepared to Sleep there for that night with three large fires burning before us, without any disturbance untill the next morning except now then a Bat would fly into the place. At the breake of day we prepared to set of, and got home to our old place in good order without anything happening and found all safe on our arrival. Now my mind began to run strongly on my new Scituation and I communicated my thoughts to Harry on the matter. He seemed to like my proposal but made objections I had never thought of, (Viz) we should be far from our Turtle Crawl, the Guano ground, and that we could find no drift wood there. That was all true, but I observed to him as the place was by far more to our comfort in all other respects I was determined to remove, and that very soon; that in regard to our Guano ground and plantation It was but to go the farther for it on occasion; and that after we were settled we would plant afresh nigher home, and make us a new Crawl for our turtle at the most convenient place we could find. And so far we all agreed.

We had fixed the day of our leaving the Cave when on a Morning shortly after, as Harry was out after wood on the shore, he espied a Canoa and came running away to us almost out of breath, crying, "Boat! Boat! Canoa boat!" Away I ran with him, Luta in the greatest fright after us, not understanding the meaning. When I came on the beach I saw a Canoa standing right in for shore about a mile off with three Savages in her standing quite erect with their paddles, intending to land about half a mile below us as I judged. Upon this we all three retired into the bushes. What means to take in this critical moment I knew not, but concluded first to observe how they would act. Now I found that Harry and Luta became uneasy altho they had been so much for my going with them before, but I spirited them up the best I could and thus we waited their landing.

They soon came to shore and haled up their boat. Soon after, one of them pointed direct for our dwelling and then they began their march toward us. Now, thinks I, they have certainly seen us or our smoke, so resolved to meet them at all hazzards; and in this I was the more bold as I could not entertain an Evil thought of them. After they came within 200 yards of us I told Harry to go down on the beach, and I then took Luta by her hand and followed, she trembling with fear. We were all three as naked, in a manner, as those we were going to face Except that I had a pair of Striped trowsers on and my bonnet upon my head. The instant they percieved us they stopt short. Upon this I hail'd them and they answered me. Then to shew that I was in no kind of fear I advanced boldly up. Then an Elderly person call'd out, "Espania?" I answered, "No, Englese." On this they all said to me, "Signor Capitano, bon, bon!" Now I took care to style myself an English man from what I had learnt from Harry and his Sister. I then made signs for them to follow me.

After I found them to behave friendly I told Harry to try if he could understand them, but how much was I struck when I saw Young Harry fly up to one of them in a transport of joy and call him by name. They all three got about him, but to give any just discription of their transport is beyond my power. He then pointed to his Sister. Here I had no need to enquire any way about the matter. The true language of the heart display'd it self amply, for I at once saw them to be old acquaintance. I could see that during the heat of the conference they cast a look of great esteem on me. At length I could contain no longer but joyned company, when Luta, throwing her arm round my shoulder, gave them to understand I was her husband. Then all three saluted me kindly in their way and made a regular survey of me, remark'd that I was larger than themselves, they being all three light low men but well proportioned.

The Reader may guess of my wanting farther information, and I told Harry to invite them home with us. I cannot but remark their great wonder and amazement when they heard Harry and Luta talk English to me. They would often lift up their hands over their heads betokening admiration, crying, 'O wah, wah he!" As we went on I asked Harry what and who they were. He told me that the Elderly man was Komaloot, his Sisters own Husbands brother, and that the tallest of the other two was Futatee; but as to the third he did not remember his name because he was not much acquainted with him. This pleased me highly and, shortly after, we brought them to our cave. I now bade Harry and his sister to sit down with them and talk over every thing, and Luta soon became full of chatter. I found her topic to be upon their own affair of being lost; and I then bad Harry pre-

pare a sort of mess for them. This he flew to obey with speed.—I remarked one thing peculiar to these people, (Viz) that they all shewed
their teeth much, never closing the lips in conversation but rarly.

Now I wanted to learn if accident or designe had brought them to
our habitation. Therfore I put Luta on that Enquiry and she related
it to me as thus, that there had been a great Canoa lost lately and that
her friends had been out in the great water to it for what they could
find. I told her to enquire if any of the people were saved. She said
no, but they found four dead Man and that they buried them; but if
true none could tell. I then enquired whither they were English or
Spaniards. They replied they were the latter by their cloaths and
little wooden crosses with beads about their necks, saying they knew
the English threw such things away unless they were made of Gold
or Silver, as they said the English did not use woodden Gods because
they thought them little worth. This made me smile. Upon this Luta
said something which made them all laugh also, and on enquiry she
had told them I had no God at all that she ever saw. I asked her how
she could tell that, when she made me such an answer that it closed
up my mouth, (Viz) if I had one I had never shewed him to her.

But to return. I asked Luta what they said concerning their being
lost in ye Canoa. She told me she was informed by them that they had
been out all along the coast but had given them over long ago, thinking they had perished at sea or that some vessel had took them up and
carried them away; that the old mans wife was dead, also one of her
Sisters called Niuxa. When she mentioned her name I could see the
tears fall. One of those Indians enquired whither I was not afraid to
live there on account of the Rainey times. I bid her tell him I was going to remove to another place, and that I would shew it them before
they went home again if they would stay a day or two. Harry told me
they said they would, and were going to make a small hutt to sleep
with us awhile. Then we all began to eat of such things as we had,
and after this Harry and one of them went and brought round their
Canoa.

When it came I observed they had collected several things out of the wreck by which I knew she had been of the Spanish nation. There were 3 pair of uncurried leather Shoes, 2 small brass Kettles, a large rowl of Sail cloth, Some woollen frocks and trowsers, a good Firelock but no powder or Shott, a great number of Spikes and small nails, a parcell of knives without springs like our clasp knives but open with a back stopper behind, about 20 balls of twine, 6 hatchets, some chizzels, three Saws with plenty of fish hooks and a pair of Shark hooks, a dozen of Fish grainges tied togather quite new, two felt hats and above a dozen new ones made of Straw, a bag of fine Lima Beans, four hammers and one mallet. But there was one thing gave me some concern, (Viz) a bloody Shirt. This gave me cause to suspect their honesty, but possibly they were innocent notwithstanding. I did not care to meddle with their booty, so what might be hidden underneath I knew not. Mr. Harry made very free to examine their cargo, and I curbed him as fearing they might take a pet and leave us, and anything of that nature would have given me much concern.

Chapter 8

I had been on shore about 4 years and 3 months when that these Indians discovered us. After this they began to cut down stuff for erecting a temporary hut for themselves. Harry lent a hand and myself, also, which pleased them much. During this they enquired in particular how I was cast on their shore. Now as I found they had got some knowledge of it from Luta I bade her give the whole relation to them.

In about three hours the tent was finished close to that of Harry. After this they prepared to rest for the night; and on the morrow I proposed for Harry and two of the Indians to go out a striking[1] fish, (Viz) Futatee and the other, keeping Komaloot with the Girl and me. I ordered it thus as a precaution, but my suspicions were groundless as I found afterward. They returned with some fine fish, and then I ordered some to be cooked for our Voyage.

The next morning we all put off and had a pleasant trip of it. When they arrived on the Spot they all concluded that it would suit much better than the old habitation, but that I must expect to be troubled now and then by the Tigers and Wood Cats, and that Harry must keep a good look out after the Piccaries and Warrees[2] or they would devour all our Yams and other things. This was a new hint for I had never once thought of any thing of the kind, having never sceen any in all my time. Nevertheless I was determined to settle on that spot, and I observed to them of my never seeing any Tigers while I lived down at the other place. They told me that was very likely as those Cretures never frequent the low Mangrove grounds, being much disturbed at the noise of the Ocean and finding little game in such quarters. But they observed that when Ever any visited us we should shew them some fire and they would soon run off, observing that the very Smoke continued for a length of time seldom failed to make them quit that quarter; then, pointing to the Deer, observed that she would be apt to draw them about us. But I was determined to stand the chance as I was passionately fond of the place.

We took a general view of the place while Harry prepared some fish, and after dinner we all got into our Canoas and returned to the old habitation again. On the Morrow I proposed to go out after the Turtle, and off we went. The party consisted of Futatee, his companion, Harry and myself, leaving Komaloot with the Girl at home. We followed it up for two days, in all which time we caught but 6 Tortoises alias Turtles. I reserved but three of them for our selves; the others they roasted in their own slovenly manner on coals for their use as they returned home to their friends.

They now began to talk of departing. I then put Luta upon begging

1. With a fish spear rather than hooks.
2. Peccary and warree: species of wild hogs.

them to bestow some few of the articles out of their Canoa as we had no means of providing the like in our poor condition, intimating that we should be very ready to assist any of their people should they come our way in any distress. Upon this they held a council togather, then asked what we desired and they would exchange with us. As to any Exchange I bade her tell them they could plainly see that I was very poor. Then Komaloot took me to the Canoa and asked Harry what I wanted. I then pointed to the Hatchets, Kettles, Twine, &cc, but what I seem'd most to require were the very things they were the least willing to part with; but he took up the Shoes and offered them. Upon this I gave them to know that I was now become an Indian like themselves, and that my wants must be quite similar to their own. This put them on a fresh consultation. At last Komaloot and Futatee spoke a great deal to Luta, which she thus delivered to me—that they advised for us to go and reside among them; that they were certain every one would treat me with kindness as I had been so good to Luta and Harry. I now began to think this an evasion not to part with any of their ill begotten goods, as I suspected, And acquainted them that it was quite uncertain if I did go to dwelle among them I might through ignorance give them some cause to be offended with me, and that I did not chuse to be within the knowledge of ye Spaniards. So it was best for me to abide where I was, but that I should always be glad to see any of them at my poor habitation when I was Removed to the other place, observing that if Harry had any mind to return with them to his friends I would by no means desire to detain him. But in regard to his Sister I had all the reason in the world to think she did not desire to leave me, as we lived in great love and harmony. Upon this they observed that they had no room for Harry if he would go, their boat was so full.

Then Luta retorted on them sharply that, altho they had so much, they would not part with any thing to her. This caused a loud laugh, and after jabbering among themselves they took her by the hand and brought her to the Canoa to shew them what she wanted. On this she laid her hand on one of the Kettles and they gave it to her. Then they asked me what I chose. I told them Harry wanted an Ax. They gave him one, then I observed they had many knives and we wanted some, and they gave us three with some of the twine. I then asked for a few of the Lima beans as to plant; of those they gave us readily as many as we would have. And now finding them in giving strain I asked for some Sail cloth; that we had also. But it was with much difficulty we could extract a few Spikes and nails, these they valued greatly. They gave us also 5 of the Sambraros or straw hats. Some time after this I took it into my head to try what flattery would do, And advised Luta to intimate what a great fondness I had concieved for Komaloot. The bait took, and before they went he gave me a Shark hook and two of the new fish gigs; these I valued much. Also they gave me a hammer and a Saw, with a parcell of the small fish hooks.

The next day they prepared to leave us, but when Harry found this he took Luta aside and desired that she would entreat them to procure him a Wife. This caused much mirth; but as Luta and I joyned in the petition they said when they got home they would advise among the people. They then observed that if they came we must expect them in canoas as they had never been to our place by land. After this they took their leaves in a friendly manner. We went down to the beach to see them off and remain'd there above an hour; and it was wonderful to see with what Expedition they paddled away, full as she was, so that I would not have trusted a favourite Dog in her unless he could be near enough to swim for his life.

While they remain'd with us I used every art to learn what part of the coast I was upon, but without effect unless that they told me I was upon the Continent and not an Island as I had conjectured. Sometimes they would mention Carthagena and a few other places. They told me no Indians lived within 4 days journey of me. They said there were Many great Indians to the Northward of me, with whome they never talked or walked. When we returned back to the cave I was surprised to find the Shoes and Gun among the mangroves, but judged they had gone and forgot them. Now Luta and Harry became Very dull and remain'd so for two or three days.

It happened soon after, as I went into the Cave I saw on a ledge 3 Dollars. This surprized me and I called Luta to enquire about it. She told me she had them out of their Canoa from under the sail cloth, and that they had as many as would fill a woodden bole. This concern'd me little as such an article was of no use to me as being to far from market.

The next business I took in hand was a thing of such a nature that I believe few of my own Countrymen are accustomed to do, (Viz) no less than making my Lady a petticoat out of the fragment of Sailcloth, and by help of twine and a Sail needle I finished it, then shewed her how to put it on. She was so highly pleased with it, as I told her my country people wore the same, that for two or three days she was constantly viewing it as she walked along. She was so awkward in it that I could not refrain from laughing, the shortness rendering it the more comic as it did not fall above a foot below her waist. If any of her own sex should ever read this they will excuse me when I plead the want of stuff to make it longer. One day as she was advancing toward me I took it into my head to learn her to make a Courtesy, and Harry to make a Bow. Now as I knew so little how to instruct her she did it in so diverting a way that I laughed immoderatly. After this when ever she observed me to be duller than usual she would be every now and then dropping a Courtesy before me untill she forced me to smile.

I in the next place determined by help of my tools to fit my Canoa as a Sailing boat. I cut the old boats Rudder and made a thout [thwart] to fix amidships, then cut me a small mast not lant[3] [sic] as my store of Sailcloth was but little. When my Sail was made I then cut me a spreet [sprit] for it. When the mast and sail was ready I took a small trip in her with Harry and his Sister, and she worked very well. The next matter was to examine her bottom, and for this purpose we got her capsized on the beach. After this Harry and I pegged up all the wormholes with peggs, then we covered her over with a large quantity of boughs to keep her from rendering while we went in quest of a Shark or two. According, the next day we went in the small canoa on the hunt and was a long time before we succeeded; but at last we hooked a Shark, and after we had killed him towed him home, rendered his

3. Possibly intended to be lank, in the sense of long or tall.

liver in our little brass kettle, and then paid all her bottom with it. Some of this oil we used to burn in a shell at times, but they soon cracked and became unfit for farther use. But Harry knew of a kind of Wood which burnt like a flambau which we made use of at times.

Now being on our removal I took care to mark it down and found my account to stand thus at our departure—4 years and 6 months. We carried all our movables thus—Harry had the Deer and a few things, the rest I stowed in my large canoa and then took in my Lady, bidding him to paddle away ahead as I had a large wind. But I soon fore-reached him and got there first, where I landed my Spous and waited his arrival. He came in about half an hour after. We then carried up all our materials to the Castle, as I intended to term it, and then gave up all for to go astricking. Harry was a dab at that work; we were not long before he struck a fine Snook fish, enough for us all at two meals. When the evening came on we then made three large fires before the Castle gate as a guard against the Tigers; and when this was done we got a few Palmetto leaves out of my canoa and laid them as a bed for the night. Then we retired within the enterance but had little sleep the whole night, the place being strange to us, but nothing disturbed us in any other way unless a Bat now and then flew out and in.

Erly in the morning Harry and I went down to the Lagoon and cut a way into the Mangroves, leaving a good shade over head. There we docked our two Canoas. The rest of the day we employed in putting all our matters in order; yet It was a full Week before I could reconcile myself to my new habitation, the thought of Wild Beast ran so strong in my mind. But my two companions slept well enough; their native innocence protected them.

The first thing we went upon at our new dwelling was to make a Stool for each of us to sit on and a new table. N.B. These were to be made of boards, but those boards were first to be procured. I then put Harry on felling a few small trees such as we could best cope with. These I undertook to cut in lengths and then saw through. Much labour it cost me before the work was finished and rough enough they were when made, but served us well enough.

I chose the inner part of the Castle as our bed chamber and to that end made fire in it least any damps should anoy us, and to banish the Bats from it. The outer part was for Harry, so that we lay some distance asunder and hid from each others view. And thus we went on without any interruption for above two months. I was quite charm'd with the dwelling.

But one afternoon we heard an unusual noise. Harry ran out but soon came running back to me bawling like a mad fellow. No sooner did I get out than I beheld poor Miss Doe flying home with a Tiger cat sticking fast between her shoulders. Rage possessed my mind at once. I snatcht up one of the Hatchets and flew to her aid. Harry was soon up with me and we soon brained it, but the poor Deer was so mangled that I at once knocked her in the head. This made Harry look at me in a strange manner, but I soon gave him to know my reasons for so doing as I then saw she was so torn that she must needs die of her wounds; and by my putting her out of pain and misery it would prevent a like disaster in future.

All this time Luta kept a distance, and indeed I was surprized at my own ferocity, when the affair was over. Harry said that he was not timmid in the least had he but a Bow and arrows in his hand; and his merit in that way was great for certain, having seen him hit small birds flying, Guanos and Lizzards running, and that at a distance of thirty yards. We were now provided with a Venison feast when we least expected it, so fell to work in skining her. All the time this operation lasted Luta did nothing but weep. Indeed we were all three concerned at the loss as she was so diverting a poor Creture, so cunning and tame to the degree of a Spaniel dog. However, so it must be; and we eat of her carcase untill it was no more fit for our use. The rest I told Harry to throw into the Lagoon for fish meat.

Some time after Luta observed to me that it was a bad omen, and that we had better to have remained at ye Cave. I laughed at her, for by this time I had got the better of all Superstition so gave myself little concern on that head. What gave me the most concern was how to fall on the best means to keep off those Devils for the future, and for this purpose we made it a rule to make up a large Bonfire twice a week. This answered our purpose so well that we seldom saw any more for years. Notwithstanding, we always took Luta with us when we went abroad, fearing what might happen in our absence.

After we had been here a considerable time we went out one day along shore to the Southward of our Lagoon. Here we found the water to be very shallow with a small current setting North, and as we were paddling along I espied a long range of a small kind of Red rushes in the water, as I thought, but on a better examination found them to be the horns of multitudes of Crayfish. We then put the Canoa close in among them and grasped handsfull of their horns, plumping them into the boat; we could have loaded her if we had been so disposed as they were not very shy. These Crayfish are of a light freestone colour spotted with black and yellow; and some of them Harry has struck often since weighing perhaps 4 pounds apiece. The discovery of these fish proved afterward of great service to us as a variety of food. We returned home greatly pleased with our cargo, and continued to live quite happy togather.

The Deer Skin Harry cured Indian fashion and I took a notion to make me a kind of Jackket of it with the hair side outward, without sleaves as I was not Taylor enough for that part of the work, but I finished it after a sort. I was not a little proud of it as it spared what little dudds I had by me; for I had one great anoyance when naked of such a nature that I could but ill withstand, which was A Sort of Fly called a Doctor fly. This Insect is about the size of our hive bee and shaped much like it, but its head is of a bright Saxon green. No sooner do they find an object than they dart at it and instantly make the Blood fly forth like a lancet touch.

I shall in this place give the reader a short view of the usual dress we appeared in, (Viz) In the first place a huge Sambraro or broad brim'd straw hat on my head, my Deer skin jackket without sleeves reaching to my hips, a piece of striped cloth round my waist below that, Mrs. Penrose in her short canvas Petticoat and a Straw hat, lastly Mr. Harry with his Straw hat and a scrip round his waist.

By this time Mrs. Penrose was advanced far in the way of Increasing our family, and on that account I took more than ordinary care of her. Her brother was so proud of it that he would be ever talking on the subject, asking me what name I would give the child if boy or girl. And now we began to clear us a good road up the hill with our hatchets that we might the better come at the top of the clift over our Castle enterance. This we did by spells, a day now and then, untill my reckoning proved that I had now been another year compleat on this shore.

Chapter 9: Sixth Year of My Residence

After we had cleared round the top of the Clift we could survey the whole coast far and wide, and I plainly percieved the great danger ships of burthen would be in if they approached too Nigh—nothing but rocks, sand banks, Reefs and currents with Eddies and breakers to be seen all the whole coast along, so that I wondered no more that I saw so few vessels pass by.

One day I took occasion to ask Harry if he could tell me what his name meant in English. This put him to his trumps a little. At last he consulted his Sister on the thing and they agreed that Ayasharry signified a Swift Runner or a light footed person. I then bade them translate Luta's name, and they said that it signified a Green Grove; that Komaloot meant a finder or sercher; and Futatee a Bald Eagle. I then asked what Codu-uno meant, (Viz) the old man who died in their boat, and they said it signified a Man of great strength.

One day as I ascended the hill to look out, as was my usual way, I thought I saw something like boats off a point to the Southward. On this the Spieglass came into my mind, so returned down for it. Harry was at that time gone out afishing. We both returned up the hill and I plainly saw them to be boats or Canoas. We then came down and stay'd untill his return, which was soon after. When I told him of it away he ran and soon came hurrying back, saying that Komaloot was coming with three Canoas. Upon this I revisited the eminence but could see no more than two, he having exagerated the thing out of ernestness; and I laughed him almost out of countenance by observing that one Canoa was large enough to bring him a Wife. This made him shake his head, saying he believ'd they would not do him that service now that his Father, Mother, and old Codu-uno were dead. Sometime after, they came round the end of the Long Key and put right away for our new dwelling. By this time I could count 8 people, then we all three got into my Canoa and went down the Lagoon to meet them. As soon as we got out, we landed and made up a fire. This they soon saw, and when they came within hail we gave a good shout. They answered us; and then I bade them both dance and sing like me. This I did in order to shew them how very glad I was to see them.

The first man who jumped out was Komaloot. He ran to meet me, and I him. After embracing he said, "Yallut-ta?" I pointed to the fire where she stood; he then ran and took her in his arms, shook hands and hugged Harry. By this time the rest were all landed. Now a fine scene represented itself to me. Nature began to display itself in her full powers. They all ran togather in a cluster, fell to weeping, laughing, hugging and even to bite each other. One of the men threw out of the boat some arms and fell to dancing. This I well knew betokened friendship, and I kept dancing and singing at such a rate that had any of my own countrymen beheld me they would have though [thought] me as much a savage as the rest (but this by the way). I knew it to be my province so to do, it being of the greatest moment to me as a poor stranger.

My Visitors were as follows: Komaloot and his Brother called Vatte-queba—this person was the Husband to Luta's Sister; his Wife Lama-atty; Owa-gamy—this man seemed to be a sort of principal; Futa-tee, who had been here before; Dama-Sunto and Zula-wana; and lastly Cara-wouma with a little boy in her arms aged about two years called Quearuva.

We then all embarqued again for our Castle and arrived soon after. When they were all landed I made signs of the great joy their presence gave me and then lead them all up to my Castle, where I told Harry to tell Komaloot to place them before me according to their dignity. When he understood this he took Owa-gamy by the hand and seated him first. I then bade Harry to bring me a few flat stones, and with the point of my knife I scratched his name on it. After this I asked him what it was in English; he told me it was a Traveller. This I wrote beneath it and laid the stone in Luta's lap. The next that came was Zula-wana; they told me his name meant a good Canoa-man. This I put down and delivered the Stone. Then came Vattequeba, alias an Excellent Fisherman; Futatee, alias the Bald Eagle; then Lamaatty, alias Transparent Water; Carawouma or a beloved darling; and lastly the boy Quearuva or the Councellor. The whole time this was doing they all sate very serious and looking fixed on me. But as soon as I had done it Owagamy enquired the reason in a very ernest way, and Harry told him I did it on purpose to learn their names. This pleased them all, so that Owagamy, pointing to them all, told me their names over again.

After this Komaloot stood up and took the young woman called Carawouma by the hand, then began a long harangue to me, now and then turning to Owagamy and the rest who all answered in one tone like an Amen in the Church. When he had finished his speech he sat down, leaving the Girl standing. During the time Harry would smile and look at his Sisters, they nodding their heads in return, so that I gathered enough to inform me of what was the theem. Then I desired Luta to give it all to me in English the best she could, and she began thus:

"Komaloot says when he went back to my people he told them that they had found out My brother and I, no more dead, because one white lost man who had a Heart as big as a Great friend had lifted up our lives again, and covered over the bones of their old friend; that Panoly had made one of three people,"—so that they all agreed I was a great hearted man, and that made Owagamy come with them to drink clear water with me. And out of the great love they bare to Ayasharry they had brought him Carawouma for a Wife, she being willing when she heard [he] was come alive again. When she had finished I took the Girl by the hand and called Mr. Harry forth, then made them joyn hands in presence of the whole company. Directly they all gave a great shout of approbation and thus ended the ceremony.

I now began to think it high time to refresh my Visitors, but was forced to bid Luta inform them that they must Excuse us as their coming so erly in the day had prevented our making a provision suitable for them, so that I must beg they would help my brother Harry in catching a few fish. Immediately two offered their service, and I told Harry to take them away among the Crayfish, so off they went. While they were absent Luta took them about by my advice, and I shewed them all our manner of living and sleeping. Owagamy observed many things to her in regard to our future happiness. This she interpreted to me and put me in mind that I should get water and drink with the men, as it was their custome with friends. I then told her to fetch me a Callabash and I then went to the streem and dipped it full, then took Owagamy by the hand and drank to him. This pleased him I found, and he recieved it from me. After this I tasted it with all the rest. No sooner had this ceremony passed than they all began to Sing, dance, and laugh with me after a much freer manner than hithertoo.

Soon after, the Canoas returned with plenty and they fell to cooking, and when ready all hands sat round and got their fill. As for our liquor, it was the pure stream which ran from the rock. After we were all refreshed I bade Harry sing them an old song I had learnt him, (Viz) "Welcome Brother Debtor," as I used to chant it frequently when I reflected on my own condition. They all seemed much delighted and were very desirous to know the true meaning. I then told Luta to give them the sense of it in their own tongue; this she did after her way. Then Owagamy made this remark, that he believed Alexander must have been a Spaniard by his travelling so far, and one of those who first came into their own Country to murder his old fathers, but that he must have been a great boy to cry because he could not kill them all. For had it been so, their sons could have had no Indians to murder in the mines—at this time expressing some words I knew not, with great bitterness. After this they all got up and took each other by the hand and fell to Singing and dancing after their own rude way, which I thought to be barbarous enough. I took notice they had little motion, being no more than a gentle trott, stopping now and then to give a kind of Whoop. This being passed, they all went and fell asleep in the porch as I may term it.

I took so great a liking to the little boy that he began to play with me, but when ever he chanced to touch my beard he would shrink back to his mother again. This made her ask Luta why I did not pluck it out as their men did. She told her it was not the custome of my country to do so but that the White men used to cut it off with sharp knives, but that I had none of them fit for the purpose. On this Lamaatty observed she would not like to feel her husbands face so. Luta laughed at her and said she must take great care never to touch her husbands head neither, but that she was then with her cheek on the head of the child.

Luta said her Sister informed her they had brought some things in their boats for us, which I was glad to hear mentioned, and told me also that Lamaatty said she was glad to find her with child for that would make me love her harder. "But," she said, "I told her that could not be unless you were to eat me."

This made me laugh so loud that it awoke the Men and they all came out to us. Shortly after, Lamaatty said somewhat to Zulwana, when away they went down to their boats and brought up to us a bundle of Bass rope, 4 Earthen pots made of a very fine red clay, about half a peck of Lima beans, a kind of very small pease, Rotten Oranges, long sweet potatoes and other sorts of roots, about three handsfull of Indian corn, Mammees, Avogatos, Cashoo nuts, Squashes, Pompion [pumpkin] and Gourd seeds all in the planting way. They also gave us 5 Coconuts and some Cotton seed, with several other things I knew not by any name. Now I had my Eye on two Dogs they brought with them, differing much from our dogs. They were of a middle size, coloured like rusty Iron, with their ears erect and broad faced, having sharp snouts and stump tails. I could have been very proud of one of them but could not venture on begging one, as I did not care to appear greedy. But Owagamy, perciving my fondness, made me signes I should have one when they went away, to drive away the wild beast.

I shall now observe the odd behaviour of Harry toward his new Lady. Every now and then he would take her by the hand and lead her off from the company, and when he got her out of our Sight, as he thought, he would caress her with fervancy, so that he soon brought her into a pleasant mood.

The Indians now began to talk to Luta about planting and gave her advice about it. I then asked them concerning my planting a sort of fence round our abode to guard us from the Tigers, &cc. This they strongly objected against, saying the more trees we had round us the more Moskeetos would anoy us. I took their good council; and they continued with us for the space of 5 days, when they began to prepare collecting what could be gathered for sustenance on their return. I gave them what I could spare, doing every thing in our power by way of retaliation. Just as they were upon leaving us Zulawana took and tied one of the Dogs fast to a stump for me. Then they all took Boat and we accompanied them out into the bay, where on parting I made Harry give them the Song again. After he had done they all sang in their turn. Now just as we were on parting, and hearing the Dog howl all the time, I took occasion to ask how we should feed him as we got so little flesh. They laughed and said he would eat fish or fruit as well. Then I desired to know when they intended to pay us another visit. They said after many Moons, when they could walk by their neighbours with good countenances. By this I judged they were at war.

This observation was very appropos for me; and I desired Harry to inform them that it was my great desire that they would never communicate my being on this shore to the Spaniards as my nation was ever at war with them, least if they should catch me they would send me to the mines and I should forever be lost to them and Luta. They then one and all made signs that they would sooner be burnt with great fires than betray me; and I veryly think they were truly sinceer in what they said. We kept company as far out as the Long Key and then took leave amidst much lamentation among the women, especially poor Luta—she wept bitterly on parting with her Sister.

And indeed I was much moved myself, the cause being truly reasonable. (Viz), Here I was to part, perhaps never more to meet, with some of the most disinterested mortals, a people who out of common humanity had done the utmost in their way to be the generous relievers of my wants, had come so many leagues without any expectation of reward. And this I blush to own was not done by Europian Christians but by men we are pleased to call brute Savages. So I may with justice remark, where is the advantage they have gained by the Spaniards' discovery of this New World? Have they not done all evils among them, destroying and Enslaving under colour of Exchanging one Idol for another, while they committed such crimes among them which ought really to point them out as the most infamous and inhumane Savages on earth? I say, had not those poor cretures been in a much better state so to have remain'd untill God should have been pleased to have brought about their Redemption in or by some more Apostolical means?

After our return our first business was to make some woodden Shovels to turn up the earth withall. These we were forced to make out of the Sollid limbs of trees the best way we could.

Now I began to council Harry as to his conduct toward his Wife. I insisted that he should behave in all respects to her as he should observe me behave to his Sister. As he observed me to be remarkably serious he made me a reverend bow and said he would do all the good to it he could think of. After I had done he brought Carre-wouma before me and desired I would give her a new name as I had done to his Sister and himself. Upon this I told him we would call her Patty. He asked me what that was in English. Now that being the first name which came into my head, I was at a stand so told him It meant a fine Girl. That pleased very well, as perhaps any other would. And now my family was increased to five including the dog.

The next business was our planting. This I considered would be best at the old burnt ground near the old cave. As I did not know how much we might be troubled by the Wild beast, and I had never seen any on the low coast nigh the sea, I judged that the most promising of success. These things took us up above a fortnight; and now we found the Turtles draw in for the shore, their time of laying being near. After this we went out a Stricking every day, taking the Girls with us, untill we had caught Eight. And then it came into my mind that we need not be at so much trouble, observing to Harry, should we watch them when they came on shore to lay, it would save us much trouble and by that method we should get all females, the males being at that season very lean. This practice we followed soon after, and turned so many that we were obliged to desist.

While we were at this Sport on a fine Moonlight night, Harry being too impatient for the turtle to fix herself; upon that she espied him and was making back for the sea again. He, observing that, ran and got astride on her back and grasped the fore part of her Callipatch.[1] I, seeing that, ran and got behind and Patty came and clung round my waist. Nevertheless, She was so large and strong that she scrabbled us fairly into the Sea. The Girl tumbled off backwards, I slid on one side and lost my hat, but Harry stuck on her untill she sunk him up to his chin before he left her. We had much laughter on the occasion, and Luta she enjoyed the scene all the time from the beach. After I had regained my hat we returned home for that night; and the Next day we returned to the scene of action and by hard labour got them all into our crawl, being Eleven in number the least of which weighed nigh three hundred. We had at the same time Eight Chicken turtle. We now and then got Sea grass for them with Concks and Wilks, and it was a surprizing thing to see with what ease they cracked the shells altho they were as hard as flint.

We spent our days quite easy as we wanted not, yet I had not tasted a morsel of bread for years. What little cloaths were left I husbanded with strict care, knowing I could obtain no more unless by the Ship-wreck of my fellow mortals; and that, God knew, was the farthest from my desire.

My Lady now became nigh her day, and we had the sad misfortune for Harry to fall sick. Patty was very tender over him; and how to act in this case I could not tell, but he took to his poor bed of leaves and was in a high fever. The Girls had some knowledge of herbs and made kinds of tea. I prepared weak soups for him, but he would be now and

---

1. Callipash, that soft part of a turtle next to its upper shield or shell; wrongly used for carapace, the shell itself.

then lightheaded. At such times he was for going a fishing or to see his Sister Lama-atty. The business now lay on my shoulders so that I was obliged to go to the old cave for Yams and Turtle alone, also a fishing. Now as I was going on one of these errand one morning very erly, no sooner had I got out of our lagoon than to my great alarm I beheld a Sloop at anchor off the end of the Long Key. I plainly saw men walking who had a sort of Sail tent on shore. Now, thought I, what a fine pickkle am I in, but I had the thought to put back directly within the point, being pretty sure they could not see me so close under the land. I directly put up the lagoon and the first thing I did was to put out the fire. My Girl seeing me much gravelled would need know the cause, but I waved it. Yet when she saw me get out my Glass and run up the hill she asked me if any people were coming. That was enough —out came Harry, ill as he was, and would follow me. When we got up to the top I could plainly see some 5 or 6 men cloathed and that they were Spaniards by their broad hats. While I was thus viewing them they kindled up a large fire. Some of them went off on the ramble, and I saw the smoak of a gun. Now I was sure they were not Indians which was enough for me, being determined to have no manner of concern with them if I could any way avoid it. I was quite amazed to see Harry—he acted as tho nothing ailed him, and wanted for us to go off to them.

But as I was eagerly looking out and carelessly leaning over a Crooked stump of a tree, it gave way by the roots and off I went down the declivity for some yards untill a rugged rock brought me up, much scratched and hurt, so that I lay quite helpless. My leg and back was torn by the stones. Harry went and call'd Patty and between them they convey'd me down the hill. Now I was laid up, unable to move much. Patty gathered medicinal herbs and my Wife boil'd them and then they washed my wounds, she being also very nigh laying down. Harry gave me trouble least he should relaps, and the Enimy at the door—all these things added togather became a great load on my mind. But contrary to expectation, either by my fall or the sight of the Spaniards Sloop Harry kept his legs. After the Girls had bathed my wounds

I found my Spirits recruit, and that I was not hurt so much as I then thought. I then bade him go hunt the Glass and keep a good look out. He came back with it, and the strangers tarried there all that day. The next morning he went up very erly and said they were there as yet and were going about in a boat. I had no longer patience—up I got, and found my right leg to be very stiff so that I could hardly put it to the ground; yet I must needs hobble up the hill supported between Harry and Patty. When I arrived they seated me; I then took the glass and found they were stricking their tent. We had eaten nothing from the time they first appeared. We then eate a few turtle eggs dried. They remained there all the next day, and we spent the second night like the first; but on the morrow Harry came down and said they were all gone. Away I went with my best leg foremost and could see no more of her, but found her soon after by the help of my glass standing closehaled to the eastward. And who they were or on what errand I never knew to this day, but was glad enough of their departure.

This happened about 5 years and 3 months after my landing on this shore. And the next day Luta had a son. I gave him the name of Owen, that being the name of my father. The following day was remarkable also by my espying a large Ship in the Offing. When I first observed her she was a great way out, standing to the westward. We soon lost sight of her as she never nighed the shore. This was the first large Ship I had seen near the coast in all my time.

A few days after this there began an Aloe to bloom directly before our dwelling, and it was surprizing to see the great progress it made in a short time. I had taken notice of them before but never had one so fair within view. In a space of a fortnight or twelve days it grew to the height of thirty feet as I judged, full of most glorious tufts of Yellow flowers and scented the place all round. The Humming Birds, Bees, Wasps and Flies were feeding all the day on its Sweets so that it became a perfect habitation. In particular there came one sort of the Humming bird which had two feathers in its tail three times the length of the bird. In one point of view it was profoundly black but in another shone like green gold. Harry knocked one of them down with a blunt Arrow, but struck away one of the long feathers out of its tail. I kept it by me a long time untill some vermine eat it away.

It happened on a day as Harry was out on his rambles he chanced to see a Green Parrot fly out of the hole in an old Palmetto tree, and found two young parrots in the nest which he brought home scarcly fledged. These birds he took care of and raised them on guavas and other wild fruits. At last they would eat Yam and Plantain, we having got access to several of that kind in the Woods; and Harry had planted several from suckers. We had also plenty of good Squashes and Pumpkins coming on, for every thing seem'd to thrive rapidly.

Patty came on in her English very fast, and as to her own Person was really a fine Girl, taller than Luta and of a lighter colour but not so full fleshed and, as I judged her, something older. When ever we went abroad any where Luta had a broad piece of bark to fix her child on, as in a trough; and this I know, It cost me a pair of trowsers for baby linen with which she used to wrap him up so as to carry him at her back. We lived after the same sort as usual for a long time, never seeing one Soul save our own little family. We eate, drank, lay down and got up as we listed, without the least disturbance. Each day was a kind of Coppy of the foregoing. Add to all this, we were blest with a good share of health; and my companions knew no other mode of life.

Yet I must needs own that I could have been much pleased to know how the world went on, and to have had the enjoyment of a good Companion of my own country. But as this perhaps might have cost me some unforseen trouble it gave me no great anxiety, as I knew my self at this time by experience as that if I was taken from the joys of this busy world, I was amply recompensed by being removed from the reach of rancour and malevolence. And now I found to my great comfort that a Young man might live, if so disposed, without vice; and I am certain, had I been removed from this forlorn place into life's great hurry, I had gain'd so much over the vanity of my own heart that I verily think I never should have dipped again into such a scene of dissipation. So that finding myself the gainer, I became quite easy nor had I a desire to return for any reason what ever Excep the joy I concieved in beholding my dear Mothers face once more.

I took a great distaste to the Parrots as their noise was the most ungratful to my Ears, but as I found them diverting to the Girls I put up with it, they being fine birds to the sight. Yet when they began to chatter I could not help talking to them at times. Luta, observing me, would divert her self sometimes with them at my expence, As thus. Getting one of them on her hand she would talk to it thus: "Cut it off! Cutt it off!"—meaning my beard; then say: "Where is your father, your mother, Penoly? Where did you come from?" and the like. All this the birds learnt pat, and to call them by their names also. And if at any time they grew dull, they had no more to do than to give each a bunch of Goat or bird pepper, when they would both begin to prate at no small rate so that I could have been glad their tongues would cease. And if at times Luta found me dull she would threaten to give the birds pepper.

Some time after, Harry came home and reported that he had seen the Wild beast and a great many more than an hundred. This surprized me and caused me to ask how he had escaped them. He replied that he was not in fear of them. I then wanted to know of what kind they were. He told me they were a kind of Hog with white faces. Therfore I Imagined them to be what I had heard called Warrees. "Why did you not set the dog to hunt them?" said I.

"No, no," said he, "too many. If the dog catch one, all the rest will bite him to death." I knew Harry to be the best sportsman so gave up the point, but I was determined to contrive some scheem or other to trapan them. Now in all this time I never saw above two Tigers, and Harry one. We found that setting up a loud shouting made them turn tail directly, so on their account I was become a little easier in my mind but took care never to suffer the Girls to wander far in the woods alone.

One day Patty brought home some of the Candle fruit or Cassia Fistula. They are about the length of a foot and when green hang dangling like Mirtle candles from the tree; but when ripe they resemble black pudding in colour. She told me they were good put in hot water against pains in the bowels or costiveness. The substance within resembles tar and is very sweet, so that I used to dilute a small quantity of it in water and squeeze a lime among it. This made tolerable beverage but in colour it resembled Coffee.

We had not tasted a Guano for a long time; there was none frequented our quarter, the soil being in no way sandy. The next thing was a Voyage to Towers Field on a party to hunt Guano's. We took all the whole family along to prevent harm. We fastened in the Parrots with plenty of victuals in their rude Cage we had made for them, and then put away down the lagoon, My wife, child and self in the large Canoa, Harry, his lady and the dog in the other. Thus we proceeded unto the old dwelling; there we went on shore and took a repast.

Now as we were all out togather I took a notion to visit the Key opposite where the Spaniards had been lately. When we arrived we went on shore and found the marks of their Tent, with a boom of an old oar made of green heart and exceeding heavy. At some distance we found an old Jarr would hold about three Gallons of a course earthen ware, round at the bottom. Harry picked up a case with a knife and fork in it, very rusty, but I took care to scower it so as to become fit for use. I found they had been so generous as to sink a barrel into my well as a legacy to those who should touch there in future times. We shipped our things, and just as we were putting off I picked up a good fishing line and sinker without a hook. When we got over to the other side we stood along shore and got to our hunting ground. There our dog ran down four Guano's and we gathered a parcell of limes, and then put back for our old dwelling where we all slept that night, and the next morning sat out for home where we found all secure. But the joy the poor Parrots shewed on our return was wonderful—they talked the whole day long.

Now as a man is never too old learn, I got Harry to make me a new Bow that I might learn to shoot at marks with him, as thinking it would be of use to me. What spur'd me to this was, Harry the day before shott a duck as she flew over our place. Our Dog hunted well altho he had no likeness to a Spaniel, and took the water freely. I gave him the name of Swift. This Dog never barked, but in the night would give a long howl at times.

Nothing of note happened from this time except the rains, untill I found I had been here now 5 years and 9 months. At this time we kept much within door, as I may say, altho we really had no door at all. And now the beauty of our fine Cascade became quite changed to a great Cataract of Red water, thick and muddy, and continued so for above a fortnight. Therfore we used to fill our large Jarr and the Calabashes and set them by to settle. Providence never failed us; and we had either a boil [or] stew, and at times a roast. (Viz), We had the duck roasted. Harry made a woodden short spit and stuck the bird on it; this spit he fixed in the ground inclining toward the fire, turning it round in the ground now and then untill it was done. As for our Guano's, we allways stewed them.

After the wet season was passed by, Harry proposed to go out to Strike some Sting-rays, telling me they had bones in their tails good for Arrow heads. As to those bones, I had seen of them, having been to catching those fish before. And as it is a fish little known in England I shall give it a description here. They are formed much like to those fish called Thornbacks. I have seen them would weigh above 200 lb. Just at the dock of its tail are fixed those bones one above the other. I have seen them with three, point behind point. These bones are very sharp at the ends with exceeding fine teeth each side as they lay flat on the tail. Those teeth are in a contrary direction to their points so that when the fish becomes vicious it erects the tail and darts these stings into its enemy, tearing out the flesh wherever it strikes, and leaves a great anguish in the wound for a considerable time afterward, as I felt by experience. Their Skins are sharp grained like unto a Shark.

There is another Species of that animal whose skins are Exceeding hard and rough, and are transported to Europe for the use of our Cabinet makers. This fish is called a Rasp-ray. There is yet a third sort of these flatfish called the Whip-Ray. This fish differs from the rest having the head resembling a Tortoise almost. The back is blewish with studds of small white circles all over it with the Skin exceeding smooth and shining, with a tail black as jett and of such a length that a fish of the size of a common Thornback shall have one perhaps Six foot in length.

After those fish Harry went in his own canoa and was out almost the whole day. He came home with about 7 bones, having struck three of those fish. What had detained him so long was this, He said the last fish was a very large one, and as he struck it the Staff slipped out of his hnd and the fish made away into deeper water with it sticking in back; and had it not returned again for the shore he should have lost the whole, and that was what we could but ill spare.

Chapter 10: Seventh Year

This year commenced with an ugly stroke of fortune to me, as thus. We all took a small trip to the Cave after Yams and potatoes, and while I was there I took a notion for to wash myself in the sea but I paid heavily for it. As I was about to come on shore I felt somthing dart into both my feet attended with instantanious pain. I directly swam to shore but was obliged to fall down on the sand. Harry ran to know what was the matter with me and found both my feet full of the darts of Sea Eggs. By this time I was in such an agony that I expected to faint. He directly ran for the Girls and they Got me into the Canoa, put on my cloaths, and then hurried me home as fast as possible. By that time my feet were Swolen so that I could not budge, and they were forced to carry me up to the bed and laid me down. After this Luta got Prickly pear leaves and split them, then toasted them at the fire and applied one to each foot, binding them on. From that time almost untill the next day I remain'd in a high fever. When it abated she took off the leaves and my feet appear'd as tho they had been boiled, but the thorns came all away with the leaves and I was quite easy. But I could not walk for three or four days, my feet were so tender; but they soon came to order again.

These Sea Eggs are of that class of beings who never move from their first stated fixture. They are of many different Sorts, shaped like to an Orange, divided with curious lines of partition, and spotted with Green, black, Yellow, red and brown. Some have no thorns at all, but the sort from which I recieved my injury have darts four or five inches long and are black. These darts they have the power to play about in the Water, directing them as a man would point with a Sword any way as they list.

Soon after this we were intertain'd with a very diverting scene. One of the Parrots had got away to a distance and was perched on a Cashoo tree where she sat refreshing herself, and a parcell of wild Parrots passing over espied him or her. Upon this they all came and settled in the same tree. Patty saw them first and came to call us out to share the diverting farce, and indeed it was a scene truly comic. They would walk side way up to her and place their heads parralell to her, then give her a peck. Another would get over her head in the mean time and do the like. Ours would hold up her foot as to ward of the blow. Others would take her a slap with one wing. At last they gathered as by consent all round her and fell to paying her at a sad rate. Upon this the poor thing began to call out, "Harry! Harry! Owen, little Owen!" as fast as possible. But no sooner did she begin to speak plain English than off they all flew, screeming like so many mad things and quite frighted, no doubt. Directly our Parrot began a loud laugh and flew home; but when she got into the cage she began to prate away to the other as fast as her tongue could go, the other bird saying, "Hay, hay, hay!" as if it understood the relation. This diverted Harry to so great a degree that he rolled on the ground laughing.

Shortly after this Harry expressed a desire to go after the Flamingos and I consented, so off went Toby[1] and his Dog the next morning in the small canoa. He did not return that day, but as I knew it to be a

---

1. Evidently the author's *lapsus memoriae*. Toby is not introduced in the tale until later.

good distance I was no way uneasy as he had fire works with him, and that made an Indian at home every where either by day or night.

The next morning was ushered in with a new adventure; it was thus. I call'd to Patty to rise and make up the fire, saying her man would be home soon. This she went out to do, but she had not been out long before she came running in to us crying there was a great thing dog fell down by the fire from the top of the rock over her head. What this could mean was quite beyond my comprehension so I got up and ran out, but just as I came to the fire down came another. This amazed me but I rouzed up my courage and went to examine them and found they were Piccaries, and both of them embowelled. Now, thinks I, this must be a piece of Messmate Harry's gamut; but as the Dog did not come in first as usual, I could not think what or how it could happen. At last a loud laugh began over our heads. Directly I ran in and snatched up an ax, being determined to stand my ground. When I came out again I heard a voice call down from the Clift, "Yallut-ta, Yallut-ta!"

Upon this I cried, "Come down, you Scoundril! Come down. Let us have no more of your dogs tricks!" And indeed I was at that time very angry with Harry, as I thought. My spirits were so hurried that I never adverted to the pronunciation or difference of Voice untill an Indian shewed himself and called down to me. Immediately I saw it to be Komaloot. Upon this I call'd out the Girls quite overjoyed. I then made signs for him to meet me and away I ran up the hill. There I found Komaloot, Owagamy, Zulawana and a young Indian I had never seen before called Sama-lumy. I saluted them all, and they returned it. They were all four armed with Bows, arrows, and Mascheets [machetes] or Cutlasses. When we got down to the house great joy commenced directly. Komaloot took the child in his arms and hugged it. They then asked after Harry and Luta told them what he was gone after.

I then enquired how they came so secretly behind us, and that they had scared us not a little. Owagamy then told Luta a story as follows— that they happened to be out after game when they came to a fine open country, and there Komaloot made a proposal to find out our place.

To this they agreed, but that they had overgone the place; this they learnt by getting up a large tree from whence they discovered a smoke on the right near the coast. This they concluded must be the place of our abode and turned off for it. Shortly after, they fell in with a few Piccary hogs and killed two of them, that they gutted them and cut out their navels, intending to bring them as a present to us. N.B. The navel of this animal is on its back, and if not cut out as soon as the beast is dead the whole carcass taints soon after. He said they discovered us at last by the great smoke the Girls made, for that Samalumy was then got up a tree not far from our habitation. They soon after got within sight of our place where they call'd a counsel and concluded to proceed after the manner they had done, least their suddain appearance should alarm us too much. I told Luta to return them my thanks for their good conduct.

While Patty was preparing a little of what food we had, the dog came running in. I then knew Harry was not far off. The poor animal was quite transported at the sight of his old masters. At length Messmate Harry made his odd appearance dressed in Scarlet from head to foot with his Flamingos, his great straw hat on his head; in one hand he held his bow and arrows and in the other he had a fine hand of Plantains. But as soon as he saw our family thus increased he made a full stop. I called him to come on, but as soon as he found who our company were, down went all his cargo at once, and much joy came on.

Harry enquired after their Canoa. When they told him they all came overland he asked them how many Tigers they had seen. This question made them send the young Indian off, who soon returned with the Skin of a Tiger on his shoulder, they having forgot it where they first saw the girl. This skin Owagamy presented to me. There was such a piece of business between our Dog and two they brought with them that he lead them all over our grounds. Now we began to ask after their families. They told us Lama-atty had another child, a girl; and that they had made friends with some other Indians after a long variance.

I then asked if the young Indian who came with them was a Captive or not. They said no, that he was a relation, but that he was under some trouble and that they wanted to bury him. I could not judge the intent of this dark speech, so put Luta to enquire of them what they meant by it. Then Komaloot took Luta on one side and held her in talk for some time. After this Luta told her brother to take the young Indian and shew him all round the place, so away they went together. When they were gone Luta told me that it was the desire of her friends that I would consent for their leaving Sama-lumy to live with us for a time as they had a great reason for it, that my consenting would shew I had a true regard for them, and that they should be ever willing to oblige me in all things, and that Sama-lumy would serve me even to the hazard of his life. Now what to think or say I knew not, but in the first place I desired Luta to request that they would be plain with me in regard to the subject in hand.

Owagamy then took me by the hand and gave me a look most powerful, and then proceeded to talk nervously to me for a time, then bade Luta interpret the same. (Viz), She told me that as her friends understood I was much in dread of the Mines, and that they were so far from discovering me to the Spaniards that they would sooner suffer death than betray me. Therfore, as Sama-lumy was now under the same terror at this time, they had thoug [thought] best to bring him off to me that he might be concealed untill such time that it should be forgotten. As he was young they thought he would grow out of their knowledge.

Directly I took them by the hands, and by Luta's help told them to confide in me as their sure friend in need. They thanked me, and then I told Luta to give me a relation how the misfortune had happened. She then said they told her that Samalumy had been to visit some of his relations who lived among the Spaniards, and that by ill luck he had made free to hang round his neck a String of beads with a cross to it; and as they were all playing together he had the misfortune to break the Cross by stricking another with it on the back. This was percieved by a little girl who ran and informed a Padre who was not far off. The Padre came and reviled him, called him "Pero Savage,"[2] for presuming to meddle with it as being unbaptized; but that he would soon find him better employmen in the Mines, then left him in great anger. This so terrified him that he took the first opportunity of sliping away to his friends, who on his information had shifted him from place to place untill they thought of this scheem to bring him to us.

Now I fathomed out the whole drift of this land visit, And think they plaid the part of a good polititians on me. Owagamy told me when any of the Padres fell out with those who had nothing to pay for an offence, they never ceased persuing them by all their arts untill they had obtain'd their revenge—and yet pretend great pitty. But as sure as they were taken hold of by an officer they then never saw the Priest's face more perhaps, nor was it in yr. [their] power to withstand it unless at a great risk.

Miserable subjection this (thought I), where every poor Indian is obliged to carry an insolent Priest on pickpack. Surely nothing can be more agravating, especially to a People who have recieved all the reason in the world to hate and detest them as the Devil hates holy water. All this I know of a certainty, what ever others may report to the contrary. And many barbarous stories are related of them—I mean the Natives; and, in truth, they may make their report good among people who know no better. But let us first enquire who were the agressors—I have resided so long among them that I know the error to fall on the Christian side. I myself have been Eye witness along the Coast of Florida when Indians have been wantonly shott at because they were in dread of coming on board our Vessel. And never was there a greater truth than this spoken in the world—but this is enough on that matter.

When Harry and the young fellow returned they had the affair laid open to them. Harry became marvellously pleased to have a companion, and the young Indian came and made me many signs of thanks for consenting to his stay. I then asked Harry to get me a flat

2. *Perro salvaje,* wild dog.

stone and I would set down the translation of the lads name. When he brought the stone I asked what Sama-lumy was, and Luta conferred with Harry saying that it was a mountaineer. I then put it down and ordered the stone to be placed away among the rest. After this they asked how our seeds came on and were informed that we had most of the things now in plenty except the oranges and Cocoa nuts. Ogamy (alias Owagamy) said that would be many, many long moons first. He then directed his discourse to the young Indian and as I was told charged him to mind all my directions and be my true friend, and to be sure to oblige the women. Sama-lumy then asked them to leave him his Dog. This they did and then took their farwell, saying they would come again when they had time.

After the Indians were gone I began to think I had brought an Old house over my head by having this Indian left with me, fearing that if the Spaniards should come to the news of it they might use me very ill; so determined if such a thing should happen that they found me out, in that case he should be gone out of sight. This was hinted to him and he promised to obey me in all things.

One day as we were all three shooting at a butt Harry told me Sama-lumy wanted a new name that he might be thought as one of our family. I told him that was but right and that he might call him Toby if he pleased. He enquired if that was a good name. I told him it was, that it was the name of a young man who took great care of an old blind father. This was sufficient, and we called him Toby from that day.

We lived on very friendly for a long time togather, and our little one began to daddle about. Mrs. Harry became bulkey and threatened to add another to the family which made her spouse very proud. Mrs. Penrose commenced a Schoolmistress, and nothing could be more innocently so than to see her sitting with them at it. At times Harry would contradict her; she would then appeal to me, and what I said was a law among them so that all disputes ended on my saying a word.

I had now no trouble on my hands to care about the family provision unless I went out now and then for my own pleasure. Now one day as the lads were on the look out they came down and reported that they saw a vessel out at sea. When I came to examine with my glass I saw three, one without the other; they appeared to be standing in for the land with the wind at west. As they came in shore I found two of them to be Schooners, the other a Sloop. But they put about soon after, and we saw them no more untill evening when they stood in again, then tacked and left us for good. I made a memorandum of it on the side of the rock with my knife.

About this time I put my two mates on digging pitfalls for catching the Warree and Piccary. This they laboured at for several days togather. They dugg six of them and we baited them with Plantains, Yams, potatoes and the like. Now and then we used to catch one but we were obliged to knock it on the head before we dare go down, they were so fierce and couragious.

I shall now observe one circumstance which lead us to a good discovery. I happened to ask Harry if he had ever seen a lizzard with two tails, I having been informed there were such seen at times. He said he thought he had, and enquired of Toby. However, one day as Toby was out on his rambles he imagined he saw such a thing run under a bush, but in going to poke his head under the bushes he met with a sad disaster. I was the first who saw him when he returned, but he was so altered that I scarce knew him. He was stuck full of lumps of red clay, one on his cheek, another on his leg, two on his thighs, and one on his breast. Some of them he had bound up with a long sort of grass. He cut such a strang figure that I called them out to behold him. This made him laugh, but then the scene became heightened beyond all discription. His eyes were almost closed up, and his under lip swollen bigger than five lips shewing his teeth so odly that they all laughed at him immoderatly; but as I was ignorant of its true meaning I could not laugh so much at him. However, he made a shift to inform us of the whole adventure and then the Girls made use of the old receipt for him and by the next day he was as well as ever again.

But to hear him relate the affair in broken English was drool enough. The poor fellow thought he saw a two tailed lizzard run under a bush, and in satisfying his curiosity he ran his head into a Wasps nest or that of a Hornet where they had peppered him to some purpose. His discription ran thus: "Twotail go in go. Toby good look, bush. Maum come. Maum maum bite Toby. Run Toby, run Toby. No see two-tail tomorrow!"

Whatever pains he had been at to find this clay I know not, but am certain he paid for it. Nevertheless I found our burning it in the fire proved it so that good Earthenware could be made of it, could we but shape it into any sort of Vessels. But this was a kind of manufactory I little understood. I now resolved to set my two messmates to work on the Clay and they lugged home a parcell of it where I made them temper it; and the first trial we had was thus. I got one of the large Callabashes and oiled it round, and then I palmed clay all round it without and by this means made a huge ugly sort of Yabba. After it had stood by to dry a time we burnt it, and it answered very well to hold our Water and would boil things very well had it not been so un-weildy. After this we made several other utensils for our purposes, fitting enough for our use.

Chapter 11

About this time I made a fresh calculation of my time and found by my best judgment it was 6 years and 5 months or more. I every day became more composed in my mind studying to subdue the passions as much as in me lay, so that by this time my spirits were so calm that I never fell in any kind of hurry excep the time I mistook the Indians for Harry. A few days after this, Mrs. Harry brought forth a Girl.

I was by this time tollerably skill'd at the Bow but never could attain to the nicety of either Harry or Toby's judgment. For instance I saw Toby one day hit a small Huming bird as it was spinning on the wing before a blossom at twenty yards distance. If this be not credited how

shall I advance that they could knock down the Butterflies as they
flew? Yet the reader is left to think as he is pleased. Yet before I drop
the subject let me make one or two remarks. I know there are those
who implicitly credit every romantick tale told by travellers be they
ever so absurd; when on the contrary others will presume to deny that
things known and attested by Men of real Veracity could never be,
or have exhistance, because they had never seen the like, or because
Penmanmour or Cader-Idris in Wales did not produce such things,
nor had they ever been heard of among the wonders of Derby Shire.

Considering this, I may gain but small credit with some folk by my
discription of the Pudeling Wythe, a kind of vine which after it has
aspired to the top of the proudest Tree in the forest drops down perpendicular like a number of Bellropes all of a thickness untill it comes
down within 4 feet of the Earth, when it sprouts out resembling the
tail of an Horse, but on touching the ground takes root afresh and
reascends as before. Also the shrub called the Flying Prickly Pear
whose minute thorns are so subtile that when the wind blows and any
person be to leeward of them, they will insinuate through his skin im-
perceptibly at the distance of 20 or 30 yards. N.B. I advance nothing
but what has been demonstrated to me through the testimony of my
own senses.

About this period we became annoyed by a most disagreeable smell.
The wind was then Northeasterly and the stench at times became very
offensive. I enquired if they had left any fish garbage about but could
find none. At last it came on to such a degree that I was determined
to find out the cause. Therfore I went with Toby in the large Canoa
along the East shore, but when we got beyond our old dwelling the
smell became intollerable in puffs. At last I thought I saw something
on a point right off Towers Field, as I termed it, resembling a Ships
long boat bottom upward. But we had not gone much farther before
there came such a strong hogo [*sic*][1] directly into our mouths and
noses that I began to suspect the true cause, therfore made a Stretch
out in order to weather it. When we got to the windward side of it I

1. Stench, bad smell.

found it to be a dead Whale laying on its side. When we drew near to it Thousands of birds were flying in all directions about it. The fish were as numerous below. I saw some of the largest Sharks I ever beheld measuring 15 or 16 feet. There were Snappers, Barrowcooters, Cavallos and many of other kinds in abundance. This Whale measured as I judged above 60 feet. I then asked Toby if he had ever seen so large a fish before. "Not up," said he, "but much, out in the big water. Blow water like wind blow." It was the same with myself, having never seen one so plain before. The mouth was wide open and gave me the opportunity of learning that what is termed Whalebone among our tradesmen lies round ye roof of the mouth, supplying as I judged the place of Gills, or as a kind of Strainer wherby to retain their prey.

Having thus satisfied my own mind at the expence of my Nose, we returned and made our report at home. I now and then sent the lads out to take a distant view of it, and we had this ugly hogo for above a week longer when the breeze stood our way. It was above a month to be seen above water. In a short time after, I paid it another visit but the scene was quite changed; all the ribs were parted and most of the fish was gone.

Some considerable time after this the Younkers went to Towers Field after Guanos and limes; but we had lime trees already planted about our place. Now as they were fond of Sailing they took a stretch out to the remains of the Whale, and as they were thus satisfying their own curiosity they they [*sic*] saw a Vessel wrecked away to the North-ward. On this they made their best way home to inform me. I enquired if they saw any people. They said no. Now how to order it at home was the thing, as I judged it to be at least 5 leagues by their account. At last I came to this resolution, to leave Harry at home and set out the next day well provided with my second mate Toby. According, the next morning I took leave and away we paddled down the Lagoon. After this I stood directly out for a considerable stretch and then fetched almost beyond our old dwelling. The next tack was fetched almost as far as Towers Field, and thus we proceeded untill abreast of the Whale Point from whence I could see over to the Wreck. It was evening before we got thither, and she proved to be a Brigantine and appeared to have been lost some time. Her bows were sunk in the sand. Her Main, fore, and foretop masts were yet standing, but the maintopmast gone; the bowspreat was gone also. Part of her fore sail was yet to the yard; the boom hung over the starboard side with part of her mainsail yet hanging in the water over the starboard quarter; her hatches were gone and I saw much sand in her hold, through which I percieved chimes[2] as of barrels. Everything was gone from the quarter deck, even the doors of the companion. The cabouse[3] lay sunk under the bow. This Vessel seemed to have been about 70 tuns burthen. She had a black Stern and on it was wrote in white letters Sant Pablo.

I then asked Toby if he would go down into the Cabbin, as she was but little beneath the surface abaft. This he did and brought out a jugg of a long shape well stopped. Then he went down again and brought up an old hat, the third time a small sheet. I then cut away the forebraces and one sheet, and then put to shore where we remain'd for that night, exposed enough. The next morning we went off again; it was then quite calm. I then cut away several pieces of her Sailcloth and left her. We were now forced to paddle for it, and did not get home untill the third day in the forenoon. We found all well and much rejoyced at our return. I then tasted of the bottle and found it contain'd some fine Aguadienta.[4] I then laid it up as a reserve against any one should fall sick; and this was the first liquor stronger than water I had tasted for above 6 years, nor did I like it in any shape.

Our young Lime and Orange trees came on finely and two of the Coconuts were burst out of the ground to the size of flour barrels and had shott forth most ample leaves. The Guavas came up wherever we dropped the seeds.

After this I sent the Lads away on the Wreck, giving them charge to make the best observations they could along the bay for anything which might have drifted on shore, and to bring what they could home with them if of any use. They were gone three days and on the fourth they came in about noon. They had a barrel in their boat which on

2. The ends of the staves projecting beyond the head or bottom.
3. Cabouse: wooden galley or ship's kitchen.
4. Spanish *agua ardiente*, probably brandy.

sight I took to be Pitch or Tar, more of the smaller rigging, a wooden bole, part of the companion, two small boards, a bag of nails, with an oar. They had rambled the shore and had been at the labour of par-buckleing[5] it into the canoa altho they did not know the use of it at that time.

The next day Harry went a fishing in the Lagoon and came back to tell me he had hooked a monstrous fish, and that it had carried away his hook. "It is a Shark," said I. "No, no," he replied, "it was a large brown fish." I then judged it to be either a Rock or Jew fish, and away we went with three concks for bait with the Shark hook. When we got to the place he shewed us I threw over the bait and was not long before the Gentleman took it. Away he towed the canoa up the lagoon untill he was quite Spent. Our shouting brought down the Girls so that they were present at the sport. It was a Rock fish that weighed at least 60 pounds. We got a paddle into his mouth and then reved a rope through his gills and made him fast to the Mangroves. Harry recovered his hook also.

Just as this sport was over Toby told Harry to listen. We all stood in suspence for a few minutes, then we all heard the tooting of a Conck shell as at a distance. Away ran the lads and were on the Clift in a minute. There they fell too hollowing out, "Yo, yo, yo! More canoas coming!" We directly got the Glass and up I went, where I could count 7 Canoas all under sail and standing right in for the lagoon. This I thought rather over many, but as I had ever found them faithful I plucked up my Spirits. I then got into our Canoa with Harry and went out to meet them; there I lay by for them. As they came in I hailed and they all then began to sing. We then stood away ahead untill they entered the lagoon; I then hailed them again. I was answered, "Amegos, Segnior!" from my good friend Komaloot; and I could not help smiling to hear him salute me in Spanish as I judged he had not many words in that language or he greatly decieved me.

Our ladies were waiting their landing with their children, and when they came on shore I could have wished half of them back again, they

5. Hoisting by means of a rope sling.

being no less than 25 in number male and female. We shewed them a kind reception and took them all up to the Castle, where such greeting began among the Women that the like was never. They admired my Son for his light colour; and I found this to be a Visit of downright curiosity to see in what way we went on.

Our Harry ran away directly to the brook to fetch me some Smoth Stones to mark down their names. Upon this my friend Komaloot ordered them all to be seated and he then stood Spokesman. He first presented me his own wife Inna-tary, and Luta said it meant a Yellow flower. Then came Owagamy and his wife Lama-atty, her couzin call'd Quali-rema or a tall Vine; then came a brother of Mr. Toby whose name was Yova-wan or a paddle-maker, Nocana-bura or a commander, a Girl call'd Ina-linca or mellow Fruit, Noonawaiah or the dreamer, Razua-bano or a great hunter, Kona-sove or a basket maker, Futatee here before, Mattalinea or Red fruit, Soro-teet or a crab catcher, Gatto-loon a forecaster, Latto-gamy or the Returner, Shoa-tate or a bird catcher, Wayatuza or a Comptroller, Zulawana here before, Gayna-sunto a bewildered person, a boy call'd Faribeed or a Singing bird, another call'd Muzzo-gayah a fighter, a third call'd Koura-coon or a Spie, a girl call'd Vina-qusta or a favourite, and one yet younger aged about 13 years and call'd Jasa-wina or a honey sucker.

After this I ordered all the names to be laid up safe and they looked on it as a great honor paid them. Our visiters were dressed and Painted in a very gay manner according to their taste of things. Owagamy had a string round his head stuck full of Maccaw feathers. Over his back hung the tail of a Fox; at each ear hung a Raccons tail; round his waist was wrap'd the skin of some beast, and a larg bunch of Sharks teeth at his breast with other things I knew no name for at all. Komaloots garb was much after the same sort except that he had a piece of Looking Glass hanging at his brest by a red string. The Ladies had little ornament on their heads except a fine tuft of Cotton on each side, but round their necks hung many strings of Shells, beads and the like, also round their arms and legs; and every one had small wrappers of Cotton stuff round their hips. The men had each a piece of Bais [baize], the young boys not any thing.

Komaloot ordered one of the Indians to go down to the canoas and fetch up some things, and among the rest was a valuable article indeed—no less than a pair of Scissors and they were presented to Luta; a piece of looking glass; a few rattles of Callibashes for the child. Owagamy gave another Masheet. They gave us half a dozen matts such as they use for sails and for to sleep on, some very fine shells, Arrowheads made of a very hard Green stone, a few fish darts, one small hatchet, a few Paddles, and a Mackaw bird of most noble plumage. All this I returned them great thanks for, observing that I was sorry we had nothing to give them in return. Upon my saying this Owagamy laughed and said, "What we give to our Brothers and Sisters we never ask for again like children." Upon this Lama-atty enquired the name of Patty's child, and on being informed that it had not a name as yet she desired we would call it her name, which was concluded on, and from that time it went by the appellation of Matty.

I now began to take notice that a Young fellow whose name was Soro-teet alias Crabcatcher kept constantly by my Harry and held him in talk. This made me ask him if he was not a relation of his. "Up the side," he replied, but said that this Indian remembered me very well, having seen me a long time before. This put me on the enquiry where he could have seen me. Harry then made me understand that he was the same Indians son I found on the Long Key at my first landing there from the Schooner—all which might be very true but he was now grown quite out of my knowledge. I then bade Harry ask him how they came to run away and leave me to starve for want. His answer was the great fear his mother was in that I should illtreat her, as I looked then so fierce.—So that here I had the Christian represented fiercer than the Indian Savage.

I then told them that the Great One had sent us a fine fish against they arrived, and sent Harry and Toby to fetch it up. I then had the handsom pots or Yabbas of our making brought forth, which caused some mirth. They then fell to cook the great fish, cutting in into junks [chunks] for a stew, Roasting plantains and Yams &cc. Two or three pots were put on for our Beans, pease and the like so that we made out tollerably well altho the Company consisted of more than 30 people. Mr. Toby waited at the table, which was the bare ground except the place where the ladies sate; this was by way of compliment for they had the matts under them.

When all were well satisfied Owagamy told Toby that he might return home again with them, for that Padre Bastano was now dead, and that he had never been enquired after at all. Toby, hearing this, gave me a sort of Side look. I then told him that as his abiding with us was only during his own pleasure, he was free to return whenever he listed. Upon this Toby casting his Eye on a young Girl in the company whose name was Matta-linea or a Red Fruit, and asked whither she had a Husband or not. This put the whole company in a roar. The girl looked like a fool, got up, and went off to the fireside. Upon this Toby cried out, "No man! No man!" I asked him then if she chose to become his Wife would he then choose to stay with us. Upon this he went down on one knee and began a Speech in his own tongue in order, as I judged, they all should understand him. I then told Luta to translate it as I saw them all well pleased, and she began thus:

"I protest before all these my People you to be my good friend and brother. When the Sun gets up and goes to sleep, when his Sister the Moon comes after his [him] to give light in the night, when blackness covers the trees and the wide sea, when I am dead in my sleep, sick or lame, And while I am able to Shoot with an Arrow, hunt or catch fish, dig Yams or potatoes, fetch fruits, &cc, &cc, &cc, let me remain with you. But if you, Panoly, say go, then Sama-lumy goes with his people."

All the Ladies were in tears the whole time. Now it became my turn to speak, so told Luta to inform them that I desired nothing more, as I liked the Young fellow well. Upon this they all gave a kind of "Hah!" as liking what I said. They then interrogated Toby and he said he should be glad to stay if the Girl would stay with him as a Wife, for then he could be always by me, learn my talk, and hear me speak about the strange things beyond the great water. But if the Girl would not have him he was willing to go back with them to speak for a Wife. Komaloot said they could not answer if she were willing to give her away as she had a good Father and Mother, but that they would represent the matter when they came home if the Girl thought well of it. Luta then call'd her and put the question to her. She said she would go home first. Finding her very pleased, I asked Toby if he would go with her. He answered, "Yes," and thus the discourse dropped for that time.

Among the things they gave us was a piece of rough Stone resembling our Grindstone which became of great use to us for Sharpning our tools. And now as there were so many Men with us I expressed a desire of making up a kind of Shed by way of a Kitchen. This they all came into, and soon after fell to cutting of uprights with one accord, desiring I would direct how I would have it—so concluded as we were hands enough to have it large enough. I then laid out the ground about 40 feet by 30 feet. After this was done I ordained Harry, Toby, and 4 of their people to the fishing department and the women to stand Cooks. When all was settled we went all to work, and in about 5 days we got it compleatly thatched in with Palmettos. My Turtles went to pot freely so that there was no want all the time. There was a door way at each end and two places open at the top for the smoke to pass out.

After all was compleat they began to prepare to return home after being with us twelve days, and Toby went with them. We went out as far as the Long Key with them. But when we came to part Luta said she had entreated one of the young Girls to tarry and live with her, but she was ashamed to ask the Men. I then told her she should have told me of it before if the Girl had a desire. Very much, she said, for that she had no father or mother. I then hailed Owagamy off the point and bade her mention it to them as my desire. Directly on their finding the Child willing she was put into our boat and return'd back with us. This was Jasa-wina of the Honysucker. We then wished them all safe home and brought home our new Maiden; and I soon found the Girl as glad to be with Luta as she was to have her; and thus matters stood with us. We gave this Young Girl the name of Jessy afterward.

We had not seen above half a dozen Monkeys in all the time of my living here, but after we had Indian Corn the matter became much altered especially while in its green or tender state; and then we were played a fine game eere we found out. This discovery was on a time when we were gathering Squashes at the old ground. We saw perhaps twenty of those Geniuses make off and mount the trees. This was a difficulty to surmount, but as soon as I got home I went to work and contrived a sort of Wind clapper to fix on a pole. This took the desired effect—not one Monkey was to be seen for some time after; but I determined to plant some at home least we should be totally deprived of all.

It was not a little diverting, nevertheless, to see those little Toads sit on the limbs of the trees with an Ear of Corn in their hands and husk them as dextrously as we could do it. There was one scene truly diverting. I once observed an old Monkey seated on a limb with two young ones; to these she gave a corn or two as they sat on each side of her. Others handed it over their shoulders to those on their backs so conformable to the human species that I could scarcely begrudge them a portion.

We had no account from the Indians for a long time so that I began to think Toby had quite gone off from his intended measures or that something extraordinary had happened. But one day as Harry and I were on the look out we heard a noise as of people at a distance in the woods and talking very loud. Harry asked me if he should hollow out. "By no means!" said I, observing if they were coming to us they knew the road, So ordered him to follow me down. In a short time after arrived Mr. Toby and two other Indians, one of them his brother called Yova-wan or the Paddle Maker, and Noona-waiah or ye Dreamer who had both been here before. They brought two Guanos with them and a sort of Bird unknown to me. Then they asked for the Girls who all came and welcomed them. We then got victuals for them, and I observed to Toby that I thought he was dead or had determined never to return to us again. Upon this he shook his head and then laying his hands on his knees, said, "Toby here now, know all trees here grow. I want see them one more time."

"But where is the wife?" said I.

"Oh, she see one tomorrow time."

Now as I found him a little in the dumps I left speaking and took myself off, as thinking Luta would soon pick out the cause of her not coming with him. After this Luta told me Toby had informed her when they got back the old folks called a counsil and were all well disposed for it, but her father would not give his consent that she should leave her home. But as they found the young pair had got a great mind to each other, to prevent farther trouble they determined to give her to another, and accordingly did so. That this affair made him grow very sick untill it happened that a few neighbours came to visit them among whome was a very fine young Girl called Rava, with whome he fell greatly enamoured, she being much bigger and hand-somer than the other. And that she had by her friends consent agreed to be his Wife if that we would suffer her to return now and then to visit her friends. That Owagamy had given his word for that, and they had promised to bring her in Canoas next time, observing that his brother and Noona-waiah were to tarry with us untill their arrival. I then desired to know when he expected them. "See," said he, "one Moon and half a Moon when cotton was done."

"Now," said Harry, "we are strong to go on the dead Ship."

"You are a fool," said I. "She is all gone to pieces before now." Nevertheless he was all for it, and in two or three days after away He, Toby, and his new Messmate Noonawaiah went, leaving Yovawan to tarry with us. They were absent four days and now the Girls began to be a little clamorous, and I was a little uneasy also. But on the 5th I saw them coming round a point to my great joy. It was not a Wonder they were so long away. They told me when they came there they could not find her; that the two trees were gone out of it, but the long tree which hung over the side was driven on shore in the bay. They said they found ten barrels on the shore and had hid them in the sand. This I liked very well. After this I sent them again and they brought home four barrels at two trips. As to the rest, they remain'd there.

The next thing we went upon was to pay both the Canoas bottoms, and then remained in expectation of seeing or hearing from our neigh-bours. The lads kept a sharp look out every morning. I now caused 5 of our Tortoises to be turned adrift, they being become exceeding lean through want of proper food, reserving but two against the com-ing of our friends. And thus we went on day by day. The Lads sup-plied plenty for our table every day by Stricking or with the line. And now my year wanted but a few days of expiring and we spent it in common and usual occurrancies.

Chapter 12: Eighth Year

Having now been on this Shore full 7 years, I told Luta we would have a sort of Feast so concluded to kill one of our turtle, and this was done. After it was brought home I had them get every thing ready such as Yams, Plantains, pepper, Salt &cc, and made a good large feast on the next day, and to go out in the mean time for a good mess of fish for that I expected they would have company enough tomorrow to help it off. This I spake as a joack, not thinking that it would really prove so. But the next day as two of them were out fishing they espied Canoas coming. Away they pushed with the glad tidings, and now Toby became quite another man, having been on the droop for a time before. I then took my Glass and went up the hill and soon saw three canoas coming in. I directly ordered our Sailing boat out and for them to get the mast and sail ready, and then dressed myself in my best attire, (Viz) first my Sambraro on my head with two fine Maccaw feathers stuck in it, my Tigers skin then made into a jackket the hair side out, round my waist a belt of bass rope in which hung my hatchet, at my back my bow and arrows, with a Mascheet in my hand; and in this garb I seated myself abaft, Harry and Noonawaiah as my two mates.

When they came nigh I bad Harry to Sing; directly they begun the answer. I now found them to be 6 Men and three ladies. They proved to be Owagamy, Futatee, Nocana-bura, Komaloot, Ruzuabano, and Gaynasunto, Owagamy's wife Lama-atty, the Girl called Vinaquota, and Rava the bride. The ladies were dressed and painted wonderous fine, especially the Bride. We escorted them all up the lagoon, and they were mightily glad to see our ladies waiting on the shore to welcome them. They were all landed and we then took them up to the house. Great comfort this to Mr. Toby certainly—he took the young lady by the hand and spake a few soft things to her; and While this was doing I had a full survey of her person And must needs own she was the finest Indian Girl I had as yet seen.

After they had been in conversation about an hour or so with our Women I then Enquired of Komaloot if all parties were fully agreed, and was answered they were. I then told them by Harry to assemble in a circle round me, which they all did. I then called Toby to me and bade him take the Girl by the hand; this he did. Then I enquired her name and was told it was Rava Ocuma or Ravacuma. On this I joyned their hands and bade Luta tell them that I should always esteem them as Man and Wife. Upon this they all fell to claping their hands and shouting. This done, I bade Harry fetch me one our brooms and I caused them both to jump over it. Now Harry, observing this, very politely stept up to me and asked why I had not done the like with his sister, so to please him I took my partner by the hand and did the like. Upon this he snatched hold of Patty and they repeated the same to the no small diversion of them all. Owagamy wanted to know the meaning of it, when I told him it was a common Custome among my people when they had a mind to be merry.[1] After this we all went to feasting and spent the remainder of the day quite

1. This old folk custom to bring good luck and to ward off evil was current in Germany, England, and the American South and Midwest, and doubtless elsewhere.

happy. The young couple were put to bed in the kitchen, and the next morning they turned too and built them a small Wigwam opposite our dwelling. They remain'd among us for above a week and took their leave of us in a very friendly way to return home.

Now my family stood thus: Myself and Luta with our son Owen, Mr. Harry and his wife Patty and daughter Matty, Mr. and Mrs. Toby, and the girl Jessy, nine in number and we all lived in love and true good fellowship untill about 6 weeks after, when Fortune began to envy our happiness. Luta was at this time nigh her time, and soon after was delivered of another son but survived only a few days. This I thought would have gon nigh to break my poor heart, and especially as She left me a young babe to bring up I knew not how. Patty had milk as yet so was forced to become Nurse afresh. This Child I called Morgan, which signifies born on the coast. We had lived together upwards of 4 years in strict conjugal love, and never had Man a more loving partner.

As soon as I could summons up my Spirits I was under the hard necessity of ordering the funeral myself with a Leaden heart and at last called the two Lads to me who, poor cretures, were both in as much seeming trouble as my self. Patty became almost mad; she would not leave the Corps one moment. I signified to them that they should dig a Grave among the Orange trees after the best fashion they could. I was forced to oversee it my self. They dug down about 5 feet and then came to the hard rock so were forced to desist. Now the Reader may picture to himself a scene moving enough, To behold me sitting at the head of the Corps in a stupid sort with my poor little Owen asking me when his Mam would get up. Patty stood on one side with her child in her arms Silently weeping over the body, and Ocuma with Jessy like two cretures quite lost to all sense, especially Jessy. This poor wretch did nothing but look on me and howl, for she loved her mistress greatly as the deceased shewed great respect to her.

Before she died she desired that I would sit down by her and I took her by the hand, which she squeezed, and said she was then going to the Old People of long times and said it was her great desire when she was fast asleep that I would return back to my own country with her two Children, if the Great One would let me go; and if I did, to say to my country women not to be angry with her for keeping me there as she was sure, had I been so much beloved by one of them, she should never have heard of me at all for that I should then never have come so far to get a poor Indian wife. All She desired I told her I would perform if God pleased, and then was forced to go out to vent my grief. In about half an hour after she expired, leaving her hand in the same position as I had left it.

After she had been dead about thirty hours I was forced to give order for her burial. Patty and Ocuma bound up the corps a little as they could, and then I told Harry to go to the head and Toby to the feet, then they lifted up the Corps. I took my poor boy in my hand and the three Girls came behind with the children in their arms. After the body was laid in I made signes that they should cover it up with the Earth. But now was my poor heart rent with the outcry of my little Owen when he saw his mother covering with mold; therfore I told them to take the children back to the house. In all the time none of them spake me a word but now it brought on a general lamentation. I then returned, fell flat on my face in the enterance and gave full scope to my passion. I lay thus above an hour, but finding no end like to be of this clamour I got up and call'd them all before me and thus began:

"You very well know, my good friends, the great regard my poor Luta had for you all, and you certainly must be truly sensible to what a great loss such a good Woman must be to your friend Penoly; but you know that we must all die. The Great One has now taken away from me what I most loved on purpose to see how you will use me when I am troubled. Therfore I hope you will all do the best in your power in standing my friends as long as you are with me, that you will shew by your best endevours that you will make up my loss the best way you can. Love my children for you know they have no mother more to look upon."

Hitherto Harry had never spoke one word to me or any one else from the hour of her death, but now they all declared they woud stand my friend even to life and limb. I thanked them, and then resolved to compose my mind the best way possible. A short while before her death I had intended to clip my beard with ye scissors, but now determined it should continue to grow.

Harry and Patty would frequently go and seat themselves on the grave for an hour or two conversing together. I became so indifferent after this had happened that I cared little how it went except I took good heed to my two children, and I must say Patty and Jessy used their best endevours to discharge their duty toward them. Ocuma, being as yet incapable of speaking English, could do no more than silently bemoan me and the Children. About a month after this had happened Patty lost her daughter Matty in a kind of fitts, and we buried her by the side of Luta.

Chapter 13

The place became now quite melancholy So that I went out oftener than before with one or other of the Lads, and it was on one of these trips that we found a large lump of Ambergriss, as I judged it to be by its strong smell altho I had never seen any of it in my life. It weighed 150 pounds or so. We laid it by on a shelf of the rocks and laid Aloe leaves about it as I found some sort of insects eate it. This stuff was of a dark grey colour and of no manner of use to me; but as I thought if it was really the true thing it must be of much worth could it be transported to Europe.

One day as I returned from fishing with Toby, on my entering into our dwelling I found Harry and the Girls very ernest over those stones I had inscribed, for I had placed them on a row above the childs reach in order to preserve them, and had added one for poor Luta. On enquiring what they were about Harry said they were learning them to talk. "How so?" said I.

"Oh," said he, "we know who they all are very well." That cannot be, I thought, but on my making trial I was astonished to find they could call them all over distinctly by name. I could not but wonder at it, but it plainly shewed they were capable of remembrance so as to be able to learn all those stones by some distinct mark, colour, shape or magnitude; but it came into my head that they must have learnt them as they were ranged. This I was determined to know, and told them all to withdraw while I changed their places. This I did, then called them in again, but to my confusion they were still as perfect as before I moved them.

Some time after this we had a few days of very dirty weather With the wind from the Southwest and great Thunder, lightning and rain. Now it chanced as Harry went to look out after it had lulled a time, he came driving down to me open mouthed and said there was a Great Ship coming to us. Thus put us all in a flutter. Up I ran and saw plainly a large Ship heeling on her larboard side on the Key Reef with her head to the shore With colours out as a signal of distress. I then got my glass and could percieve as I thought them Dutch Colours, she being about 6 miles from us in a direct line.

How to act I could not tell as I was not certain of her being a Real Dutchman, but the cause was to do good if I could. In the mean time the wind shifted and fell more. Now, thinks I, go I will some how or other, and ordered them to get ready the boat, with fire tacklin. I then got out a Shirt from my poor store and in I jumped with Toby. When we got to the point of our Lagoon we made up a good fire and I fixed up my Shirt. Soon after we percieved a boat put off directly for us. On this I got into our boat thinking that now I was in for it, I would give all up to Providence; and back we hurried as fast as we could.

When I got home I dressed myself as I had done when the Indians came last and took my little Owen in to the boat with me. Harry, seeing this, said they would come too. "Well, then, first get your arms," said I. He was not long before he came down to the point after us, bringing the poor Girls and children also. This vexed me highly but as I plainly saw he did not know what he was doing I held my peace, having enough on my head at that time. When we all shewed our selves at the fire they Shewed a White flag abaft, then a Dutch jack and white flag again. Now was I strongly agitated between hope, fear and desire.

As they came near I told Harry and Toby to follow me and do all they saw me do. Then we left the women and children by the fire and away I Marched with my two messmates behind me to meet them. When they came abreast of us a Man stood up in the boat and hail'd us. I clapt my hands to my mouth and answered, "Hollow!" On this they pulled in for the shore and there they lay on their oars to view us. I could now plainly see the boat was Dutch built and that there were nine men in her. Seeing them thus in suspence I called out, "From whence came ye?" They answered but I could not make it out and then came in for to land. Now a Man jumped on the beach and, saying something to them, they put off from the shore again. He then called out to me, pulling of his cap at the same time. I returned the compliment but could not understand him. After this I went up to him and held out my hand, saying, "An Englishman."

Upon this he shook me heartily by the hand and told them they might come on shore, as I judged, for so they all did and gathered all round me in amazement, then shook me by the hand. My lads seeing this did the like, but what to make of us was their greatest wonder for not a Soul of them could speak English. But I gave them to know the best I could that I was cast away like themselves and had been on this shore above 7 years. I found they could understand 7 years by their aiming to repeat it. Then they survey'd me from top to toe, lifting up their hands and saying, "Ah, boor Mon!"

Now I found they began to fret because they could not understand me. But a lad said, "Godart Somer Engels spraken en der Schip." This put them in a good humour again and I invited them to walk with us to our fire. This they complyed with so far as to accompany us in their boat. Here three of them landed again. No sooner did my people see them than off they ran, but I call'd them back and they came trembling with fear. One of the men asked me if they were my Vrowen, as I thought. Then they said they would go "on the Schip bring Godart Somer comen on lant" with them, but I made signs for them to go home with me. This they declined but concluded one should stay with me. As it was his own offer we all shook hands then and off they put for the Vessel.

After they were gone I asked this man his name and he said it was Jan Brill. Now finding the time grow so heavy on our hands for want of understanding each other, and as he appeared quite disconsolate I told Toby to go with the small canoa and fetch some victuals. In the mean time the man and I walked too and fro on the beach. He held me now and then in talk, but as I could not understand him it was of little purpose; and thus we remained untill Toby returned. Now Harry and Toby were so full of it that they would have fed the poor man. Harry would now and then take him by the hand and say he was like me, meaning cast away.

Sometime after, we saw the boat go along side and about dusk they returned and brought Godart Somer with them. They had not been landed long before it came into my head that I must for certain have seen the young fellow before as his countenance appear'd familiar to me. I then enquired from whence came they. He told me the Texel and that the Ships name was *Dertroost* and that they were bound for Buenos Ayres. "Did you never Sail out of England?" said I.

"Yes," said he, "three Voyages."

I then asked him if he ever sail'd on board a Ship call'd the *Harrington* out of London. He paused awhile and the replied, "Oh, no, neet! Over Ick vas on bord dat Schip. I been gon on shore en der Gravsend." Directly I found him to be the person I took him for, as he was one of the Supernumeraries put on shore at that place. They were all pleased at this and began to grow impatient for him to ask me questions as whether I knew the Coast well, and that their Skipper desired I would come on board with them.

I told him I was so far from knowing anything of the coast that I knew not where I was myself, but if they wanted to be informed about the shoals any where nigh my habitation I was at the Captains service; but as to my going on board It could be of no manner of use except to oblige him, and told him that I did not care to go then as I expected another squall from the same quarter. And as for their impatience, it was my opinion that she would never more be got from that place for that she would sow down in the Sand and perhaps was bilged now; but they would not think so and begged I would come off as erly in the morning as I could to shew them some channel if they could hale her off by any means. Now it came on to rain again, and we soon lost sight of her. Shortly after the wind it chopt round to the Southward and freshen'd up and increased so that I did not chuse to remain where we then were with our little family. I then told them that I must return home and if they chose to go with me they were welcome, as I thought they could not pretend to get on board that night without danger of filling by the great sea which would soon set in if the wind should increase. But they chose to make the trial and we parted.

All this time the wind strengthened, and when we had got round the point we were as safe as in a mill pond. They laboured at their oars for some time while I remained within the point and much troubled in mind as thinking should it come to a gale, what an unhappy condition those poor souls would then be in. But a few minutes after it increased so strong that I saw them pull round for the shore again. Directly I landed Harry and told him to run along the shore and wait for them, then get into their boat and pilot them in. This soon after was the case and away they came in after us, and soon after we all went on shore wet as drown'd Rats. I shewed them into ye kitchen and got a large fire made up to dry their cloaths for them. They all looked much cast down as expecting a miserable Account of things next morning.

I took John Brill and Somer up to my lodging as thinking they might want to have some counsil with me, for Sleep never once Visited us all the night. Thus we sat and talked, but Mr. Brill wept much. At last We got up and went to look out, visited the kitchen, and found them all as fast and snoring as tho no trouble had befell them. I then called Ocuma and told her to order some torches and bring them in. After Toby had fixed them he kindled up the fire. And now the wind abated; at length toward morning it fell stark calm. Then I proposed to Somer that we would awake the people and go in quest of the rest, as I told him we might depend they never staid by the vessel for that I was certain the Sea would make fair breach over her on that reef. This they agreed to, but when we came to rouze them they were so ignorant of their scituation that they acted very foolish, running against the thatch and asking nonsensical questions, as Somer told me. But trouble soon brought them to reason, and I ordered Harry to get our canoa ready to go with me.

This was about 4 in the morning and away we all went, leaving Toby with the Women. When we got some distance out we saw the Ship had swung round and lay on her beem ends. No boat appeared to be near her. Mr. Brill then wrung his hands like a man in despair. Somer told me he wanted for me to go on board with him and to come into their boat. This I did and we put the canoa to a killick. We then rowed away for the Vessel. Soon after this Somer call'd out in Dutch that he saw their longboat. I soon saw her and people walking on a point above the old Cave. On this we got head round and pulled away from them. When we came in with the beach I saw 5 men who all ran and shewed much gladness to see their shipmates again. Mr. Brill then asked for the Skipper. They said he insisted to abide by the ship with 5 more and that they knew not whether they had survived the dreadful night or not.

Now there was no time to be lost, so off they put for the Ship but soon returned saying there was not one Soul left alive any where on board. I then asked Somer which was the Mate and he pointed to him and I went and shook hands with him. I then desired Somer to inform him that I desired they should all return back with me to my place and there we would hold a consultation on what was first to be done as the Ship was past all redemption lost. While I was speaking I observed one man who went up the beach and seated himself on the grass to bemoan his wretched fate, as I judged, but to my great surprize saw him very deliberately draw out of his pocket a pipe and pouch of Tobacco, then fill his pipe. After this he drew out a Tinder horn, struck fire and lit his pipe, then with much composure clasped his two arms round his shins and began to puff away without any seeming concern at all.

They soon came to a conclusion and away we all put for ye old Cave. There we landed and got a parcell of roots and the only turtle we had in store. After this we all put away and put Harry on board his Canoa and so returned to our place where 14 of them landed, being all who were left alive. Now I had enough on my head to have so many mouths to feed and knew not for what length of time. And should they take it into their minds to have full possession we had no power of resisting.

Then I asked Somer what was the Mates name and he told me it was Jacob Van Tulden. Upon this I welcomed him to my poor habitation as an asylum and desired him that he would favour me so far as to be a friend in endevouring to protect our Girls from any insult which might be offered them. This Somer told him in Dutch privatly and he then took me by the hand, promising to do all in his power on that score. As these Men talked a language unknown to all my People the Girls kept aloof, being not a little afraid of them. Mr. Van Tulden, observing the colour of my children, asked if one of the Girls was not my Wife, but I gave Somer information and he told him of the loss of my Wife, and that two of those were wives to my two friends. After this the cookery began and we all eat togather excep the females and children.

I then made Godart Somer my interpreter, speaking always through his mouth, telling him it was highly necessary for them to appoint some to fishing with one of my men; otherwise we should soon come to a Starving condition being so many. Van Tulden and Brill, who I found was the boatswain, said that it was a just observation. The next thing was to order others for fresh gangs and after a while it was settled thus: the Mate, Somer, My Self and 5 others to go away in the longboat for the Vessel; Some to cut wood; Mr. Brill to have Toby with him to guard the Girls and children; while Harry went with others after our food. When things were all adjusted we prepared to go off to the Ship. The Weather was as calm as a clock so that we got along side of her in a couple of hours. The first thing which struck my Eye was a Yellow Cat running along the windward side mewing in a sad manner. The Ship we found bilged with all the lower tier under water above a foot or two. Then the Mate sent some of them down into the Stearage where they remained for some time. I now bade Somer inform the Mate that as I was very certain there were no inhabitant excep Indian for many leagues along this coast, I could advise him nothing better than to get what they could come at out of her for their own use. Otherwise I was sure the Natives would come and plunder all as soon as they espied ye Wreck. This alarmed him; and then we got down into the Cabbin where we found everything all gone to leward and capsised in a confused manner; but what was singular, little water was to be seen abaft. This I attributed to her being so high abaft, and she was more by the head also.

The rest of the hands I found were got into the hold, and as they came on the deck were all in liquor, but as all were now become masters and nobody left to throw the water out of the Longboat, as the Sailors term it, I had not a word to say. The Mate found a Keg of Gin in the Steerage and took a small sup, then handed it to me, but I declined it. Just then casting my Eye round I espied one of those precious things call'd a Biscuit. Eagerly I snatched it up and said, "God be praised!" then took a bite, tasting of Bread once more after being above 7 Years without one morsel. Now observing Somer to grow intoxicated a little, I made a bold to chide him, saying they knew not how precious their time was, and that if they did not bestir themselves with speed while the weather held fair perhaps all hopes would be forever cut off. This he took kindly and told the rest what I said. They seemed to be a little more on their guard after this, and Somer told the Mate that there were two of the people dead in the forecastle, as they told him. There were two of the hands who had perhaps done that miserable folly, as seeing death before their Eyes, took their fill of liquor to forget death. He said their names were Verwilt and Poersen.

After this I happened to ask Somer to beg the Mate to look me some paper if it could be come at. "Paper," said he, "dare is more as a boat load on board de Schip." Nothing could please me better. I then asked him to mention it to Mr. Vantulden, who as soon as he could be made sensible of my desire took the hint, and runing forward by the mast clapt his hand on a vast bale of it. He seeing me so elevated took out his knife and began to cut away and soon discovered me paper enough, then going aft into his Cabbin produced me a bottle of Ink as I thought. These articles I took plenty of and got them into the boat. He then went to work in the Cabbin and got out a parcel of cloathing, several Guns and pistols, some bedding and other things, then he brought out a Quadrant. I then took out a Compass as it seemed only to be unhung; and all these we got into the boat. The people got out two barrels of beef and some bags of bread, with three Kegs of Gunpowder, Brandy and Gin; and then we put off for the first time and got back safe to our company where I found the Girls were become more free. This was owing to Brill's good conduct.

Now the Mate reflected he had forgot to hunt for the Logbook, to bring Shott, bullets and other things of material use. But away they went the next Morning by day light for the wreck. I remain'd at home. About the same time in the evening they came back chock full. This they did dayly untill they had brough off a prodigious quantity of things untill the wind came round to the North and then blew fresh, so that the sea then beat in full on her uperworks.—I forgot to observe that the Cat jumped into the boat as we came off the firs trip, but no sooner did he jump on shore than he fell so greedy on the fish garbage that he became unable to quit the place untill Nature, being so overcharged, threw it off again or it must have died.

After they had got all from the Ship which could be got at, they began to consult what was the best step to be taken next. This I could have no hand in as I knew no more of the coast than a child, so left them to their own counsel for that.

Chapter 14

Now while matters were thus in agitation how they should act for the future We had much trouble to encounter, as thus. Altho Mr. Vantulden and the Boatswain used every method to keep good Order while on Shore, yet as there was plenty of Liquor it was totally out of their power to keep the people sober. Then Somer acquainted me that if I did not provide to secure some of it for my own use, it would soon be all gone, and privately conveyed by Mr. Van Tuldens order four Anchors of Brandy and some few kegs of Gin away by the assistance of Harry and Toby, while they were all sleeping.

After they had concluded to go to the southward in ye longboat and to leave the Yawl with me, I asked them where they intended first to touch at, and they told me at Puertobela[1] if they could reach it, that they intended to keep in shore along the coast. I then desired they would inform me what lattitude they thought we were then in, and they said they judged about 11d and 30 m North. Then I enquired what name the country bore, and they said they believed it was Costa Rica.[2] I desired Mr. Van Tulden to leave the date of the Year and day of the Month as I was quite ignorant as to any certainty about it. He then asked me for the bottle he had given me and I told Harry to fetch it, then expressed a desire that I would contrive some sort of a pen. This I was under the necessity of being beholden to one of the Parrots for, and made a sort of a pen with one of her feathers. He then

1. In Panama, also spelled Puertobello, Portobello, etc.
2. The boundary between Nicaragua and Costa Rica now lies at approximately 11° 30′ N.

bid Harry get a little water in a small shell, and when it was brought he took the bottle and emptied forth a powder of a grey colour and then with his finger produced Inck, being the first Ink powder I had ever seen. He then told me that Somer should speak it in English or I should not understand his writing, so I had best to write it myself. This was done and I found that It was thus: Anno 1754 and the Month of August the 5th day; so that by my own account I had missed in my reckoning about six week, some how or other, but it was a matter of no great moment to me.

Now there were Two Fellow among them who were absolute bruits and void of all Grace or generosity, by name Clause Deckker and Adam Brandt. These two Hell hounds, for they deserved no better title, took occasion to pick a quarrel and demanded the liquor that they said was missing. All argument had no Effect on them. Brandt went about raving and cursing like a devil as he was. I offered it back again but all the rest insisted I should not return it by any means, for that I had been a true friend to them all. About half an hour after this as Mr. Vantulden and Brill were sitting at victuals with me we heard a Pistol go off. Up we jumped. I snatched up a Mascheet and they took each of them a Pistol and out we ran. The noise came from the cookroom as I thought. The Girls were runing away with the children up the hill, screeming like distracted. Now my blood began to mount and away I flew to the Kitchen. But just as we entered off went another. We then ran back and stood togather, not knowing what to do, when out rushes Somer like a fury with a pistol in his hand. We then all three stood on our own defence, but he call'd out to me saying, "Never mind, Skipper, never mind! Dat divel is gone pon Hell now!"

"For Gods sake," said I, "Somer, are you gone mad too? What is the matter at once, or I will cut you down."

"Vel, dan, dat divel Brandt he vill say Toby hites da chin. He say neet him do ut. Dan dis Hellson he shoot him in van minuet. Out dan I rones and plows out his pranes, unt dat is all."

We then ran into the kitchen and there found poor Toby rolling in blood. I stood like a Man thunder struck. And now all became confusion and noise. The Mate and the Boatswain then call'd Somer and me out to them, and then demanded who were of their side, when one and all came over to us—even Deckker himself as thro fear perhaps now his coleague was dead. After strict enquiry we found there was no kind of plot at all, but that all had taken rise from that wretches own jealousy of my poor Toby, poor fellow, innocenly lost his life by it, to my great grief.

Every one highly commended Somer's action, and after all became a little quiet again I gave orders for the burial of my poor, unfortunat, faithful friend, and they laid him by my own Wife on the other side. Ocuma would not be seen but shut her self up, and all my pleadings could have no power over her, but she remain'd in the back part of my dwelling for two days without being seen at all. At last by much entreaty we got her out so emaciated that it was wonderful to see in so short a time. But I was forced to let her have her own way as I knew she had lost so great a friend, and I as fine a tempered a fellow as ever was born.

Now some of them talked of burying Brandt, but I absolutly refused it saying no murderers bones should be laid any where nigh my peaceful habitation. Then the Majority said he should be taken and sunk off at sea for Sharks meat, and this was done accordingly.

They then began to talk of leaving my place and made me an offer of a place in the Longboat if I had any desire to leave the place I was then in. But I thanked them for their kind offer and said as I had two young Children left me to take care of, I thought it my duty to stand their true father as perhaps should I leave them they would become meer Savages—and that would remain on my spirits the longest day I should live.

The Mate, soon after matters became a little reconciled again, call'd me aside and told me that Brill and Somer had been talking with him on an Affair of much concern to him, meaning Somer. "Well," said I, "can I be of any service in the thing?"

"Yes," said he, "I bin saying met Mr. Vantulden, as you vil Ick sal stay hare unt liven met you, as I ben feared for Deckker he vil go put me pon Chail ven Ick sal comen en Oland, as you knowen for vat."

"Is the Mate willing?" said I.

"Yes, besure," said he, "all mine people sayen so, it is petter for me."

I then asked him if he had a Wife; if so, that I thought it more expedient for him not to remain with me but to retire to some other part of the world where there was a propability of providing for his family. But he answered that he had none to care for but himself, and that he was no way inclined to run himself headlong into danger while it was in his power to prevent it.

"Come on, then," Said I, "Old Shipmate, and I shall be proud to have you for my Companion, so now you may let them all know that you and I are one, and you are fully out of Deckkers power. Now you can bid him defiance." Then the Mate call'd Brill the Boatswain and they both shook me by ye hand, then told Somer that what ever they had not a direct call for to carry with them was for our use. I told them that we must Certainly acknowledge it a great favour at their hands. They made answer that they were all certain I owed them nothing but good will, and they should take care to report my Christian like behaviour to their owners if ever they lived to return to Holland. Mr. Vantulden then told Godart Somer to call all the men togather, and then retired into the house where, seating him at my table, he took Pen, Ink and Paper and drew up a sort of protest in Dutch, then read it over to them and they all with one accord signed their names to it.

The Substance of which was that after the loss of the Ship, Captain Meert, with part of the Crew that a certain friend, a Subject of Great Britain shipwrecked or cast away on the same coast years before and there residing, had through the kind assistance of Providence been greatly aiding and willingly did do every thing in his power toward their immediate relief. To which he asked them all if they were free and willing to put their names. They all answered, "Yaw, yaw, yaw," and kindly shook hands with me all round. The names of those who signed are as follows: Jacob Van Tulden, Jan Brill, Adam Oest, Harman Byvank, Wouter Meyer, Abert Dubbels, Godart Somer, Claess Deckker, Peter Bylert, Cornelius De Man, Teysen Willems, Davit Oert, and Joust Van Drill a boy.

I then begged that Somer might translate it for me that I might have a coppy of the same for to keep by me, and they told me to do so which

I did. Mr. Vantulden then mentioned to them the affair of Somers remaining with me, and they all agreed that they thought him much in the right so to do. Nevertheless they all said what he had done was no more than common justice as that they thought the taking of Brandts life was ridding the world of a great Villain. After this they made all ready as fast as possible, having fitted up the Longboat to the best advantage for the run and got on board all they could conveniently carry. The Carpenter Adam Oest had calked her afresh and now they only waited a favourable Wind. About three days after, it came round to the North East and then they began to Muster all hands, being 12 in number. I then told Somer to speak to the Mate and tell him that it was my ernest request he would do me the favour not to mention any thing concerning me being here when they should come among the Spaniards, as he knew my reasons, And that he would not fail to forward my letter to my Mother by all means possible. All this he faithfully engaged to do if he lived to get home again. And now as they were just on the go I summon'd all my folks. Mr. Vantulden then kissed the Girls and Children with the tears floating in his Eyes, shook hands with Harry and all the Crew followed the example, then turning to me offered to put a few pistoles[3] into my hand. But I bid Somer inform him that I should think myself almost as bad as Brandt should I dare to take it, as knowing it could not be of any use to me as I was so scituated but it might prove of great benefit to them whither they were going.

He then laid his arms over my shoulders and said, "You ben wan goot vrind, Mine Hare," then turning to my old Shipmate said something in Dutch and dropt on his knees. This I took directly and as they all knelt I made a motion to my folks and we all joyned them, And by his behaviour he seem'd to me very devout. They then began to Sing a psalm or rather a sort of Hymn as I thought. When they had done they all got up and took their leave of me and all the rest in a most hearty way; but just as they were steping onboard I call'd for a large bottle they had Given me and made them all take a parting drop

3. A Spanish gold coin worth about $4.00.

of Brandy with me. Then they shoved off and we gave them three
Cheers. After this ceremony was passed they began to row away down
the Lagoon, and we all ran up the hill to see them out. When they got
out so as to give the Reef a good birth then they bore away before it,
and about two hours after, we lost sight of them as they doubled a
point.

They were with us from the first time of their landing about three
weeks, and took their departure on the 30 day of August anno 1754.
And now I must make my candid declaration that as to Vantulden,
Brill, Bylert, Oest and indeed all but that fool Deckker behaved to us
in all respects like honest men. During the whole time they remain'd
with us I made All the three Girls sleep in the internal part of my
dwelling as I judged that precaution best, finding some of the men a
little too fond of Jessy; but Ocuma kept a keen eye over her by my
direction.

I now began to think it necessary to begin a sort of new regulation in
the family, as Toby was dead and another in his room who it was
possible would not be quite so tractable as the other, to my mind. And
soon began a serious conversation with Somer as that his stay with me
being absolutly his own choice, I begged he would take my advice in
all respects, knowing as I had been here so long a time I for certain
knew the natural tempers of the Indians better than he possibly could;
and that if he strictly studied to be my friend I should use all my best
endevours to make all things as easy to him as lay in my power. That
he had won the love of Harry I was positive by the noble part he had
acted in revenging the death of his countryman and friend.

Somer said that he should abide by my council as I knew full well he
was a Stranger. I then told him he might fall too, and Harry should
help him to fit up a good birth in the Kitchen to sleep in; and then
they went about it.

Now I resolved to take Ocuma to my self as a Wife. This I had the
greater mind to do as thinking perhaps Somer might pay his addresses
to her. And for to put it out of all hazzard I took an opportunity to
give Patty notice of my intentions, and to mention it to her in their
own language as she had not English enough so as to understand me.

After this in about an hour Patty came and call'd me aside and told me that Ocuma said she must do all things as I would have her to do if I thought her good enough, and that she would willingly serve me and my children with all her heart. "Then tell her to come into the house to me," said I, and away she went and brought her. I then told Patty to call Messmate Somer and the rest in. When they were all assembled I took Ocuma by the hand and declared before them all that I took her as my Wife and mother to my children. Nothing could go beyond the joy they all expressed on the occasion; and thus I became a married Man again, as I may say.

The Ship shewed herself above water for a long time after this and Somer went with Harry now and then off to her, bringing back what they could come at as they found opportunities. I had now been here approaching to Eight years and everything proved quite agreeable. My new friend acted in all respects as became his Condition. But one morning erly Godart came in and informed me that he saw 5 Indians coming down the hill and caught up his Gun.

"What are you at?" said I. "Don't terrify yourself, they are all my friends; you may be certain of that. But go and call Harry and his Wife here."

Now when the Indians observed that I had another White man in my company they halted untill I beckoned them, when they advanced saluting me in a very kind way. These Indians were Vinniquote or the Smoker and Brother to Ocuma, Selacato or a joyous person—these two Strangers were conducted hither by Owagamy, Futatee and Noonawaiah, my old acquaintances as I may say.

Owagamy asked directly for Luta. Upon this I withdrew to a distance, leaving Harry and his wife to recite the whole melancholy story which took up almost an hour. All this time I kept out of sight to give them the opportunity. After this I returned and seated myself alone, but no sooner had I done this than my three friends came all to me and shewed the greatest tokens of compassion in plain and unfeigned condolation. They then all hugged Somer as though they could have eaten him. They told Harry they were well pleased to learn I had took poor Toby's widow for my own Wife, as it shewed the true regard I had for him as they also did the like among good friends. They told us they had seen a boat full of White men pass by their shore. Harry told them they were Messmate Somers friends. When they learnt this they said had they know that and they had landed among them, they should have used them as well as ourselves, observing if I used their people so favourable it was their duty to do the like by mine—drawing this parrallel.

Owagamy told Harry that firm friends were to be compared to a Strong Man whose two arms assisted each other to fight and defend the body from injuries, While his two legs were the mutual supporters of his body while he ran, leeped, &c. I answered that Mr. Somer and I were greatly beholden to him and his people and should use our best endevours to continue the old friendship. Owagamy then desired me not to be cast down, saying that As to my loss he thought I was well recompensed for that the Spirit of Luta was now centered in the heart of Ocuma, and that of Toby in the Soul of my new friend, pointing to my Shipmate Somer, saying did he not possess as good a Spirit as Toby he would not have revenged his death. Then he observed we did not perhaps take the same conduct as they did when ever they took Fool-Water, for on all such adventures it was their standing rule to lay aside their arms and to order a certain person to take care of the true things least when they should become as foolish as the Water was itself they should revenge the deaths of their Old fathers Old fathers a thousand moons ago.

The Indians stay'd with us four days, and I gave each of them a piece of Wollen cloth we had got from the wreck. Somer desired Harry to ask if they would bring some Tobacco with them when they should next visit us, and they said we should have enough. Then they departed. Shortly after they were gone Ocuma asked Harry if Somer was not younger than me. I told him to let her understand he was my elder and that she would soon see his beard become long also from want of a Razor—and this remark put me on triming my own with the Scissors. I had humoured my whiskers so that they turn'd up finely. As for Brother Harry, he plucked his out by the roots after his own country fashion.

It was wonderful to see what a quantity of goods we had got together from the Wreck; it took us two days to stow things away for our own advantage. We could now dress ourselves in Dutch cloaths, which I did at times to divert the Indians. We wanted not for Strong liquors, yet at times I could have wished not to have had one drop as my Friend Harry had got to great a relish for it.

This put me on a scheem to wean him if possible at once. I took a good time when he was abscent and convey'd a quantity of Groupar Slime into a bottle, then filled it with Brandy and Gin mixed, then hid it for my view untill a fair opportunity. Soon after this he asked for some. I then took occasion to tell him if he loved it so much it would cause him to hate all his best friends, saying it was not made to make men mad but to use when they were sick. So a drop served for that time; but before night Harry told me he was sick.

"Are you very sick?" I replied.

"Yes, very, very!" said he.

"Oh, then you shall have enough of it, Harry, to be sure; and when you have taken what quantity you like, go to sleep." This took, and I gave him the bottle. He took it off quite pleased to his lodgings, and was not long without a good suck, undoubted.

Now as we did not see him for some hours I sent to Enquire after him. They found him fast asleep nor did I see him all the Evening. But after we were all gone to bed Patty came to waken us and crying that Harry was sick, sick. Now as she stood with a torch of Pitch burning in her hand and shewing a most dismal face it put me in mind of the midnight opperations of Witchcraft. Nevertheless, we got up to save appearances and I shewed much seeming concern. The poor Girls were all in tears so that Jessy ran to call Somer. No sooner did he come than like a true Dutchman he cried, "Oh! Dat felow is Tronken, he is tronk, dat is all."

And indeed the poor fellow had taken such a quantity that I began to dread consiquences. He had almost finished the bottle, and it had worked him fore and Aft at no small rate. The next morning he began to come too a little but was very stupid and sick. No reason was to be got from him all the day. I told them to inform him how vexed I was, and to say if he had died his friends would lay his death at my door. Soon after he came to me and begged pardon, saying he would never have one drop more in his life. I then told him if he was resolved to go after poor Toby he could not lay his death to me, having been informed of its true use before, but that he would not take my advice.

"What would you have had to say," said I, " if it had made you mad as it did the White man Brandt, and you then had shott me?" This was enough, "No, no, my good brother Penoly! The Great One make me sick on purpose."

"Well," said I, "do you want any more of it? There is enough left." But off he ran, nor one drop more would he ever taste. As for the Girls, they could not be brought to taste it at all. This turned my Shipmate against it, so that we had it in plenty without much use.

It may not be much out of character if I mention the odd behaviour of Our Indians when they first saw me begin to write my Journal. They would gather round me and whisper to each other, and if they chanced to croud me too much, if I did but put my pen toward them they would jump back as much terrified. And one day as I was reading it over to Somer Harry said that now he was sure I was a very cunning man for that I could make all my old words speake again quite new, and that I could make dead people talk.

"How so?" said I.

"Did I not hear my Sister Luta talk to Mr. Somer," said he, "just now? And she is yonder in the grave," pointing that way. This made me smile and I observed to him that I would make little Owen do so soon. "Ay, ay," said he, "when he has got a beard as long as yours." Sometimes he would touch the nib of the pen and say no wonder birds could learn to talk, but that he supposed it all came out of their wings. —I met with great difficulty in getting a knife sharp enough for penmaking. My pens, too, they were of a brittle kind of quills as of Turkey buzzard and from Hawk and Bald Eagles.

After we became all well settled I asked Somer one day where he was born. He told me at Middelburg in Zeland. "Do you not remember Peter Cass and George Neilsen your countrymen on board the *Harrington*?" said I.

"Yes," he said, "very well." I then told him Cass died at Kingston that same voyage. This discourse brought on more, and talking of the war he observed to me that it was peace now between England, France and Spain. I asked him how long. He said in the year 1748 peace was made. I was glad of the news as thinking should the Spaniards find me now perhaps that I might meet with more favour from them.

I had been for a considerable time at my Journal day by day before I could bring it down to this period of time; and as to what has preceeded it has been all collected as I could best remember. But I persuade myself nothing of any note has escaped, remembrance having been carefull to retain all I thought any way worthy. But I must observe here that in regard to Indian informations, Spelling their names, and the like I do not affirm them to be exact as a Man must be born among them before he shall be able to give a true pronunciation or be able to coppy their Ideas and manner of conveying sentiments.

Chapter 15: Ninth Year

Ninth year commenced. We had much business on our hands the last year, much interest and much trouble, and now it was become June the 15, anno 1755. When as Mr. Somer and I were both sitting by the light of a torch reciting over old adventures in former travels, A Monstrous Beetle struck him in the face and gave him a terrible black Eye. These Beetles I had seen frequently in the Woods in the Evenings. I have found them as large over as an hens Egg and of a dark green colour. They have a long kind of forceps like to the claw of a Crab set with teeth, and has a black polish so that nothing can be finer. With these forceps they lay hold on young twigs of trees such as they can grasp, then expanding their wings begin to whirl round the branch with great force or velocity and by that means cut the bark through to ye Sap; then by hanging under they suck it in.

Our Girls used at times to produce a sort of Musick with two or three of these Inscects, as thus. They made them fast as our Children do Chaffers[1] at home by long strings, and then hung them up in the Cavern passage way and leave them to Spin round; and it was surprising to hear the sound they made, Even like to the deep pipes of an Organ. Sometimes, according to the magnitude of their wings, they would strike chords most sweetly. Messmate Somer's Eye happened to be of the discord order and was not well for above a week or more, but we took Indian methods of cure for it and it was at last quite restored again.

I shall now, being on this subject of Inscects, describe a kind of Ants in this country. They are of a dirty white colour and shaped quite different to other Ants. They build their nests on the limbs of trees, stumps of old trees and rocks. Their nest is as large as a Beehive and of a consistency resembling coarse brown bread. From this Nest or general commonwealth they have generally three or four high roads composed of the same substance. These roads are arched over and of the size of a mans little finger so that all their works are deeds of darkness. They never fail to have one of these paths leading to water; and if at any time accident should damage this causway, which they lead up and down bodies of trees, rocks and the like, they never fail to repair the breach again; but the matter of which they compose is not of the same colour when new, being then grey. Should you break any part of this road you will soon see two or three make their appearance but retire back again as informers; then incontinently forth comes a multitude in the greatest hurry and confusion imaginable. Yet if you watch they all forsake it again, leaving the breach as it is; but if you go thither the next morning you shall find it fully repair'd. But then should you take a fancy to break it down a second time in that case they will not repair it as before, but they carry it round circular or in a large curve but joyn it as before. The Indians say the nest burnt

1. Chafer, a beetle; in U.S. chiefly a June bug.

to ashes is good for many disorders. As to that I can say little; but that they destroy wood is most certain, having eaten off an upright of my table in one nights time. They bite intolerable, so that when ever they took a notion to lead a road our way we were under the necessity of routing them by fire.

But, Oh! how often have I been soothed in this Solitude when the divine Works of Nature have insensibly drawn me into deep contemplation. Then have I sinfully and anxiously desired to have my youthful associate Bill Falconer[2] to be with me to explore these real beauties and record them in his sweet juvenile Verses. But alas for me, and I hope well for him, it was not to be his lot. No, I parted with him in old England and there may his bones rest in peace, where I am perhaps never more to put footing. Come, Fate, then, deal me out that portion which is to be my share and let me patiently submit to the blessed will of Providence with all due resignation.

My Messmate Godart often expressed what a loss he was at for a Pipe and Tobacco. This was a thing not easy to surmount. I had some old stuff by me but of no use through length of time; but a pipe was the difficulty. He observed there were pipes enough on board their Ship, but we never saw any. I told him if he and Harry could but find some substitute for tobacco I would soon mak a pipe by hook or crook. We then consulted Harry, as his people smoked frequently when among us but they smoked it in rolls like to the Segars used among the Spaniards. Harry said he could soon find a plant his people used when they were out and without tobacco or the right sort, as he called it. This leafe he soon produced. Then I told Somer if he would cure his leaves I would undertake to make pipes. I then bid Harry kneed up some clay very fine, and rolled it round a wire. This was by way of a Stem. Then I botched up an ugly bole; these I joyned togather by raising a mouse[3] of clay over them. After this I ran the wire through it

2. William Falconer, born in Edinburgh about 1730 and as he says "condemn'd reluctant to the faithless sea," achieved some fame for such nautical verses as "The Midshipman" and his *magnum opus*, *The Shipwreck* in 1762. He was lost at sea en route to India.

3. Mousing (nautical): turns of a small rope to unite shank and point of a hook.

again, and after it was dry we burnt it. This put Somers genius to
work; he made a good kind of mould with his knife and after this
we never wanted pipes.

Seeing Godart so pleased when all this was accomplished, and observing him to talk with more spirit when he had his pipe in his
mouth, I then began to practice it myself so that we all three soon became good smokers. And indeed the Girls, too, in a short time after;
and as the stuff we used was sweet and no way disagreeable I indulged
them in the notion for we were never visited by any very polite company so that it was no inconveniency. And now you might have seen
the whole family quaffing togather of an evening at no small rate.
Now and then Somer and I indulged ourselves with a drop of Liquor,
but very sparingly altho we had a good quantity by us, but I had very
cogent reasons for so doing.

I now began to think of instructing Owen in the Alphabet, and
these I made with my pen the best way I could. And during the time
I was shewing him the rest would sit by so that they all learnt togather. And now I would have given a thousand dollars for a Bible,
had I been worth them. The little fellow could say the Lords Prayer
as well as I could, and perhaps was the first of Indian natives who had
ever done the like on this coast in the English tongue.

And after this sort I used to amuse my time, now and then with my
Gun but this was seldom as we had not plenty of shott; other times at
Writing, fishing and the like. Somer employed himself in making A
mast and sails for the Yawl, and when he had done we got her keel
up and paid her bottom with pitch, tar and sand as thinking it Would
warn off the Worm, and found it answered midling well.

And now, notwithstanding we were in far better circumstances, I
began to find my peace of mind disturbed not a little, as thus. Somer
began to alter much in his carriage. He would get his pipe and retire
to some distance and remain for an hour or two by himself, yet he
never shewed any ill Blood to me. Yet it gave me much uneasiness
scituated as we then were in this Vague part of the world. I had observed this behavour for some time before I chose to mention it to him,
but as I found the man continue in the same mood I took it into con-

sideration and resolved to have a serious talk with him. Therfore on an evening I said, "Mr. Somer, suppose that you and I should take a trip over to the Long Key, perhaps we may find some things drifted on shore from the wreck." With all his heart, he said, "Well, then, Harry shall get the boat ready tonight. We will take our Guns and lines and Swift shall go with us."

This pleased very well. Accordingly the next morning off we put, with our pipes in our mouths. I put some brandy in the boat also. I left Harry governor and told him if any thing should chance to happen he was to hoist a piece of an old Ensigne, being a part of a Dutch ensigne from the wreck.

Now it happened some time after we arrived at the Key and were walking toward the point, Somer cried out with an oath, "Dare is von Schip comen!"

"Avast swearing, Shipmate," said I. "Shew me her."

"Dare, met mine fenger," said he.

"Well, pray, don't be so hurried," I cried, then taking out my glass percieved her to be a Small Sloop standing to the westward. "There, let her go, and a good passage to her!" I said.

"Oh, that is not the thing," he said. "I want that she shall come in here, come here!"

"What do you want with her, pray? She is some Spaniard bound down the coast, I suppose."

"O, that is the thing always with you," he said. "You dont want to leave those Indian Women. You are no more a Christian man. You will live here all your time."

Now, thinks I, this is a fair Slatch for me to begin, beter late than never. But just as I was about to begin he took notice that our Signal was out at home. I then proposed to return as thinking the vessel perhaps was not the only cause. When he found this he said, "What, you will go then?"

"For certain," said I.

"I thought that you can't wait to see how the ship steers."

"Not I, indeed. I know she never means to speak us, being certain they know nought about us."

"I suppose Harry is got drunk again," said he.

I chose to put up with it all, knowing there was no other help but patience. So away we went. When we were seated, "Mr. Somer," said I very calmly, "I now percieve plainly that you cannot reconcile yourself to the blessed Will of Providence, and it gives me much concern indeed To think you cannot conform like a good Christian to the will of your God."

"Oh, vat you vil say!" said he. "Dare is neet Brode, neet Flais, neet oder dings."

"How can you talk after such a manner, Godart?" said I. "Do you want? How would your case have stood had you been cast on this shore as I was, to find nothing but shell fish to support Nature and those to eat raw, without a fellow Mortal to converse with, expecting every moment to be knocked on the head by Savages? Think on this, my good friend. How different has the Almighty delt with you. Has he not spread you a table in this wilderness, a thing you had no right to expect? Have you not got me to converse with? And was it not your own choise to remain with me rather than to run the risk of being executed for taking the law into your own hands?"

This touch'd a little. "That is all true, Mate," said he, "but I am not used to it as you are. I think I shall not live here so long as you have."

"As to that, no Man can foretell what he is to go through in this life. But let me advise you to be fully resigned to Gods will, as it is my determination so to do. If you only take this resolution every morning at your first rising you will soon find your heart more at ease. This is my daily practice. Nothing is more certain should Providence so order that I shall see my native country again, I shall be thankful. But if I am to remain where I am or wander to the day of my death I am still resigned. My nam's Content."

"Well, say no more, Mr. Penrose," said he. "If I must die in this country I cannot help it. The same God is in every place. You are my good friend; and so knock it off, knock it off, and I will think better."

When we got home we found company arrived there. We found Mr. Owagamy, Komaloot, and Vinnequote brother to Ocuma. Now commenced great joy on all sides. Somer put on a more placid air than lately, and we entertained them with the best we had. Now I must observe to the reader An odd turn on Somers Humour, as this. He took me aside and desired that I would treat with Owagamy to procure him a Wife. This I promised to comply with. And now I though within my own breast What a poor, fluctuating Creture is Man; today he passionately hugs the very thing he totally rejected yesterday. But as I concluded this step might prove greatly in my favour I desired Ocuma to mention the thing to Komaloot and ye rest. When they returned this answer: that if Somer desired such a thing he should go to look for a Wife along with them, for that it was not the custom among them for the Girl to go about to hunt the Man as men went out to hunt deer in the woods. This brought on a laugh at poor Somers expence, but he was pleased to joyn in their opinion. Upon this I observed such a thing would become a great difficulty to us as we knew not the way to their home. Komaloot then archly asked whether we desired for them to bring all the Girls in their Nation for him to chuse one from the whole body; and if they came they would eat up all we had before my new friend could find one to please him.

I desired Harry to tell Komaloot that I thought his remark very just, and that we had no other Way than for my Messmate to return with them and make his own market the best he could, and that Harry should go along with him on condition Vinniquote, my new brother, staid here in his stead with his sister until they returned. In about two hours the thing was agreed on, although not to the Satisfaction of Patty, she being nigh her time. Somer now began to act a new farce between hope and despair, but I bid him keep up and never fear for that my friends would treat him civilly on my account.

The day came when they were to set out and I was for the first time to part with my good friend Harry, and that with a reluctancy for I truly esteemed him. But off they went well armed. My Shipmate was dressed in a very odd garb, a pair of Dutch breetches with a little short jackket, and one of my sambraros on his head. At their departure I gave Owagamy a piece of cloth and some trifles to the rest; this was by way of sweetning their tempers.

Now was I in a different plight to any I had been in before. As for

Patty she was all in tears, the poor Children crying after Harry, and my self not in the best of tempers fearing some disaster should befall them; but I was obliged to bear all with patience the best way I could. Now I was forced to go with Ocuma's brother on all errands as he knew not one word of English. After this sort did we remain for a whole month.

Now we began to keep a sharp lookout as we expected them by Sea if Somer succeeded. In their absence we got one Warree; at another time Vinniquote, being among the traps, espied a Tiger devouring a Piccary in one of them. He ran to informe me. Directly I got my piece charged with two balls and soon dispatched him. No tumbler could have shewed better postures than he did, but Vinniquote soon put an end to his gammut. He then drew him out and draged him home, where we skin'd him and spread the skin out to dry.

Five weeks were now passed, and no signs of our Quality. This made me grow very uneasy, thinking often within my own mind: Oh! how much happier did I live when I had none but Harry and his Sister with me. But those days are now passed by, and what the future may bring forth God only knows. When I first landed on this forlorn coast what would I have given for the consolation of a Companion! Since that day I have feared leas I should be overcharged; and now, whither I should have too much or too little was the question. Thus are our poor Souls never to one stay, Tos't about on this Ocean of human life, ever greedy for this or another change like the child who soon grows weary of his plaything; and the last use he makes of it is to be satisfied in what it is composed of—when that is done he throws it aside and becomes anxious for a novelty.

This reflection brings back to my memory the observation Somer made on a certain day when he saw me playing with Ocuma. "I wonder how you can be so fond of those yellow women," said he.

I made him this reply: "When a man is in Rome he must comply with the Roman custome or he will lead a miserable life there, Somer."

"But I can let those Indian Girls to them selves if I do not like them I suppose," said he. I told him me need never to stand in any great dread of being ravished by any of them either a Wake or in his Sleep. But what a change took place! My poor Messmate had the natural frailty of Man working strong within him, and knew not that to be the principal cause of all his uneasiness. Could he have had only one of our fine blooming Girls transported to our habitation from Europe, all perhaps would then become Elesian Fields to him. Alas, how little do we know what we are, thought I; and now is my Messmate gone to look for the very thing he so much despised.—So have I rejected dainties at my Mothers table, but Want brings us to a due sense of things and we eagerly jump at the rejected crust we so late dispised, and heartily thank our gracious God for it. And sure I am that he who studies to make any state of life which shall fall to his lot easy, even tho it were at the very Gate of Despair, yet by due reflection he may obtain comfort if he will but zelously put his confidence in God his Maker by daily imploring his divine aid, He being Omnipresent.

I had contrived me an Angling Rod and line with which at times I used to amuse my time at the head of the Lagoon with the small fish. Now as I was one day at this sport and in one of my Contemplations I heard the sound of a Conck shell. Directly I quitted my sport and returned up to the house and informed them of it. I then got out our Colours and my Glass and mounted the Hill. I soon percieved three Canoas coming round the point of the Key. I then came down and put on a suit of Dutch seamans cloaths, and told Ocuma to put on my Tigers jackket. I then gave a piece of Red cloth to her brother and a blue piece to Patty, and thus we got into the Yawl and went down the Lagoon to meet them, leaving Jessy with the children. They soon came into the Lagoon and met us, blowing their shells.

No sooner did they draw nigh than I heard Shipmate Somer begin a Dutch song, display his hands, and shew every token of joy. So, so, thought I, you are pleased again, I hope; and I waited to see the Marketing brought home. Shortly after, Harry began his song. This was all my desire, but poor Patty burst into a mad fit of crying for Joy. Soon after this we landed and they all came in. The first Man who jumped on shore was Harry. He ran with open arms to hug me, then his Wife and all the rest. Then came forward Somer and shook me by the hand most heartily. I observed that he was now a doubloon, I hoped.

"Oh, yes, yes!" said he. "Over I vill shew you mine bretty young Vife Wanee." Our company consisted of Komaloot, Futatee and four more Indians who had all been here before, and 4 ladies, Mrs. Komaloot, Mrs. Owagamy, The Bride, and another Young Woman. As soon as we got up to our dwelling Mr. Godart brought his Lady by the hand and presented her before me and said, "Dare is Madam Somer, as you bleases." She was a good Jolly Dame aged about 18 as I judged.

"Well, now, I hope you are cured of the Mully Grubs," said I.

"Vat is dat, dan?" said he.

"Why, have you not been feeding on chopt Hay for a long time before this?" I said.

"Vel, over all, Mr. Penrose, dare is neet comfort for man if he bin out von goot kirl, unt dat is drue!"

I then welcomed them all, and desired Komaloot to send away a gang to Strike fish as we were not provided for a Wedding. Upon this Harry cried out they were married already. "That is not to my purpose," I said. "I am determined to have it celebrated here anew."

"Dat is right," said Somer. "Come an, dan!" This was made known to the whole company, and all whooped for joy. I then went and made up a brave bole of Grog for them, and then we enjoyed it with our pipes. The Ladies soon after retired into the house to chat by themselves. As for my Shipmate, he was now become quite a new Man. No long silent puffs of tobacco—his tongue ran to me the whole time on the reception he met with among them, and of their manners and customs.

After this sort we spent the time untill our sportsmen were all return'd with plenty of fish and fowl. Now Evening came on, and I told Harry to make a good parcell of torches. By the time all our sportsmen had drank round they had swallowed down 5 of my great Pans of Grog which was at least 7 or 8 gallons—yet none were drunk for I kept a tought hand that way least Sport should be spoiled. About 6 in the evening I ordered a Broom to be brought out, and now the Indians knew what was next to come on. Then the Ladies were called forth and we made them both jump over it. After this I saluted the Bride and all the Ladies; this was followed by all the rest to the no small Mirth of the whole company. I then bade Harry tell Komaloot to make all as merry as possible, which he soon put in practice. After Supper we all fell to Dance, sing and play untill the Sun rose upon us. At last all became so weary that we were glad to turn in to rest, not a man being much the worse for liquor. Thus ended Messmate Godarts Wedding, and I must own this, I was never merrier in my days. What gave me such Spirits was to see my Comrade so much altered; and he afterward declared he believed his whole melancholy proceeded from his being, as it were, bird alone without a Mate. So that Nature is the same throughout the Universe.

The Company tarried but 4 days with us, then took Vinniquote away with them. Mrs. Somer and my lady soon became sociable, And every thing was now in a fair way again. But Harry told me I had forgot one great thing, which was to give My Wife and Mrs. Somer new names in English. "Well, then," said I, "in the first place what is the young girls name?" Somer told me it was a long one and he could not speak it well. Then Ocuma told me her name was Mattanany or a sweet taste. I then desired her husband to call her what he thought proper, and he called her after a Sister of his own Eva or Eve. "Well, then," said I, "we will call Ocuma after my Sister also"—which was Betty, which names became established.

I now told Somer it was high time for us to think of Turtleing, the time being come; and we followed it up with good success for a time. And on the 7th day of January Patty brought forth a son to Mr. Harry. Full of Joy he came to me with the news, but it was all smashed at once—little Morgan was missing and could not be found. At last I had the melancholy news brought in that he was drown'd in the Lagoon, having been with a stick aiming to catch fish, and had been dead perhaps above an hour. I took this misfortune as cool as patience would let me; and after the burial was over Harry came over very innocently to know what Name I would give his son. This coming so abrupt on me, I said, "Call him Job."

"Job," he said, "what is Job?"

"Patience," I told him.

"Well, that is a good name," said he.

Nothing happened worth my notice for some time so that I but seldom went to my book, and we all lived together very friendly. We were now nine in number and Jessy grew to be a fine young Woman, quite obedient in all things, and would have sacrificed her life to Serve either My Wife or self. So that I now enjoyed my full peace of mind, nor had I once a Wandering thought in my heart. And thus I closed my year as to the state of my own reckoning.

Chapter 16: Tenth Year

On a day I stood leaning against ye side of our Kitchen with my face toward our dwelling I was so struck with the scene that I imagined in my mind, Could but some Ingenious Artist have a sight of it twould certainly make a curious Picture, as thus. First was to be seen the mouth of a large Cavern, somewhat resembling a very high Cathedral door way excep the arch much wider. On the right hand was to be seen My Betty with Patty sitting behind her braiding her long black hair. A little without the Cave enterance was to be seen my Young Owen taking aim at his Uncle Harry, who stood on the other side of the enterance with his back against the Rock as a kind of Butt for him, and catching the Arrows as they came in his hand; Somer sitting against the side of the rock within, with his red pipe in his mouth, tayloring with an old dutch cap faced with furr on his head; Eva recieving a bole of Stewed fish from Young Jessy before the door. N.B. We wore but little cloathing when within doors, the Girls seldom any more than a short breetch cloth.—My Self as sitting about the Center within at my table, Writing, the table covered with a piece of Sail Cloth; Patty with her young child slung at her back with a scrip of cloth; the two dogs and Cat before the door way; and our Parrot cage on one side of the Cave, but the Birds on the top of it in general, the cage oblong and square. From a chinck in the Rock projected a long stick with an other to sloop toward it, whereon Moggy the Macaw bird was in general to be seen. Over the Cavern was to be seen huge rocks overhung with trees excep a place wher stood our flagstaff, the flag about 7 feet long and 5 deep consisting of only two stripes, the upper blue and the under white.

Now it came into my head to ask Somer for a regular account of the Journey when he went a Female hunting. He told me that now and then they caught Land Crabs and roasted them. The Indians killed two Monkeys which they feasted. Then they went over one very long and high hill with but little wood on it, and then descended to a large pond or inland lake. Here they walked 5 miles as he judged, and in it he saw numbers of large and very frightful animals with very long tails, both in and on its banks. These I judged to have been Aligators. He said travelling hard made his feet full of blisters, so that his guides were forced to walk at his rate and were ever willing to halt when ever he shewed a desire. On the 5th day in the evening they came to a place where some Plantain trees grew, and there seating themselves eate all they had in store. But instead of making up a fire according to custom They got up to put forward, which did not a little dismay him finding Harry had known no more of the way than himself untill now. He then enquired whether they were going to travel all night. "No, no," said he. "We are now come," and that in a short time they heard ye Crowing of Cocks.

Presently after that they came to a large Wigwam. Here the Indians seated themselves And began to make an odd noise with their hands held hollow before their mouths. This brought forth two Indians who directly knew them, and they all entered the Wigwam; here they slept till ye day appeared.

At this time a number of Voices were to be heard, with conks blowing &cc. Soon after this many Indians from all quarters came and saluted them, among them bothe Women and children gazing with much curiosity. Then finding himself in the midst of them he offered to shake hands with some of them, but none of the younger sort would touch him by any means. Then Owagamy came and took Harry by the hand and lead him about from house to house as a great curiosity or lost sheep found again; but in a day or two they behaved more free and would gather round Harry and him to hear them speak English, with which they were highly delighted and frequently aimed to repeat the words after them.

He said it was above a fortnight before they took the least notice of the affair he came upon, and that Harry advised him Komaloot should be pushed on in the affair. This was done, and his answer was that he did not percieve the Girls to run away from him. Soon after this Harry told him there was a Girl at the next Wigwam with whome he had conversed and that she expressed a sort of desire to live with Ocuma; so that if he was but to get her brother once to concent he was sure she would have him, as he had given her great encouragement in regard to the love Penoly shewed his own wives. He then got Harry to speak to her brother. This he did and soon after Owagamy and the rest assembled on the occasion; and Harry told him they so managed the affair by representing me to such an advantage that her brother gave full consent. He then begged Harry to ask the Girl before them all if she was willing to go with him, as he desired they should all be thoroughly satisfied before they took their departure. The Girl then had the question put to her, to which she answered in the affirmative. As this all became settled the brother took her by the hand and delivered her to him saying, as he was told by Harry, "You are now my brother flesh." Here ends Somer's account of his journey & reception among the Indians.

I had suspected my new lady to be pregnant before she became mine and now found it really so, but an affair soon happened which reversed the matter. Harry happening to be chiping at the flint of his Gunlock, the piece went off, and as his own Wife sate very near him he had like to have shott her. This so terrified my Dame that she was soon forced to retire, and therby lost her Child. She remain'd quite ill above a week and on this account we procured her every little article of nourishment in our power.

Now it so fell out as she was sitting on a day before the door with a little Crab soup before her, She call'd to me and desired I would take notice What a large Guano there was on the Green among the Lime trees. On this I called to Harry and said, "See, there is a fine mark for your Bow and Arrow." He then took them in hand and shott but missed the mark as it just at that interim passed behind a bush. On this he snatched up a Mascheet and gave chase to it, and soon after he call'd out, "Here he is." Upon this I followed and came up just as he had killed it.

The Guano had got into an odd kind of Nook covered with bushes. Now as I was thus surveying the place I percieved through the bushes farther in a heap of Stones piled up like a kind of Piramid, about the height of 4 feet. "Here has been Some Indian buried," said I to Harry.

"No, no," he said, "we dont do that way." However, being flushed with curiosity I told him to go and fetch Somer, and I shewed it to him to know his opinion. He said he could not judge what it signified, and stooping into the bushes drew out the bottom of a glass bottle and said he now thought it was the grave of some Christian person. "Well," quoth I, "let us move away the brush and make a serch farther into the affair."

"Oh! no, no," he cried. "Dont offer to disturb any mans bones."

"Never mind that," said I. "Come, Harry, let us begin." So to work we went. After we had been employed for some time I told Somer, laughing, "You shall have no share in the prize if you don't turn too and lend a hand." Upon this he began. After we had worked a considerable time we came down to a thick Plank. "Now," said I, "let us lift it up." When we had removed it we found beneath it a part of a Skeleton with its head almost intire but much decayed. Now Godart would have no more to do in the business. Then finding it lay between three other boards I told Harry to move the bones off to another place. As he was at this work I took up the Scull in my hand and found a cut on one side of it as with an ax or some sharp Wepon. I shewed it to Somer, saying this had been foul play some time or other. When all was cleared off and the Under board removed I percieved the neck of a large Bottle above the Ground and close stopped with a black substance as of pitch. This I bade Harry to dig up with his Mascheet. By this time they were all got around to satisfy curiosity.

This Bottle I carried away with me up to the house and there seated myself, then taking out my knife cried, "What say you, Godart, will you go shares with me?"—and began to work round the neck of the bottle.

"I think your a Man of strong heart, Mr. Penrose," said he.

"Well," said I, "here goes!" But I found unless I broke it the business would prove tedious. I knew it did not contain any quantity of liquid by its weight. Upon this I got a stone and prepared to knock off the neck but when I came to the breaking part, Somer shewing the example, they all left me and ran off to a good distance least some Hobgoblin should make his escape and devour them all. This made me laugh, as it was impossible to refrain. With a Mascheet I soon clinkt off the neck and found the contents to be a roll of Paper. Then I bid Somer draw near but he absolutely refused so to do.

I then determined to overhall it my self and found three Rolls of Paper one within the other. The first contained the contents of what the Seamen term a Round Robbin, and as thousands may not be acquainted with the true meaning of such a thing I shall give it after the most simple way I can. The true meaning is this. When ever a Conspiracy is forming for to carry any scheem into execution Either on board or on shore among Seamen wherby to gain the point intended, then the Ringleaders form a circle on a piece of Paper round the margin of which they sign their names, causing the rest of the conspirators to sign their names round in rotation untill the whole be filled up, by which means it becomes imperceptible to the Spectator who was the person did first put his hand thertoo. This being done, they then bind themselves by Oath to stand by Each other, let what difficulty arise to oppose the undertaking even to life itself if it be a thing of desperat consequence.

The Second Paper contained a most infernal Oath devised by some of the Devil's own principal agents, undoubted. This was accompanied with some of the most horrid Imprecation ever uttered by man Against any He, or they, who should presume to disturb that place unless he had their own infernal right so to do; also against anyone of their own party who should dare to betray the secret to a Stranger or any who were not propper claimants thertoo unless they previously knew the rest of their diabolical old fraternity to be dead and gone.

The Third Paper contain'd some very odd characters mixed with readings, yet not so artfully contrived as to put it wholly out of a Mans power to unravel ye Secret. Had it indeed been otherwise I am certain many of those Ignorant reprobates would have been far enough to seek in any length of time; but fate ordered their hellish plot and booty should remain unmolested by them forever.

After I had thoroughly examined these papers and formed the best conjectures I could concerning them, I then called to my friend Somer telling him he need not give himself any Superstitious conjectures about the matter; that it was Some of the Devils manufactory was certain but he knew God to be above him; and as he saw I was in no way moved about it, he as a Man should never give way to any such Idle Ideas. This brought him to me saying, "Vat you have gotten dare?" I then gave him the papers to look at but found he could make nothing of them.

Now I should have been all of a piece with him had not I learnt while In the Island of New Providence many odd relations concerning that detestable class of People denominated Pirates. Therfore, to render every thing concerning that excerable set of People as clear to his understanding as it was in my power to do, I told him nothing was more certain but the very things I then held in my hands had previously been the darling theme of those abominable wretches. And then to give him a thorough taste of what Man can say, write and act when he has once rejected his Maker, I recited over the second paper, but with no great desire as to my own will. When he had heard its contents he cried "Put ut to da Divle!"

"That I shall soon do," said I, and then rammed it into the flames before his face, saying, "Go and follow up your curst Inscriber as fast as you can post!"

I then told him that It had been an old custom among those odd wretches when chance threw any very larg treasure or Booty in their way, then in that case fearing to carry it about with the Vessel, they used to hide it on Islands, Keys, and in secret places along the Coast, using a most diabolical ceremony at the interment of their cursed riches, as thus. After they had in the first place signed their round Robbin they, instigated by the Devil, decreed privily to sacrifice some poor unfortunate Spaniard, Mulatto or Negro and there bury him, leaving his Spirit as a kind of Guardian or Centinel over their ill begotten wealth untill such time as they should return. And then it was they drew up those detestable articles of their faith and buried the whole in a Bottle with the Corps and riches to preserve if from moisture or any other injury of time.

The Round Robbin

After I had well considered the affair I went and laid the papers up in a safe place, as Somer seem'd no farther curious about it. So then I took Harry back to the spot and we threw all the stones togather again, and dug a hole on one side where we deposited the bones. And thus this uncommon Adventure ended for that time; yet I thought I was clear in the thing that Money or some other things of Value were there hidden.

The Round Robbin exactly transcribed from the Original Manuscript as faithfully made out as the Badness of the Characters and blindness of ye Ink would admit. N.B. Those names to which crosses are added were such as could not write, as I judge; and I take notice there are Negros names among the rest such as Sambo, Cudjoe, and perhaps others of them were of the mixed breed as the principal character necessary to become one of Such a Banditty was that of being an approved Reprobate. If he could once recommend himself capable of Robbing Father, Brother or Relation, Force a Rape on Maid, Wife or Widow, Swear Black was White or the contrary, or even Stow a poor unfortunate Man in Davy Jones's locker he was then the man fit to be sworn in as what they styled a good Fellow.

NIMROD'S PORTION.

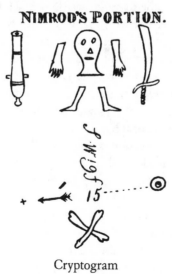

Cryptogram

A faithful Representation of the Third Paper as to the matter and due form, with what I deem to have signified Watch Words. Now this Paper was what I conjectured to contain the whole secret. Nevertheless I kept the affair to my self, Knowing full well could it make us as Rich as ten Jews it could by no means render us one farthing the happier in our condition. I often pondered on the thing in my mind. Night after Night did I dream nothing but Pirates, Either that we were diging and beset by those kind of People, that the Ghost of the murdered Victim was petitioning us to relieve him or we were Sharing money, so that frequently I raved and started in my fits of agitation. And heartily have I wished Harry had never gone after that Guano; then, thought I, we might ever have remained in total Ignorance and been yet as happy as heartofore. But after a time those Idle visions vanished as we talked seldomer on the Subject. Yet I cannot say but a great desire would at times rise in my heart to satisfy my own curiosity; and had not Somer been so backward and Indifferent on the matter we should not have been long eere we had made the trial.

Some time after this I proposed to Shipmate Godart that we would take a Voyage along the coast Eastward, to which he agreed, in order to make some farther discovery that way. I was put on this by his desire of seeing the great Stone Harry had told him of at Towers Field. Harry was to be left as guard to the Women, and when we had laid in necessaries off we put down the Lagoon in the Yawl and stood along the shore til we got to the old Cave. There we landed and got some Yams. From thence we stood out about an hour, then tacked and stood away for the next bay and after a time got the length of the Creek, where just as we were going to land Swift jumped on shore after a Guano and he soon killed it; we then put in.

We then took through the bushes but missed the true tract so that I could not find the Stone for my life. Now as we remained thus in suspence our Dog at a distance began to howl, and were sure he had the sight of somthing or other. We follow him Cutting our way with our Mascheet until we open'd into a large Pond. Here we heard noises resembling the murmers of young whelps or puppies. The place was overgrown with large Reeds, and my Messmate cried out there were some of such "Divel cretures" he had seen when traveling with the Indians. Directly I called off the Dog who, poor toad, trembled much. I varily think we saw above twenty of them. We directly quitted that repository of greedy devourers, who many of they lay sunk beneath the surface of the water with only the nose out. After we got off I could not help thinking how happy had been my lot to be landed where I had so long resided without knowing such monsters were so nigh me. But as I knew those Animals seldom quit the ponds to ramble into the uplands I was not much concern'd.

After this we returned and I struck as near as I could for the Rock and by chance soon found it. We then took a good Survey of it and Somer took it for the remains of an old tower, but when I observed to him there was not the least signs of any cement or morter to be seen he gave over that opinion. As we came away he observed that that place had also been frequented by the Pirates too. "Undoubted," I said, "as they were acquainted with the whole Coast, it being their general maxim to lurk within a Lagoon, Creek and the like with a man posted Either on a tree, hill or masthead From whence they could Espie a sail to a great distance when, waiting a proper advantage, the [they] popped out and captured the poor Culprit at once by vertue of those laws themselves had made."

After this we went to the Palmetto Grove and caught three more Guano's, then stood away for Whale Point as I termed it, but saw no more than ye Scull and some ribs sunk in ye sand. When we got round we landed, and kindling fire we roasted one of the Guano's and had a good meal with it and a Yam.

After this I proposed we should range the long bay which now lay before us perhaps 5 miles in length, thinking that we might find somthing drifted there. Some time after, we came up with the Brigs boom; farther on we found 3 barrels of Tar sunk in the Sand by our own lads, perhaps; and thus we trudged on for above 4 Miles as we judged, being more ground than I had gone over at one time for several years before. We now concluded for to return, finding nothing worth stooping for. After we got back to our boat I proposed to explore round the next point. He agreed, and we were forced to give it a large birth as there was a Shoal and Surfe ran out from it. When we got round we found the land trend away to the left for about two leagues, then fetch a compass round more Eastward again as far as the Eye could see. Now as we were exploring these new Scenes I observed a large smoke to ascend about 3 leagues right a head of us. "There are people," said I, "yonder, of some sort or other."

"That is nothing to us," said Godart.

Then did I retort on him, "How long since you fell into this way of thinking, Launsman?"[1] Directly on speaking I descried a Sail in the Offing standing to the Southward right before the Wind, So nigh in that with my glasses I saw she was a very large Ship. "What say you now?" said I. "Shall we stand out and shew our selves?"

"No, no," he said, "let us take down the mast and lay snugg." This we did and got her in behind a parcell of low bushes. Here we remain'd for Some time, and saw another fire yet nigher.

"Now," said I, "Somer, I am Certain they are Indians or Spaniards, for it they were folk in distress one fire would be sufficient as a signal." The Ship kept her course and after she had passed by about an hour we got into Our boat, steped our mast, and put away round the point with a flowing sheet. After we got abreast of Towers Field we hall'd in shore and landing there concluded to sleep under our Sail for the following night.

The first thing after turning out next morning was getting a fire made, and after we had refreshed our selves with a good meal we went in quest of some limes, and then stood along shore homeward, put in to the old plantation and gathered a parcell of Yams, potatoes &cc, and then put off for the Castle and arrived about noon. But how amazed were we to find on our landing Our Kitchen was burnt to the ground.

They all came runing down crying and clapping their hand, full of joy at our return; but I stood like a mope, not knowing how the thing could have happened. But finding them all alive I took my Wife in

1. Probably meaning landsman (as opposed to seaman), from now obsolete *laune* or from Welsh *llan,* ground or land.

one hand and Owen by the other, walking up to the house in silence, seated myself, and then enquired how such an affair could happen. Harry then told me that Owen had gone into the kitchen and got playing with the fire as he innocenly told them, and soon the whole was in flames but that he, with the Womens help, had saved all the valuable things at the great hazzard of their lives. "Well," said I, "I am heartily glad things are no worse." But the loss of our Kitchen was a matter of concern to us all as we had been so long used to it, and its being a Hall of reception when any Visitors came among us.

The next thing to be thought of was rebuilding our Kitchen, and we had one thing much in our favour as they had dragged down the thatch where the fire would let them so quick that all the uprights remain'd unhurt, being of a very hard kind of Wood. Now Somer and Harry were employed in fetching home Palmetto for our thatch; and after this we went cheerfully to work but It was a full fortnight eer it was compleat, and at the last did not Equal the Old Temple seen in former days. Nevertheless altho it was not quite so Ship Shap as is the Sailors term, yet it answered our purpose well enough.

Now as I expected a long series of Rain I proposed to Godart that we should lay in a good store of Roots and other things of that kind, as this conduct had hithertoo been much neglected. And I determined to lay them in the back part of our dwelling least another kitchen blast should take place. And now speaking of these long rains I shall observe they come on twice a year, but most about October, and then hold on with but few intervals 3, 4 or 5 Week more or less. And on an Evening when it would hold up a little, Mirriads of Fire Flies then swarmed in the air twinkling like so many Stars. And of a serene night when all was hushed I have heard the things Grow. Several times Somer has cut a tuft of grass for that end, and we have found it sprung 3 inches in perhaps 30 hours time. The most disagreeable thing at this Season was a kind of tree Toad whose noise was the most doleful that can be concieved.

We remain'd chiefly within door during these times, our employment being chiefly making Pipes, pans, pots, and ordering our tobacco. The Girls spun thread after their way and sewed also with Sail needles.

Sometimes we took a bout with the bow and arrows at marks, at other times playing Quoits.

But at last my good Messmate Godart fell bad of the Rhumaticks and became so lame in both Arms that he could not feed himself so that his poor Wife was under the necessity of doing that office for him. It then left his arms and fell into his legs. Now was I forced to undertake a new task, (Viz) Making a pair of Crutches for him; and by these assisted he would hobble down to the boat where he would sit and fish with his pipe in his mouth by the hour. For to give him his due he ever hated Idleness if he could possibly Stir.

He remain'd in this condition above 3 months and then got better every day untill he threw by the Crutches; when, like A true Dutchman, he must begin some employment and this was no less than making a Tub. I thought it beyond his skill, but to my great wonder he made it after a sort, but it suited So as to hold water and became of great use for many things.

We had nothing worth notice from this time forwards but the Sight of one Sail which passed by to the Eastward, untill by account I had compleated my Tenth year and began the next, in the same constant bond of Harmony.

Chapter 17: Eleventh Year

Eleventh Year began. Now it chanced on a day as I was at my table Writing And Somer with his pipe standing behind overlooking me, He took it into his head to ask wher I had put that "Divels Paper" we found in the grave. This was what I expected would come out one day or other, having concluded it should rest so untill it came out of its own accord. I then closed my book and turning round arose and said, "Here is the paper safe enough, but let us not go about things rashly.

Let me light My pipe first and then you and I will take a Walk and have some conversation on that affair." So off we walked and seated our selves down among the Orange trees where I began thus:

"Godart, I think in regard to this Paper It imports there is a Sum of Money hidden in or near the place where we found it."

"Oh! you dink so? You ben choakin?" said he.

"No, no," I replied, "I have no bone in my throat. I think I speak clere enough and think I have found out the whole secret, to. Observe here"—shewing him the paper—"you are to observe here two words. These are the Watch words which none were privy to but the very parties concern'd. In the next place observe here is a Mans head represented and these his arms and feet. This means the Person buried there, whom they killed, to be as a Spirit to guard over the treasure there hidden."

"You dink dat?" said he.

"Yes, I verily do," I said. "As to this Gun and Sword perhaps they were what figures they carried in their Colours, as also these Cross bones. But now take notice. Here is 19 feet southwest, and thence 15 feet to the very spot or Else the same distance as this dart directs; and within such a Circle lays ye Cash I dare say, if any may be there; and this is my judgement."

"Well," said Somer, "suppose we should make a trial of it?"

"With all my heart," said I, "if you think you have courage to undertake it, Messmate."

"Oh, I am neet fearen da Divle," said he.

"Come on, then, we will fall too. But now I think of it it will be better to postpone it a little longer untill you gather more strength."

"Youst as you vil for dat," said he, and the thing was dropt for the present.

Soon after this we had a Visit from the Natives. They brought with them an Indian White as an Horse and seemingly very purblind. I soon found our People were well acquainted with him, and as such a Sight was an odd Object to Somer and me I desired Harry to give us his account of it. He observed that now and then, but very seldom, such Objects were born; but as to the cause he could give us no better

information than that they call'd them Moon-lights, and that people
said they were concieved at the minute the Moon was at the full.
"Then," said I, "one might think you might have more of them." But
he could say no more Excep that they were not beloved among them;
none would wed with them; but that they lived and died as they were,
as being of no service unless on Moonshine nights and that then they
were as brisk as other Indians, seeing very sharp, going to fishing with
their darts when other people could not see at all. I observed his Eyes
appeared to be inverted as to ours like an Inverted Crescent, keeping
them much closed in the day time. This Indians name was Erreawa
or White Shiner. The Indians who called to see us and had brought
him at his request on the Visit were Muzo-gaya, Damasunto and
Vattequeba. They remain'd with us about 5 days, and in that time
made a perfect cure of Somer by means of Roots boiled in water with
which he was bathed; and I told Betty to learn the true knowledge of
them before they left us.

Soon after they were gone, and finding Godart began to stand
stronger on his pedestals, we took a new voyage westward on the discovery. We took our departure from the point of Long Key and stood
down along the Coast about 3 leagues, when we came to a bluff head
land. Nigh to this in a small sandy bay we went on shore. About this
place were multitudes of Mullets with Porpoises in persuit of them;
they were so thick that we knock'd several on the head with our Oars.
These Mullets have often in their Company a fish of a much larger
size call'd a Calipiver, differing little in form from the true Mullet.

After a short stay we put off again down along the shore with the
wind Easterly untill we saw a long sandy bay, at the farther end of
which ran off a Rocks with a small hummock directly off that. This
we rounded and then ran into a little cove where the Water was about
three feet deep. Here we landed again and Godart shott a White Poke
or large kind of White Crane. These Birds are so exceeding white
and tall that I have many times mistook them for a Sail, especially
when they have been standing out far from the shore on a flat with the
Sun shining strong upon them, as at such times they have loomed exceeding large, and when nothing but the margin of the Horizon could

be seen behind them. And certain I am that at such times I have per-cieved them at the distance of 3 Leagues untill, either by flight or a suddain move, they have undecieved me.

In this place we spent that evening, but on the morrow the Wind came up fresh at South so that we came to a determination to go no farther and put back right before it untill we got the length of our Long Key. After we had got round the Reef the wind fell and it soon became a dead calm. We then turned too and rowed, getting into our Lagune in the Evening not a little fatigued, without either profit or much discovery, and thus ended that cruise.

After we had been home about three days We got the notion of examining our Pirates corner. Our Indians could not think what were our designes but we got the shovels and marched to the Spot. In the first place we cleared away all the low brush and then I cut a Stick night to a foot in length as I could and got to measuring the ground. When this was done I told Harry to begin digging. He worked for some time with such poor wooden tools as we had, but to no purpose. Now and then we had hard roots to cut through with our Mascheets. However, we worked down about 3 foot and then desisted for that time, finding nothing.

Then Somer began to laugh at me and said, "All de Monix [moneys] is dare I vil put in mine eye, and dan Ick sal see, too!"

"Well," said I, "now we will begin directly so far on the other hand, and if that fails we will then begin in a line from the foot of the Skele-ton." Then to work I went my self, then Harry took his spell, and Somer joyned him. But they had not got down 18 inches before Harry discovered some hard surface. I then began to joak Somer in my turn, saying, "Here is the prize, my Soul!"—being at the same time just upon giving the whole affair up. I then bade Harry clare away the dirt and we discovered a smooth substance like lead. "Huzza, Somer," cried I, "here it is, here it is!" We then fell hard at it untill I plainly saw a round circle; and we soon got up the prize and found it to be a huge chamber Stool Pan. Directly on this I took out my knife and began to scrape it and found it to be good Silver.

By this time Harry had got to work at somthing more and found it to be two more laying on their Sides; these we lugged out also. After this, found 17 Dishes of various sizes all of the same metal, 4 large and 26 small oblong plates, 6 Basons would hold 3 quart each, and above 50 smaller things for table use. Beneath these we found cups or cans and then came to a vast body of Cob Dollars.[1] And as we were thus viewing it Harry observed a thing of another shape among them but could not stir it. We then fell to and cleard away and found 7 large Candlesticks above 4 feet long, these were all doubled to make good Stowage; 10 more about half that size; and after we had got out about one half of the Dollars we came to a very large Bason with 4 rings to it, and within it was a large sum of Gold coin. This Bason we found stood on terra firma so that we then desisted, all three in a copious sweat. "Now," said I, "Messmate, lend me your hand. You are by far a richer Man than when you turn'd out this morning if money can make you so; and I heartily wish you had a part of it safe lodged in the Bank."

Some of the Plate had rich raised work on it with coats of arms display'd, Lions heads, Chevrons, Shells and stars; and on the feet of some of those Candlesticks was the Name: Isabel Rubiales D. 1605.

Now after we became possessed of this vast booty we really knew no more how to dispose of it than so many Idiots, and many arguments Somer and I had about it, as to think of Enjoying it was to us absolutely vain, it being not of the least worth to us. It was true I could have trusted Owagamy or Komaloot with the secret; but the matter was how they could conduct the thing in such a manner as that the affair should never be tract [traced] to its first origin, as the Spaniards would easily discover it to have been their property. Sometimes we thought of melting the Vessels down, and thus it went on for such a length of time that it became a matter of little concern to us. There it lay just covered over, useless and no more regarded than if we had never found it except we kept out some few of the gold coin wherwith the Women adorned themselves and the Children.

I then made Harry plant a parcel of Lima and Guava seeds before

1. In the form of lumps or balls.

the place, which in a few months time threw a masque before the whole. After this was done we gave all our Indians charge never to speak of that affair before our Visitors, least by that means we might all be involved in trouble before we were aware of it. This they all promised steadfastly to observe. And many times have we diverted our hours in acting the part of dealer, Contractor, and purchasers. Sometimes Somer was the Merchant and contracted with me as a Carpenter to build him a Ship of such a tonage or burthen. At other times I purchased large tracts of Land from him. And in this way we amused the time with little variety untill we had a Visit from the Indians.

These were Owagamy and three more and informed us that Komaloot was dead. This threw us all into unfeigned Sorrow for the loss of so good a friend, which made me observe that altho he was now gone and could never more pay us his kind Visits, Yet it was our ernest desire they would not think of dropping us on that account. Owagamy then gave a suddain Start and replied that he knew a friend from an Enemy by the feele, and that he did not leave touching him until death made him too cold. I returned him my hearty thanks for his good opinion of us.

He then took occasion to enquire where we got the gold he saw on our Wives and Children. I told him we found it by chance on the Sands by the Seaside. He then said he supposed it to be some of the money my Merry Countrymen had hidden when they came along the Coast to plunder the Spaniards in his old fathers time, Observing that when he was a little child there died among them a very old White Man who had been one of those people, and he remembered his name was Yaspe. Moreover he said his father when talking with him heard him tell that he had been at the plundering Churches and getting great riches; and that on a time he with a number more had buried some once on the coast to the Northward of their dwelling, where they belayed a young Molatto fellow to keep watch over it. That his father and some of the other Indians, among whom was old Coduuno who died in the Canoa with me, proposed to go with him in serch of it; but that Old Yaspe told them in case he was to find out the Very Spot he nor they could be any thing the better for it as it would, on their digging, continually keep sinking lower in the Earth. On their enquiring the reason for this he told them the Spirit would Sink it as knowing he had no title to any part of it because they, on a Quarrel with him, had landed or marooned him with a Curse so that it rendered him totally incapable of being any how partaker. This was the superstition of that Old Vagabond.

On this I directly got Harry to pronounce to me that Old fools name but it could be brought no nigher than Yaspe; and on going to my paper I found one of the mens names who signed ye Robbin to be Jasper Cary, who undoubted was the very person. Owagamy signified. Our friends stay'd but three days with us and then departed for their own home. We all desired they would bear our sorrow away with them to our friends at home on the death of Komaloot.

About this time Shipmate Somer had a Daughter born which he was pleased to call Anauche or Hannah; and three days after Betty brought me a Son. Him I called Rees.[2] Now we were become Eleven in number, a little society hid away from all the World as I may say, perfectly happy if we could but be content as we wanted for nothing but such things as we could well do without. For instance, we had a large Bank. If at any time our ladies were a little out of order we could on such a pressing occasion procure a Duck, Diver, or some other fowl; yet this was attended with rather too much expense—our ammunition growing short—as I valued one charge of Powder at the rate of ten dollars, and could have well given 50 of them for 5 pounds of that infernal composition.

I shall in this place take notice of a diverting scene we were every now and then entertain'd with. (Viz) The Indians when last with us brought with them a very young Monkey as a gift to Owen. This little creture, being but lately taken from its Dam, became much taken with our Dog Swift, so that when ever he lay down it would get on his back and place itself between his shoulders. This came on at first by the Child putting it to play with the Dog. From this time forward it was ever on his back, go where he would, the Dog never

2. Doubtless the Welsh name Rhys.

offering to snarle or refuse. This was what in future opened the Ball, as I may say.

Harry would call the Dog by name, then set off as hard as he could run, the Dog after him with the little Jockkey sticking at his back. By frequent trials the Monkey rode to admiration. At length Somer made him a little Cap and Whip. Now and then Harry would get privately among the Woods and then call eagerly for Swift, when off would set the Dog and rider full speed, who was become so great an Horseman that he never once fell. But what went beyond all the rest was to see the great address he shewed when the Dog would push thro a thicket, for then he would dodge his head first to one side and then to the other with such care that I would defie the best Huntsman to push through a Brake better.

If ever we attempted to send the Dog into the Water the Monkey would be off his back in an instant, let us take all ye precaution in our power at such times. Nothing could be more diverting than to see the little Toad run home with his Whip in hand and Cap on his head. No sooner would he arrive but he would go up to my Wife, get on her Shoulder, and there begin to chatter as tho he related his grievance to her; but such tricks would make him quit the dogs back perhaps for two days.

I think it quite unnecessary to recite over all our ordinary customs as they are in general one and the same round, in order to avoid being too tedious. And now another year had revolved since I first came on this foreign shore, but I am content.

Chapter 18: Twelveth Year

Twelveth year began. On a day as Somer was going thro the trees he told me how he had been beset by a Small bird; and as these birds are somewhat remarkable I shall mention their nature in this place. It is called by some the Hanger. There are several sorts of them but all fine feathered. They are about the size of our Starling and make their nests to hang down from the outer branch of a tree by a string. The nest is oblong like to a Cabbage net. Many times as I have passed any where nigh to one of their nests the bird has at once darted down from a limb full into my face, fly back and then return in a furious way as it would pick out my Eyes, so that I have been forced to beat them off.

These birds are fond of a particular kind of Insect which is altogether singular in its way. I always found them on the Cedar, Cypress and such kinds of trees. These Insects make themselves a kind of house resembling the Shape of a Ships Buy [buoy] and of a Substance so tough that it is impossible to break it with a mans finger. They fortify this Buy with particles from the same tree in a very curious way. At the uper end of this buy the Insect appears, about half its body out, where it is constantly spinning its threads, lowering itself down and then haleing itself up hand over hand, as is the Sailors term, with great dexterity. I have seen above a thousand of them hanging from one tree like so many bobbins. It is curious to see how dextrous the Hanging Bird catches them as he flies, then putting it under his foot on a limb of the tree disengages it at once.

We often found Land Tortoises. These Harry told me were choice good eating; otherwise I should never have thought of such a thing. Of these we made Excellent Soup. It is almost incredible to think how long those Animals will retain life after the head has been taken off. I have known them to move 10 or 12 days after that operation if kept in a shady place. This is an absolute fact.

One Day this year, being out about half a mile back of our home, I proposed for us to make our way back into the Country to see what we could discover, And on the next we armed ourselves for the purpose. For some time our passage proved exceeding hard and difficult. At length we made our way so far that we came to an opening of clear ground well grown with fine lofty trees, after that to a bare country. There we espied three Deer runing Swiftly; our Dogs put after them but soon lost them. We then came to a place where there was a kind of morass, on the other side of which was to be seen a long range of broken banks. Here we Saw multitudes of Wild Parrots flying over our heads.

Now as the Scene was quite new to us we were the more curious, and Somer observed at the foot of the bank a monstrous scull of some Beast or other; it was as much as he could lift. The jaw teeth were many of them yet in the head, quite Sound, but could be drawn out easily. Going a little farther on, I pulled out of the bank a Rib of monstrous size. We then found more Bones pertaining to the same kind of Beast. Now what species of Animal it could be I knew not, but Somer insisted it must be an Elephant, having seen one, but I never had. However, we cam off with three of the teeth, and we found all the bits of wood or stick which fell into the water was petrified. We made a shift for to mount the bank, from whence we could see far away round us. After we had so far satisfied our curiosity we returned. When we got home a council was held again over the teeth, but all were ignorant. Only Harry said he had heard the old folks say they had found such when hunting. And thus it rested, nor could we make any more of the matter.

Shortly after this Somer proposed that we should have a general day with the whole family in the boats, it being fine weather. Accordingly, the next morning, every thing being got ready, off we went in two boats. And thus we proceeded—Somer, Wife and Child, my Wife, children and self in the Yawl; Harry, his wife Jessy and child with ye dogs in the great Canoa. Our Voyage to the old plantation was very fine. From thence we put off for the end of Long Key and there we landed the Women and Children. I stay'd with them and kindled a fire while Somer, Harry and Owen rambled along the south shore. In about a hour Harry came back and informed me that they had found a very large boat like that Mr. Somers brothers had gone away in to the South, but that it was full of Sand, and that he desired I would come to see it. I then went with him and found her to be an English longboat with a bilge in her bow, on her starboard side, painted black and yellow and seemed not Old altho much weather beaten. As we found her there we left her for that time.

I return'd to the Girls, and they went after the birds. When I got back I went to work with my line at throwing out, and caught a couple of fine Mutton fish. These with a few Redshanks and Scapies they brought back with them gave us a plentiful meal, under an awning Somer and Harry raised for us with our Sails. After this we comforted our selves with a little Toddy and our pipes, and in the evening returned to our Castle again with our ladies in high spirits.

Shortly after this Somer and I undertook to go and clear out the boat we had discovered. This cost us some trouble but we patched her up so as to make her swim home very well. The next thing was for to get her up. This we accomplished by the help of rollers when all hands were mustered; and she was got up so that Somer could get at her very well, for he was Carpenter, Sailmaker, Calker and Cooper on all occasions. The geting of her up cost us much labour, doing it by Spells inch by inch.

Now as I observed my Shipmate so very earnest about putting this Longboat into repair I asked him one day wherein lay all the necessity for the great labour and pains he was at, as when she was refitted we could have little or no call for her as we had two sail boats and a canoa already. But he said it was diversion to him, and for that reason I held my peace. But when he had done I told him that he and Harry had only created a new jobb for themselves. "As how?" he said.

"Why, now you must fall too and build a shed over her, or else she must be launched again; otherwise the Sun will soon do for her." And in order to preserve her from the worm they built a shed over her. After this she remain'd where she was.

The next thing we fell upon was melting down our silver plate, as thinking by that method we migh some time or other get it off. For this purpose we dug a large hole. Harry was employ'd for some time in cutting billet wood. When all was ready we made up a kind of cross pile and laid all the different things thereon, and Harry with Jessy were to stand Stokers; and after the whole was completed it formed a huge piramid. But altho the fire was well kept up yet it was above 5 or 6 hours eere the whole was ran down, and then we left it to extinguish of itself. In a day or two we cleared away all the ashes and got a noble mass of Plate, ran into many odd shapes. These we were forced to reduce into smaller pieces and it cost Harry work enough, but he had time enough on his hands. What by bending and the application of an old ax he reduced it all. We then buried the pieces in a private place against a time (if ever) they might also become of use to us.

Nothing of any signification came on untill I proposed that Somer and Harry should take a trip along shore southwest of the Long Key. Accordingly they took the large Canoa and left us the next morning. After they were gone I took a march with my Gun among the Traps, not daring to go far in their abscence. In one of the Traps I found an odd kind of Beast of a brown colour. It had been there so long that it was in a state of decay, so that I left it there untill such time the boat returned. This day also I shot a beautiful kind of Parrot which was quite white as Snow except a fine crest of Yellowish feathers on the head. This bird I shewed to my wife who said it was an Auckco but observed that they would never talk much.

My two friends did not return that night and I began to grow very uneasy on their account, fearing they had met with some disaster. That night I slept not as the wind blew off shore. Thus did I wait in suspence untill the next afternoon when to my great joy I saw them coming round the East end of ye Long Key. They brought home a very large kind of shark such as I had not seen before. This fish had no teeth, and its skin was exceeding rough to the fele. They had also in the boat a good lump of Ambergrease, differing in colour from that which we had already. I then enquired what kept them out all night. He told me they ranged the shore above 5 miles, where they found a cask which he imagined to be either Beef or Pork, but had left it safe on the beach untill I should go and pay it a visit. That shortly after, they saw a Vessel standing to the southward, upon which they unshiped their mast and retired among the trees, but that in about an hour she tacked and stood out to sea. And by this time it grew late, which made them conclude to remain there for the night as there was a pretty small Creek running up about 40 yards, at ye head of which was a charming run of fresh water where they had staid all the night, plagued to death by the mosketoes. I could not think how that Vessel escaped my sight except she was too far to the Southward for my Eye.

After this I took Harry to the trap and shewed him the Animal I had found in it, and he lugged it out and gave me this odd account of it. He said those cretures live chiefly by catching Ants, saying they will creep slowly on towards a nest, laying flat on their bellies, then put forth their tongues to a great length, which never fails to atract multitudes of those Insects upon it. When the beast finds by their strong biting that he has got his freight, he then whips in his tongue and swallows them, and then begins the same process. The tongue of this animal when Harry drew it forth was exceeding long, narrow and round.

It happened one day as Somer and I were walking by the Shore near to some low flat rocks we had a curious scene of an Amour between two Sea Crabs, and as there are not 2 in 20,000 who ever happen to see the like I shall touch upon it. (Viz), I was sitting on a long stone perhaps 20 feet by 15 feet in length when a Crab came up the side of it and marched slowly toward the middle of it and there squated down. About one minute after that up came another on the opposite side. Directly as the first Crab saw the second it erected itself on its legs as tall as possible. The last comer then advanced very slow for about three feet toward the other in the centre and there made a full stop, the other facing of it. The Second Crab then began to move in an Oblique direction but slowly to a very wide angle, from right to left so as to form a kind of curve or semicircular motion to the Crab in the Centre. This he repeated for a considerable time, and making his regular advancement by contracting his curve, increasing in Velocity as he advanced so that by the time he had made about two thirds of his progressive motions his Velocity became so exceeding quick that the Eye could not catch the motion. The Centre Crab constantly moved at the same time as fixed on a Swivel or pevit untill the male Crab became very nigh, when in an instant the female became willing to sit still, flang back the . . . and an union commenced.[1]

1. In the MS the words between "when" and "an union" are inked out.

Godart's attitude the whole time was very expressive of admiration. He stood with his two arms before him and hands clenched, then burst into the following expressions: "How crate is our Got vat mak all dem his tings. Shipmate, He is here, He is dare unt al over da vorld, unt dat show us He bin in dis lant mit us, dis minute."

"Most certain," I said, "His almighty Eye never slumbers. Therfore should not you and I watch also, messmate, that we may not forget we are ever in his holy view where ever may be our lot to be cast in this life?"

This naturally leads me to make some remarks on the other sort call'd Land Crabs. There are of an amphibious nature but their chiefest residence is on ye Land. There are two different sorts or colours of them, the one of a Chocolate colour, the other that of a Mulatto. The dark sort are reckoned the best and are to be found even so far up land as some miles; yet they have their anual time of coming down to the Sea which is in the breeding time, about March. What is very wonderful, when they are on a march they never turn either to one hand or the other, but if a huge Stone, log or trunk of a tree chance to lay in their passage they mount over it, and that they do should it be as high as one storie of an house. At which seasons they come down from the country by thousands; the Males are then so vicious that they have frequent battles and fight furiously, giving each other such blows with their great claws that the sound may be heard twenty yards as their claws are much larger than those of the Sea Crab, especially one of them. When one of them finds himself rather the master, he will strive to sieze the other by one of his large claws and thus holds him for such a length of time that his antagonist, finding no other means of escaping, gives such a suddain snap with the joynt next his body that he leaves the whole member to be devoured by the other and thus makes his escape.

This sort of Crab divours every thing indifferently as it can come at it. They burrow deep into the Earth, having generally two holes, the one for to make their escape by, perhaps, or for some other reason. If a corps should be buried without a coffin, as is many times the case abroad, they never fail to find it out and devour the whole flesh from the bones. They are so swift it is out of human power to overtake them if they have a fair field for the chance. These crabs differ in bodily shape from Sea crabs, being of a round and compact body. The Lizzards take particular care to avoid them, knowing by instinct that if they come but within a snatch of their claws there is no redemption.

My friend Somer from this time fell into a kind of melancholy, and one day I asked him the cause of his dullness. "Oh, my good friend," said he, "I am thinking on my wickedness."

"So should we all," I told him.

"No, no, Mr. Penrose," said he, "you have not been so great a sinner as me. Did I not shoot Brandt?"

"Pray dont give your heart so much trouble on that account," I said, "for it is my real opinion that you were appointed by the Great Judge himself at his instrument to be the end of that Wretch. Know ye not it is His divine decree that whosoever Sheds innocent blood by man shall his blood be shed?"

"That is true," he said, "but then I sent him to hell without my giving him a chance to ask pardon."

"Leave that reflection alone to the great Author of our being, and pray let us drop ye subject." So to divert him from it I asked him when we should go and examine that Cask they found. "Tomorrow," he said, and we went accordingly.

Away we went next day in the Yawl. When we came to the spot I scuttled it in order to examine its contents and we found it to contain Hams. We then got it on board and returned home, but when we came to examine them to our great surprize we found they had lost all their saltness in a manner. We hung them in the Sun to dry and dry they did, sure enough, becoming as hard as sticks. Our Indians would never taste it after the first time so that they hung by for a long time, excep Somer and I now and then cut a piece and Eate it by way of novelty.

And now I shall give the Reader a sample of my own courage when put to the test. One evening Mrs. Penrose and Harry took it into their heads to divert themselves a little at my expence. She knew me to have a custom to cut a bit off those hams in an Evening to eat with a plantain, and I usually sat on a stool without. Now as I was sitting with my pipe smoking, Betty took occasion to ask me why I did not take a bit of the Ham for my supper. "I think I will," said I. Now they hung back in the cavern, so up I got and opened my knife for that purpose and marched in to ye intent. But when I came to advance toward the place, whistling as I went, All at once I was struck with one of the most horrid sights I had ever beheld. Back I ran much faster than I had entered, and was making for my stool with my hair standing on End. My Wife, observing me to be so much alarm'd, burst into a great fit of laughter. This brought me to my self a little. She then told me the Secret and rallied me not a little, saying she wondered white men could be frighted at such trifles who were not dismay'd at the Winds and great Waters. When I had recovered my thoughts again I went in with her to get a fair view of it, and yet the sight was truly odious. It was Mr. Harry who had got 4 of those Fire Flies I have mention'd before; they are nigh as large as chaffers. These he had fixed, two of them between his teeth and one in each socket of his Eyes, then placed himself in a dark corner, the greeness of whose light cast such an infernal gleem over his face togather with his mouth and Eyes appearing to be all on fire that I defy the bravest heart not to be daunted should he come upon it unaware as I did.

Somer happened to be then down by the water side, and Betty when she saw him on the return told Harry to place himself again as before. When he came up I asked him if we should get a bit of ham each. "With all hearts," said he.

"Go, then, and cut a bit for each of us," said I. In he went freely but in a short time we heard him hollow out but did not run back as we expected. But out ran Harry in a great hurry, calling to us. We ran in and found him laying in a strong fit. I bid them run and get a torch directly, and it was nigh an hour before we could get any sense from him when he was so far recovered as to converse. I got him some Gin, and asked him what was his disorder, when he began:

"Oh, Donder, Donder! Ich sal never liven much longer!"

"What has terrified you, man?" said I. "You stare like one mad."

"Oh, Shipmate, I have see von spook for Brandt."

"Pshaw," said I, "dont be foolish, man! You have fallen in a fit. You are subject to them, I suppose." He said he never had above one in his life to his knowledge. Now I would have given a thousand Dollars this trick had never been plaid. The poor Indians were all terrified to death, and how to contrive the matter I knew not. I advised him to go to Sleep, strictly charging his wife to watch by him, and that he should not know anything of it untill ye next day. The next morning he seemed quite recovered. I then told him the real story, and that they had served me in like manner. But he could not be persuaded untill it was repeated the next evening, and then it was all passed off in a joak the best way we could.

Few young people give themselves the time to reflect on the dangerous consequences attending a great fright; yet how frequently they practice the thing altho thousands in the world have been rendered useless to society by it, to the grief of many a family.

Chapter 19

It was now about the middle of July when as Somer and I were on the hill looking out to Seaward I thought I saw some kind of a Vessell in the offing, therfore call'd down for my glass. When Eva brought it up to me I found it to be so, but what to make of her we could not tell. She was as we thought under no sort of Sail and too far out to be at an anchor. It was about noon when we first discovered her, and there she remain'd all that day. The next morning I went up again and found she had not drifted half a mile from her first station. This put us on disputing—Somer was for going out to reconnoitre her, but that move did not suit then with me, as not knowing how things might turn out. This I found gave Messmate Godart uneasiness, so I told him if she remain'd that way two hours longer I would consent to go out with our Yawl and get a more satisfactory view of her. He observed that as he was convinced she was in distress our duty called on us to save life.

"What would you say should it prove a sort of decoy?"

He then made me this reply: "Dont you always beg me to hold fast on ye Divine Providence, and where are you now, man?"

"Say no more," I replied, "but let Harry get the Yawl ready and in Gods name we will go." By this time the whole family were got interested, and we kept a constant eye on her.

Now as I found my Wife not fond of going, I told Somer that he and Harry should go, giving them strict charge not to go too near her unless they saw absolute necessity to do so. So away they went with a light wind, leaving me full of concern untill their return. Every now and then I took a fresh lookout. At last I saw they lay too. Some time after this I saw a small thing put from alongside of the vessel and joyn ours; and as I was thus under my cogitations I saw both boats go alongside of the Vessel, and I hoped to some good end. The reader may easily think what a taking I was in while they remain'd on board of her. When I went up again I saw they were put off and stood right in for our bay. I waited with impatience for the upshot of the affair. At last I could percieve my own people in her; but no sooner did they come in than I ran eagerly down, crying, "What news? What news?"

"Oh, give me some water to drink!" said Somer, "and then I shall tell you all."

"How came you to be out of Water?" said I while they were drinking.

Then he began and said it was a Sloop from St. Jago da Cuba[1] in great distress; that they had been struck by lightning which had carried away their mast about 6 feet above the partners,[2] two hands struck dead; and that they had not one drop of Water left when they came

1. Santiago, on the south coast just west of Guantanamo.
2. A framework of timber to support a mast as it comes through a hole in the deck.

onboard them, having finished the last the day before; that they drank
off all they had carried out in the Yawl at once.

"How did you come to understand them?" I said. Somer then told
me that he believed the captain was an Irish man, for he could speak
English very well and his name was Dennis Organ, and that he
ernestly begged my kind assistance if possible. "How many hands are
they?" said I.

"Only 3 men and a boy."

"Well, then, come on. Let us in the first place carry off some water
in one of our empty Caggs, for we can pretend to do nothing farther
untill she is had in to an Anchor."

"I have told them to go for water to the point of Long Key," said he.

"That was right," I told him. We then got in some of our provisions
and put off directly. As we got out of the lagoon we saw their boat
rowing for the Key point. We hurried off to them as fast as we could
and when we got along side the Captain stood crossing and blessing us,
making bows to me. I jumped on board directly, when he came and
eagerly Kissed me saying that we were Jewels of Angels Sent from the
Holy Powers to be sure to save their lives. "How long have you been in
this distress, Captain?" said I.

"18 days, my dear," said he, "and out 29 days." They had not one
spar left. They first got up the Square sail yard to the boom as a mast
or rather jury mast, and lost that three days after, being carried away
in a gale of wind, and now had nothing more left, saying that if they
had, they were become so exhausted in strength that they could not
make any hand of it. I told him we must first get her in shore to an
anchor if we could, and then we would try to cut him a small tree
down and endevour to get it stepped for him according to our
strength. Then he asked us down below and offered us some Aqua-
dienta, but I told him it was a thing we were not used to, so begged
him to excuse us.

"Oho," said he, "my dear children, you are the first Sailors I ever
knew in all my life who dont like a drop of the Silly cratur." I told
him I would inform him more on that head another time.

Now as we were thus sitting in conversation I took up a book which lay on one of the lockers. Curiosity made me open it, when I found it to be Spencers *Fairy Queen* in English. "This is the first book I have seen in many a long year," said I.

"And is it, troth?" he said. "Why then, Honey, I could gratify your desire by the fist full, if that be all, but first let us be getting the Sloop in to an anchor, by your laves."

"As soon as your boat returns," said I. Some time after this we turn'd too and towed her in to 12 fathom water and there came too, it being now become evening almost. I then took my leave of them as I did not care to remain onboard of her all nigh least somthing should happen at home. I asked the Captain to go on shore with us, but he did not chuse to leave the Sloop.

I slept but little that night but about three in the morning rouzed Harry and told him to call Somer. We then put off down the Lagoon and were obliged to row off to her as it was flat calm. They were all turn'd out waiting our arrival. "Good morning to you, my sweet Babes," said the Captain. "Long life to you!"

We then jumpt on board and he took us below. I observed one of his hands to be a Spaniard, the other two Negros. The Capitain then took out a bottle, and holding it up to the light said, "Well, now, what may your name be called, I pray?" I told him Penrose, and at his service. "Penrose," said he. "Was you ever on board of the old *Namure* [*Namur*],[3] young man?" I answered in the negative. "Well, troth and faith, then; I was well acquainted with one Davy Penrose on board of that Ship in the year 38."

"But you must understand," said I, "those days are too old of date for me."

"Faith, and that is true for you, I believe," he said; "but however its the same thing, maybe he was your elder brother."

"Some relation, perhaps," I answered.

3. This ship was built in Woolwich in 1697, and after service in the Mediterranean was wrecked with her 640 men in the East Indies in 1749. A second *Namur* was constructed in 1756.

"Oh, then, by my Shoul you dont gain great credit by your kin, joy; for he woud be after milling and pilliareing[4] any ones Dudds he could lay his hands on, so that some of our knowing lads would be after remarking dat he was one fishermans boy, each of his fingers a fish hook. But that is nether here nor there. Take a bob a piece of this, children"—holding out ye bottle and glass to me—"As you would not take any before." So to humour the thing we took a little of it.

After this we returned too and got up the Anchor, then leaving the Skipper at the helm we got three into each boat and began to tow her farther in. While we were thus employed the old man asked me if I knew a good birth for to bring too in. "I have not been here so many years not to know that," I told him. After we had been towing about the space of an hour he called the boy Perico on board and ordered him to cook us a good mess of Chocolate. The sound of Chocolate revived my heart. Shortly after we all took about a pint with a good Spanis biscuit each, and then brought her safe to an anchor opposite our old plantation where she lay in about two fathom water snug enough.

When matters were brought thus far I gave the Captain to know I should be glad of his company at our poor habitation. He said with all his heart, so leaving the boy to look after ye Vessel we came away to-gather. As his two people and Harry rowed we 3 sat, and I then ran over my story in brief to him. During ye time the Old Man would cry, "Salve Domine!" At length we came to our Barcadera, when I took Capt. Horgan by the hand and bid him welcome. The rest of our family had gathered round to meet us, but no sooner did they fix their Eyes on the Negro man whose name was Rodrigo but away ran the Children, and the Girls began to move also as it is my opinion they had never seen an African before.

Now I told this kind old Hibernian that without any more adoe or ceremony he was free to make use of our place as he listed, and that Mr. Somer and I would give him all the assistance in our power; that we had plenty of those things needful toward the Support of

4. From mill: to beat, strike, or overcome; and pill: to rob, plunder, or pillage, from OF *piller*.

human nature, but as to dainties we had long since learnt to live without them; and that when we were a little refresh'd we would take a hunt among the trees after some sort of a Mast, and Mr. Somer generously undertook to make it. I now took the opportunity to ask him how much Powder he had onboard. "Indeed," said he, "it is not long since I was in great dread I had too much of it on board when we had that misfortune of ye lightning." I then observed that we had a fine lump of Ambergrease by us, and should be proud to make an extchange with him for Powder. "Oh," said he, "you shall have what I can spare for nothing, joy," since we were so civil to lend our help in his distress. I then told Harry to bring the Woman and children to me. They came and I presented them before the old Gentleman and he recieved them cordially; and as the Negro fondled on the children they became more free with him.

After we had dined Mr. Somer and Diego the Spaniard took a walk in serch of some sticks to cut for a pair of Sheers[5] while Mr. Horgan and I hunted out a tree fit for a temporary Mast. After this we returned and chatted over our Pipes, he observing that he had not done the like for 5 years before as they always made use of Segars. He then said he would present us with some tobacco, with a little Sugar and Chocolate. I then began to ask about Twine, Needles, Nails, &cc or any thing he could well spare, most of which we afterwards obtained in some degree.

The next day they went to work and felled the trees, then Somer and Diego went to work on them and in about 5 days they formed a tollerable sort of Mast. Now what is surprising as the Captain told me, they never once had sigh of any Vessel during the whole time, being frequently becalm'd for days togather. He also told me that two casks of Water were stove by the thunder in the hold, and 5 long bars of Iron were fairly melted; that when they were first struck he imagined all his people to be dead as they were all down, but that Pedro Gomez and Martin Galvan never came too more so that they commited them to the deep ye next day. I then Enquired whither they were bound

5. Shears: two or more spars rigged as a hoist.

and he told me to a port call'd Madalena,[6] and that he owned half the Sloop himself. She was about 60 tons burthen, quite old and much out of repair.

The next day the Captain and I with Harry and the Negro went away to the Sloop, taking some Yams and beans for the boys use. Now while we were on board and having leasure I asked him to give me a sight of some of his books. He then call'd Perico to get out a square box. When it appear'd I was struck with an odd circumstance. The lid had the following directions on it done with black paint: "To the care of Mr. Aron Manby, Kingston, Jamaica." "This has been prize goods, I suppose," I said.

"Indeed it was all that," said the Captain. "They have laid a long time At St. Jago in an old store unheded as few or none could read them, so I bought them, child, for a trifle."

I then said, "What will you take for them by the lump?"

"Why, as to that, hony, I dont care to part with them at all, do you see, case I know some of my acquaintance where I am bound who will give me a good price for some of them, as we never have any English books come among us but by the Wheel of fortune, as I may say."

"Come, then," said I, "in a word will you take the value of 50 pieces of Eight, as you say you gave but a trifle for them?"

"Indeed, Mr. Penrose, I can deny you nothing at all, at all. And now, Faith and Soul, if you will give me 70 dollars you shall have them and cheap enough, to."

Now, thought I, you are an Old Fox, that is flat. "Well, then, I will give you in good sollid silver the full value of it. Is it a bargain, or not?"

"Shew me the money," said he.

"As to money," said I, "where should I get cash? But you shall have it full weight in Silver when you come on shore."

"Are you on honour, my love?" he said.

6. The reference is probably to Rio Magdalena on the south coast of Cuba west of Santiago, rather than to the area of the much larger Magdalena River in Colombia.

"For certain," I told him.

"Well, then, my jewel, you may have them, so say no more but take them with you when you go." And to mend the bargain he gave me a bottle of Cordial. I then Call'd Harry and he with the Negro boy got the box into our Yawl. I was now become so eager to be on shore that I knew not where I stood. Now just before we were going to put off, and waiting for the Old Man who was down in the cabbin, I was surprized to hear the Negro fellow talking English with my Harry, and laughing.

"What makes you so merry, Blackie?" I said.

"Master, I was saying to your Man that the Old fellow was well paid for those old books."

"How so?" I replied.

"Because I was with him when he paid for them, and he gave but 5 pieces of Eight."

"Never mind that now," said I. "Pray, where did you learn English?"

"I was born in Spanishtown, Jamaica, and was carried off by a Privateer from Old Harbour about 13 years ago when a boy."[7]

"Are you a free man now?" said I.

"Yes, Sir," he said. "My Wife bought me free. She is a Spanish Mulatto of Rio Madalena."

After we came on shore I told the Captain I should convince him of my honour, and then produced a quantity of plate in pieces and bade him Examine it well. He then began to cut it and ponderate it; at last he said: "By the Holy St. Columb it is good Plate, sure enough. And where did you find this, now?"

"By chance digging for turtle Eggs," said I.

"Well, then, by the Blessed St. Patrick you were a very fortunate Man, Capt. Penrose, To find Turtles that laid Silver Eggs."

"Now how shall we weigh this said plate?"

"O, leave that to me, hony," said he.

7. Spanishtown is inland some ten miles west of the present Kingston; Old Harbour lies to the southwest.

"Yes, but I hope you will let me have a hand in the affair, Captain, too," I answered. Then taking up a piece I asked him what he valued that at.

"About 8 dollars," he said. And thus we went on untill his averice became fully satisfied. When this was done I wrote a Receipt and he signed his name to it, Dennis Horgan.

After this we went to visit the Mastmakers and brought them down to the house where I made them a good Yabba of Toddy out of our little store. And then I sent out the Canoa a Stricking, and in about two hours they returned with a fine mess which was directly cooked. And as we were Eating, the Old Man took occasion to ask me if I were a Catholick or not. I answered in the negative.

"Ah, that is your misfortune," said he. "But no matter, hony, if you are to be saved, you are; that is all. It is no meat of mine, Child, only it is a great pitty and an Error in judgment among your People to be quitting the true and only Old Mother Church."

"Never mind dat," said Somer. "Dont you see how the goot Got mack his sun shine pon all? You vil neet call us for da Divel when we mack you von goot mast wan dime more." And thus it ended. Then the pipes were call'd for with some of our friend Horgans choice tobacco. After this the Old Man went up the Hill with Somer and Diego to see the work.

In the mean time I took the opportunity to examine my purchase and found the contents as follows: The Fairy Queen, Popes Essay, Spectators, Seneca's Morals, Chaucers Tales, Don Quixot and Ovid's Epistles; then Josephus,[8] Ansons Voyage,[9] Ramsays Songs,[10] Foxes Book of Martyrs,[11] and a fine large old Bible with great clasps, the

8. Flavius Josephus (37-c. 100 A.D.) was a Jewish scholar and historian, onetime Governor of Galilee and later a Roman citizen. There were at least fourteen editions of his works in English in the 17th and 18th centuries.

9. George Anson, *A Voyage round the World in the Years MDCCXL, I, II, III, IV*, London, 1748.

10. Allan Ramsay, *Poems*, 2 vols., London, 1731.

11. John Foxe, *Actes and Monuments*, known as *Book of Martyrs*, London, 1563, and later editions.

Spectacle de la Nature,[12] some of Baxters works,[13] with Virgil, Homer and Horace, and many Pamphlets unbound. These Books had layen so long neglected that the Worms had passed through them but not hurted them so much as to spoil them. Nevertheless I thought the Old Captain well paid for them, altho I would not have returned them for double the money, as I looked on it to be a chance among thousands for me to meet with anything of that kind in this place. And so highly proud was I of them that I stowed the Box away with the greatest care imaginable, valuing it as an inestamable treasure.

The next day we sent off the Sheers and a small boom. As for their other boom, they had in the first place cut it in order to make it suitable to the strength they had to raise it for a kind of jury mast. And when the new mast was finished we mustered all hands and with rollers and handspikes got it down to the lagoon in two days, from whence it was towed along side. I then made Somer master Rigger, and the next day we raised the Sheers. After this was done I mustered all our whole force which could be spared from the Shore. I sent off Patty, Eva and Jessy, so that they now mustered nine in Number. On the Morrow Harry and the boy came in and told me that Mr. Somer had got the mast in, and that the Captain desired I would let him and the boy go out a stricking fish for them while they got up the Shrowds and other things. Accordingly I dispatched them away with some roots and what I could spare.

It was above a week after this before Mr. Somer had got her any way in readiness; and then they had her Mainsail to cut less, to suit her mast as it was neither so taut or stout as the former. But in about a fortnight they got her in a sort of condition for to proceed, and then we made a kind of frolick on shore and were as merry as so many poor people could be expected to be on the occasion, and the Old Gentleman was as liberal to us as he well could Spare, like a true Hibernian.

12. Noel Antoine Pluche, *Spectacle de la Nature; or, Nature Display'd* . . . Translated from the original French, 2 vols., London, 1748.
13. Richard Baxter, probably his *Life and Times, published from his own manuscript*, London, 1696.

They remain'd with us almost a Month, living chiefly on provisions from our plantation, fishery and Gunning. In the mean time while they remain'd with us we got about 30 weight of Powder and about a hundred weight of bar lead. The Captain gave our Women some boxes of Marmalade. They had a quantity of Dry goods on board of several kinds; I got above 2 dozen Barcelona handkerchiefs, a variety of Ribbons for our Girls with which, like true females, they afterward dizen'd themselves out. Mr. Horgan presented me with a small pocket Compass, a thing which gave me much joy. He gave Somer a plane and a pair of compasses. Harry for his share got an hour glass, which pleased him to such a degree that he would now and then lay himself flat on the ground with it before him and watch it the whole run, frequently striking the Glass to cause it to run the faster as he foolishly imagined. We got store of twine, Thread, Hooks, Needles, Pins, two Penknives and many other articles we stood in need of. And the time drew nigh that they were about to go, and the Old Man and I settled. I paid him for all we had almost, as we scorned to take any thing for our labour, as Mr. Somer and I looked upon it no more than our duty to relieve the Distressed—having recieved a sufficien example from the poor Savages, our sincier friends.

After all things were settled, the Old Man asked me to take a walk with him in private, when he began thus: "Mr. Penrose, how is it possible that you could live so many years here among these Savages? If you will but leave them and go with me in my Sloop you may there become a Very happy man. We have several very holy men with us who will be proud to bring you into the true way, I mean the bosom of our Holy Church. What can you expect to be after spending your life in this Wilderness?"

I made him this reply—that as to my living among Savages I had sufficiently found my account by their faithful services that they were my true and experienced friends; and in regard to my Scituation I was so well content with my condition that I would not of a choice Change it unless such a thing should come to pass that I could be once transported with my Wife and two Children in some English Ship to my own country again, and I well knew my removing among the

Spaniards could never prove fortunate to me, being determined never to change my Religion; and that I was well assured my friend Somer was steadfast of the same mind, saying that if we did not Enjoy the Superfluities of the busy World we were over and above made amends by living in a state of Innocency, and in no great dread of wanting what was sufficient to support us could we but be content.

"Well, then, my dear jewel," said he, "I shall have no more to say."

"Now," Said I, "Daddy, I have one petition to beg of you which will cost you no more than the keeping of a secret, (Viz) that you will never discover this our residence to the Spaniards your acquaintance, as our being on this shore can never prove any way detrimental to them, being in no way concerned with others, nor have we evil practice in our hearts." He then grasped my hand and declared by the Holy Spirit that he would ever be silent on the matter, and that he would manage the affair so that none with him should be the means of its being discovered.

A few hours after, he proposed to go off, and we waited on him to the Sloop. When they had got up the Anchor, I then stood Pilot untill we saw them clear of the Long Key and then bid them a good Voyage, returning safe back to our old mansion. And I hope we discharged our duty by them; and perhaps on ye whole they made a saving voyage for they got both pieces of Ambergriese which must be of great value. And thus ended this new adventure.

We were now become so happy as to read and hear the Scriptures, a thing which proved of much comfort to us. Now after they were gone I repented we had not sold the Longboat to the captain, but Somer observed it could never have answered as they could neither hoist her in or out, and to tow her would impeed their way too much. "Let her be," said he, "who knows how soon we may want her ourselves?"

Some months after this my messmate Godart became much out of order, with spitting of blood; and I thought his great application to reading might be the occasion, as he became so fond of it after I had learnt him that he would be at it hour after hour. I therfore begged him to refrain, and that I would read my self when ever he had a desire, advising him as we now had Powder to go out with the Gun or a fishing with Harry at times. This he complied with and soon became much better.

Chapter 20: Thirteenth Year

It was now become the latter end of June and time rolled on after the old sort. Nothing happened of note, only my School advanced apace. My Son could now read midling and Harry almost as well as I kept them to it daily, each in their turn; so that I had Six Schollars and all were very zelous.

One Day Somer and I took a notion to count over our treasure, for hithertoo the whole had remain'd as when first we found it. We began with Gold and it amounted to 557 pistoles and the Silver to 7,944 dollars—a brave sum to be divided between two poor Jack Tars. "Now," said I to Godart, "suppose you and I had shared all this from a prize in old England, how do you think we should have behaved with it?"

"I think," Said he, "it would all have been shared among Whores, Fidlers, Pipers and Publick houses."

"How so, Messmate?" I replied. "Do you think we should not have found out some more honourable way?"

"Look you, mine goot Vrindt," said he, "we are not now such mad, Skipping Drunken fools as we were in those days. We are now Men. The Great God has disposed of us another way. It is nothing more than the work of the Devil himself when men act after such a manner, Mr. Penrose. He has always his friends ready to instruct others, so the boys learn it of the men."

"That is very just, messmate," said I. "The Devil is never at a loss for an agent."

"But now what do you say," he replied, "to Privateering itself? Is it not robbing of the honest trader of his goods, if you please?"

"Do they not act after the same sort by us?" said I.

"Yes, that is true. But nevertheless you may plainly see by the way we and many others live that Men, if they were truly just, could live without Cutting each others throat and plundering innocent people who would live as harmless as we do now."

"All this is very good," said I. "And yet, Shipmate, I do remember the day when you had a strong hankering for the publick World again. And what was all that for but to indulge your vicious will again?"

"Ah, my good Man," said he, "at that time I was more at ye Devils service than now."

"Pray, Somer, be plain and honest. Would you not of a choice rather live in Holland, provided you could at will convey what money you are master of thither?"

"That I should prefer living among good Christian people and to be above want is true, but not to loose my good state of mind for the whole world."

"Well," said I, "make your heart easy. We are like to remain as we are. But I could have left this place with Capt. Horgan if I had been that way inclined, as he made me the kind offer."

"And by this time you would have been begging."

"It may be, perhaps, so indeed," said I. "So how do we know but what ever is, is right, as Mr. Pope says in that book we had reading last night?"

"Very true," said he.

"Yet I could wish to know whether my poor dear Mother be yet alive," I said.

"What good would that do you?" said he. "I have no father or mother to mourn for me for they are both dead."

"So let us drop it, and learn to live so that we may never be in dread of the day when God shall call us off."

This dialogue, whose topick began our counting over ye Dross, Ended as we returned from the place, leaving it in its native Soil as we found it first, and made no more account of it for the future—leaving all to the divine will of God and making ourselves as cheerful every day as we could in innocent amusements of some kind or other Such as shooting at marks with bows and arrows, Playing at Quoits, setting the Girls and children to run races, making utensils, Singing of Psalms, and sometimes a jumping at distances. In a short time after, as Somer and I were talking on a few lines I had been reading in Josephus, I took it into my head to propose a Sort of worship on the Sabath day. This he seem'd much to like. Upon this I proposed it should be his province strictly to observe the day of the week. This he took upon him; and I ordained that every Sunday after breakfast we should say at my table the Creed, Commandments, and Lords Prayer, then the first Chapter of the Bible, so to be continued in rotation as they came, and to conclude with a Psalm after the best way we could. As to myself I could sing but one, which was that of ye 104th tune; but Somer could sing several Dutch tunes a few of which we adapted the best way we could. And thus our form was settled, and to begin the next Lords Day.

According, when the day came I told Harry to collect the whole family, and when they were all met I took my place and gave them all strict charge that they did not make any noise. During the whole time the most profound Silence was kept as I read, untill Somer and I began to Sing the Psalm. The Parrots then began to hoot and sing at such a rate we were forced in future to remove them to the kitchen when Sunday came to avoid being pestered with ye screeming. And indeed we found need to do the like with one of our Dogs. This would set the other to work often, so that at such times we were forced to put the whole disorderly crew in durance togather. Nothing could be more singular than the behavior of our Women when they were at this service. Their looks were so profound and Seriously innocent that it gave us much plesure.

The next thing Godart went upon was to make a kind of desk for me to read at. And thus we kept irregularly on unless some unforeseen thing hindered us. And here I must remark that once on a Sunday as we were in the midst of our Psalms there came three Indians by land

and walked up towards the Cave, where they halted and stood in a very serious attitude of attention untill we had finished our ceremony.

These Indians were strangers to me except one who had been here before and was call'd Gaynasunto. Another of them was named Owasotas and a kind of half brother to my Wife, by two fathers as he expressed it. These Indians brought seeds of Tobacco from Owagamy and a Piccary they had shott. This was dressed afterwards and we made a plentiful repast with our friends.

I shall in this place take notice of somwhat singular in regard to the Old Bible which I purchased of my friend Captain Horgan. On the first unprinted leaf of this book was the following memorandum: "Samuel Shaddon was born May 4th anno 1670. Joseph Shaddon, his Son, was born in Westminster on the 12 of August, anno 1701. Mary Shaddon was born on the 9 of October, anno 1703. Nicholas Shaddon was born on the 23d of November, anno 1705. Elenor Shaddon was born on the 2d of June, anno 1708." Then on the inside of the Cover was thus written in another hand the following singular lines:

"Thomas, This is the last favour you can possibly expect to recieve from my aged hands. Take notice and remember that it is my ernest request that you strictly peruse this book, and the more this World frown on you, open it the oftener. If you truly examine its contents you will find consolation, the one thing needful, for no man knows the severe trials in this life. Never part with it if possibly you can avoid it. But rather, when you or yours have by frequent useing of it rendered it necessary to be rebound, reserve the old binding in your own family as a piece of antiquity for the sake and remembrance of the Donor who wishes you all happiness. James Rogers, 1719."

About this time as my Wife and I were walking on the other Side of the Plantain walk I took notice of a small kind of Bird to her, telling her we had a bird in my country much of the same size which we called a Wren. Nothin can exceed these pretty cretures. They go always in pairs. Their shape and magnitude togather with their actions are much like the bird above mentioned, but their colour Exceeds the Parrot in greeness and under the throat is a large spot equal to the

Ruby in colour. They are not very shy, seldom mounting above the low shrubs. She told me they call'd them Manune, which word I could get no better interpretation of than mutual love; and well adapted, I thought, as they are ever togather. When one flys the other does the like. When or wherever one pitches the other alights close by its side. They frequently bill like Pidgeons. This conjugal love so apparent in such diminitive cretures renders them highly to be admired and immitated.

But now how shall I draw the sorrowful scene which we both soon became witnesses of? As we were ernestly admiring them I observed one of those little innocents begin to flutter its wings and chatter much, then run along the spray and return to its mate. This I at first took to be a kind of courtship, but shortly after as it flew down to the ground Betty pointed to a long and very Slim Yellow Snake which was quoiled up with its head in the centre erected, and playing its tongue at a great rate. The little Bird would run too and fro, fluttering with its wings and make a sad noise, then fly up to its mate again. Every time it came down it still drew nigher to the Snake. At last the Snake threw itself at its length but still kept its head directed full toward the bird. Betty then told me I should soon see the Snake open its mouth very wide and then the bird would run and play close before it, when the Snake would give a dart with its head and take it in.

"How can that possibly be," said I, "seeing the head of the Snake to be no bigger than the end of my finger?" But she insisted it could take in the bird whole. "But that shall not be," I reply'd, "if it is in my power to hinder." Then with some warmth I cast my Eyes round, and finding a kind of twig I ran and gave it a stroke athwart the neck which soon spoiled its enchanting power, and by that means restored the poor little innocent to its Disconsolate mate who sat all the time on the limb crying chirp, chirp, and trembled at a sad rate.

I then turned to Betty And recited over the circumstance of Our first mortal crime in the credulity of our Mother Eve. Upon this she said I was a very big cunning, that I could tell her any thing I pleased as it happened on the other side of the great Waters. But she was sure such a thing had never happened in their country, because when ever any of their Women chanced to espie a Snake they ran from them, or it, as knowing they would Poison them, and not to wait to hear what they should say to them if they could talk.

Chapter 21

One day as I was passing into our dwelling I took notice of a White circle on the underside of the Archway of the cave, and as I had not observed it before I was a little the more curious about it. But on a nearer view I saw now and then a kind of Brown Wasp come in with a bit of the same matter and begin to fix it thertoo. This Circle was about the size of a quart bottle and in the course of a few days they had formed it into the shape of a small punch bowl. Thus they went on untill they had got it to the size of a large bottle when they began to contract its bulk so as to bring it to the likeness of a neck, still working downward, so that by the time it was finished it was almost a foot in length, leaving only a small hole sufficient for one to enter at a time. After this they daily went too and fro during the hottest hours. The Girls wanted to knock it down least they might sting the Children, but I forbade them. When I found they had all forsook it I told Harry to cut it down with a large knife carfully; and when I came to examine the internal parts nothing could be more curious. The cells were ranged circularly one with in the other, so that it form'd one compleat spiral line. As to the substance, it resembled our sort of course white paper but much stronger, and did not weigh above an ounce or two at most.

There is a sort of Insect here of a very odd form, being in length about four inches yet so slim in one part that it is not much thicker than a small thread. It has eight very long legs and two horns 6 inches in length tapering to such a small point that it is as fine as any cobweb to appearance. The whole Insect, wings and all, is of the fine hew of a watchspring, but what makes it singular is its smell, as no Rose can have a finer scent. It has the power to fold up those horns as in joynts or can at pleasure lay both horns at length backward in a direct line.

There is another Sort which resembles a Wasp but three times its size, and in colour like amber with a Yellow head. I never could see above one of them at a time. The manner of its life differs from that of all other Insects of that class. It burrows in to any dry and sandy place and to the depth of a foot or more. To this receptacle He brings all his Prey, being very furious after all sorts of flies and the like, which he catches either on the wing in full pursuit or by stratagem when they are on a leaf. He has two legs much longer than the rest; and as he always carries his prey between his feet, he by a movement of the joynts of those two long legs poises the load, if it prove rather heavy. When he brings home his prey and has descended below you shall hear a kind of noise the whole time like to a person drawing a fiddle stick over the smaller strings. When this noise once stops you may expect his return. Directly on his coming up he then proceeds to work with his two long feet backward, and in a short time covers the enterance so curiously that the place is not to be observed; and should you make any alteration so as to decieve him, yet he has the sagacity to find it out without fail. I have opened these repositories and have found at the bottom several small Cells in each of which were stowed numbers of Insects of different kinds.

This leads me naturally to another sort of being with which we were amused at times, A kind of large Beetle of a black colour. This Insect whenever It finds the dung of any animal or other kind of pulpy offall, it there takes up its residence untill the whole be consumed. But as ye manner of its providing for itself is the most curious part of the story I shall inform the Reader. They always fly by night or in an evening. They have a most powerful knowledge in the finding out of any of the above mentioned stuff, even should you lay it in a very secret place. When they first find it out, and if the surface of the Earth be not of too hard a texture, they begin to work down through the centre of the Mass to a considerable depth, bringing up the loos earth as in yr. arms. This they lay all on one side untill the whole business of that sort be finished. Then they begin to gather up arms full of the matter just as one would do with Hay or Straw. When it has cleverly got up as much as it can grasp it then walks backward to the edge of the hole and throws itself backward, load and all, and thus tumbles to the bottom of its pit or cell, then returns again and acts in the like manner untill it has industriously collected the whole. If you dig down some time after you shall find the whole mass curiously made up into a round ball, and very close packed togather. But when you break this ball, in the Centre is to be seen its young Embrio; and as that comes on to maturity it has a sufficiency ready provided. It then begins to eate on the internal part. The old one does the like externally, so that by the time they have eaten up the whole, the young one is become capable to provide for itself. But if it should prove too small a quantity in that case the old one goes in quest of more and fly's home to the cell with it in her arms, as I may say. And this she continues to do untill her young is fit to go abroad. When that time comes she brings the young black bantling up in her arms and there leaves it to its self.

About the latter end of August Harry had a Daughter born and he chose she should be call'd Luta after his Sister who was my first Wife. And as Somer and I were passing a joak concerning making out fortunes for our children we happened to mention the word dross, meaning the Money those Sons of Jolly Roger had buried. Now my youn Owen chanced to stand by us at the time and Said, "Father, there is Dross in the great Bible book."

"I know that, child," said I, thinking he meant the clasps.

"No, not the clasps," he said.

"Go along, you blockhead, and hold your tongue," I cried.

"Indeed, daddy," said the boy, "there is Dross in the boards of it."

"Come, Somer," I said, "let us see what he will be at." When we came to open the Bible the Child at once shew'd us a place within the cover where appeared a piece of some shining stuff, and on examination I found it to be a piece of coin. Upon this I went to work and got it out and it proved to be a moidore[1] sunken deep into the cover. And on farther serch I found there was a range of them. We then turned to the other lid and found it the same. Somer then lookt at me and I on him; but after this pause I said, "Now do I discover what the Author of those lines written on the cover intended." After this I laid it all fair again the best way I could and observed to Godart that the Old Horgan, could he have discovered the secret, would never have let me made the purchase. Upon this Godart, taking up his pipe, went out of the house in a most extravagant fit of Laughter. It was some time before I could get him to share the mirth with me. At last he Said he concieved that he saw Old Mother Fortune standing right foreagainst him and making game at he and I. "In what shape?" I said.

"Vat shape? Shapen as two nunuchs [eunuchs]," said he.

"How so?" I replied.

"Why, she is given us monix like as von mountain, unt she know frall dat we been neet petter overall."

"Well said, Messmate. That is a comical observation, indeed."

Now as I had good reason to think both covers were full there could not be less than 60 in each. And then we fell to ruminating on the cause or intent therof, when I came to this way of thinking.—That this book had been presented to a Person who had perhaps been some great spendthrift, and that the good old Author had ingeniously taken this method to supply his wants as thinking he would be in a better state of mind to recieve so good and great a relief while frequently perusing this Holy Book. But alas, His godly designe miscarried and perhaps had gone through several hands untill by the wonderful turns of fortune It came into this remote corner and into the hands of those who must needs prize the book far beyond the riches of its binding.

Soon after this discovery I remember Harry and I were walking in the Woods and I observed to him a kind of Vine growing up a large tree and hung full of a kind of Beans. I asked him if they were fit to eate. He said the Indians eate them at times. The Pods of these Beans

1. A Portuguese gold coin.

were a foot in length and about the breadth of our Windsor bean but much flatter, and the Bean small in proportion to the pod. As they were nigh ripe we gathered a handful or two of the Vine and carried them home where we stripped them and stowed them in a lockker Godart had made. Now it chanced that a few days after this I happened to set myself on this box, when on a suddain such a loud report went off that up I got and ran out quite surprized. The Girls ran in to know what noise it was. But on Harry's lifting up the lid they all began and fired away at a brave rate. Some of them jumped quite out, and before they had done we had above a Royal salute from them.

On the 4th of December as Patty and Jessy were out on the hill looking for some leaves for a burn they came down and informed us there were many large boats out on the Waters. Away we ran up the hill and saw 7 large Vessels with 3 others of a smaller size all standing to the East. They being so far out, I got my Glass and found some of them to be large Ships, others of two masts. As the wind was at west and but little of it they remain'd in sight for several hours, and in the Evening we heard a Gun. Harry and I then took another look and found them all huddled togather. Erly the next day we went up again and could but just percieve them with the Glass, and in about two hours we lost sight of them. That it was a Squadron of King's ships Is my real belief and belonging to Spain probably. The next day we saw a large Sloop standing the same way, which was one of the Same squadron perhaps.

Somer now took a most romantick whim, (Viz) that perhaps they were on the serch for us, saying that it might be the Irish Captain or some one of his people had informed against us. "That is a most rediculous imagination," said I. "Can you be such an idle man to entertain a notion that we are of such great note or consequence that the Vice Roy should fit out a squadron for no better purpose than to rout a coupple of poor Jack Tars? Let not such vain thoughts enter your mind. For if the case stood that they did know of us they need do no more than send a small armed launch and she would sufficienly do our business, should they think it worth their time. So think no more of that, Messmate."

Nevertheless, when I first saw them huddled togather when the gun was fired I must own I became a little flurried untill I let reason take place. For, I thought, what could induce them to make it a point to rout a couple of poor Seamen who had committed no crime, but landed there mearly to save life. Yet I make no doubt had they but known of the cash we were possessed of, they would not have failed to visit us but for no other intent than to leave us as naked as when we first landed. And should this prove the case we could have spared it and have then remained as happy as before.

Once or twice a year we were visited by numbers of Pidgeons of Two sorts, (Viz) Bald Pates and Sprig tails. I should have given a hint of them long before this, but as I could never command any of them for want of amunition they flew by unheeded. The Bald Pate, as I call them, do not breed about us as I never observed any of their nests. This bird is small and, what is not very common, is quite Black except the Scalp or pole, that being quite White, feet and bill crimson with red circles roun the Eyes. The Sprig tail is a fine Bird about the size of the English Wood pidgeon or Quist and much resembles that spieces. When they fly the tail appears as terminating in one long point. This bird is so swift of flight that it is my sincier opinion they can fly 7 miles in one minute. I do not advance this as a rodomontade but by ocular judgment, having at times stood on an eminence as a large flock has been coming; when no sooner have they hove in Sight which could not be less than two miles, yet eere I could cock my piece they have been right over my head. Nay, the Indians as I once was observing this to them, insisted they could fly above a Thousand miles in the course of 24 hours without once resting. And this I really can credit, Owagamy's reason for it being sufficiently convincing—he saying that his people had shott them with a kind of red berries quite fresh in them erly on a morning, which berries did not grow within two moons walk of them away to the Southwest as he directed with his finger.

Now I am speaking on these birds I shall mention another species of Pidgeon or Partridge, as it seems to partake of each kind. This bird is in size about that of a partridge, short and full, but in regard to its colours I have not words to express its great variety, many parts of it being of the changable kind. The Indians call it a deciever, and with propriety. They are never to be seen in any exposed place but ever in the hilly country among rocks and bushes. Their flight is but of short duration depending much on running; and so exceeding subtill are they that if they are persued they squat and will not stir altho you should tread close by them, But on your passing them they artfully run back again with a flutter, by which means they are often betrayed. If by chance they can get no shelter when persued, in that case they will squat behind any small stone on the off side so that you may know to an inch where the bird is, yet cannot shoot it. Therfore they must be taken either on the run or wing; all other means will prove of non effect. These birds are excellent dainties.

About the end of December my beloved Shipmate began to fall off again, and he declined so fast that he became Skin and bone. Now what to do for him I knew not, it being totally out of my power to give him any relief. At last I proposed by Harry's advice that they should take a journey to visit the Indians, thinking the change would prove of some benefit to him. This proposal he seem'd to like and soon after undertook the journey, being become a little stronger. I was loth to part with a man I so much valued, yet my heart earned [yearned] so much toward his happiness that I would have given all the treasure then in our power for his health. When they came to depart, for Harry was to accompany him, he ernestly requested that if he never lived to return I would be a father to his child. And early on ye morrow they prepared to depart, not without much concern on all sides. I now proposed that he had better take Eva his wife and her child with him as perhaps She might prove of service on the journey. This she was glad enough of. Accordingly off they went; and enough had I left on my hands—Patty and Job in lamentation, my Son howling after Somer and Harry, for there never was a greater veneration between Mortals than between them.

Now we were left to shift the best way we could. The whole business fell to my lot, And after they were gone we seemed like lost sheep. My heart was frequently heavy as thinking perhaps I might never see the

face of my Esteemed friend more. I then began to repent that I had
made such an idle proposal, pestering my Thoughts day and night
that he might die in the woods, being in so weak a state. My Wife
administered her best consolation, yet I laboured the harder in my
breast.

Thus was I forced to drag the time along, Patty ever on the dumps
as she had the young children. And as I expected to hear from them or
they would return in about a month, when that time elapsed I became
very uneasy as thinking he certainly must be dead. The thoughts of
his Departing among ye savages almost drove me wild, not that I
once had a notion of their neglect but to think myself the Author and
the very hindrance of my discharging my dutiful last office in laying
him under ground.

Now it happened very late one evening my Wife woke me and said
She heard a Conck blown. Up I got and ran to lite a torch; I then
called Patty. I then asked my Betty if she had not been dreaming. She
said no, and that she was certain. I then got a Shell and gave a strong
blast. Shortly after, it was answered as at a great distance. Now the
ugly thought struck me that perhaps the sound might not proceed from
my friends, and when this had once took possession I marched about
like a man in a state of Stupidity. But soon I heard the Sound again.
Well, thinks I, let what come, will. I am now determined to stand the
brunt; and then gave another blast.

By this time the Morning began to peep which gave me new spirits.
"Make a good fire up," said I to the Girls. On this the shell sounded
and by the sound I knew they were not far off. Before the fire we stood
for a time, and then I sounded and was answered from ye Lagoon.
On this I gave a Shout and was answered by Harry's well nown
whoop. Then we all ran down to the landing and waited untill they
all came in. The first man who jumped on shore was Owagamy. By
this time it was light enough to see plainly. "Where is my dear Shipmate?" said I with a loud voice.

"He is here," cried Harry. Then came on shore my poor Godart. I
took him in my arms and lead him up to the house. But before I could
well recover myself I saw another White Man and a Spaniard as I

thought. This startled me much but I was so overjoyed at my friends return alive that I took no farther notice at that time. Somer then told me he had been much worse or he should have returned before, but nevertheless he was resolved if his time was not long he would die with me, his friend.

Now, thought I, the secret is burst at last. The Spaniards know of our being here, and farewell to all future comfort perhaps. Yet I determined to keep up my courage the best I could, and said, "Harry, how many are you in company?"

"Ten," said he.

"Welcome all," I said. "And pray who may this stranger be?"—taking him by the hand in order to clap a good face on the matter. But how astonished was I when in plain English dialect he said:

"A poor, unfortunate Wanderer long lost from all comfort in this life."

"The more welcome to me, messmate," cried I. "This is a pleasant mistake indeed. I certainly took you for a Spaniard. But think yourself at home, friend. And pray what part gave you birth?"

"I am a subject of Great Britain born in the Shire of Buchan."

"Oh, you are a Scotchman I presume; and pray what may be your name, my friend?"

"My name is Norman Bell, at your service."

"Make yourself as welcome as you please," said I, "and if I can by any means contribute toward Your future happiness, command me as you please, with all my spirit, messmate."

I was now got into such an odd mood that I knew not how to behave, so divided was the Passions of my poor heart. On one hand stood Patty and Job quite overjoyed; on the other hand poor Eva with Jessy recounting her troubles, while the tears fell from her face; my new friend gazing round him like a man on enchanted ground; in another place Owagamy and others chatting with my Wife and Owen; Harry with the rest in another knot; so that the Reader may paint the scene to himself if he can.

When it was fair day I told Patty to get water in one of ye Yabbas and then I made some weak toddy for my poor fellow pilgrims and another for the Indians. But when I presented it to Bell he declined it, saying he had not used the like for a long time. But by my desire they drank, and then Betty made them up our Bed, being both of them weakly. They slept for about five hours, where they rested well. In the mean time I told Harry he must be under the necessity of going to the Crawl for a Turtle. Away he and another Indian went and when they returned it was killed and dressed for our entertainment.

When my two friends awoke I joyn'd them and had them out to the Indians as I chose to give them my company as much as possible least they might grow jealous by my paying more respect to my own sort than them. Mr. Somer said he found himself in a greater flow of Spirits than for a long time past. This was good news to me; and after our meal we all enjoyed our Pipes and were the largest company of puffers I had had togather since my first landing. I asked of Mr. Bell how long he had been among my good friends the Indians. He said not above three weeks, and had enjoyed more comfort in that time by the conversation of Mr. Somer than for some years past. He was pleased to say that my friend had delivered himself so much in my favour that he thirsted to be with me.

I then took the opportunity to ask Owagamy his opinion concerning the teeth we had found, and after the Indians had handed them from one to the other and conferred notes togather in their tongue Owagamy Told Harry that both his father and self had seen of them, and that they knew of a deep valley wherin were many of them but it was far to the South. That he never could learn any of their old people had seen one of those animals alive, saying they knew those cretures had white horns as long as an Indian for that some old people related that they had seen of them—instancing Old Wariboon, a great hunter, kept one of them a long time by him, but as he lived a great distance from them they had never seen it. Upon this an Indian whose name was Kayoota, and present at the time said his father had seen it so many times—holding up his fingers; from all we gathered that the Beast then talked of must have been an Elephant and that those horns they mentioned with the teeth of ye animal. But how the whole race became exterpated remain'd to us a riddle unless the natives time out of mind had unanimously joyned to destroy them. Yet one should naturally imagine the task was of such a copious undertaking that they could never have succeeded; or as the continent being so extensive, all the natives would never have joyned by mutual consent as being seperated thousands of miles asunder and quite unintelligent to each other. But I leave it to the learned to put what constructions on this great mistery they may think proper.

Chapter 22: Fourteenth Year

Nothing worthy recording happened from the time my new friend Bell came to reside with us, and it was now become the mont of June and by my computation I had been here compleat Thirteen Years, not much within or over. And by permission of my new acquaintance I shall relate a short account of his life from his own remembrance. (Viz), he says that his father, Angus Bell, was born in West Lothian and had followed the Pedlars calling and died when he was but 10 years of age; that some time after he was placed with a Carpenter in the Shire of Fife, as his Mother was of those parts. From the Carpenter he ran away when about 15 years of age, and got onboard of a Vessel which traded up the East country. After that he went some trips from Aberdeen to London and there left that Vessel. In the War time he went out several Cruizes and was taken and carried into St. Malo's[1] where he lay in prison a long time, but that during that Space he learnt to play on the German flute from a certain fellow prisoner whose name was James Alexander and one of his countrymen. After this they were exchanged and he came again to the City of London, and then got on

1. In France.

board a Ship bound for New York. That on his return he went to learn the French horn and Trumpet, but by a foolish prank of Wrestling got a kind of hurt in his back So that it rendered him unfit to follow the Seas at that time. And some time after this he chanced to fall in with a set of puppet shew folks who, finding he understood the Trumpet, engaged him; and soon after that he commenced Merry Andrew with these people. Then on the rove he travelled over part of England, Wales and Ireland.

His next connexions was with a Quack Doctor with whome he travelled two years and took every opportunity to study his arts, saying he had ever been adicted to mimicry and could with ease take off the French, Dutch, Irish, Welch &cc. But as he had long since got perfectly cured of his Strain and coming to the City of Bristol, he took a fresh notion of going to sea again, Shipped himself, and was taken by the French and carried into Leogan[2] where he lay so long in prison that in order to obtain his liberty he Engaged with one Capt. Ruiz, a Spaniard then bound to Carthagena,[3] and he procured him his discharge. With him he sail'd for some time, and went afterward to Maracaybo[4] from which place he used to follow the coasting business.

And there chance brought him acquainted with an old man who was born in Dublin, by name McGill; and as he constantly used his best endevours to obtain the Spanish language he could speak it a little fluent. Now this Old fellow told him he could recommend him to a match of good advantage to him if he could fancy the person, and that he was sure he would succeed as he knew full well, having heard her express as much one day when he was sounding that day with Pantoja's trumpet, he said. "I suppose you mean Maria Bela, the Mulatto girl." "Yes," he said, and that she was possessed of four or five slaves, a good house, and money also.

Upon this he determined to follow the old mans advice and soon after Married her. That he lived well with her for about 5 years untill he became daily plagued by one of the Padre's on the score of religion.

2. Leogane is a small harbor in Haiti, not far from Port au Prince.
3. Cartagena is on the Caribbean coast of Colombia.
4. Maracaibo is in Venezuela.

This Man left no stone unturned to draw him from his first princi-
pals; but altho he had lead a very abandoned life, as he said, yet he
was proof against all his art. But little did he think what a scene of
trouble was coming on at that time. But on a day as he returned from
his little bark or sloop he had purchased, he found matters to appear
too glaring not to suspect his Ladies honesty; but as he had found
sufficient cause long before to think Father Martin and she were too
great, he took no manner of notice at that time. It was lucky he had
no children then alive. But when a fair opportunity came he gave
her a gentle reprofe, saying he wonder'd how any man in the state
Father Martin was could think of converting him when he so highly
stood in need of Conversion himself; that for his part he thought it a
strang kind of Religion, indeed, which forbade the marriage of Priests,
yet indulged them access to the ladies at all times even when all others
were quite Excluded, under colour that they were father confessors.
But to make short, from that time he never enjoyed one moments comfort, as the unfaithful Hussy had communicated all his sentiments to
the Old Rascall, as he termed him. Martin from that time carried a
higher hand than ever and one day, being in a kind of pet, said: "Sr.
Bell, I am sorry you would never be advised of my kind council. Therfore if any Evil befall you it is of your own seeking. I think you should
have left the Church alone, by all means, after being so well recieved
Among us."

He wanted no stronger hints, he said, knowing that fire and hot
fury was at his heels, and that he must either implore Martin to
cuckold him or undergo Catholick resentment and persecution. From
that time he became miserable, untill he resolved to leave those parts
to wander he knew not whither. But for some time before he put the
scheem in practice he soothed the Scoundrel in the most abject manner, and when he had softened him down a little he determined to
make his flight. But as he could find no fair slatch [?] by Sea he was
forced to take his land tack onboard, leaving the following lines—
that as he found his life lay at Father Martins mercy he had bade them
an Everlasting adieu, being determined to live no longer.

After this he wandered away in the night with but nine pistoles and a few little articles in a small pack at his back, being determined when he should get beyond all knowledge to turn lunatick or Buffoon; and after that sort he had wandered above a thousand miles too and fro. By this method he had evaded all suspicions, passing for an Italian, and gave himself the name of Giovannetti saying he put on the air of a slighted lover ever Singing Love-sonnets or telling merry tales, so that he never wanted relief wherever he came. And thus he rambled for the space of 4 Years untill chance brought him among our Indians where, finding my friend, he determined to pay me a visit and to take up his residence if agreeable.

"Well," said I, "you have padded the hoof to some purpose, and have had a large draught of this intoxicating world."

"Mr. Penrose," said he, "I have sowed my wild oats long since. I have laid all my follies aside, I can assure you."

I then took an opportunity and observed that he must have collected divers Nostrums in his travels, and that Poor Somer stood in great need of his help if he had but any drugs. "As to that part of the speech," said he, "I think him in a deep decline, and before many Weeks he will no longer be our companion in this life." This gave me much pain as he seemed to pronounce his doom, as it were. "But," said he, "I know ye Virtues of several American plants and Roots and will use my best endevors to administer all the comfort I can. But this I know, he will linger away gradually, changing at times so that you may be flattered into a conciet of his recovery. But he will go off at once when you may not expect such a thing."

Mr. Bell soon became a hale Man, but my worthy Shipmate he wasted away daily. Yet he was ever of the opinion he should weather it, saying now and then, "When I can get a little stronger I will do this and that." Nevertheless he every day grew weaker. At last he became a real object of pity, Walking about like a living skeleton. The colour of his skin became of a dark brown; the trowsers would hardly keep on him; his Eyes became so exceeding hollow with a fixed stare; and his lips shrank in such sort that he became a terrible object to behold. When ever he drank we could hear the liquid rattle within him.

His poor Stomach became so depraved that he would long to eate things unfit for the food of Man or Dogs, yet he continually walked about.

At last he left his darling Pipe and grew exceeding fractious, altho he was ever much to the contrary when in health. There was no thing we could procure would please him; but we took this with all generous patience, and what ever he wanted he had, if going miles could procure it for him. At last he took a notion for me to make him some fish broth; this I went heartily about. When I took it in to him he raised up in the bed and fell to feed heartily, saying he liked it much, and finished above a pint of it. He was then on my bed in the cave. I then asked him how he found himself. He made me no reply, but fixing his Eyes against ye other side as tho he saw something, and in an instant threw the Spoon against it with great force and, falling back, gave an odd kind of hollow sound and Expired.

Upon this I turned out of the cave and went to incline my head against the Rocks, as none were by. When I came out they knew not the cause, but Bell coming up as seeing me thus, soon suspected the cause and went in. When he came out he call'd Harry and told him that they might not disturb me. But soon the information circulated and a general din of Lamentation began; and if ever true grief was expressed in its full scope it was then—so I need not be prolix on that head.

My most worthy and truehearted Messmate departed this life on the 21 day of August, anno 1760, having lived with me in perfect brotherly love above 6 years, and was as much my brother in a Sentimental way as tho we had been twin born. Thus did I loose my darling partner and fellow Sharer in all my difficulties and advantages, one who out of a true sense of reciprocal regard had continually made it his study to concur with me in every social interest and recreation. Godart Somer was a Man of true fidelity.

Chance had brought us together in England. Our first meeting was on board of a Ship at the Red House, Deptford, but as we were at that time all strangers to each, little intimacy passed between us; nor do I know that we ever held a conversation above once when on board of that Ship as at that time he spake English but very indifferen. On our Ships dropping down to the Nore He with several more were discharged and put on shore at Gravesend as above our compliment of hands; so that Claus[5] only made a kind of Visionary appearance, as I may say. And altho our junction was at that time but short, yet Providence had ordained it that, let us make whatever traverses we could on the Main, we should meet again at a certain period of time to become the mutual comforters of each other. Shall we say that this is Fate or Chance?

Another thing similar to this has happen'd to me in my time. I once was going out as I thought in a Snow of Bristol call'd the *Swan;* this was in my erly time. Now it happened that as I was walking on the Gibb[6] I went into the Shop of a block maker. Seeing a young fellow there at work, my intent was to ask the favour of him to touch my Penknife on their Loadstone. This he complied with and asked me among other things what Ship I belonged to. I told him ye *Swan* Snow; that I intended to bind my self the next day to the captain as he had no younker at that time. "I fancy you are wrong," said he, "young man." But I insisted to the contrary. He then told me that wrong I must be, for that he had been bound to the same Man that morning, and that he was sure he would not have two apprentices. On this I made enquiry and found the thing So to be. This circumstance made us become a little acquainted, and I took my course another way soon after. Yet not withstanding he had fairly outed me, as I may say, of that Birth, still we were to meet again another day, as thus.

Long after this, when I was Taken in the *Harrington* and carried into ye Havannah, as I came on board of the *Conquestador* to which Ship we were committed as prisoners I Observed a Young Fellow sitting forward on the Windlass in a sickly condition, whose face appear'd familiar to me. And as he was dressed in a blew wollen frock and

5. Evidently a slip of the author's pen unless this might be a nickname for Somer.
6. The dock area near the old "Floating Harbour" of Bristol.

trousers I turned to one of my Shipmates and said, "There sits my old friend Jemmy Fishers—Revenge!"

"Who is it that knows Jemmy Fisher?" said he. This made me stare as I had untill now concluded the person to be a real Spaniard.

"Did not you belong to the *Swan* Snow once, Messmate?" I said.

"Yes," he replied.

"Then I am such a person"—mentioning my name. With that he shook me by the hand, and turning out a round Oath swore he was heartily glad to see me. "Well," said I, "you see I have fetched you up with a wet Sail at last, so that the difference lies only in the departure. But as to the Lattitude, Bearing and Distance it is the same; so that if you can only recollect the last subject we were upon when on Bristol Gibb, we have time enough now to finish that discourse."

This young fellow told me that he had been prisoner at that place above two years, during which time I had rambled too and fro many ways, and after all found myself safe moored alongside him. Such are the great frolicks Miss Fortune is pleased to divert herself with, now and then, with us poor Mortals of the wandering tribe.

I Now looked upon it as going to begin a new course, as the natural drift of Mr. Bells temper I was yet a stranger to. And I had enough on my mind. All the family took on unfeignedly so that, what with their sighings and my Sons innocent remarks on the actions of the Deceased, I for some time went about with a dagger in my heart. Norman and Harry prepared a resting place for my beloved friends remains, and we conveyed it to the Grave where it was laid to rest among those who had preceeded him. After this I returned up to the house, and they all came and seated themselves in very melancholy postures round me.

After some pause I broke silence to Mr. Bell, ran over the many good qualities of my departed friend, and intimated that I then looked up to him as Successor appointed by Providence as he had so very opportunly been directed to my habitation, saying that as one Island had given us both birth, in a manner, I hoped he would never fall from that integrity so long held by a man who was not my countryman, but had learnt by a proper feeling of misfortune to know himself and shew a true Christian benevolence to his fellow under the like circumstance. He then made me this answer, that he should always think it his Duty to concur with all my desires as I had so generously treated him on his first arrival, saying he well knew the stress of a forward fortune and that he should seek all opportunities to render my life easy and agreeable to the utmost of his power.

Godart was a man possessed of a generous Soul, faithfull to his friend so that he gave me the most convincing proof man could. And when his poor Worldly passions were once subdued he became a most valuable and constant creture to me and all with whom we were connected. His Soul was ever on the desire to do good, so that Idleness was a torment to him. His genius was always busy, and many things he made fit for our purposes which are too tedious to mention here, as one circumstance will be sufficient to convince the reader that he never gave up a point when once took in hand. I shall observe Some few months before his death he undertook to make two Chairs for us; and altho many things stood strongly against him, yet he went through with it and compleated the work with only such tools as we had. But how much commendation do I owe to the memory of so valuable and worthy a man! He is no more.

We Passed our leasure hours in reading chiefly for some time, and I found my new Companion a very agreeable and Sensible Man so that I by degrees recovered my spirits. But Eva soon became sullen and Sad, would seperate from us so that I knew not what to think of her. But as my Girl and I were one day alone I asked her what possessed Somers Wife; she refused to be comforted. She then said, "I have picked out the secret from Patty at last. She tells me that if Mr. Bell will not take her for his Wife she is resolved to go back to her own people again, because the Vine of Unity is become broken now, and that we all will soon look on her and her child as a Dead tree with her young branch withering away as of no more use."

"So, So!" said I. "Here is a fresh piece of work cut out for my hands. But how can you or I doe any thing in an affair of such a nature unless

Bell should broach such a thing of himself? And perhaps such a notion has never once entered his brain." But soon after this Bell talked of going out with Harry to catch Guanos, and as I knew that matter would take up some time I told Betty to give Harry his lesson to sound him while they were abroad togather. This was done and when they had fairly laid the plan Harry proposed going off the next day, and went accordingly.

Two or three days after they had been home I asked Betty how the theem took. She informed me that Norman was determined to have no manner of connexion with Eva, having told Harry that he had a sufficient reason against taking a Wife and desired him never to say any more to him on such a subject. "Then it is all an end," said I, "for I am resolved my friend shall use his own discretion. So let me hear no more about it. And if I find her still obdurate she shall return with the next canoas, when they may come, for I am resolved none shall remain here unsatisfied on any account."

Some time after this I found Messmate Bell to become very serious and on my mentioning it to him he told me what he had learnt from Harry, and that he must own it fretted him not a little as perhaps it was a thing I desired, saying he was ready to oblige me in any reasonable thing but he hoped I would not insist on his taking of Somers Widow as a Wife as he had thoroughly experienced enough of Womans infidelity. "Mr. Bell," I replied, "you may rest assured I never promoted a thing of the kind. Yet I know the girl would be fond to have it so, but I leave it wholly to your own self to act as you think propper. She shall return to her kindred by the very first opportunity, so pray make yourself easy on that score."

Now when Eva found the thing was past all hope she continual honed for her departure. My Lady finding her to remain in that obstinate humour began to take up the cudgels and told her one day, when she refused to come to Victuals, that she thought her very greedy indeed and a great fool into the bargain to want a Man without a heart, saying that she thought Jessy had the most right to such a favour, but that she had patience enough to wait untill the Man brought her the basket of love flowers (an Indian custom). This vexed her to a high degree so that she became from that time quite dumb.

I must in this place make one remark least I should forget it. Some time before My friend Somer's death, a few days, several large birds of the Vulture kind came and settled on a large old dead tree in our neighbourhood; and the nigher his end approached the more came thither and there remain'd to the hour of his death. But no sooner was he departed than they all took wing and kept floating in a circular manner untill night, then alighted again. But when the body was buried they all left the place, to a bird.

These Birds are of such a voracious disposition that their sagacity is hardly to be credited. Nothing is more certain than that they smell a body when death has siezed it for miles, and this is to be proved thus. On any such thing happening should the body chance to be then on a plain without a tree nigher than a League or two, yet they never fail to be in at the time altho none are to be seen any where before that period. Now the reason we assigned for their visit was this: my poor friend for some time before his exit became very offensive in his breath so that at times we could not well bear it.

This Bird is in size about the magnitude of a Young Turkey, of a Black colour, and has those odd excrescences round the neck like that fowl. They never kill, but patiently wait untill the animal is dead, and as they know the time to an instant they then drop down from the tree, if any be near, when the master of the ceremony begins first and eats out the Eyes and fundament, then leaves it and the rest fall on. They never quit the place untill the whole be consumed. I have been informed when in Jamaica where there are plenty, that a Law was enacted and a penalty of 5 pounds against the shooting of one these birds as they are found servicable in clearing off all carrion. I once made Harry shoot one of them in order to have a fair examination of it, as he said their stomachs were full of very large worms and found it realy so. But what is surprizing, when I came to lift up the bird to my great wonder it did not weigh much more than a pound, being no more than bones and feathers. Another thing as singular is it has no tongue.

Chapter 23

As I happened to see Eva one day sitting on the Grave of her husband I went to her and found her weeping. "Pray, child," said I, "let me beg the [thee] not to renew my trouble thus."

Upon this she held up her Child and said, "Take it, for I know you intend it."

"What has put this whim in your brain?" said I.

"I know it is white blood," she replied, "and you will not let me have her away with me when I return to my people."

"Who filled your head with this nonsense?" I cried.

"Patty says she knows you will not suffer me to take her away to my country because you loved her father so much."

"Do tell Patty that she is a fool and that I am very angry with her for giving you so much grief. Do you think I am worse than the Wild beast of the woods to go about to rob you of your young one? No, Eva, you shall take your child home with you when your friends come next to visit us. Yet I must needs acknowledge that I should have been pleased for you to have been the Wife of my new friend Bell, but as he says he has had one very wicked Woman already he is resolved never to have another."

Upon this she flew into a rage and began to twist and drag her hair like a distracted creture, saying, "Am I wicked, wicked?" The poor child began to screem and this brought my Wife and Jessy. I told them to settle her rage the best way they could and left them. And this was the greatest fude we ever sustained in all our time, but I experienced one piece of experience by it—this giving me a fair opportunity of learning the natural genius of these people when chagrined, and I found they can be as implacable in their rancour as steadfast in friendship. Such tempers as those should be used with delicacy. A While after, they brought her up to the house somwhat composed, When Mr. Bell began to cheer her the best he could, telling her he did not reject her person for that he liked her very well; but as he had been very unfortunate with his other Wife he chose to remain Single, and that she could easily obtain another Man among her own people when she returned.

Things remain'd thus for some time untill the arrival of 4 Indians who had been out on a journey and paid us a visit on their return. These were Vattequeba, Gattaloon, and Wocozomany with a youth call'd Outaharry, his son. The two last had never been at our place before. We recieved them in a friendly sort, and the next day I put Betty and Harry on broaching the affair concerning Eva. After a time I found them to grow very serious but some time after, Harry came to me and said Gattaloon wanted to make a speech to me. "Tell him I am ready," said I.

Upon this he advanced up to me as in an hostile manner and throwing out his right arm with one leg advanced, he began to deliver his discourse or rather Oration. This took up a long time, and his behaviour the while was quite in the Heroic strain. Every now and then he would appeal to his comrades, who all answered in one short word as one voice. I then desired Harry to give me the substance of his speech the best way could, and this he did, (Viz):

"You far water stranger, Your Skin is whiter than ours, White like the Moon shining in the night. Can you expect our actions to be whiter than your own? What is the things I know, I hear, and see? Has not the wind of voices gone through the trees and by the side of the shore That my Brothers and Sisters have given their Flesh and their Blood for a mixture with yours? Shew me more friendship than this and we then shall own it is whiter than ours. Now we hear the voice in the wind saying 'Oh, the blackness is coming of the Bird which devours the dead.' Must we not all go to sleep? Are you not picking off the flesh from the bones? Our Sister here must return without a covering of love because her love is gone to sleep. Could she keep him awake any longer? Or tell us, did she put him to sleep? You will say, 'No no!' Awaken his Spirit again, as it is in your power, that she may find joy and laughing hours, Least the Winds carry the sound of Black sorrow among our People and they should forget the way to this place."

This was a thundering broadside, and I then thought should once my friendly connexion with those people be broken then farewell to all future comfort. The whole time Harry was giving us the interpretation My friend Bell stood with his arms folded and his face to the ground; and when it was finished he turned round on his heel and marched too and fro. But on his observing the great trouble in my countenance He came up to me and said, "Let me not be the cause of my friends disquiet, no, not for a moment of time." Then going to Eva he took her by the hand, and leading her up to Gattaloon took him hold with the other and thus advanced up to me, when he began thus: "Observe me well. I here declare before you all present That to wipe away all animosities, oblige my Worthy friend Mr. Penrose and all those with whome he holds friendship, I do now take Eva as my Wife," and then kissing her said, "Tell these good friends, Harry, that I will use my best endevours to blow away all the Blackness they expected, by rousing the Spirit of our departed friend for the comfort of their Sister in my own Person."

Directly I bade Harry run over what Mr. Bell had declared, when joy illuminated every countenance and I took my Messmate by the hand, saying I was much indebted to him as he could never shew me a higher token of his veneration than in this generous act. "And now in order to disperse all those black clouds of impending troubles let us shew our selves as merry on the occasions as we well can before these our friends." Then Harry flew away for his broom and we made them perform the old ceremony to the great mirth and satisfaction of the Indians. And thus was ended an affair which I greatly dreaded would terminate in trouble and vexation enough to me.

The next day the Indians took leave of us and went away in good spirits. It was now become the middle of December and Bell proposed that it would be much better to make a new crawl for our Turtle within the mouth of our home Lagoon before the next season came on. This I approved of much, and he and Harry went to work about it. This piece of business took up a fortnight of their time.

One day while my two Messmates were down at the new Crawl I took a notion for a peep into Mr. Bells little Budget or Kitt, and ye contents were a Clasp Knife, a Razor and Hone, a Lancet and some other trifles. But there was a small Rag made up very curiously but I did not chuse to cast it loose least it might give him offence, so left it as I found it. When he came home I asked him What he had so curiously bound up in the bit of linen among his gallitraps. "Did you not see it?" said he.

"Not I."

"Then I know no reason why you may not,"—and went for it and after he had took much pains to undoe it shewed me a Stone about the Size of a common Sleeve button and said, "This is a very valuable Diamond," and that he had purchased it of an Indian from the River of Plate for 15 pieces of 8. There were in the rag 4 more not one quarter the size. Now as I had not seen any thing of the kind in its natural state I should have put but small value on it, but he told me they were worth above 1,000 pounds sterling.

"Well, then," said I, "you are nominally a Rich Man, not worth one single farthing." On this he gave a Spanish shrug with his shoulder and made use of a common phraze among those people, (Viz), "totus une, tambien" or like to like.[1] And I must remark that I should never have suspected him to be any other than a real Spaniard as he had been so long among them he had contracted all their gestures and manner of speech. Add to this his hair being long and black, it gave him the very look.

One day as we were sitting all at victuals and being in a good mood I said, "Well, Messmate Norman, I hope you like your new Wife, as I find she seems pleased again."

"Ask her that question," said he, which I did.

She smiled and said, "How much did you like Luta?"

"A great deal," I told her.

1. Perhaps, "*Todo uno, también.*"

"But she is gone to sleep now," said She; "and how do you like Ocuma Betty? Here she sits with her Eyes open, then."

"Oh, you all can see how much I like her every day."

On this she burst out into a Laughter and ecchoed me: "Oh, you can see how much I like my New Flesh Also, if you have a mind to peep!" This made us all very merry and I observed that nothing could make me happier than to find our family restored once again to its old state of love and tranquility, saying we should have found affairs in a poor condition had we incurred the ill blood of our neighbours.

About this time I had a mind to learn whether Somer or Harry had ever communicated the secret of our treasure to Mr. Bell or not. For this purpose I began about the bush, as is said, concerning Piracy and of their hiding money, &cc. He said he had learnt enough about them from the Spaniards, but I found he was quite ignorant as to my drift. So one morning as he was busy with his Razor and Hone, for he shaved himself, I asked him what he would take for his Diamonds in ready Cash. On this he gave me an odd smile, saying "Do you know any jeweller in this City who chuses to purchase?"

"Yes," said I, "I do. Suppose I am the Jeweller, what would you value them at?"

"Ay, ay, that will do well enough," he replied.

"Will you let me have them on paying down 500 dollars?" I said.

"I should be glad we were safe in England with as good a sum each," he replied.

"No trifling, are they mine or not?"

"Yes, yes," he cried, and put them into my hand saying, "Down with your dust."

"Come away with me to my counting house"—and took him by the hand.

"What game comes next?" said he. "You are in a flow of Spirits I think today." But to make short I disclosed all my treasure to him, but when he cast his Eyes on it he became fixed as a Mast.

"The Diamonds are Mine, Messmate," said I. "There is cash sufficient to discharge the contract."

"Troth, man, I believe it is true; but if it is, pray how came ye by it?" I then gave him the whole story at large. "Weel, by the Cross of St. Andrew it Winnelskews me, and I can hardly believe my own sight."

"Friend Norman," said I, "call for your Cash as soon as you please."

"Troth, man, it is as safe in yere Bank there as in onny other part I can remove it to, so let it remain."

"Well, now, I think I have fairly laid my Anchor to the Windward of you," sd. I.

"Not in the least," he said. "Go take your Jewels to market and make the most of them!"

"Come, come, take and put them up in your Pack again," I said. "What is mine is yours."

And then squeezing my hand he said, "And mine yours, reciprocally, with all my Soul."—And thus Ended this piece of drollery for that time.

On the 9th day as I think of February Betty my wife brought me a couple of fine Children at one birth. The Girls were all three so highly pleased with the novelty that they got round me, hugged and clung about my shoulders in such a manner that I thought they would have gone wild for joy. A day or two after, a Small altercation came on among them what names they should have, the one being a Boy and the other a Girl. Upon this I said I would do my wife the honor to call the Girl after her country, (Viz) America. When she found this she seem'd much pleased, and said if I was willing she would give the Boy a name she knew surely would please me. On my asking what that might be, "Somer," she replied.

"Thou art a good creture," said I. "Nothing could ever be more adapted to my liking for certain. Oh," said I, "let his good name remain among us to the end of our generations, henceforth."

Now I had taken it into my head to contrive a kind of addition before our enterance, and for this purpose Messmate Norman happening to be out in the Wood cutting a few poles, a large Tiger seemed to be after him. He came flying down the hill in a great fright, crying and bawling out, "Harry, Harry! Messmate!"

Out I ran and said, "What is coming on now?"

"Oh!" said he, "here's the Deel coming down the Brae as fast as the wind."

I ran and snatched up my gun and said, "Where is it?" By this time Harry was running with his Mascheet, the Women scrambling away the Children. "Come, come," said I to him, "take up that little hatchet and follow us." So away we went up the hill but could discover nothing. "Where is your Deel, Norman?" said I.

"I am sure I saw a terrible Leopard or a Tiger."

"How do you know what it was?" I answered. "Where did you ever see any of those cretures that you know them so well?" He had seen them in Shews of Wild Beast, he said. I asked his pardon. "But this proves a Vision, I think." But all at once Harry cried, "Yonder he is, over the Clift behind the grove!" I ran and fired at him, but to little purpose. I then ran down and got up a Shell; they did the like, and he soon quitted the field as we began sounding; and we saw no more of him nor had we seen one for a long time before.

Now as this flurry was in going on Harry said he was sure he heard the sound of a Shell at a distance. This I thought to proceed from the great hurry he had been in, but he was positive, as he said. "Then go and take a look," said I.

He soon began to cry out: "Boats! Canoas!" We then went up and plainly saw three Canoas.

"This is a visit from Owagamy as sure as we are living, on the old affair," cried I. "So now you must all put on every art to treat them with the greatest civility. And you, Norman, pray lecture your lady the best you can." I then ordered the Yawl to be got ready and hoisted our colours, then leaving the women, down we went to meet them and in the first place gave them three Cheers, in the next place we began our old Song. They answered, but not so heartily as in times past. However, we preceeded them up the Lagoon, and there landing I recieved my old friend Owagamy in the most friendly way I possibly could. Messmate Bell and Harry did the like and did the same with them all round.

They were nine in number and all armed which was not their general custom. After we had given them some drink out of what little remain'd in store, I called for our pipes, but they declined the offer. I now began to tremble as thinking on future consiquences. After some short time Owagamy, begining to survey the place round over each shoulder, asked some questions of Harry. I now got a little warmed and boldly bade Harry to let me know what was the thing Owagamy enquired after. He said it was whether we all lived in love and peace togather; and that he had informed him never more so, and that he replied that was well. "Tell Eva to stand forth," said I, "and if she has any sort of grievance on her mind let her declare it before them all."

Now I had never seen an Indian then present, who was her Brother, before; nor did she take the least notice of him all the time. Owagamy then questioned her a few words, when I observed him to cast his Eyes on Norman and smile. "Now, Now, merry well," said Harry.

"How so?" said I.

"Because she says she knows Mr. Norman loves her."

"Well, come," said I, "Betty, give your friends the whole account of the affair from first to last, and also my friend's objections at the first, and I suppose they will then be all reconciled if they have any reason left within them."

She then began and I could see much confusion in Eva. When Betty had ended her narration Owagamy burst out into a fit of laughter; all the Indians did the like. Upon my enquiry into the cause Owagamy lead up Eva's Brother to me and my friend Bell and made us joyn hands in good fellowship. I then asked Harry what caused that Horse laugh. He then replied: "Owagamy says Eva made all the cold blood herself; that she should have let Mr. Norman alone to chuse the Plantain himself and not have began so soon after her husband was dead; but that he judged she liked White flesh so much that she grew mad, fearing young Jessy should snatch it from her, and therfore she took care to bespeak him as soon as possible; and that she should think herself much obliged to him if he gave her two Children every year so that her family might never be without the breed; and that he would take good care to fasten her well by him by having them remarried in their presence, if I pleased."

Up I jumped and cried, "Harry, go fetch the Broom." I then turn'd to Norman and said, "Now, Bell, if ever you were a Merry Andrew in your life I pray turn out and shew us something or other by way of diverting away this dull gloom which has hung over our heads so long."

With that He ran and took his Wife by the hand and in an instant had her on his shoulder, when he fell to capering and sung the following lines from and old Scots Ballad:

"Fye, let us a' to the Bridal
For there will be lilting there,
For Bell's to be wedded to Eva,
The Lass with the Coal Black hair."

After this he cut such odd freaks over the Broom that it amazed me, much more the Indians; as he was a Man full Six foot and she but light in person he made no more of her than a feather. Now all faces wore new aspects, and my friend Owagamy was the first to call for pipes and we all sat dow to Smoking togather. Then Bell arose and desired a ring should be made, when he began his pranks again and of all the Mimmicks I ever beheld I never saw his fellow. He then said he would shew them a specimen of his slight of hand with a small stone. For this purpose he stript himself to his buff, then put the stone into his mouth, in a short time produced it from under his armpit, and thus he conveyed it from one part of his body to another to the great amazement of the Indians. He then Tumbled, walked on his hands, and the like. Now as he was doing this Eva ran and caught fast hold on him as dreading he should fall. This made Owagamy laugh and say that she was in terror least he should break in two pieces, he supposed, as she knew if he were once spoiled there was neer another White man more could fall to her share.

I thought the Indians would have eaten him up alive. They then said they supposed I could do the like if I was pleased, but I bid Harry inform them to the contrary. They kept it up the whole day, and thus ended the wedding to my great comfort. The next morning I thank'd Mr. Bell for carrying the thing off so well, but as he had been for many years out of practice he was so stiff in his joynts he could scarce walk.

Now the Indians first gave us to understand that one of their men in company called Loosoyamy was brother to Eva. I asked why they had conceal'd that matter when they first came. Harry said it was because they thought we were turning black. I bid him inform them that they never should find any blackness to proceed from our side; that the whole mistake had proceeded from Eva's imagination; that I intended to send her away from among us. Owagamy then told Harry that they could stay no longer for that time, as they had other affairs to transact when they returned, and took farewell the next morning accordingly.

The Day after, Owen brought me a Skin of a Snake almost intire as a curiosity. This put Harry on giving us to know that at the time those reptiles want to discharge themselves of their old coats they go on the hunt untill they can find out any old knot of a tree or some such apperture. Through these holes they pass and by that means leave the old coat behind them, after which they are obliged to keep retired for some time as theyr new skin is yet too tender for traveling. At one season of the year in their breeding time I have seen multitudes of snakes gathered nigh some Run of Water or other in bunches or masses, and twisted in such strange combinations that it is wonderfull to see. And thus they tumble and roll about, at which times you may approach as nigh them as you please without dread of harm, they being in no wise capable of seperating. I have seen perhaps a dozen in one bunch thus, and of different kinds.

Chapter 24: Fifteenth Year

My new friend had resided now about a year with me and we were become very happy togather. And it fell out soon after that we both took a ramble with our guns in the Woods. Now as we were going he took a plant, and shewing it to me observed that it was a fine Narcotick, as he termed it; and he after this shewed me others saying, "This is a very fine Stiptick, that a Diuretick."

"You deal much in Ticks, Messmate," sd. I. "But if you had once about a dozen such thumpers as I have seen our Harry pull off our Dogs at times, well fixed under each of your arms, you could not make so ready a conveyance of them as you can with a small stone with all your slight of hand.—You have a great knack at your Scots Songs," said I.

"Did you not observe a book of them among my things?"

"Oh, you have a fund of humour then, I can assure you."

"If you have such a thing," said he, "it is a good cordial for low Spirits."

"If I could read them—" I answered.

"I can do that for you," he said.

"Well, pray then, let us have it now and then," I answered.

He then said that as Harry and he were one day out at Towers Field he saw plenty of large Reeds growing, and that with a little patience and contrivance he imagined he could form some sort of a German Flute with them. "Pray take good heed your Music dont bring you to mourning," said I, "for that place is full of Aligators, my friend."

"Never fear," he replied, "we will find out some way or other to get some of them. Tis but to make up a good fire and they will all retire."

"Ay, ay," said I, "and that work may bring on such another Bonfire as I made soon after my landing here, which I verily thought would never be extinguished again."

"Well, leave all that to Harry and me," he replied.

Soon after, they went to fetch home Salt and while they were away got some of those canes which they brought home. After this nothing but making flutes went forward, and he got me to make an Iron round in order to burn the holes. This I contrived out of a Spike nail. After many unsuccessful trials he produced a sort of German flute, but for want of knowing how to adapt the holes according to the bore they would prove fals in tone. But error learnt him experience, and he at last made one tollerable good and true. The next thing was a book to put down notes in, as he said. "And pray where are the Tunes to come from?" replied I.

"Let me alone for that," said he. "I have a method of my own, and that you will see."

The Book was made and every now and then he would be at it, pricking as he termed it. Now as I understood Music as much as a Goose does conjuration, It appeared all misterious to me. Nevertheless by his strong application Our Wild forest became acquainted and learnt to Eccho the charming melody of "Tweed Side," "Etrick Banks," "Invermay," and many other such tunes; and many an hour has his pleasant pipe charmed away for me in this forlorn place.

Harry became so enamour'd with Music that he was ever tooting. This made Messmate Norman instruct him and he soon came on to a great degree. Our Girls caught the Sounds and learnt all the Tunes they plaid. The Indian Women have a charming natural sweetness of Voice and often joyned in accord with them. Ye children took it from them, so that it was common to hear Owen, Hannah and Job chanting it every day. And now may I say of a truth, we lived in perfect harmony togather; So that the Lord was graciously pleased to raise me up a new consolation when so nigh being severed from my worthy Somer, for whom I had so great a veneration.

Thus time went on untill the middle of August, and as we were one day out after the Tortoises I Espied a Vessel in the Offing standing away to the Northeast. Now Messmate Bell observed to me, what was there to hinder that we could not leave our place. "As how, pray?" I said.

"Why could we not go off in that Long Boat?"

"And provided we could, where would you propose to go too? Surely you cannot think of keeping the Seas long in an open long boat."

"Could we not keep the shore aboard always?" said he.

"But where bound?" I cried.

"Why, I think we might get to the Coast of Carolina well enough in her."

"What, to round all the Bays, points and Reefs, my friend? Only consider the vast Bays of Mexico and many others, and all the unthought of difficulties beside."

"Well," said he, "but you must consider if we but once surmounted what you object against, we then should horse through the Gulf of Florida in a short time."

"Dont reckon without your Host," I replied. "Let me hear in the first place how you would lay your plan in order to such a grand undertaking, and then if feasible, well and good, friend."

And thus he began: "I would raise her a streake[1] higher, make us a sung Cuddy[2] forward, with lockers abaft."

"And this would take time," I told him.

"Hoot, hoot, what then?"—if he did not begrudge the labour.

"Well, admit matters were come thus far," said I, "then comes her suit of Sails next."

"We have canvas enough for that," said he.

"That is all settled," I cried. "But there is the grant But yet to come, Shipmate—Provisions, my friend."

"Oh, as to that matter, have we not enough of several kinds and water plenty?"

I then became more Serious and said, "How long can you think such vigitables and things we daily use would last? And where is the room to stow so much of our Water necessary for the Voyage, as there must be room for our family, certainly?" As to that he said there would be no need to carry "more than Your Wife and children" with his own Girl. "So, said I, "and how would you dispose of all the rest?"

"Let them return to their own people again," said he, "as I suppose they would prefer that to going along with us."

"Do you not know that I look upon Harry as a part of my self?" I replied. "Have I not had his Sister to Wife by whom I had two Children? How then in conscience, think you, can I be guilty of yt [that] extravagant piece of cruel infidility to such an honest and faithful poor creture who would at a word of mine brave the Whole

1. Strake: a longitudinal board or plank.
2. A small cabin, sometimes a cook-room.

Ocean to bare me company throughout ye Universe? Pray, have you so soon forgot that fine lecture the Indian gave us some time ago? Let us beware that we become not Black as he figured it to us in the character of the Vulture. Let us not forget that we have been once baptized and, as he observed, Nature had made us whiter than his race and, as he observed, the more we should shew our selves White in all our actions and deeds. But laying all this aside, I know that such a scheem would prove abortive."

"But self preservation, Messmate," said he.

"Are you not preserved already?" I replied. "But it is evident to me that the method you propose must inevitably bring on our utter distruction unless some miraculous act of Providence should bring us to a safe deliverance. And after all, perhaps, we should not find our account by the exchange of conditions. You think this, that as we abound in worldly trash that would give us the command every where. But pray consider, my good friend, how many temptations we should become liable too amidst Strangers. Let me beg you will give your self five minutes time to reflect on such an Important a matter, and then let us have a fresh conferrance on the subject.

"I daresay it has originated from the anxious desire you have once more to revisit your native Soil. This is a natural and worthy thing in all degrees of Men; but if we cannot do so in a commendable and easy way then let us een abide where we are, a Gods holy name. Know you not that those homelings in our Country who have never experienced the Cold, heat, and unheard of hazzards of such as Travel oft times in penury and want and frequently naked also—I say they, having never been far from the smoke of their own chimneys, Expect all travellers to return home Rich. The reason of which is this—they seldom hear of any other than the Rich bruited abroad on their return to their respective homes. For those who have been prudent and unfortunate have rather chosen to remain and end their days where they were, than to return in Poverty among their old friends and relations, whose kindness can never be long trusted to, least you should become burthensom. And certainly should that be any poor fellows case, Reproach ensues. They will then querie, 'How did you spend your time for such a length of years? And what is next to be expected? You have been either a Drinker, Gambler, or a very Idle and inconsiderate Man at any rate.' And least your Cup of mortification should not fill to the brim they will in that case gall your Spirits with recounting that such and such an One left Home later than you and was returned with a large fortune, and during his abscence was continually supplying his poor relations. But you may every now and then hear by the slant that you never was of any worth, Egg or Bird.

"But, alas! Let us see how many of these Rich, Honest and Brave fellows return to spend the remainder of their days in Ease and plenty. Oh, how few are they when compared to the vast multitude of those poor unfortunate objects who have perished abroad throughout the Globe by one kind of Death or other, and quite Unregarded as unworthy remembrance."

"Havast, take a turn there, and Belay that, Messmate, if you please," said Bell. "I must confess nothing but the natural and longing desire a Man has to see his country before he dies prompted me to what I have advanced. I now can see farther than before, for I dont think you can be averse to seeing your country again more than my self, were all things agreeable to that end."

"You have said nothing but what is absolutly true," I replied; and thus we finished or belay'd our argument for that time.

It was now about the middle of October, and at about 10 in the Evening there came on such a terrible Gale of Wind that before two hours it blew a Hurricane shifting all round the Compass. Every small article was blown down; and had we not been sheltered by a large Grove of Trees in front, with a Wall as it were, and a strong shelter two thirds round us behind, I know not how we should have fared. Yet the Wind would come with such an Eddy and whirl round our place that I ordered all our fire to be extinguished, fearing it might be blown among the thatch and so fire our kitchen again. But about three in the morning the Wind fell, and Eva called me out of ye Cave to come and see. "See what?" said I.

"The great blaze in ye Clouds," she said.

When I got out Bell called to me and asked what I thought of it "I cant imagine," I replied.

"Let us endevour to mount the Hill," he said. We were forced to baull as loud as we could for the Wind was yet so high that we could hardly keep on our legs. But when we got up We could plainly see a most dreadful fire at Sea distant about three leagues as we judged. On this we knew it must be some poor unfortunate Vessel all on a blaze, knowing the fire could proceed from no other cause. And thus She burnt for two hours longer, and how long before we knew of it we could not know. And as the day came on we saw no more of her. About noon it fell quite calm, and left our Apurtenances all scatered at a strange rate.

"Well," said I to my friend Bell, "were we not provided for this last dreadfull night, think you? And what would those poor Souls who belonged to that Vessel have given to have been then among us?"

"Alas," he replied, "either fire or water has been their destruction before this hour."

"You may be pretty well assured of that," said I, "for sure I am no Boat could live. And is it not a standing warning to us, Messmate, to be content with our lot as thus instanced? Suppose now the case had stood that you should have proposed the affair of our leaving this place about a month or three Weeks ago, and I had came warmly into that risk.—You nor I could have never be supposed to know of this Hurricane at that time hidden in the hollow of the Almighty hand. And should we have been at that time on the Ocean in a poor open long boat full of one incumberance or other, what would then have been our dreadful condition, think you? Ask your own concience and say you have no need now for the space of five minutes reflection to make me an answer on that head. You will naturally reply, 'To have been back at our old mansion again,' without all dispute."

"Messmate," said he, "one ounce of due consideration is more in value than fifty weight of folly."

"Let this dreadful example then remain imprinted in full and evident Characters on our souls," said I, "my fellow Pilgrim. And henceforth let us never repine at what we call Fortune; for we know not, poor short Eyed cretures, but it may be Fate. Let lerned Casuists compose volumes to support argument pro and con if they please; it is no study of ours. I am determined to remain stead fast and resigned to the Divine Will, and I judge by the feelings of my own heart that is the only thing can bring me off in my last hour.

"What does not Man undertake or undergo to obtain a portion of the very Articles with which you and I abound copiously? Does not this shew the man of true content what a small portion would Suffice to make him happy? Witness your Diamonds and my Dross which lies yonder in an useless heap, and why, truly, we do not want it."—

Mr. Bell is in no measure chagrined at my writing thus, knowing that I mean no other than a generous advice in regard to our common good and interest of the family. And here I observe, as he stands by me and may have hourly access to my Journal, any thing that I write or note down if disagreeable to him He has my free consent to erase the same, if he may imagine it any way prejudicial to his credit should our book ever fall into the publicks hands.

The next day we proposed to take a run out and examine the Shores, thinking that by some favour of fortune a remnant might be found and saved. So we got the Yawl and went away to that end but we were forced to return without the least discovery, finding nothing. And who they had been or whence from we never could learn. Not a Stick of her ever came on shore sufficient to indicate any thing to that purpose. Staves we found at times half burnt; these we took undoubtedly had belonged to her.

About two days after this melancholy affair as our Harry was away to the old plantation in the Canoa a poor Dog came creeping to him almost starved to death. He brought him home with him, having lifted him into the Canoa as the poor thing was not able to do the like for want of strength. I ordered that all possible care should be taken of him, giving him but little at a time. This Dog is a black and white Spaniel of the largest breed and perhaps much valued by his owner as he seem, altho in so low a condition, to have been very handsom. This poor beast had certainly belonged to that unfortunate Ship; but in what manner he came to land we could not think, as the Sea ran so exceeding high, unless the Crew had happily made their escape and had Either left the dog behind them or he had been lost before their departure. But if that were really the case they must have landed away round about the Whale Point as we could have no sight of them.

"Who knows," said Mr. Bell, "but they may yet be there?"

"God only, and them selves," I replied, "but if so they stand highly in need of relief as I know by my own experience." He then declared it was his desire to go and satisfy himself as to certain whether or not. "Go, then, by all means, my friend," I cried. "Let us save life if possible." I then told him Harry must stand Pilot as my friend had never been that way before. And I proposed that they should take the Spaniel along with them, thinking that if perchance any folks were there the Dog would soon find them out. And away they went Erly the next day, and did not return untill the next in the Evening late. The first thing I saw was the spaniel who came in to me with great Joy. On this I ran away down to the landing and called out, "Yo ho, there!" When they answered, "What news?" said I.

"None at all of any Service," said Bell. They then came up with me and reported they had examined the whole coast even into Boom Bay as I call'd it, and as they were on the beach the Dog put off and ran away ahead to a thing they saw at a good distance; that they followed him, and when they came up found the Corps of a Young Fellow; and that he at first intended to bring it home in the boats bottom but that the smell forbid it. And as he fount it so, he and Harry had stripped the body and buried it in the Sand, bringing the cloaths with them, Saying they were certain the Dog had a knowledg of the deceased as when they were digging the grave the creture sat looking on the whole time. But when they came to strip the body and remove it to the place of its Interment the poor animal began to howl and whine sadly. When they had covered it up he went and laid down on the Spot and stay'd there, looking after them untill they had walked away about 50 yards; That they then called him and the poor Toad then got up and followed them freely to the boat.

Mr. Bell describes the Corps thus: that he took him to have been a young Man aged about 20 or upwards, middle sized with sandy hair, his dress a striped fine shirt, Petticoat trowsers of a good white linen, with a Jacket of the same kind to which his Hat was fastened by a Lanniard. He had a pair of white fustian Breeches on under his trowsers; and in the left pocket he found a Clasp knife and a small bunch of twine, in the other a note from which we learnt his name to have been Richard Green. And in one of his trowser pockets was the following Song in manuscript, "Early one Morn a Jolly brisk tar, &cc" by which we judged they were English, or at least we were certain that the Youth had been a Subject of Great Britain. No more could we learn of the matter.

We took pains to find out this Dogs name and by calling over numbers discovered it to be Rover. And in about a months time he was so well recovered as though he had never been reduced to the degree we found him in. And I believe nothing but distress of hunger brought him so soon to relish Fish.

About a month after this My Son Owen shott a Snake of the Barbers pole sort and came in a great hurry to inform me that he had shott a Snake with Two Heads. I laughed at him and said, "That can never be, child."

"Hoot, Hoot," said Bell, who was then standing by, "the Boy is Winnelskewed, as I thought myself when ye shewed me a' that geer yonder in the Neuck [nook]."

"Pray, Bell," said I, "explain me that word if you please."

"Why, it is a saying among our people in Scotland when ever they mistake one object for two that the Moon is in the Hallier[3] or clouded, and at such times they are Winnelskewed or their Eyes decieve them."

Upon this Harry went with Owen and they brought it up to us on a stick, when to our great amazement the thing became verified. This Snake was not above two inches round and in length about 4 feet. About 5 inches from the natural extremity of a Single head began two necks to branch out, terminating with two fair and perfect Heads compleat, both capable of performing all their necessary functions. And

---

3. Halliard or halyard, from ME *halier*, that which hales or hauls; here in the sense of partially hoisted.

this we were all witnesses of as the creture was not yet dead, but opened each mouth and plaid with both tongues alike. This wonderful phenominon I made Harry skin with the strictest care, and we have it by us as a proof of what I advance should any Traveller by chance pay us a visit. I asked Harry if he had ever seen or been informed of the like before, but they all agreed they were ignorant and that they had never seen the like before in their lives.

Nothing came on from that time untill it was become December 23d by our account. And I took notice to Mr. Bell that I well remembered my Mother always took care to have a Goose at Christmas, and that we would have somthing like it if possible on that day. "Where will you buy it?" said he.

"We must try for a Substitute," said I. "You and Harry may go away to the Bird Key with your guns and there you may find game of some kind or other." So away they went ye next day and brought home three Boobies and 5 Redshanks. "Now," said I, "Bell, if we can catch a couple of fine Red Snappers I think we shall be well provided for a good Christmas dinner."

"Come on, then," said he. We then got our lines and away we went down the Lagoon but had not the success I hoped for, when as we returned my Harry caught a large Barrowcooter. Now I observed to my Messmate that those kind of fish are apt to be poisonous, and asked him if he knew how to prove them. "Well, then," said I, "when they go to cook it, boil it alone With a clean piece of Silver, and then we shall be sure." This was done the next day and the fish proved to be good. Otherwise it would have turned the Silver quite black by their feeding on mineral bank, as is imagined. And that day we all dined together which was not our daily custom, as Mr. Bell and Wife dined chiefly with my Wife and me.

The next thing which happened was the loss of my friend Godarts orphan Daughter Hannah of a fever. My Messmate used all his Skill in his way but to no purpose, and we laid her alongside those who had left our little society before.

About a month after Christmas Messmate Norman became lame in one of his hands. He had been out to fish alone in the Indian canoa, and among other fish he had caught was one wch. is call'd a Doctor fish from a sharp bone it has on each side of ye tail. This bone is not perceptible to a man unacquainted with that fish, as it has the power to lay it close to its side or erect it at pleasure; but this bone is so keen that no Lancet can be more so, and much resembles it in form. The whole fish is of a purple brown and about the size of a midling Haddock.

He brought home at the same time two others of a peculiar kind and construction. The first is called by our Seamen a Parrot Fish and with great propriety I think, as the whole fish is green excep the fins which are red. It has very large scales, but its bill or mouth is not formed like to fish in common, having a pair of bones as resembling the beak of a parrot with which it mashes or cracks small Shell fish. The whole ruff [roof] of its mout is also one hard bone.

The other or Second kind is almost a coppy of the above mentioned Except that instead of its being Green, on the contrary it is perfect blue and is called in Providence the Gillambour. Whence they derive the name I know not unless from the Spanish.

Mr. Bell's hand remain'd bad for above a fortnight and at times gave him great pain. At last my Dame took it in hand and proved the more successful Doctor of the two. She cured it in about 5 days by applying the juice of herbs to it. When it was well I joaked him about ye Doctor fish, saying that two of a trade seldom agreed. "I shall take care for ye future," said he, "when one of them happens to pop his nose into my Shop to let me know that I will be Master."

On a day soon after Harry brought in from his traps a very curious little Animal the like of which I had never seen, but my Messmate knew it at once and called it an Armadillo, saying there were numbers of them away to the Southward. This animal was of a light ash colour of the size of a young sucking pig, and resembled that creture only much slimmer made and the tail much longer. But what makes it the most remarkable is they seem to be absolutly in an armour of shells. I asked Harry if they eat them. "Yes," he said.

"Cook it then," I said, "and let us taste it." Bell said no Chicken could be finer, and I found it so in reallity.

Now I proposed to Norman that we should turn up our Yawl and large Canoa in order to examine them thoroughly and repair them after the best way we could. This we went about, and I found my poor old Canoa like a Honeycomb. Upon this I set Owen to peg making and with those we pegged her all over the bottom. But she was now become old and worn much for the waves by the length of time I had her in my possession. As for the Yawl she was full of the worm also, but yet in a much stronger state than my poor old Ark of preservation. But I found by mixing a plenty of Sand with our pitch and tar was of service, and we did all in our power toward their preservation.

After we had compleatly fitted up our two boats and mended their Sails, made a pair of new oars and some Thouls,[4] I proposed that we would make a Day of recreation for the whole family; and accordingly when the day came we all mustered with what was necessary and put away down the Lagoon, My Self, Wife and three children with Harry in the Yawl; Mr. Bell, his Wife, Patty and Jessy in the great Canoa; Owen, Job and Luta in the Indian cano. Owen was boatman and could paddle very well as he was now between 9 and 10 years of age, but when a little wind sprang up I took them in tow and thus we arrived at the Old Plantation safe, where we all landed and left the Ladies with their children and Harry to guard and attend them. After this my Messmate and I and little Owen went out into deep water in order to catch a few Grouper and the like in our Yawl. We laid her too in about 12 fathom Water and let her drive over the patches of the Rocks, as you can see the bottom distinctly at that depth in these parts of the world. We had not been long on the ground before fine Sport came on. We haled in and baited as fast as we could; but it happened that while I was bound with a large Groupar a Shark came up in full chase after it. I pulled as eagerly as possible, yet he caught it hold before it came nigh the waters Edge and left me no more than its head to the hook.

Now as we were thus at contending which should have the fish,

4. Tholes: wooden pegs inserted in a boat's gunwale to hold the oars in position.

another Shark being in chase of it at the same time by mistak in the
great scuffle bit his antagonist. In a few minutes after this as we were
both very merry on the circumstance, as he put the laugh on me for
catching no more than the head of a fish, he became at once bound
with a witness; and being not so much used to the sport as Harry and I
were I cried, "Hold on, Messmate, and play him well."

But he through Eagerness fell down backward in the boat, crying,
"Hoot, Hoot, Mon! What for sort of Muckle horned Deel is dealing
with us now thats just luging us aboot?" For by this time I had got
hold with him. Owen laughed to that degree that he lay down and
kicked with his heels. But soon after, we tired the fish and he sheer'd
alongside. I then up with an ax and soon gave him his quietus, and it
proved to be the very Shark which had snapped away my fish from
the hook. The other had bit him into the Bone through a part full 7
inches thick.

After we had caught as much as we wanted, which we did in less
than an hour, as we had been desirous we might have filled the boat,
I then gave the line into Owens hand, he being like all children full
of novelty and ambitious to do great things. But he soon began to
hollow out, "Oh, Daddy, Daddy!" I then took him round the waist and
bid him pull with all his might, but he soon began to cry lustily and
quietly resigned the line to me—otherwise he would have been overboard inevetably. I haled the fish in for him, and then we stood in for
the old place where we had left our ladies, and there found a rowzing
fire burning, my Wife saying she had Got it ready agains we came
as she could see plainly with the glass that we had good luck.

We had not long landed before we heard Jessy cry out lustily. I
sent Harry to know what was the cause, but he soon came back and
snatching up his Mascheet flew off like a dart and we after him.
There we saw Jessy standing with a load of dry wood on her head
and Harry chopping at a large black Snake which lay right in the narrow path. This Snake was at least 6 feet long but not venomous in
the least, as Harry said. This Snake he brought with him to the fire
to roast and did so, offering a part to us but we declined it, keeping

our stomachs for better fare. "Well, well," said he, "he had no business to be there to frighten Jessy, and I would serve forty of them so if they came in my path."

"Deel stick ye weem [worm]!" said Bell.

"I forbid that," said I, "so belay that speech, Messmate."

"Hoot, hoot!" said he. "Thes Indians wad devoor the auld Whaap-nab[5] himsel, gin he were weel cooked, and sup his broth after that, Ime thinking. Foul fare on such beast!"

"Why, Norman," I replied, "you dont know that I have eaten of them before now with him, and really they tast well enough."

"Weel, then, ye had better, the next ye find, be getting one of ther muckle tree paddocks[6] for sauce too ut," said he.

In the Evening we all embarqued and got home safe to our abode. Our stock of liquor was now become very low so that we seldom touched it but on a case of necessity. The next thing came on was to repair the damages we sustained in our thatch during the late Tempest, and this business took up some length of time. Our Plantain trees suffered also. After this time matters went on in the old channel with little variation of circumstances untill such time as I had compleated another year.

Chapter 25: Sixteenth Year

Sixteenth Year began. It happened as Harry and Owen came in from fishing they brought up to me a curious bunch or Whipp of some living substance much resembling Catgut and of the same hue or pale yellow colour. It was so interwoven that we could not by any means

5. Deel and Whaap-nab: the Devil.
6. Toads or frogs.

seperate it, neither could we discover either end so as to find head or tail; yet it kept continually in motion appearing like to a hand full of thread animated, and might be as we judged 12 fathom long. I had seen one of them before which I found in the stomach of a Groupar, but if bred in the maw of the fish or taken in as food we knew not, as this which I am now describing came up on the hook.

This singular Insect leads me to a discription of one I found in the Woods on a day about 4 years ago. It was lying on the ground, and as its shape was a little peculiar I took it up to examine it and found it to be of a hard substance black as jett, and in make the true form of our Barbers curling pipes and in length and bulk of that magnitude. It seemed to be composed of a rang of scales and at each end had a small aperture, and when on the ground could advance slowly with either end forward, and that with ease. There were neither Eyes, mouth, or any detached member to be seen.

Many extraordinary things which are absolute curiosities of Nature have escaped my memory, especially such as fell under my observation in the first years of my residence here, for want of means to record them as in those days I little expected to become master of materials for that purpose. Yet whatever came within reach of my speculation never escaped my inquisitive inclination, having from a Child ever taking much delight in prying into the works and wonders of Nature. Now what ever I have or shall advance, I declare has passed within my view; and as thousands have passed or traversed over many part of this vast continent they may confute me easily if I advance falshoods. But where could a Man, scituated as I am expect to recieve a benefit from by imposing untruths on the World?—especially as I have but a scant expectation that what I write may ever fall under the inspection of my own Nation and Brother Tars, for whose information in chief I thus amuse my time. As to the lerned I stand not in any dread of their sensure, being a man of no Education my self, therfore beneath their scrutiny and Envy. Yet I may venture so far as to think they will not carp at what may be honestly advanced by me, who am but an Illiterate Sailor.

I make this digression on account that perhaps many things which may in the great length of time I have resided here have been seen and described by my pen have never been noticed by any others before. The reason is obvious: they keep moving from place to place and perhaps give themselves little concern to explore the beauties of this Universe, When on the contrary I remain as a Man consigned over to such a purpose, with time sufficient to answer all such ends.

One Evening about 5 oclock as Messmate Bell was reading over some of the Scotch Songs to me and giving me the explanation of some of the old words in them, All at once the Earth began to lift us up and down, twice. Upon this we began to stare at each other wildly. Bell threw by the book, crying, "It is an Earthquake. Bring away the children from the side of the hill," said he. "Perhaps it is not over yet, and some of the stones may give way." Just after this we had another motion but much weaker. I had never felt the like in my life before, but my Messmate said he had felt several since he had been in this country, and had been shewn large Hills and Clifts split from clew to Earing[1] by them, as we sailors term it—saying there was little danger where we were as there were no Volcano's in our neighbourhood that he knew of. And as I found our Indians heeded it not, it passed of, they carlessly observing it was only a sign of heat which really was the case soon after.

The Butterflies now became more numerous than I had seen them in all my time before, and now I have mentioned them it may not be improper to say somthing concerning them. In the first place they all differ from any I know in Europe, are much wilder and swifter, in general flying up over the tops of the loftiest Trees in the Woods; but as to discribing their plumage it would be endless, there being so many different sorts. But I shall remark that I have seen some full as broad as ye palm of my hand and many much larger, and I have often found Pods of the Silk work sticking in crevices of the rocks and clefts of Trees. But there is one sort we find at times fixed to the limb of a small twig 5 times the size of the ordinary, and in colour of a dark Brown resembling Ocum.

---

1. Literally, from the lower corner of a square sail to the rope attached to its [upper] edge, used in reefing.

These pods are so strong that it is hard to Rend them asunder. The Fly which it produces is as broad as a Mans hand and of a beautiful variety of colours, Grey, red and white, with a pair of fine yellow feathers in front of its head. There is Yet another Sort of a Brimstone colour with a circle in each wing which is as transparent as Glass, with the after parts of their wings tapering away like to a Swallows tail. We sometimes see a sort which are yellow with bars running thwart in a very regular manner of black; another kind Green with black bars transverse to the other sort.

But I must observe one thing truly remarkable and beyond my comprehension, as follows. At times we found a kind of Brown Wasp which, falling head formost to the Ground from the Trees, there takes root, from whence springs up a small plant through their bodies. Mr. Bell's opinion was that it proceeded from some kind of Seed they swallow which intoxicates them, so that when ye Wasp falls to the Earth those seeds take root and immediately spring up again.

We were now Visited by a Single Canoa from our friends. In it came Soroteet or the Crabcatcher, Yewarrabaso and Kayuaza; the two last had never been at our habitation before. These Indians came out of curiosity to see us, and brought with them a pair of Young Fowls as breeders, saying they were as a present from Owagamy with his heart, as they termed it; and that he had them sent to him from over the great hills. Nothing could have delighted me more. Among other things they informed us that they had another of thos People call Moonlights born, a female, but that she soon died which all were very glad of. This put me on making another enquiry about these odd beings, but to no manner of Satisfaction. After they had been with us about three days they left us, but after Soroteet had got on board of the Canoa he reminded Harry of a flute he was to make for him, and I gave him to know he should make it.

Some days after the Indians were gone we heard a great noise among the fowls in the Kitchen. Eva sent Job to see what might be the cause, when he came running out and said Jackko had got one of the new Birds in his arms and was pulling out ye feathers. This fired my blood and off I ran. When I got in, there sat Mr. Monkey with a fowl in his lap picking out its feathers one by one. Directly he held out the fowl to me. On this I took the fowl in one hand and him by the head in the other, and thus brought them out. The fowl was not much hurted, but to prevent his doing the like we Tied him up and with a small switch I made Owen flog him while Job held the Fowls feathers to his nose. After this disciplin he was dismissed, but he grew so shy from that time that whenever one of the fowls happened to come nigh him he was off in an instant. But when one of the young Cocks began to Crow the Monkey would rave and run into the first corner he could find and there clap his hands before his face, which caused much diversion among our younkers; but he never touched them afterward. Yet to give him his due character, he acted the downright Skulker on board of a Man of War, alway at hand when any thing was to bee shared.

But among the multitude of his tricks I think one of them merits recording. One day I observed his Impship very busy down among the graves and sent little Luta to learn what he was at. The Child came back and said Jackko had got a heap of round things in a hole there. On this I went down myself and found a hole wherin he had deposited 50 Dollars or more. Altho it was true we stood in no need of it then, yet I thought some day or other we might have a call for it. I then bid them Call Norman who was then down at the boat. When he came I shew'd him that Jackko had found a treasure likewise. "Ay," said he, "and yours is grown less, I dare say." How he came by the discovery I know not, but must have seen us at it, as he had been at the labour to remove many Stones before he could get at it. But to prevent the like Messmate Bell and Harry removed the whole in the night so that none knew where it was except us three.

About the middle of August we had a most tremendous Gust of thunder, Lightning and Rain but no wind, scarse, during which the large tree wheron those Vultures lodged at my friends death Was split from top to bottom so that it parted like a pair of sheers. I had all the family within the Cave the whole time, not above three quarters of an hour; and all becoming calm we ventured forth again. "Well," said I, "we are all safe, thanks to kind Providence." But shortly after as my little Rees was runing about he came and told his Mother that one of our Indian Dogs was so fast asleep that he could not get up; but when Jessy went to see it she said the Dog was quite dead, struck by ye lightning as we supposed. We could percieve no mark of violence externally, yet he was stone dead.

Chapter 26

It was not long after this before we had a dismal stroke befell us, attended with fatal consiquences to us all, as thus. The while we men happened to be out in the bay after the Turtle the cursed Monkey overset a Yabba as it was boiling on the fire, by which my son Owen got one of his feet scalded. This so greatly alarmed them all, as they knew how much I prized him, that my Wife packed Eva off into the Woods after certain roots to stew as a remedy. The poor creture went off with speed altho then with child. We did not return untill about 4 oclock. When I went into the house I found the boy with his foot lap'd up, and had the story in full. My Wife said Eva had been gone a great time after herbs or roots, and wonder'd what detain'd her so long. I took no notice at that about her, but ordered the Monkey to be drown'd at once, being determined it should never be the cause of more mischief; and Harry settled that point with a stone about its neck in the Lagoon.

Now as the evening advanced Mr. Bell grew uneasy about his Wife, saying perhaps She had rambled beyond her knowledge and had lost herself. "How can that be? She has been all over the wood diverse times." said I. "But you and Harry had better go off in quest of her with one of the Shells." And away they went and did not return untill

Sun down but without any tidings. Now I began to be much alarm'd and advised that they should get torches without loss of time, arm themselves and off again at once, dreading her being alone in the Forest after night as I made no doubt of her being devoured before ye morning. We heard them almost the whole time tooting and shouting. I ordered Patty to make up as large a fire as she could as a direction for them back again. Every now and then I blew a Conck, and thus time passed until midnight. Now all were in tears about me; and if I did not hear their sound now and then my Soul filled with horror least they should all three be lost.

At length about two oclock they came in. Mr. Bell was almost frantic with distress. No Eva could they see or hear of. I now becam sensibly touched both on account of the Woman and my disconsolate friend. I put on all the most favourable circumstances and used all my skill to keep up his spirits, yet I feared much we should never see her alive more. Thus we remained untill the dawn, and then I proposed to go in quest of her myself. I took Harry with me and left Norman with the Women as he was in so much trouble. We scowred the woods in the strictes manner untill high noon without any discovery, and then returned.

Now I began to reflect heavily on my own neglect so as to leave the Women at home without a guard, but I was by the length of time become self secure, as I may say. Poor Norman, observing me to fret at such a rate, said with his Eyes full of water, "My friend, let me entreat you not to charge yourself as being any way the original cause of this my sad disaster, for had you stay'd at home the misfortune might still have happened."

"Pray let me have my opinion," said I. "From henceforth nothing shall ever delude me so far from my reason as to neglect a thing of such consiquence."

"My good brother," said Harry seeing me in such a preturbation, "perhaps She is gone home to see her Brother."

"Blockhead! Fool!" said I, "could she go so far without Victuals and alone?"

"You dont know what the Indians can do when the great ugly Spirit is on them," he said.

"I cannot be brought to think such a thing unless Messmate and she have differed lately."

"We never have as yet," said he. "Yet who knows but she has took some mad fit in her head and may be gone off thither. But such a thought would not have taken place with me had not Harry hit on it."

"I shall be glad we may find your tongue true," said I, "with all my soul."—Yet at the same time I could not entertain such a mad notion.

And thus our time passed on in a dolorous way for three days longer. Now Harry said to me that if Bell was so minded he would go over land with him to their people. "Go and call him to me," said I. When he came I mentioned what he had hinted. Upon this he said it was highly needful, he thought, as otherwise we knew not what constructions the Indians would put on the thing. "That is a very just observation, indeed," I said. "Therfore if you are willing, pray go; you have my approbation so to do."

He came at once into the motion and, arming themselves, went off the next day with a few trifles of provision and the dog Swift with them. I charged Mr. Bell to have his Eyes about him and strictly to follow Harry's advice as he best knew the country; and if in case they found her there to bring her back by water, but if it proved abortive in that case for to return as they went, by Land, as by that conduct we should be the better prepared on their arrival. I then said, "I give you a fortnight and if you return not in that time we shall be wretched."

After they were gone I formed many conjectures about the Girl, as somtimes thinking that perhaps some Strange Indians had found her and took her off with them, or that she might be drown'd in some pond. Again, that she had roved so far beyond her knowledge that she had starved to death for want. But the chief thing I dreaded was that she was destroyed by Wild beasts, and the Women joyn'd in that opinion.

Thus we remain'd twixt hope and fear day after day. I never left home once farther than to go down to the lagoon to catch a few Grunts and the like, living chiefly on vegetable diet. In about a week after this about 9 at night Owen cried out that he had heard sombody hollow. We all ran out to listen but could hear nothing. A short time after, he said he heard it again, and we soon heard one of those birds I had mistaken on my first landing for a Yoho. This threw us quite aback again, and we all turned in with heavy hearts. And thus it went on untill the whole time elapsed for their return, and no appearance.

About 5 days after this Swift came runing into the Cave. "Here they are!" I cried in a transport. Upon going out I percieved Harry and another Indian coming down the hill. My mind now misgave me at once, and I ernestly call'd out, "Where is Bell?" When they came in Harry said they had left him there, being sick. Now, think I, Eva is not there for certain. Harry said Eva never went there. "What is the matter with my friend?" said I. "Tell me at once."

"He will return with some of our friends in a few days," said he. I then told Betty to sound Gaynasunto, the other Indian. She told me that after Bell and Harry arrived there the Indians held a private council. When they had done this they told Harry that they concluded Eva was either took off by some strange Indians or eaten by the Tigers, saying they knew me to be such a true friend that I would not give consent to Shewing any blood as they could never find, by all their industry and vigalance, so hard a charge against their White Brother in blood and flesh.

"Surely," said I to her, "have they then had Spies to watch over us and privatly to observe our conduct? Tell me, I charge you, have you a knowledge of any such proceeding?" She then frankly own'd that some of their People had been deputed to come on such an Errand and had actually been at times so nigh our habitation as to get a fair view of all our behaviour. This news startled me, but as I know full well they came for no other end than to make their observation after what manner we treated their Women I soon became cool again. Yet I could not but wonder they should take so great a trouble mearly to satisfy curiosity. But when I once reflected that from that source arose such a mutual friendship between us, I could do no more than highly commend them in so doing.

All this time Harry seem'd to be on the reserve, as I took it, And I asked him the reason that he did not give me a full account of all that had happened during their abscence. "Oh," sd. he, "Owagamy told me to keep my mouth shut, saying he will be the Mouth when he comes back next time with Mr. Norman, and then Gaynosanto is to go back with him."

"What occasion," said I, "can they have in giving me so much uneasiness? If Eva be there let her return with her husband."

"No, no," said Harry, "she has been meat for Tigers long ago, or starved to death."

"Then if it be so, why did he not return with you?"

"Owagamy sent me off with that Man," said he, "as thinking you would grieve, but they will come soon and that is all I know." Well, thought I, if he has taken a conceit as to reside among them, a' Gods name I must reconcile myself to my first manner of life the best I can.

Above a fortnight elapsed, and no news of Bell. Then an odd notion popt into my head that perhaps the Spaniards had got knowledge of him and the Indians had given him up. Then I thought such a conjecture was dealing unjustly by my friends. But about two days after, as Harry was coming out of the Bushes he espied about three Canoas coming into the bay. "Hoist our colours," said I. We then got the boat ready and went down, to have them entertain the better opinion of us as I knew not how matters had changed from the time Bell left me. Gaynasunto and I were only in the boat as I had charged Harry to abide by the Girls.

We met them at the mouth of the Lagoon. Now observing Women with them I began to think they had some Sort of Sport to play off and intended to surprize me With a sight of Eva again. I gave them a Salute and put away in before them. When we landed Owagamy and Bell jumped on shore and saluted me, which overjoyed me. I saw two Women in the canoa but strangers to me. When they came

out I lead them up to the house. After some talk I asked my Messmate
who those ladies might be, as my Betty knew them not. Then taking
one of them by the hand he presented her to me as his Wife. "O ho,"
said I, "if that be the case much joy to you!" He thanked me and said
the whole business had been conducted by my friend Owagamy and
his council, and that he had condesended not from Choice but as
knowing should he decline the proposal it might prove of an Ill consiquence in future and involve us in much trouble. "You were very
prudent, Messmate," I replied, "and I am heartily glad the matter has
come to so pleasing a conclusion."

I now gave order that things should be provided that we might shew
them every civility possible. They were all in high spirits. Owagamy
desired that the ceremony should be repeated, for he said they had
done the Broom work at their place already to the great mirth of all
the Indians; and it was repeated accordingly. I then learn'd that the
Bride was a Widow. She seemed to be about 25 years of age and named
Aanora, or a thing desired. Mr. Bell satisfied me the next day as to his
remaining so long with them, as follows: That after they well had
weighed the matter they called a council and that they took him to it
in a large Wigwam, and after they had all got togather he was placed
by Owagamy's side. Then a profound silence held for the space of
about half an hour, during which time about 12 of them kept smoking.
At last an Indian got up and spake to Bell in Spanish, saying that his
people desired Gattaloon (meaning himself) to be the one mouth or
Voice through which he was to hear them all. That they knew of a
certainty he was a fair or true Man, and that they saw his heart
through his Eyes. They knew he had lost his wife some days before
he came to visit them, and they were satisfied much in regard to his
coming to them on that account. Otherwise they should have entertained an opinion of him far different; but now knowing such a sad
misfortune to have befallen him, not of our own seeking but through
an oversight, their council had—finding him to grieve so much for the
loss—determined to keep him among them untill they could find a
plant propper for his cure but that it took them some time to find it

out, but that they had now found one. It was a little drooping for want of nourishment, as it had been a dry time lately where it grew. Then an odd kind of noise was heard and there came three women to the door, one of which was call'd in and Owagamy, rising, took her by the hand and said: "This is a Woman not of our Nation but our friend. She has lost her nourisher, and we give her thee by her own consent. Nourish her as thou hast so done by Mattanany our sister, now lost from life. We think it hard you should be without a Woman, as you know so well how to respect One. We sent our valuable Brother Gaynasunto with Ayasharry least our great heart White Brother Penoly should stand in need of friends in the mean time. We will return with Aanora and thee to thy friend as soon as convenient."

I bade Harry return them our most hearty thanks for their Love and the great care they had been at in salving the late great wound my friend Bell had recieved. I had no liquor to treat them with now in store. This they were informed of. Owagamy answered that all things decayed in time except the Sun, Moon and Stars, so that he wondered not at it in the least. After they had been with us about 5 days they took their leave. Before they went I distributed some pieces of blue Cloth among them but the Moth by the length of time had eaten all such things much.

When I was about to take my farewell of Owagamy at the boat and saying what great friends he and his people were to me, he Smiled and told Harry that I had one thing to do yet to convince his people of my faith. Upon this I Insisted to be acquainted in what way I could shew them the great trust and confidence I had ever had in him and his people. "You have many times looked toward the place where we reside in the long time of your being here, but you have never put one foot willingly before the other to visit me and my People. You knew not the path through ye Wood yourself," said he, "but Ayasharry can lead you by the hand when your mind turns so toward us."

I told him that sole reason of my never doing them that duty was owing to the great charge I had on me to preserve these his Blood and Flesh consigned over to my care, but that he might acquaint his people on his return that I now made it my firm resolution to pay them a visit the first fair opportunity. Upon this they all shouted, and we went down the lagoon to see them off.

I shall in this place observe that both Harry and my self could speak at this time as much Spanish so as to be understood, as I had desired the favour of Mr. Bell to take all opportunities with us for to learn enough of that tongue so as to be able to converse, thinking it would prove of infinite service in future as we knew not what might come to pass. And this he did very willingly. I came the sooner on as I had got a smattering before while prisoner at ye Havannah.

It now came into my head, as thus. I consulted messmate Bell that I was determined to study Spanish with a full resolution, and as I knew he understood marking peoples skins in characters he should mark a Cross on one of my hands, and that I would get him to shave my beard and platt my hair behind after the Spanish mode. He laughed at me, saying how could I pretend ever to pass for one of those people when my tongue would soon betray me. "Let me alone for that," said I. "I have got my own plan."

"As how?" said I.

"Thus," I replied. "I can report that I am a native of Barcelona, went into the service of an English Gentleman at Venice when a Boy, and remained with him and others after I came to England many years, by which means I lost my Mother tongue in a great degree."

"Troth," said he, "that move will do if you can but carry it off well. And your Name—how will that answer?"

"I will fix on one for the purpose by your help," said I, "sounding as nigh my own as possible." This motion being determined on, Messmate Bell shaved off my beard in the first place and ordered my hair, but when we put it in practice it was done in my cave and Harry was at the time gone down ye Lagoon. My wife and the Girls were exceedingly diverted at my transformation, saying that I was gone back many, man Moons and had brought back a pretty little young head with me. My Messmate then put one of the old Sambraros on my noddle and making me a low bow welcomed me to his abode in the name of Signior Louis Penalosa. "That will do," said I. "Bless me, my face feels as tho the half my chin was carried away," said I. We had a kind of berries whose pulp washed equal to Soap and these we always used for such purposes.

Soon after this I missed Owen. I enquired after him and they said he was gone with Harry. When I saw them coming we all kept our countenances the best way we could, but to see the behaviour of Harry and Owen on the occasion is beyond my skill to describe. No sooner did Harry see me sitting so altered but he fixed his Eyes on Norman and looked so confoundedly simple that a man would have thought he was turned a downright fool, but poor Owen burst into a flood of tears in hearing me speak. I call'd him to come to me but he ran and got behind Patty, clung to her, and there began to bellow at a sad rate. Upon this Bell took him hold to bring him to me but he resisted with all his might, saying it was not his father. At last I call'd to Harry to come and shake hands with me. "O!" said he, "I know it is you, a little not you, sideways one way, but Mr. Norman has cut your face and made it so sharp that it looks like a young callabash now."

"I thank you for your fine comparison," said I, "Harry."

"You look like a young Spaniard now," he said, "and you always was afraid of Spaniards. Now you make us all fools."

"Never you mind that," said I. "Mr. Bell and I have done it to cheat them if we can."

"Ay," said he, "but you will never do so with my Indian people for we can smell the difference well enough."

Now Owen began to smile a little and asked Bell what he cut his father for. But the thing pleas'd my Wife highly, she saying every now and then how pretty my new head looked, only she thought it quite too small. I told her it would soon grow larger; yet I was a singular object among them for a few days.

The next thing was to mark my hand, and this Norman did with two small needles tied togather and filled the punctures with wet powder. It cost me both pain and patience before he had done. His own arm had a Crucifix drawn on it long before. I then proposed we should make some small crosses to wear at our breast occasionally, and for this end Bell went to work with a dollar out of which he cast two or three small ones. And thus we were compleated as two counterfeit Spaniards.

After this I spoke to Mr. Bell that we should give his Lady another name as it was become our stated custom. "Troth, gie her the name ye like best," said he.

"Not at all," I replied, "you must do that your self."

"Well, then, we will call her Janett if you like." And Janett was her name. I then told my Wife to inform her of it and she became mighty fond of it herself.

About the latter end of March as Bell and I were out fishing in deep water a prodigious large Shark came ranging along close in View. My Messmate said It was very different from any he had seen before. "Let us bait the Shark hook," I said; "perhaps we may catch him." Directly he whipt out the bowels of a fish and hung it on, then threw it out right before his nose; but he flew like a dart from it at first, yet return'd immediately and took it in. We let him have time, and had the Gentleman fast. He gave us brave sport for a time, sheering down below with great strength. At last he became tired out and let us hale him in sight. When we got a fair view of him we found this Fish had a piece of a three inch Rope in a knot just above his tail and that it had been on him a great length of time. The fag ends were about a foot long and had been yet longer, as we thought; it was become white as flax. This fish was about 16 foot in length and the largest we had ever seen, having many rows of teeth, and had been an old cruiser in his time—perhaps had followed some ship from the coast of Africa after the dead Slaves, was caught by one of those Ships and had been let go again or made his escape, as he was a true Tiger Shark of a blue colour with the tips of his tail and fins yellow. Fortune at length brought him hither to make his Exit. We got several quarts of Oil from his liver which was of material service to us.

Speaking of Fish I must remark that at times we found an odd animal running over the bottom in shoal places, of a triangular form about ye size of a large Flounder, and carried its head erect as a hen does, with bright Eyes, the back mottled in a curious manner. It has four feet or fins shaped like to the back fins of a Turtle with a tail resembling a fan. The tail and fins or rather finfeet were edged with yellow. This creture can run along the bottom nimbly but in deep water swims with ease. We never ventured to take them as not knowing their quality.

We also found a sort of Insect or rather reptile creeping in ye Shallow Water, of a dark olive green full of black circles. This creture advances in the manner our Sluggs do, dilating and contracting after that fashion. But the most curious part of the story is that on being once touched they instantly emit a most glorious purple liquid all round them to the distance of a yard or more so that the animal is no longer perceptible.

About the beginning of May my Wife asked Harry to procure her some Sappadillos the next time he went out in the woods. Now on a day soon after Harry told me in private that he knew what had become of poor Eva. "Say you so!" I cried. "How came you not to tell me of it then before?"

"Because I thought Mr. Norman should not know it," he said.

"I dont know what you mean," I replied.

"When I was last in the Woods," said he, "for Sappodillos—"

"Well, and how then?" I cried.

"Come with me, Penoly," said he, and then took me up the hill where in a hole under some bushes he shewed me the remains of the poor duds she used to wear. My blood ran cold at the sight.

"Whence came these?" I cried in confusion. He then told me that as he was on his ramble about two miles off he came to a thicket where he first found a rib bone, and looking about found the scull and other bones with the rags, and knowing them directly he said his great spirit came to him so strong that had 5 Tigers been present he would have engaged them all. "Well, keep it secret," I said. "I shall let him know of it at some propper time." I then went down and privatly informed my Betty of it, charging her never to presume to leave home without a guard on any occasion whatever. Soon after this I gave them the whole of the discovery when they were all together, and it proved warning sufficient from that day forward.

Chapter 27: Seventeenth Year

A few days after our new year had commenced came Gattaloon with 7 Indians more, all of them our old acquaintance. When we went to Salute them they all appeared Sad, seated themselves and remain'd silent for a few minutes. Then Gattaloon got up and held forth in a mournful strain a long discourse in Spanish to Mr. Bell, but I soon found it fraught with the melancholy news of Owagamys death. After he had done, seeing me so very dejected, he took me by the hand and said, "I am Owagamy now, and I will stand by friends as long as they or I live. Your friends shall be mine and I will be his, and my strength shall go forth against your haters."

Mr. Bell became so enraptured with his speech that he clapped him on the Shoulders and cried, "Weel spaken, Hardicanute!" We informed them of Eva's fate and as they were in no great flow of Spirits they soon left us which was in two days time, saying Owagamy had charged them to be friends to us and they were all determined so to be; that they were glad I had fell on ye scheem of passing for a Spaniard as it would take a great stone off their heads which they had carried on my account a long time, but that they had born it with willingness.

Owagamy had ever been a steadfast Friend from the first of our acquaintance and was a Man of great penetration and forecast according to what might be expected from an uncultivated Native. And I must own the news of his death truly efected me, knowing full well he had always been our Best Bower Anchor when ever storms arose; and he joyntly with our good friend Komaloot were ever ready and willing to stand our Pilots in conducting us to the safest harbours of calm repose so that we might remain intirely Landlocked from wind which might chance to blow. When ever either of our poor little Skifts chanced to touch on the quicksands of inquietude they made it their principal care to tow her off into a safe birth. And remembering all these good and generous offices they had performed in the course of our acquaintance, I desired Gattaloon to signifie on their return not to forget our unfeigned condolence to all friends.

One Evening Owen came in to me as I was reading and said Mr. Bell desired I would come out to see the great Rainbow. "A Rainbow in the night, boy?" said I, as it might then be 10 oclock. But as I knew somthing more than common was to be seen I went out, and in the North East was a large dense cloud with a perfect Bow of a large magnitude in colour like to Skim milk, much more distinct than any I ever saw given by the suns orb. Norman said he had seen one before, but it was a novelty to me as in all my travels I had not seen the like, but Harry was not so great a stranger to the like.

About this time our fishermen brought in two fish of a kind I have not yet discribed. One of them is called by some Seamen ye Ballahoo if I am not mistaken. It is a fish long, round and slim shaped much like to the Garr fish, but differs much in all but the body, the upper fly of the tail being short and the under 4 times the length; but few fins, and in regard to its mouth very singular as the under jaw or mandible projects to ten times the length of the upper, terminating in a very sharp point so that it is impossible it should seize prey as other fish do. But nature has given it such an address that when lying on the Surface of the water and percieving its object it instantly darts as an arrow from a bow, piercing its prey with the lower bill, then sinking to the bottom where it remains darting of it untill it becomes no longer able to escape when it takes it in at its pleasure. And this is to be seen if in shoal water.

The other sort is a Fish constructed much like a Flying Fish but grown to the size of an ordinary Mullet. It is curiously marked with blew, green, yellow, brown and red. The Wings or fins are much longer than the whole body, tail and all, and almost transparent. When these wings are extended they spread broader than a mans hand and are beautifully variegated with many colours.

I shall now give the Reader some account of the vast variety of Lizzards we see frequently and Seldom. The most frequent and common are those call'd the Lion Lizzard. They are most numerous abroad in the heat of the day, exceeding swift of foot altho they seem to go much on the belly. This belly is chequered much like our common English Green snake but its back is striped horizontally from head to tail with delicate broad Stripes of a brown and yellow colour resembling velvet. The male is very vicious after the female, and much larger. I have seen them above a foot in length. Their conjunction is Lateral; and it is to be observed that in their courtship when the Male first espies the Female he protrudes a large bag from beneath his throat, puffing it out as full of wind & drawing it back at pleasure, so that when he is not thus employed nothing of that bag is perceptible. This is common to the Guano and all the Lizzard tribes.

Galliwasp—this is another species frequenting the Woods and lurk much in holes in ye Ground, in colour dark grey and black. They bite Sharply as the Indians say, but not poisonous as reported in the Islands of ye Westindies by the Negros. They are of the largest kind of Lizzards and if persued take to their holes, but smoke soon dislodges them. They are also very indolent, remaining long in one place.

Sattin Lizzard—these are of a Solitary disposition. You seldom find more than one in a place and that always in the shade under a rock or in the chinks and cleft of Rocks, where they lurk day and night. I have known them to remain in one place for three days and nights without once changing their position. They are striped black, brown, white and grey, and shine like sattin as they move. But it had one quality differing from all the other kinds which is, it has the power to make its body so flat that it can at pleasure adapt itself to any chink it chuses to lurk in.

I have mentioned that sort called the Wood Slave already, but it is beyond my power to discribe the whole genera of them. Some are Yellow, others black, brown, red, speckled &cc. Some come forth most in the heat and dryest time; on the contrary some kinds are seldom to be seen but after rains, and so forth. They in general live on insects and have the tongue forked as the snake.

Now it happened after the family had retired that my Betty being awake shook me, and when I answered her she told me that some one or other of them was sick, saying she heard a very sad moaning. I soon heard it my Self and got up, call'd Harry, and finding him well sent him to learn who was out of order. But on Enquiry all were well; yet every now and then we heard sad and deep groans. The dogs were call'd but they were all well enough, and what to think we could not tell. Somtimes it ceased and then began again, now strong, then weaker, and thus it went on untill fair dawn. None went to sleep the whole night but the younger sort.

Now Bell started this notion, that some strange Indians had perhaps discovered us and it might be a scheem to decoy us among the Woods, as the sound seem'd to come from a part beyond the place where we found the money and plate. "Po, po!" said I. "They have been long enough in finding us out then, and this is a poor method for them, indeed, as should they have any disposition to annoy us they could do it in a more manly way if they were so disposed."

"What if it should be the departed Spirit of the Victim they left as guard over the treasure?" said Harry.

This made us smile and I said joakingly, "By my troth, then, he has been very remiss or on some long journey thus to begin his hones[1] after so great a length of time." But the women were sure some Indian or other person must be there very bad or dying, saying perhaps it might be one of our friends either much hurted as he was on his way to our place. This carrying some weight with it, I Told Bell that he and Harry might arm themselves and take along the dogs to find out the cause.

"Come," said Harry. They then loaded their Guns, took Mascheets and away they went boldly. In about 20 minutes they returned.

"What news?" cried I. "Have you found it out?"

"Found it out?" said he with a very serious countenance. "Ay, ay,

1. Complaints, objections.

and if you had been with us you would have found it out also."

"Make me acquainted at once," said I, "let the thing be how it will, for I must be satisfied."

"It is one of the Natives of a most Gigantick size," said he, "and dying as I take it, but not of our friends as I never saw him come hither in their company. Nor do I think him of ye tribe as he differs greatly in colour from our friends. He has not the least sense we could percieve, but groans heavily." All this time our Harry kept aloof. The Girls were all gathered round the Story and standing there with open mouths. As for my part I saw Bell begin to look seriously on the ground after he had given his account.

I began to form strange notions in my brain, saying, "He is not dead yet—I hear him groan still."

On this Bell burst into a monstrous laughter and holding his head up cried, "I am to windward of You now, my good Messmate." Then came up Harry to help him, and after they had laughed their fill Bell said, "Come, come, what do you think it may be?"

"You have the game to your own selves," said I.

"Well, to clar off all farther conjectures It is yon great Cotton Tree which the lightning split. There is a broken limb fell thwart another and as the wind dies or freshens it rubs more or less with a groaning noise. But when one is near it the sound is above the tone of any dying person."

After Messmate Norman had play'd off this fit of the horrour so well with us all, I came to a determination for my Visit to see my good friends to the Southward, and for the journey I got Bell to make us a knapsack each to carry our roasted yams &cc in. Harry was to stand Pilot, and the company were to be Harry, Owen and my self with the dog Rover. When the time came for our departure I told Mr. Bell that I gave the whole charge into his hands, Saying that I rested satisfied with his conduct in our abscence to be kind to my Wife and all the rest. Then calling all togather I charged them that they gave good heed to my friends advice in every respect. And as it was a thing Incumbent on me and what I could not in fair play be off, as they had been such a number of times to visit us, I took a Sailors leave of my Wife and the rest, leaving them all in tears abruptly, and away we went. Owen wept out for his part. The novelty of the thing gave him spirits enough.

I need not to mention a discription of our road as that has been done, but we arrived all three in safety; but as I and the Child were never used to go such vast lengths our feet became much blistered. Now as we drew nigh to their residence, which was about 5 in ye Evening, Tired to death having been six days on the trampoose—sleeping on the bare Ground every night with a large fire round us, living scantly as we got no more than 4 Parrots and one Pidgeon the whole journey; but Harry shott a duck in a pond and as he could not come at it he wanted to send the Dog in for it—this I absolutely refused least he might be devoured by ye Alligators.

When we had got thus far I made my Child sit down by me and sent Harry into the town before me to find how the land lay, and inform them of our being arrived. In a short time we heard a confused noise of many people advancing toward us; and soon after we percieved a throng of men, Women and Children coming up with little bells, callabashes and immitations of German flutes making a most confused noise, with Gattaloon, Harry and several other faces I well knew. We then arose and Gattaloon took me by the hand with a generous smile on his face and gave me a most kind welcom. Such a pleasing aspect was to be seen in all their faces mixed with a kind of admiration that I never beheld the like before, and It raised my spirits much after my fatigue.

Owen stuck close by me all the way we went into theyr ranges of houses or Wigwams and stared about him as one astonished, being the first time the poor Soul had made his appearance in publick, as I may say, for the whole universe was to him one scene of wonder. As we advanced more people made their appearance. I had rigged my Owen out in such sort that he looked like a young Cupid with his sheaf of Arrows at his back and Bow over his arm. We were lead into one of their places of dwelling And at the Enterance were met by Zulawana and others. There sat on a mat a very ancient Woman to whom Zulawana lead up my Child, and she took great pains to examine him, being dim sighted. She then placed her left hand on his shoulder and muttered some few words, which I desired might be interpreted to me and it was to this Effect: "Let not an Arrow hit him, let not fire burn him, a tree fall on him or the waters choak him. All you strong men preserve him from the hot spirit of those who would kill him while he remains in the days of tenderness."

Now Harry observed to me that she was one of their good cunning Women and had told many strang things; and that an Indian had told him they expected us that Moon, she having foretold it to them for some days.

The young Indians gathered round Owen and by gentle usage coaxed him out, when they got bows and began to dastardise[2] him with feats of activity. Owen having Harry his Uncle at his side, took courage and shewed them some of his skill. Some of the children would gently touch him and look on their own fingers after it, as thinking his colour might rub off as he was lighter coloured than themselves, yet he looked much more the Indian than an Europian.

Chapter 28

Now after I had been among them two days Gattaloon say'd he was mighty glad I had turned Spaniard, as there was at that time an Old Spanish Soldier come among them and intended to come and see me in about two hours, being then abscent with two of their people; but that he and his friends had taken care to spread the report that I was a Spaniard. This put me to my trumps, so that I became under the necessity of acting my part the best way I could. Accordingly he came and saluted me in the Spanish way. I returned the civillity and a con-

2. Daze, impress.

versation commenced When I gave him my whole history—that I was a native of Barcelona but had when a boy entered into the service of an English Gentleman who was at that time in Venice, with him went to England, &cc. That In the course of time I lost much of my Mother tongue, and after a multitude of changes became a Servant to a Gentleman bound to England from Jamaica and was taken, carried into Havannah, put prisoner on board of a Spanish Man of War. That after many other turns of fortune I became lost in a Canoa on this shore where I had resided many years, part of which time quite alone.

He seemed amazed at what I related and said he found I could not speak Spanish fluently but that I looked like a Biscain or Biscayan very much. He then asked my name and I told him it was Louis Penalosa. Now as we were talking I happened to mention the passage which happened from the Ships top when I was a Prisoner. On this the Old Man gave a Start and said he well remembered that affair, being then a Marine onboard that Ship. I then Enquired his name and he said Pablo Nunez, but as that class of Men did not associate much with us I could not recollect him at first. He mentioned to me concerning a man whose Name was Nick Jones, that he had been placed Centry over him while in the stocks for drunkeness—calling him Nico Yone— and that he was a drunken mad English dog.

Now as we were thus talking, I happening to call my Owen in English, when the child came too us Nunez took him by the hand and said, "Good boy, hablar Englse? Me hablar Englese tambien. What is yournama, boy?" Owen answered. I then interrogated the Old Man where he learnt English, when he told me that he had been taken by the English in the reign of Queen Ann, said he was prisoner in a castle there by Portsmouth. That he on being released went to Sr. John Norris's fleet, was up the Baltic with him on board a Ship call'd the *Boyn*,[1] and remembered Peter the Great when on board the fleet, and recited some few things concerning him—as on the Queens birth day he refused to drink her health with the Admiral out of Silver pint can

1. The *Boyne* was built at Deptford in 1692 and saw wide service in the Caribbean, Mediterranean, and Baltic. Sir John Norris eventually became Admiral of the Fleet.

but ordered a pipe of Wine on the quarterdeck, then calling for an ax knocked in the head, took a Mess Can and dipt it into it, then lifting the can to his head drank such a quantity that Norris could not venture to do the like. Also that to please him the Admiral ordered a Sham Engagement and that Peter took up a shott in his hand desiring the Admiral would make use of some of those, as such a game was but childrens play without them; that the Admiral replied he must beg to be excused as he could not make so free with his mistress's Subjects.

In a day or two the Old Man became greatly taken with me, saying, "Brother Englese, I have no Wife or children. Neither have I any provision from the Crown now I am become Old and no longer of Service. I have been from the Old country above 30 years, and should I return to Burgos where I was born none would know me there at this day. Without Plata I have been a fool in my time and have now nothing left but rags and grey hairs." Then giving a heavy sigh said he was grown weary of time, having been put off so many times for a passage home, where when he arrived the poor portion allowed was not worth going for, in a manner; that he had for some time followed the profession of a Barber and maker of Segares untill he had rambled hither, thinking that he would end his days after the simple mode of the Indians as he had now no more care for this world, saying he need not seek after friend or kindred knowing he had none in all the country.

The Old Man delivered himself in such plain, honest terms that I at once said to him, "Padre Nunez, know ye how to keep a faithful friend when you have found him?"

He turned his Eyes toward me and said, "Where, child, shall such grey hairs as mine find interest in falshood at this day? I am now almost 70 years of age."

"Could you be content to reside with me at my place," said I, "and fare as we do?"

"Peace and quiet, Signior," said he, "with a little morsel in friendship is the utmost of my ambition. I will go with you if you will bury me in love."

"Sware, then, only this," Said I, "that you will never betray the confidence I shall put in you as a faithful friend, and then return with us to our habitation with all my heart."

He then took me by the hand and swore by the Bd. Vn. [Blessed Virgin] to be true and faithful to me and mine, in presence of all my friends. As soon as they understood it they all gave a great shout, and thus he became Elected one of our society.

After this was settled I became uneasy to be gone, and mentioned it to my old friends who were by no means against it as they knew my reasons. I then agreed with Gaynosunto to Make me two stout Canoas for which I promised them 50 dollars, and he engaged to get them made and bring them round to us in about 3 Moons. And observing Hides among them I proposed they should Bring us such, with Cotton cloath and matts to be paid for by me, to wch. they agreed. After all was settled I proposed that I chose to return by Sea as Old Nunez could not travel well so far by land. This they all agreed to, and accordingly every thing was got ready. We left then In 4 canoes after I had been among them about a fortnight, and our Company consisted of Gattaloon as commander, Zulawana and 7 other Indians with our selves.

We took the favour of a Southwester and stood away large after we got clear of their creek. This lasted us the whole day. We then put in shore and landed on a beach. The Indians soon made up a shelter of bushes and we composed ourselves for that night. Erly at the peep of day we were off again; but the wind fell so that they took to their paddles; sometimes they stood, at other times they paddled on their knees. We went at least 7 knots an hour. In the Evening we put in to a low head land full of trees, but as the moon arose soon after, we remain'd there but just to Eat and then put out again. I now found they acted with great caution, speaking with a low voice; and thus we proceeded untill about 12 oclock, then put in again, took a Small Nap in our Canoas, and about 5 they got a fair wind again.

I now found Zulawana begant to grow a little uneasy, frequently spurring on the Indians when ever the wind fell. Upon this I wanted to know the cause. They spake in their own tongue so that I understood but little now and then. At last they informed me that as the Moon was then going to turn sides, (Viz), change, there might come on a strong wind from the North and bring rain also, saying if so we must be forced to put in and perhaps remain there some days. This was dull news, but as We were not Master or Pilots I said nothing. This evening Zulawana told me that we should see the Long Key by my place the next morning if they only went to Sleep a few hours. This we concluded on and to put out about 5 again.

But we had not composed our selves long before I felt a cool breeze from the North. I then told Nunez that I did not like our birth and proposed that we should put into a small bay on the other side the small point we were then at. This was done, and we haled up the boats. Now It came on to rain; the clouds gathered, and the Indians fell to making shelters as fast as possible. And thus we remained for three days. My poor Child shivered with the stress of the weather as he had never been exposed to the like before, altho it was not cold.

When we had eaten up all we had I took Harry with me to try to shoot something, but while we were abscent the Indians sounded a Shell for us to return. We did so, and Zulawana proposed as it was now become almost a Calm that we should push for it and away we went. The Indians began to work away with all their might. My poor boy almost famished for food. At last they all began to sing, Gattaloon shewing the example. I asked the reason, when they told me they should see my place soon. This I could not well credit but in about an hour after, one of the Indians call'd out and pointed with his finger, and I saw the point of a low spit of land which they told me was where I lived; but on my standing up I found they meant our Long Key. Upon this I told my Harry to begin our old Song as I knew that would please. This gave them all fresh spirits and in about 2 hours we came in with it, and glad I was to my very Soul even as tho I had been just that momen going to land on my native shore.

I now proposed that we should land and I would go off with my Gun with Harry while others went a stricking, giving order that they made up a good fire in the mean time. After about 2 hours we all assembled and relieved our hungry bellies with what we had procured. It was now about 3 oclock and we all Embarked again. I looked out for our Signal but saw none as they had not seen us. When we got within the bay I took up a Shell and gave my usual blast, soon after which I saw our Rag flang out which rejoyced me much. When we got within the Lagoon I heard my Messmate blow, as we all had a different mode for that purpose wherby we knew each others blast.

When we got in sight of the Landing we saw them all hands dancing and singing. Owen jumped out and swam on shore for gladness. But such greeting was there when we were all landed that I need not endevour to discribe it, only I must observe that my Betty exprest her joy by a flood of tears. But to be short, Bell told me all had been well in my abscence and that they longed for our return every hour. And now was we reinstated once more after we had been abscent above 3 weeks.

We had left three dogs at home as Harry, being a mighty dog man, he now and then got one from his friends. But as they were fresking about, Rover being glad of his return, I missed Swift and on enquiry was informed he had paid his debt to nature by the bite of a snake 5 days after our departure.

My Home was so transporting a place to me now that the old Proverb was truly fulfilled, "Home is home, &cc." Daddy Nunez said if I had told him I had been born there he might have believed it, we had so vast a body of articles about us. I introduced him to messmate Norman in the fairest light and he recieved him as a friend, gave him to know that whoever I recommended to him he made it his business to Esteem.

Our friends stay'd among us 4 days, and on the third Soroteet or the Crabcatcher was missing for a time. At last he came down the Hill with a small Basket of Flowers he had composed in the Woods. These he came and presented to our Jessy to the great surprize of us all. She recieved it, which made us wonder as much, and then they both came to me and Soroteet asked me if I would suffer him to remain among us if he chose her for a Wife. I then asked Gattaloon if it was agreeable to them all as, if so, they had my free consent—supposing the thing had been made up between him and Harry while we were at their place, as I found it soon to have been the case. All agreed and they performed the ceremony among them directly, when they took their farewell of us in as much good humour as ever.

The first thing I studied was the building two new Wigwams as our family was now increased, and this they went to work about it as I proposed that Mr. Bell and Daddy Nunez should live in one and the new married couple in the other.[2] When they were finished they took possession, and we all lived very agreeable togather as I made it now a determined rule that Bell, Nunez, my Wife and I should always mess togather. And thus we carried matters on for the future, living on after my old fashion for the remainder of my Seventeenth year without controle.[3]

Chapter 29: Eighteenth Year

Soon after the commencement of this year and about 9 oclock in the evening we heard several heavy guns fire in the offing. Norman ran up the hill but could percieve no flashes. This put us all on the wonder, but how to account for It we knew not. But Old Nunez observed that he supposed it might be Guardacostas, saying the Spaniards had several out to prevent contraband trade since the late Peace. "Peace," cried I, "that has been for many years unless there has been a fresh war." Upon this he told us that they had but just then concluded a peace with the English, for there had been another war since that he and I were concerned in—all which we knew no more of than a new born infant.[1]

2. The author has apparently forgotten that Bell had brought back an Indian wife, the twenty-five year old Aanora, some months previously.
3. Check or restraint.
1. The Seven Years War ended with the Peace of Paris in 1763. Penrose's "eighteenth year" was allegedly 1764–65.

On the 17th day of July as our people were busy making torches about 10 in the forenoon all at once we heard a Gun fired as from some Vessel nigh in shore. This was a novelty indeed, and what to think or how to act we could not tell. Away ran Harry and came down with the news, saying there was a fine Ship right off with a flag out not far from the Long Key. "What, what!" said Bell. "Come away, now, Mr. Penrose," he cried, "let us see!"

When we got up the hill she proved to be a large Sloop quite in shore with our bay. "This is new indeed," said I. "How must we act in this case, think you?"

We saw them douse their colours three times. "They want to Speak us," cried I, "and have discovered us by the great fire we have had this morning. And now how we must proceed I am sure is a mystery to me."

"Get the Glass," said Bell. When that was brought I could plainly percieve She had up a St. Georges Jack.

"They are English!" I cried, "Or if Spaniards they have discovered us at last and are come to learn what we are here upon."

"Well," said Bell, "suppose they are. If you are willing we will go off to them. It is but to know the worst, and let it come. What would they do to a couple of such forlorn fellows as we are?"

"How will you order the affair?" said I. "Suppose you and old Nunez go off to them. You can act the Spaniard to a notch." This we fixed on. Now all was in a confusion, but we told the Old Man our intention and he complyed. The Yawl was got ready and off they went without arms or any thing excep water. After some time I saw them out clear of the Lagoon. I had given Bell and Nunez their cue at their departure so that they knew how to carry the thing on. When I saw them geting along side I said to my own heart—Now is this Day big with some important Event or other, and how it may go none can devise as yet. But I determined in my mind to keep up a Spirit. I thought every hour a day while they were abscent, but in about 4 hours they returned and gave the following account of the expedition.

Bell said he found her to be a Bermudian built Sloop, had guns and looked much like a smart Privateer with a bottom as white as a Hounds tooth; and as they drew near her he plainly heard, "A Rope for the boat!" call'd with a "damme" tacked to the end of the charge. That he then Hail'd them in Spanish to which they answered in the same language. When he got or board he asked from whence they came and was answered from Gillicrankey [Killiecrankey]. This he said seem'd odd to him as knowing that place to be in his own country, but that he soon found they were English.

"Well," said I, "and what had brought them hither?"

"It is my opinion they are Pirates, as Nunez says the War is over some time."

"No, no," said he, "they are what you may call Fair Traders, and we can purchase some Flour of them if you think proper."

"Thats the mark," said I. "And how did you come on with them?"

"They know no more than the Dead but that I am a true Spaniard," said he. "I have told them we live 5 miles up the Country and that we would purchase from them if they stay'd a day or two, upon which they asked where they could water and I have directed them to the point of Long Key. So now I think I have done my part so far, mess-mate."

"Well, then," I replied, "we must in the first place get out a parcel of our Dollars and boil them in hot water and ashes to get off their blackness. But what may they ask pr barrel?"

"Only 30 pieces of 8," said he.

"O, that is but a trifle," cried I, "to us but money enough, God knows, to some folks. How many will they spare us?" said I.

"As much as we want, for seeing our Signal of Smoke as they thought was what made them bring too and fire that Gun."

"What do you really take them to be?"

"Why, they are people from North America, either Pensilvania, New York, Maryland or New England upon what they call the fair thing."

Now I observed to Bell that we should be obligated to admit our New associate Nunez into the secret of our cash as it was unavoidable.

"Well," said he, "he has sworn to you to be true, yet I think it would not be amiss to sware him again on your Bible and let him know also that we are English men as he will certainly come by the thing one way or other in the course of time, as It is my opinion he suspects it already by our talking English so much and by small hints he lets fall at times."

"Agreed," said I, "and as we have little time to spare let us both take him into the house directly, and you shall open the whole affair to him in brief as you can best do it in Spanish." We then sent for him and Bell began with him to the following effect by my advice:

"Signior Nunez, My friend and I have sent for you in order to inform you of a matter greatly to your advantage. You are Well acquainted that your coming among us was of your own free will and seeking, and that you have given my friend here your positive affirmation to be true to all his secrets. What say you to this?"

"Gentlemen," said he, "I am now but a poor Old man dependant on your generous friendship. I shall steadfastly keep my word."

"Ay, hold," said Bell. "Stop there. Are you content and free, provided we make you a Richer Man than you ever were before, to sware on this Sacred Book that you will inviolably keep secret what we shall now unfold to you? We are two plain and honest Men and have no Evil in our hearts against you or any man on this Earth."

He then said, "My friends, I trust you because I see no cause to the contrary. I am at your service." I then told him the book then before him was none other than the Holy Scriptures and tendered him his oath with a Cross laid theron, and he took it in a very serious manner. After this Bell gave him to know that we were both Englishmen, and of the Money I had discovered, &cc. As to our being English, he said that was no more than what he suspected, and in regard to every thing else we might rely on his fidelity and thanked us most cordially for admitting him a member of our interest. I then set Him, Bell and Harry to work with the Dollars, but when the Old Man came to behold our treasure, "Santa Maria!" said he in an extatic attitude, "Mucho Plato per Cierta!"—or a deal of Money for certain. "Maravillosa!"

After we had got this piece of business done, Early the next day I sent off Messmate Norman, Nunez and Harry in the Yawl with a quantity of Money, Yams, Plantains, Potatoes, Oranges, limes and Beans to deal with them after the best way he could, and to present the Officers with such of the truck as he thought best; also to purchase any thing he knew we stood most in need of; also to bring me an account of what they might have to dispose of. And away they went. I had given Harry his lesson over night.

About 12 oclock the boat returned. Bell told me he had bargained for twelve Barrels of flour, and a Goat with young to be delivered to the old plantation; A barrell of Gunpowder, Shott of different sizes, a parcell of flints, Nails, Fish hooks, Clasp knives, 2 Saws, 6 Chizzels, 2 Adzes, 5 Hatchets, 3 Axes and some other articles. He said they acted with precaution and dispatch and asked about the Guarda Costas, but that he could not learn the Captains Name. But as there were diverse articles he advised me to go off my self, saying I could pass for an Irishman and then I could please my self as I liked. Accordingly I came to that resolution and as my Lady had never been on board of any Vessel I determined to take her with me.

So Early on the morrow Off we went, My Wife, Bell and I with Owen in the Yawl, Nunez and Harry in the Old Canoa, leaving Soroteet as guard at home. When we came alongside Bell went first on board and told them that I was a Neighbour of his in partnership with him, that I was born in Ireland but had resided many years in that country, and that the Indian Woman was my Wife and the Boy my Sone. Now I had charged Owen to say that his name was Muskelly if he should be asked, but otherwise not to speak for if he did in English they would carry him away with them and he would never see me again. That was enough for him.

After we had been on board for some time I asked how they came into these parts so remote, as Gillicrankey was in Scotland. Upon this they said there might be more places of the same name, and if I did not ask too many Qustions they would tell me the fewer lies. "Well, then, faith and Soul," said I, "I know how to keep my breath to cool my pottage."

I bought of them a large Grind Stone, two Watches, two dozen of

White Beaver hats, 5 pieces of Striped linen, Thread, Osnabrigs,[2] Twine. Bell produced his small Diamonds and a little fellow who seemed to be a Doctor was put to examine them and they had them for value of about 200 dollars in truck; but we observed this part of the game was plaid off under the rose or juggled up in the Round house. We bought a pair of Good Fowling pieces, another Watch for our friend Nunez, Needles, Pins, Scissors, Razors, Raven Duck, a good Telescope as that I had was but a small inferior one of the kind, some Medecines and lancets (these messmate Bell chose out), Penknives, with 2 Large Iron Pots, Cordage, a Gander and Goose with a Drake and Duck—and well did we pay for them as they had as much melted Silver of me for them as ballanced with 18 dollars. They tickled us up also in a few Quart bottles and Phials we purchased of them. We got also a Serving Mallet,[3] two dozen of Sail Needles, three Marlin Spikes, and a Dozen of Small Blocks,[4] Several kinds of small stuff such as Ratline, Marline, Spun yarn, &cc. Bell took notice to me of some small Red framed looking glasses and It struck me directly that they would prove fit presents to our Indian Neighbours as well as a few for our own use and we bought 3 Dozen of them reasonable; a Dozen of Table Knives and Forks, and many other articles I cannot mention.

After we had got what we wanted they seem'd uneasy for our departure and we wanted their company as little. But as we were put off from them with our last purchase some Ragamuffin fellow call'd to me and said, "Paddy, what will you take for your Squaw?"—meaning my Betty. Now the Chap happened to be Red headed, and Bell stood up in the boat to return him this answer:

"Ye Reed Pow'd Brute, She is now remarking ye to be the most ill faced Deel she ever beheld with her twa Eine!" This turned the whole skit on him and they directly set up such a laugh that the fellow began to blackguard[5] by way of a foolish revenge. But on my desiring that no

2. Osnaburg: heavy cotton cloth of a coarse weave.
3. A heavy hammer for driving spikes, perhaps with its handle bound around with cord or light rope.
4. Grooved wooden pulleys mounted in a casing or block.
5. To use scurrilous language.

answer might be returned and pulling away for the shore, a Man on the roundhouse spake to us with a small trumpet and said:

"Signior Sawny, you forgot to purchase some Oatmeal. I say, your Crawthumping Wife will flog you for that when she gets you home, you Renegade!" Upon this Order was given, "Come, run up our Anchor and hoist the jibb there!" And away they went close haled with the wind at south, and we for the Shore glad enough they had pay'd us the visit and as glad of their departure as we wanted no more of their company.

After we got all our purchase home safe we became as busy as Bees in a Barrell of Tar. We lodged our Flour in the Kitchen. I put a white Hat on each of their heads which made them all as proud as Lucifer. We fell too work on making Shirts, Shifts, trowser and the like so that in a Short time we appeared all of another Regiment, and had another of those fair traders came on our coast we were yet a match for them.

We were often very merry on the occasion and my Girl was continually on the new Subject as it was a matter all new to her. She call'd the Roundhouse the little Wigwam of the Great Men; the Hold she call'd the long Kitchen Of my country folks—but she thought they were very impudent for they look'd through her Eyes when she offered to open them. Owen and Harry's remarks were how so many people could find victuals to Eate, and how they could carry those great heavy Shooters. Owen thought it strange to see them run up the shrouds and hall the ropes through the blocks. But the Drum was what struck them most—how they could possibly put so much noise into that thing with no more than those two little sticks.

Bell asked the favour when on board to have a Gun fired to see what effect it would have on the Indians, and they obliged with three. But when the first went off Harry ran to me, got behind my back, stared like a wild Cat, and shook like a leafe crying, "Ow, ow, ow!" Owen fell down and roar'd like a stuck pig; but it took a different effect on Betty. She stood motion less with her Eyes closed, but after a time when she came too she desired me to be going, for she was sure another such knock would shake her head off and split her heart.

The Women had Each a looking Glass presented to them in which they were constantly looking, and call'd them Water Stones. But the Watches became the Wonder of them all, nor could We persuade them but that there must be a spider or some small Insect within them made Owyooks of, or what we may term witches, to keep them always moving and ticking. These we were forced to preserve by informing them that none must touch them but those who had been to learn how to charm on the other side the great water. The Scheem succeeded so well that not a soul of them would touch a Watch on any persuasion whatever; and Harry with Owen, if they saw Either of us go to wind one up, would immediately withdraw to some distance. This was just as we would have it; otherwise our Watches would have been soon spoiled. But what is remarkable, my young Reese could not be brought to fear a Watch in the least, so that we were forced to make fobs to carry them about with us or hang them on high in the Evenings.

After a short time we made Leven and kneeded Cakes, and Our Ladies they were so exceeding fond of them that I could have wished we had bought more Flour. But now I found this mode to be a kind of waste and proposed to Norman that we should contrive an Oven. Now as this was a large undertaking and of moment, I began to restrict them in the Flour article untill the Oven should be built. Norman proposed making Bricks and burning Lime of Shells, but Nunez told us that we need not give our selves all that trouble, saying that we could make Yabbas, he saw well enough, and that it was but to fall too and raise us a large deep Oven of somwhat the like form, then make a good Clay hearth for it to rest on—which, when well burnt, we had no more to do than laying our Bread on that hearth well heated, and then Whelving the large yabba Oven over it, covering the Whole with a Glow of coals occasionally.

This business was put in force and they succeeded happily in the process; and then Nunez got Harry to help him build a small thatched hovel over our Bakehouse. In this Oven they baked now and then as my shipmate Norman thought best, he being Steward. We commonly had bread 3 times a Week and about halfe a pound Each. But one day as they were heating this Oven hearth I observed that it would not be long before the Oven would be useless for want of Flour as we had but a very faint view of getting more in the like manner. After this at times we used to mix Yams, Plantains, &cc with the flour by way of Ekeing it out, and produced good bread for such as we were.

Thus we lived in Love and Friendship and as we were in a lone and Solitary place we enjoyed a constant round of tranquility unmolested. We wanted for no thing meet for the use of contented Mortals and we thanked God for our blessings. Nor could we in reason repine at our lot considering all things, As how Could I possibly have imagined at my first landing on this shore that the Lord would so graciously spread me such a Splendid Table in this forlorn Wilderness? Let every Mortal on Earth look inward and reflect, then ask himself, "What do I merit, after all this disobedience?" This was truly my case as when I landed first on this Shore I was in a real State of Reprobation, accustom'd to all Vice except Murder and Theft.

Chapter 30

Now it happened on a day Harry brought home half a dozen Flamingoes, and while the Children were picking them Norman observed to me that for the Sake of Novelty he would make us a Fowl Pye, and to work went he and Betty. They baked it nicely in our fine Oven, so that now we could command Boil'd, Roasted, Baked, Stewed, Barbecued &cc as we chose it.

About the latter end of September Norman and I went out on a party for Recreation And to fish in Deep Water, taking Owen with us. Now as we got out of the Lagoon the wind came round to East and my Messmate proposed that we should make some stretches into the Offing as it was a fine turning breeze, and we did so untill we got about 5 Miles out beyond the East point of Long Key. This was the greatest distance I had been right out in my whole time. And now the Wind began to die away, but we had expected to return with a fine leading breeze.

Now I proposed to stand in again. "As you please," said he, and away we went before it for the space of half an hour when it died away and became stark calm. We now found a small current running to the Westward. "How now?" said I. "Here we are, but to get back is the question."

"We must take to our oars," said he.

"And a pretty pull we shall have," I replied. "We shall drive a league below the Key before we can get in again." But too it we went, and in about half an hour got within the currents way and then concluded to fall to fishing when the water should shoal. But while we were thus chatting We observed a White Ball on the Surface of the Sea with somthing playing round it. In a short time after it bounced above the water to the height of 3 feet or more. We lay on our Oars for a time to see the curiosity and saw the thing repeated often. What it could be we knew not, But concluded to row gently toward it. When we had got within about 30 yards we could discern it to be that sort of Fish called the Hedg Hog or Globfish. This fish has the power of blowing its self up so as to become round like a ball, being armed at all points with long and sharp darts. Now round this fish were gathered three or four Dolphins who would every now and then strike it out of the Water with their tails. When the Globfish fell back to the Surface it would paddle away with its under finn to some distance very swiftly and then the game renewed. Thus they went on untill Bell chanced to make too great a movement with his Oar when it sank at once like a stone, so that we concluded it to be real sport intended, seeing the Globfish could disengage itself from the Dolphins at pleasure. Now this lead me to a confutation of what many Seamen hold, (Viz) that a Dolphin is never seen within Soundings, but I am certain to the contrary as at this time we had not above 18 fathom of Water and over patches of Rocks.

A little after this we fell to fishing in about 12 fathoms and soon had fish round us of many kinds, among which were the largest Amber Fish we had ever beheld. Now as we were very busy at our sport, now and then there would follow up the fish on our hooks a Fish such as we had never beheld in our lives before, but as he did not shew himself high enough to give us his true shape I shall give the best discript I can. It appeared as Black as a Coffin when covered with velvet, with a monstrous lofty finn on the back runing its whole length. On the highest part of this finn right over the shoulders was a long kind of whip about 16 inches long. The upper fork of the tail had the same kind of tag to it, and these he continually kept playing. The whole fish might be about 4 feet in length. It seem'd to be very active among the other fish, driving every here and there and seem'd to be very voracious, yet it would not touch our bait nor could we percieve that it offered to snap at the other fish. I could have been glad to have caught him as I am fully persuaded these Fish are rare to be seen.

Soon after a Small Cats paw came in from Seaward and we got up our Killick, sat our Sail and stood in for the bay with the wind increasing, so that we soon arrived with our cargoe of fish. Among the fish were two Sorts deserving discription; they are Called Morays. They are commonly about 4 feet long or so from the head to the tail, which end in a compleat point. They are shaped like to a Sword, having fins runing the whole length above and below. This fish is flatted and not round as an Eele but in other things acts like it, twisting itself in various knots, and bites sharply. One Sort is Green as a leek but the other is so finely mottled with White, Black and Yellow that the Leopards Skin cannot be compared with it for beauty.

By this time we had gotten several young Fowls about us and Old Nan the Goat had brought forth two Sons. They gave us our hands full of trouble at times, being so very mischievous that we were forced to keep a sharp lookout over what linen we possessed of, for when ever they could come at it they would Chew and Nibble it to a Rag presently. At last they found way to my poor Store of Paper and as fair traders began to treat themselves with it. Now as It was with great difficulty I could keep the worm from it also, I determined we should take some new method to ward off the impending danger. Now as we could all see the great necessity, so all joyned willingly to prevent the danger. Bell finding my Wattleing Work so usefull took a resolution of making a sort of Hovel for our Goats and Fowls, And we all went to work with Spirit. This business took us up Six week before all was finished to our minds.

This Work we carried on thus. It was divided into 4 apartments, one for the Goats with its own door; another for the Fowls so that they could never get out in the Morning without permission; One for the Dogs free of access to them; the 4th was our Store Room three times the Size of the others and was alloted for our dry Wood. As for our Gun Powder we kept that a good distance off under a cavern of the Rocks in the Earth.

I told Bell to build a kind of fence round the side of the stream of Water for our Geese and Ducks so contrived that they could with ease play in it without wandering too far away, with a small house in one corner of the fence. And by the time the whole was compleated it formed a kind of Farmers dwelling; and by this method we preserved our live stock from the Tigers or Wild cats, but those Gentry seldome troubled us now. And many Mornings have I been highly delighted with the Crowing of the Cock and innocent noises of the Goats, Geese and Ducks calling the boy to give them their daily sustenance.

Some short time after this and about 12 oclock in the day one of our Dogs took off up the hill full speed. Upon this Bell turned out with his Gun. I told him not to venture too far from home but away ran Harry after him with his. They did not return in less than two hours. When they came in I told Bell that I thought them foolhardy going off with only Small Shott. They said they had followed the dogs for three miles as they were sure they had scent of a Deer by dung they found, and that on their return they had found a Bees nest in an old tree full of Combs. I enquired how far off it might be. They told me not above a mile. "Well," said I, "shall we contrive to take it?" My messmate said the Evening would be the best time for the purpose. "Then there let it remain," cried I, "for me, I shall not venture my Carcase on such an errand at such a time."

"Well," said Harry, "if Mr. Norman will go with me I will venture."

Bell came to a resolution and off they went in the Evening with Fire and Powder and each a Gun and Mascheet. I was in pain the whole time for them but in about two hours they returned Victorious with a fine parcell of Combs. I asked them how they went to work and they told me they first made up a good fire, then they Suffocated them with a Squib.[1] When they were all at home I soon found the Women knew better how to do with the Honey than to make Bread.

Now as I happened to be out very Erly on the morrow I percieved a large Smoke to blow over our Clift. Bless me, thinks I, what can this mean? I called out the rest and they all seem'd much alarm'd. "Now," said I, "you certainly left fire in the Woods last night and we shall be ruined if the winds keep southerly." We then went up and found it to be the case. The fire was spread far and wide and a dreadful appearance. "Now," said I, "you have found out a most infallible method to rid us of Tiger fears."

"Weel," said Bell, "and so best."

"Ay, but now you must be at a loss for fewel unless you go farther afield for it," said I.

"O," said Harry, "it will not come down below to us." And I found it so in reallity, as it left off when it came to the Brow of the Hill, but the Smoke continued above 3 days. When I found the whole was over We took a Walk and found all the Traps ruined. Every thing was a devastated so that the place for two miles back and wide was become quite naked and bare. Yet I must needs own that I was not much grieved as I was now certain the harbour was broke for those rapacious Beasts. But we lost on the other hand as it was very handy on several accounts; besides the beauty of the place was all gone quite in a Regard to prospect. This affair happened about the 27 of December so that we had a rare bonfire to keep Christmass with.

Nothing happen'd worth notice for some time after this but we became pestered with Hawks after our Chicken so that the boys were fully employed. The Cat made bold also with a Chick or two, but by the Childrens tieing him up and giving him a trimming with a bunch

1. In British usage any sort of firecracker; also a syringe or squirt. Here probably a tube or other device for directing the smoke.

of feathers round his neck he left off the game. The Hawks we put in dread by fixing up a pole with a cross at the top to which he hung the dead Hawks we had shott. No sooner had we found out this remedy than we became a new trobbled with a sort of large Snake which swallowed them Whole, but Owen and Harry often shott them and his Uncle and he used to roast and Eate them and at last tempted Bell and Daddy Nunez to do the like.

One day as I happened to enter our dwelling and casting my Eyes on our Child America as she lay sleeping on a few Plantain leaves I saw a monstrous Centipeed extended athwart her throat. The sight startled me much as knowing should it Sting the Infant in that tender part the agony it would throw her into might prove mortal. Now dreading least its feet by a movement might awaken her, and she might perhaps put her hand up to it, by which means it would either sting her hand or her throat, I clapt my hand gently down by it and with one suddain jerk cast it clear of her, when I killed it and put it in a bottle of Brandy we kept for the purpose, as knowing it to be the best antidote against ye Poison by rubbing the part injured with it—it never failing to asuage the anguish or reduce the Swelling. These Insects are of a Yellow brown colour and their general size from 4 to 8 inches in length, and in breadth scarce an Inch. They are scaled on the back as in joynts with a pair of Forceps or pinchers at the tail, and when angry Erect them in a curve forward emitting an enormous quality through small appertures into the wound which turns the injured part quite livid and brings on a most excruciating torment which last sometimes three or four hours.

I remember on a day as I was talking to Betty and she leaning with her Cheek against a rock side I percieved a large Scorpion close by her face, wherupon I withdrew and called her aside. When I got her from the place I shewed it to her. We then took one of our phials with some of the Brandy out of the other bottle, and Bell by an artful twitch got in into the phial. But it was not in long eere it emitted a drop of some liquid, and he getting his watch we stood by it for a space of 15 Minutes before the Spirit overcame it so that we could say it was quite defunct.

The Scorpions are not large as we never saw one above 4 inches in length, most of them being 2½ or 3 inches. They are shaped in the fore part somewhat resembling a lobster having Claws, but differ much abaft as I may say, having a tail of several joynts in the end of which is inserted a hook. This they use after the same manner with the Centipeed. They are of a pale dirty yellow and carry their young on their backs, and our Indians say that if any of their young should chance to come before them they will at once devour them. Harry one day shewed me one and told me that I should see him make it kill it self. He made a circle of burning Coals round it, and the Scorpion endevoured to escape for a time; at length finding it impracticable began to turn up its Sting and in a few minutes wounded itself to death. This Insect as well as the Centipeed frequents all kinds of damp and obscure places and never voluntarily approaches the light of the Day or Sunshine.

I shall in this place take notice of the Spiders, but as to give a discript of the many sorts would be too tedious; yet as I think mentioning the characters of a few may not be disagreeable I shall begin with that of the greatest magnitude, and I can declare of a truth I have seen some which would spread the full extent of a mans finger and thumb when expanded. These are frequent and make webs exceeding strong, but they are not venomous altho they have sharp black teeth and bite if molested. They are seen at times with a large and round white Belly as may be judged about the Size of an half Dollar, but this is none other than a bag in which they carry about their young. This bag they can dismiss at its propper season, and then they lodge it against some shelve from which the young come forth at their appointed time.

There is another sort which I gave the name of the tiger to. It has no settled place of abode nor does it ever spin any Web but keeps on a constant cruise after the Flies. It is striped black and white, and nothing can exceed the craft of this Insect when lying in wait for its prey. You shall see them on the side of a tree, rock or the like in any place where flies frequent. Here he lurks as asleep, but as soon as any flie chances to fix within the distance of two feet or so of him he

directly with one suddain motion of his body faces about in a trice, and
with his short legs advances slowly toward him. But if the flie chance
to move his position in the least he then in an instant points the same
way and squats perdue,[2] then begins again to advance exceeding slow
untill such time he comes within the distance of about 8 inches when
he jumps at once on the poor victim and devours him.

Another kind, not large, which Bell call'd Red poops having their
after part as red as Vermillion—these Gentry keep in corners and the
like. They are continually spining threads and runing up and down
them. If chance they espie an object such as a grub or the like they
drop down by a thread and give it a gentle touch which instantly
kills, when they descend again and by fixing more lines to it they
draw the body up by degrees, hand over hand as one of our Jacks
would draw a buckket of tar up into the Main top of a Vessel. We
found it necessary to kill them when ever they chose to visit our Cave
as they would at times drop down and give us one of their favourable
touches, which instantly gave the patient such an inflamatory burning
that he would be forced to run to the first oil he could come at, or
the phial of Insects which laid the poison in a few minutes.

But we found at times a kind of large Spider back in the up land
which highly deserves a discription. It is Black and White. They
frequen banks which face the rising Sun in which they have cells.
Now on a day as I was out with my Gun and Harry and Owen with
me, the boy bid me look on the Bank and see the Great Spiders, how
they stopt their holes. This made Harry call to me for to halt, saying
that if I went on slowly I should see a fine thing and what I loved
(meaning a great curiosity). And soon after I saw several of those
Spiders run into their holes and slap too one of their doors after them.
On this I drew out my knife and picked at one of them and to my great
surprize found it to work too and fro as on hinges. It was composed of
a thick substance of Web and of a circular form. After I had satisfied
my curiosity thus far I told them we would all three withdraw to watch

2. Hidden, concealed.

their motions, and after some time we could see one neighbour open his door half way, then another, and so on untill many threw them quite back and came forth. But now as we were intent on viewing this wonder in nature Mr. Rover espying them, he soon drove the whole town to close quarters and so spoiled our farther interest of observation for that time.

Now it happened as Daddy Nunez was out on the hill, which was usually his morning walk, he came down and said he thought he percieved some small canoas at a distance to the westward. Upon this I took my new Glass and went up with Norman. We soon percieved two Canoas coming. "Now," said I, "these are our new boats I will lay any wager, so let us prepare some kind of a repast for them against they come in." In about an hour they came round the Key and I could then plainly percieve 10 people in them. "Get our boat ready," said I. "Norman, you and I will go down and meet them," so off we went and met them in the bay.

When we got within hail I called and they answered "Amegos" or friends. We then put off before them up the lagoon and they all came on shore—Gattaloon, Gaynasunto and 8 other Indians who most of them had been here at our place before. We all welcomed them after our wanted fashion and Gattaloon told me those were my two Canoas they had made for my use. They brought us 4 Beef hides, Matting, Cotton pieces for our Women, some Cocoas and Coffee seeds and other things. The Canoas were 18 feet long and 2½ feet by the beam, as I may term it, and would carry 8 Men each with ease. I presented Each of them with a small Looking Glass and some of our remaining Dutch Cloth, but it was of little value being much injured by the moth and time. Bell gave 50 dollars into the hands of Gattaloon, desiring they would never discover the means of their obtaining them among the Spaniards unless they reported they found them as we had done. All this they promised to observe strictly and we doubted not their integrity, having had the experience of their fidellity for such a length of time.

Gattaloon asked Daddy Nunez how he liked his scituation and the

Old Man told him he had not known so much ease and content for many years past. He then enquired the same of Soroteet. His answer was that he thought the Agago, or as they translated it The Killing Spirit, had never found the way to our place or had never heard of it, saying could they not see the Manoluvy or Manolubee was always among us when ever they came by the Laughing in our faces at all times. (By this word they mean a general amity or concord among us.)

In about three days and after our little business was settled they took their leave to return home over land, having brought Arms with them for that purpose, saying on their departure there was a Vessel cast away about half a days paddling from their place more to the West. We asked them of what People but they could not give us that satisfaction, saying they saw none of the men dead or alive and that she was all in pieces, had a white bottom, one Mast and some great Guns—from which we judged it might perhaps be our Fair Trader as the discription tallied with her.

Chapter 31: Nineteenth Year

We had nothing remarkable from the time the Indians left us, which was about the latter end of March. But some few days after they were gone Harry told me that he had got a great secret from Soroteet to tell me. "What may that be?" said I. He told me that Gattaloon had informed Soroteet when last here that we were discovered or known to be here by the Spaniards. "Ay, ay!" cried I and directly call'd Norman. When he came, "Now begin," I said to Harry, "and what ever you have learnt, Speak it, let it be what it may

Either good or bad." For I must confess it discomposed me at first, but reflecting again that it was a thing which must come to their knowledge one day or other, I became more calm again.

And he went on, saying that Gattaloon told Soroteet the affair because he knew he could talk neither Spanish or English, and that the affair could not well be devulged to me while they were among us least we should take it ill. We might attribute the discovery to their trechery but desired we would not entertain so hard a thought of them, as those who were now dead had pledged their hearts with us. That they knew not by what means we were discovered but that a Couple of Spaniards from Maricaibo had been lately among them and asked If there were not two English Men married among their people and lived somwhere along the Shore to the Northward. That finding we were known to be here they thought it a folly to deny that they knew nothing of us, but had confessed that they knew of a poor man who had told them he had been driven on shore in a boat alone; but that I had been many long Moons there before they had found me out, and recited the circumstance of one of their Canoas being driven on shore where I resided, by which means I obtained a Wife. That I was a good man and liked to live there with my Indian family, but that I should have traveled to find out some Spaniards had I not been informed they would send me to the Mines as being an Enemy at that time; but that I was so far from being an Enemy to Mankind that I had since my landing there give my best assistance to two or three distressed Spanish Vessels, and that they had heard me often say could I but be confirmed in one thing—which was that they would not injure me—I could die in a true state of satisfaction. That in regard to the other Man who lived with me, he had been cast away long since and came among them, but hearing of me he had traveled to find me out and had got one of their Girls for a Wife also. That we lived by fishing and were the most inoffensive Men that could live.

"Well," said one of them who was an old Man called Perez, "when you see them again you must inform them that they need not be in any manner of dread or fear, as their condition is not to be envied; and if they are content to be voluntary Anchorets [anchorites] none will make it their business to molest or disturb them. But they are not Bon Catholicks, we suppose." But they told them we were, that we Prayed to the book and Cross often, to which they answered, "Star bon."[1] They enquired how far it was from where they lived and they told them above 7 days distance. And thus their Enquiry ended.

We both thanked them for their good conduct in our hearts. And how or by what means they came by the knowledge we knew not unless by some of the fair traders who might have been wrecked or from Old Horgans people. However, we now became intirely easy in our minds as thinking we had made a happy discovery, knowing by the tenour of the Spaniards discourse they would not give themselves the trouble to seek us out Because we were of no consiquence to them Either for good or ill.

One day as Daddy Nunez and Harry came in from fishing they brought home in the Canoa from the Bird Key a part of some Animal Substance in long round shapes of a brown hue Exceeding smooth and of a consistancy like unto soft grissle. I asked Harry what it was and he gave me the following discription which I thought odd enough. The Old Man kept continually chattering at the same time to Bell in Spanish, but the matter was as Harry said. He got out of the canoa and was wading among the Rocks after one of those kind of fish called a Cuckold with his Mascheet in his hand, And all of a suddain he felt something clasp him round his legs clinging very fast. On looking down he saw a monstrous Lancksa, as he called it; that he directly call'd out to Nunez to come to his assistance, which he did; and by cutting with his knife and the Mascheet togather he got free, and that he had brought part of it home to shew it to us and would then roast and Eate it, which he did. But of the discription He gives of this Being it is quite romantick to me. However, as I have not beheld the like with mine own Eyes hithertoo I must beg the kind Reader to rest satisfied with Mr. Harry's account of it.

1. I.e., *"Está bien,"* that is good.

(Viz), He tells me that they are not very frequent, Especially this grand Sort, but there are three sorts of a less magnitude. That they are always found adhering to the side of a Rock or huge Stone in some place where there may be an Eddy or current of Water; that they expand forth several Arms which are continually playing about in the water and that in the End of Each of those Arms is a kind of mouth, as he expresses it, which catches all kinds of little living things, meaning Marine insects. That these arms convey what they catch into one great mouth it has in the centre of its body, but that it has no Eyes nor can it remove from the place it is fixed on. But should any part of it be torn or cut away, in that case the part so moved or seperated will soon cement itself to some other place and become a New Lancksa and act exactly in all things like the old mother it came from. That they will lay hold on every thing they can reach, and provided the Object prove too large for them to take in, in that case they suck the substance out of it and then let the husk or skin drop. All this story appeared wonderous to me, and I must leave it to the Learned to determine of what class it may belong to unless it may be that being called a Polypus.

Now I am on this Subject I must remark another kind which it is my belief may belong to the same tribe of Marine animals. These we saw when Somer and I were once out to the Westward in a place among Rocks and even under water. Through several holes in the side of those Rocks about 4 feet down seemed to grow small tufts of flowers Resembling in shape our Polyanthus but of a pale rose colour now and then tinged with yellow. But on my runing down a Paddle to shove a bunch of them off they would instantaniously retire into the Rock. This drew on a wonder in us, and finding by repeated trials that it evaded all our art, Somer took upon him to detach one of them which projected forth from an angular corner with an Ax. And to that end he got overboard and knocked the piece off, when he put it in my hand and came in again; then seating himself began to beat it to pieces and in a small cell we found a substance like to a thin membranous substance. But those part which had expanded like so many flowers were become quite contracted, yet there seem'd to be some small palpitation left shewing life remaining. I judged the Violence of his strokes had been the cause of its death as knowing full well it must be some kind of animal being or other, by others we had caused to retire now became display'd afresh; but on our offering to touch them they incontinently withdrew. This natural curiosity would ever have escaped my memory had not this adventure of Harry's came on at this time to revive it.

And now I am on the Sensative subject I shall remark some other of a Terrestrial kind. (Viz) there is a kind of long thin Grass growing in these Regions which, if you should only cast or wave a hand or even a small Switch over it, it instantly falls down flat altho not touched or approached nigher than a foot. There is also a Species of the Yam which when you find it sprang above the ground, should you then fix a stick or the like in any point of direction within a distance of 3 feet, it will in a short time find its way to it. But should you remove the stick a short time before it had reached it, and shift it to the other side or any one point of the Compass it will soon find the way round and then begin to climb up it.

There is to be found on the Seabeach a kind of Vine with a red stem about the thickness of a Goose quill with small leaves growing in pairs laterally and at the distance of two feet from each pair. But what makes the thing most remarkable is when it has extended its stemes as from one centre like to a Star to the distance of perhaps 10 or 12 feet, It there takes root in the sand and becomes a fresh Centre proceeding in like manner; so that in some places the shore will be spread with them for 50 yards and all from one common Centre. And so strongly do these red Tendrils hold in the sand that on taking hold of one of them you shall find them tought or turgid like any Ships stern fast. There are some kinds of Flowers also which have the quality of displaying their bloom after the Sun is set and keep so the whole Night through untill the day comes on, when they all close again. On the contrary, others open with the Rising Sun and close again as it sets in the Evening.

It may not be derogatory to this Subject if I should mention a thing which all the Indians hold to be a real fact, but this I do not affirm as to my own knowledge. But they have advanced to me That there is one kind of Deer who have Ears in their Feet by which means they know when an enemy is approaching even at a miles distance or much farther. And once when walking in the Woods Harry picked up the foreleg bone of one of those animals, and shewing me a gruve in the Shin part proceeding from the parting of the hoof, told me that was the channel by which those Animals heard to such a great distance. But I rather concluded that some Nerve of a very subtile sensation had lain in that hollow gruve which gave the creture such a distant warning of danger.

Similarity: There grows a kind of small tree here which bears a large Fruit shaped somthing like a Bell Pear but much larger and flat on one side, full of soft thorney points. It is of a dark green inclining to a purple toward the large End, which is of a full purple. Its pulp is white, spongey, and very full of juice with many purple seed within it. Its leaves are large and hang in an ample form. Now what is a thing much to be admired is a Small Bird who feeds on the seed of it. This Bird is in size like to our English Green finch and of that kind of Green. Its Bill resembles the Parrot. And as the fruit varies or graduates from the Green to the Purple so changes the bird in its hue exactly, from its tail to the neck and head which terminates in the purple so that when the Bird is actually on the limbs or fruit you can hardly know unless it should move or shift its place.

How manyfold are the Wonders of our Divine Creator when our Eyes behold these things. Should we not say: "In the Majesty of Thy Wisdom, O Lord, hast Thou created them to the improvement of our understanding, and to lead us step by step to a proper Idea of Thy Omnipotence"? And how thankful ought I to be thus to have so much leasure to Contemplate on them; and, as I have said, Step by Step may they bring me and all mankind to a proper sense of my own state And their own so that in the End we may all become worthy members of his divine abode through the Merits of Him who descended from whence Eternal happiness flows.

Chapter 32

About the 10 day of August Mrs. Harry brought forth a Girl and they gave her the name of Betty as a compliment to my Wife. And Harry observed on the Occasion that Soroteet had not hithertoo been renamed as was customary with us when any Indian joyn'd our family. I then turned to my friend Norman and told him to stand Godfather, and he thought proper to Call him Rory or Roderick. And from this time we heard no other Sound for two or three days from Harry, Owen and the other Children than "Rory, Rory, Rory,"—so much would any simple novelty play on their innocent minds, arising from their contracted mode of life and never being enlarged by a sight of this great worlds Hurry and Varieties.

At times Mr. Harry would amuse himself with learning the Boys to Swim by taking them on his back in the lagoon. Now it so fell out that as He and Mr. Rory were down at the Water with the Children at this sport, Norman, Nunez and my self looking on with our pipes smoking, Daddy Nunez cried out, "Un tiberoon!" or a Shark. This soon made them all quit the water with surprize as we never had seen one so far up before. But the Indians got bait and soon caught her.

This Shark was not above six foot long, yet she had 8 young ones which would not leave her so that they were all taken. These young gentry altho they were not more than 8 or 9 inches in length yet were so strong that it was a great difficulty to hold one of them in a Mans hand with a Strong gripe. It is well known the Shark brings forth her Young after the manner of Quadrupeds, but there is a great mistake among those who think her young on any suddain danger run into her mouth or down her throat, when the very Contrary is the truth. For on any approaching danger they All secreet them selves in the Womb; and this we had the fairest opportunity of observing as the thing was transacted to our satisfaction before our eyes.

The Indians brought with them when last here a few Pods of some exceeding large Beans of a full brown colour, having but two in each pod. These Beans or Kernels are about the size of a Dollar and of an Excellent virtue for all complaints of the Bowels. As they report, the Mode of using them is to scrape a part of the Kernel into warm water or Stew them, and so great is their Efficasy that the quantity of 3 or 4 grains Will relieve the most racking cholic immediately. This we have experienced now and then, as occasionally required. I have ordered a few of them to be planted that we never need be without them in future.

One day Harry and Rory brought home with them a Hawks bill Tortoise weighing about 30 pounds, of Whose Shell our artificers in Europe make great use in divers kinds of Ornaments. Yet this kind of Tortoise is not very agreeable to the taste, nor do we eate them. And as this gives me an opportunity to mention more on the Subject I shall take notice that there are 4 or 5 sorts of this Animal; nay, I might say with certainty 7 Sorts great and Small.

(Viz) in the first place, Loggerhead Tortoise. This kind is most frequent on our coast and are so large that many of them run to 400 weight. They have a very round back and are rather longer in propor-tion than the other kinds, but there is no beauty in the Shell. The Second Sort are called Trunck Tortoise as they resemble the form of our old Coffers, being ridged. They grow big and rank and are not very agreeable to the taste. The third I may term the Hawks bill as their beek resembles the beek of that Bird. Now the fourth is what they call the Green Tortoise and most coveted as their flesh exceeds all others in taste. These are known to grow to the size of 300 weight also. The fifth kind are such as never go into Salt Water but frequent Ponds and muddy places. These are of a most odious appearance to any Stranger. I have seen them of above 50 weight, and when one of them finds himself Environed by Enimies so that he can not make his

Escape he will fight with a hissing noise; and should he once fix his jaws on any object he will never quit it without bringing off the piece. They are black, rough, and have bright Eyes with circles of Red so that they cut a most formidable appearance; yet the meat of these animals stewed is very rich and agreeable to the pallate.

The Sixth Kind are of a diminitive size and frequent ponds also, but never grow to any great bulk and are of no Estimation except for the beauty of their back shell which is generally Either Yellow bordered with Black, Olive bordered with Either Yellow or Red. The seventh sort never frequent the water but keep up in the woods and never grow to any great size, seldom above 3 pounds. At a certain season of the Year they retire below the Surface of the Earth where they will remain for the Space of three months without any Sustenance.

All these several kinds are Oviparous, and there is one peculiarity in these odd beings which is they can and do retain life for many hours after the head is seperated from the body. But in regard to the Sort I was just mentioning, nothing was ever more true than that we have known A body to survive twelve days after the Head was taken off and the body become putrid. I well remember a circumstance of the Head of one of the Loggerhead tortoises being cut off about 10 in the Morning and thrown away by the head of the Lagoon. Yet poor Eva, now dead and Gone, happening to take it up on the next day in the Evening, and she wantonly plac'd her finger within the Mouth It at once fastned on her finger wherupon she began to run and whoop at no small rate; but on Harry's thrusting a knife between she got released.

We had not explored our back territories since the accident of the Fire, but Messmate Norman proposed that he and Harry should make an Excurtion as he had a mind to take a tour for a day and for that purpose they equipped themselves with Arms, amunition And provision. Accordingly, Erly on a Morning they took into the Woods, or rather Barrens; three Dogs went with them. They did not Return untill about 6 in the Evening, and to my great wonder they brought home with them 2 Small Black Pigs but had lost one of the Dogs. They told the following story—

That on their first setting out they found all the underwood burnt for the distance of a mile or more, and as Harry stood Pilot he had him to the place where we found those huge bones. That they then Mounted the bank and proceeded South about half a mile when they came to a Wood of fine tall trees. That there they seated themselves and refreshed, but that they did not go much farther before they came to a great Savannah which lay low, and that they saw here and there a single tree growing. But on their going into this Savannah they percived some small black cretures Runing swiftly through the Grass, But that they kept their Course directly for a large tree at the distance of two hundred yards or so. Now as they drew nigh to that tree Bell plainly discovered two or three of the same animals and taking sight shot one so as to cripple it, but that on their coming up to it he found it to be A Young Pig about 7 Weeks old, as he judged. No sooner did he take hold of it than it began to cry lustily, soon after which he says they plainly heard the gruntings of Hogs as when they are enraged, with a great rushing through the grass, on which Harry immediately began to climb the tree, desiring him to follow his example. But before he could get his arm round it a huge Brown Boar came furiously on him.

What to do he could not at first determine, but got on the other side and began to load as fast as he possibly could, keeping his Eye steadfastly on him and dodging round now and then. The beast would make directly at him, bouncing at a great rate and chamfering his long tusks with his mouth all of a white foam. But now as he was in this horrid scituation and just making ready to fire at him, Harry discharged his piece from the tree and took him directly in the Ear which at once laid him motionless, and gave him an instant deliverance. That Harry then Came down and loaded afresh, saying he must follow him and he did so as Harry had percieved others from his scituation. Soon after, they came in view of the female with severall young ones, and that they both fired on them, when Bell killed another of the young. The old Sow and the rest took away through the grass with the greatest Expidition but that they declined the persuit. They then returned to the tree and took a Survey of the old Senior and Bell said he had never beheld any Boar of such a magnitude in his life. His tusks were at least 8 inches in length, and that about the head and shoulders he was of a monstrous thickness. This august animal let out the Entrails of one of the Dogs in a moment, by whose death Messmate Bell preserved his own life perhaps, as by that means he gained time.

We Sent off Harry and Rory the next day to bring home a part of the Boar togather with his tusks, but they returned with no more than the tusks as they found the carcase almost devoured by the tigers or those of their own species, which was what we judged, as the Indians say they will do so constantly. They also advance that in case a Wild Hog becomes wounded, if he can but get away he seeks out a kind of tree and then fretting its bark with his teeth and tusks causes its sap to flow, with which he by rubbing against anoints his wound and Recovers again. They told me it was their opinion they were Very numerous in that quarter by the dung they saw, and that they judged they found food in that Savannah by routing in the ground and eating a kind of long nut which fell from some of the Tall trees resembling our Acorns. Whatever could be the cause I know not, but during the whole time of my residing in this place I never saw one of those Animals in our neighbourhood, but perhaps the food they are most fond of grows in parts more retired from the shore. Bell says that he thought that Boar did not weigh less than 200 Weight. As for the two young ones they brought home, we barbicued them and found them delicious.

The next piece of business we went upon was to make Masts and Sails for our new Canoas, but in regard to their Sails we were forced to be sparing in our Canvas as we had no great stock of yt. article. And as we had not been once out in them from the time they first came, we concluded to make a small voyage in them to the Northeastward; and accordingly Bell and I with Owen on a morning put out of the Lagoon in one of them which Bell Distinguished by the name of "Jannet," and the other which I called the "Komaloot" was manned by Daddy Nunez and our Rory. We stood away for the Old Plantation where I visited My old Grounds, having not been there for a long time except on the Shore when we brougt away the goods we purchased of the Gillicrankey man. I went into my old Cave, from thence to the part which I had set fire to so long ago; but all was now Become a new Forest of young Saplings and bushes. Yet every here and there were to be found abundance of those kinds of things running rank and luxurious which had proceeded from the original plantings, as we seldom visited the place for such truck because most of the same articles now grow within our own vicinity. But as we were on the return, Bell having been Rambling in the bushes, he call'd to me to come to him. When I got on the spot he shewed me one of the most noble Calabash trees I had ever beheld, And as it is a tree of a very peculiar growth I shall describe it.

Its height and size resembles much the Codling Tree[1] but the limbs, or rather the superior branches, grow Horizontally from the tree very streight and have but few small leaves which grow in pairs opposite to each other, with a pair at the extreamity of each bough or branch. But its Fruit is Most to be remarked. They grow to the magnitude of a small Bombshell, are of a pale green and full of snow white pith. Contrary to most other kinds, you shall see one protrude from the very extreamity of a limb so that by means of its great weight the bough shall bend down to the Ground in, or on, another limb. They may be seen to push out from the side, sometimes in a small Crevice between two limbs by which means they become distorted as having been cramped in their growth. Nevertheless, what ever kind of obstructions they may meet with does not deminish them much in quantity, as they will push their protuberance wherever they have vent. Somtimes you shall see one or more push out not one foot above the root of the tree; and as the stem of the fruit is so short and slender it appears to the Stranger that they are excrescences of the Fungus kind rather than its fruit.

After we had been there about an hour and I had shewn my two friends all about my first habitation, we took boat again and proceeded to old Towers Field, and there landing went to dinner, after which Bell took Up his Gun and away he went with Owen and Rory, who

1. One of several varieties of apple tree bearing elongated fruit.

was but newly acquainted with firearms. Owen must needs have my piece also with him. When they were gone I took Daddy Nunez with me to Shew him the large Stone I had discovered among the Woods. On our Arrival I asked his opinion concerning it and he told me that it Was his opinion the first adventurers, Either Columbus or those who Succeeded him, had erected it in that place as a memorial. This made me smile, saying, "I pray, Daddy, how many men do you think it would require to raise this Stone provided there may not be much of it below the surface of the Earth?" He answered 1,000. "And do you think that such a number of your Countrymen were ever on this spot at that erly period?" said I. His answer was that the Indian Natives In those days perhaps assisted them, as by divine appointment the country being revealed to them that they might have the honour of first preaching the Gospel among those Savages. I now began to draw in my horns as I did not chuse to contradict the old gentleman. He had never given me any cause of contention; therfore I let him feed on his own bigotry as it suited with his own opinion.

When we got back to the Water side we observed our people to fire and run to and fro much out on a point toward the Whale Point. What they could be after we could not think, but in about an hour they returned, when Bell reported they had surprized three Seals asleep between some rocks and that Owen had shott one of them with my piece, but as he had but slightly wounded it the animal had escaped them notwithstanding they did their best to get the seaside of him and pelted him with stones. "O," said Nunez, "if you had but given him a small stroke over the nose with the but of your piece it would have been over with him soon."

We now began to think of our return and put off accordingly, but just as I was Steping into the Canoa I picked up a small kind of a Cockkle Shell of a fine Crimson colour, from the bottom of which and on the inside grew up a beautiful Branch of White Coral of a texture smooth as glass and resembling the horns of a Stag and in length about 4 inches. At the extream points were small Studs resembling so many Stars of a bright blue. "Now," said I to Bell, "this is a real curiosity and would fetch a good price were it exhibited on some shew

box in a London Shop Window." I have it by me among abundance
of other articles yet. We got home safe without any thing more occur-
ring at that time and found all well.

We had not been home long before I observed Mr. Harry struting
about at a distance with an air of great importance dressed up in A
clean shirt of mine, my old Tiger jacket, a Bever hat, and a Mascheet
by his side and mimicking the air of a Spaniard, the Girls all tittering.
"Look," said I to Bell, "I wonder what new whim has Entered the
head of My Lord Henry today." On this I call'd to him and he came
toward us with an air of great dignity to be sure.

Bell held forth his hand to him With reverence but he put his
hands on his hips and with one foot advanced said, "Me un grande
Cabalero." Upon this Daddy Nunez fell in a hearty fit of laughter.

"Come, come," said I, "this is enough for once, Harry. You are a
great Don today, and tomorrow you will be no more than my poor
Indian Brother I suppose, unless that your fit of prodigality continues."

"Ha," said he, "I am a rich man now as well as your self and I will
buy me a Watch talker, too, When Gillarandy comes here again."

"You fool," said I, "leave off Your nonsense. I am tired of it." On
this he went off and soon came back with his two hands full of
Doubloons, the slight of which Surprized both Bell and me. "Where
got you those?" I cried.

"In the Dead mans hole," said he, "in the Old Dead Mans hole
along side."

"And how came you to find it out after we had examined the place
so well, and after such a length of time?"

"Come see," said he. So off We all went and he ran before us, and
getting there first held up a large kind of Cup to us. When Bell took
it into his hands there might remain about 20 more Doubloons in its
bottom, and on our Scraping the Vessel we found it to be pure Gold
weighing about 20 or 22 ounces. Now the place being left so long
exposed to many Succeeding heavy rains was what brought this to
light. He said that as he chanced to be there picking a few limes curiosity lead him to take a view of the place and that he saw the brim of

the Vessel sticking out of the side of the old hole quite plain, and that he got it out with ease not two hours before our arrival.

"Well, Don Hendriquez," said I, "you have had the Weather Gage[2] of us all in this discovery, for certain. And now let us know in what way you intend to proceed with your Money and Gold Cup."

"Oh, what is mine is yours, my good friends," said he, taking us off in our behaviour to each other on any occasion. We returned him our thanks and the Stuff was placed in the Treasury according to his own desire.

Soon after this we discovered a sail laying too right off our place. This was About the 19 of March and in the Morning. I got my Glass and saw she was a large Schoner. Bell proposed to speak her, but I objected as she was at the least 2 leagues out. "Notwithstanding," said I, "If you are inclined so to do, You and Daddy Nunez may take Harry with you and go out in the Yawl and shew yourselves if you are inclined. We know the Spaniards are well acquainted that we are on this shore now, and why need we be under any Restriction on that account? The Wind is favourable."

On this they Came into the resolution and of they went with a few Pistoles and A parcell of Yams &cc. They had not got far out in the Bay before I percieved a White Jack hoisted and the Schoner stood for them. Now I knew if they stood on that tack long they would certainly run on a ledge of Rocks, but in a short time they hove too again and lay by for our boat, soon after which I saw them get along-side of her.

Well, thought I, this may be another Fair trader or not. I kept on the hill constantly untill they had been on board of her above an Hour, when I saw them put off with another boat in company. Now, thought I, Bell is geting beside himself. What View can he have to bring any of those people on shore here? But I soon became sensible of my Error by seeing the other boat part company and row away for the point of the Long Key, which I understood was to get water.

2. Weather gauge: position of one ship to the windward of another.

When they came in Bell informed me that they were a Guarda Costa of ten guns from Carthagena and that the Crew was a Medly of Mortals composed of all the dips or casts from the Spaniard down to the Indian and Negro. That the White Flag as we took it to be was the Ragged Staves in form of St. Andrews cross; that the Commanders name was Zayas; and that he found among them an old foul Loon his countryman, one Watty McClintock Who had turned Papist and had been among them from the time of Admiral Vernons being on the coast, from whose fleet he had Ranaway. He told me that observing exactly such a Claspknife in McClintocks hand as we had purchased from the fair trader, he interrogated him by what means he obtained it, when he told him he found it before it was lost on a Maroon Key some few months ago, saying several of their people had one of them Each.

"They are English," said Bell. "Has any vessel of that sort been cast away lately, then?"

"Why, no," said he, "that I know of. But You must understand there are several Vessels from the north who belong to the English Colonies who are by chance driven this way by some fatality or other, and as they know full Well we are out they leave now and then a few trifles on the Keys and other places that they may not be disturbed while they take in a little fresh Water or so."

"Shake hands, Devils," said I. "Any man may conster [construe] that. But have they any things among them such as you thought of use to us?"

"Not any thing," said he. "They look more like a gang of Thieves than anything Else. I got a good whetstone or two of the Lieutenant in return for a few Yams and Potatoes, and that is all," said he. Soon after this we saw them streatching out to Seaward and before night lost sight of them. Thus ended the adventure.

About this time Bell and Nunez contrived a kind of Board In order to amuse the time at a game called Draughts, and at this they would sit by the hour without speaking many words, with a segar in each of their mouths. They frequently would be at me to play, but one game extended to the full of my patience, it being a game fitter for Cripples and Taylors than a Man who had the full use of his limbs, as I thought. Nevertheless, it Was agreeable enough perhaps to the first inventor as undoubted he was an object of a very sedentary disposition.

Harry was every now and then bringing home one curiosity or other as he knew such things were what I frequently used to amuse myself in; but in this article he at times was much Out of his judgment, often fetching me trifles of no beauty or rarity. But now and then a real Curiosity presented it Self before his Eyes. (Viz), he brought a few days ago a sort of Marine plant growing to a large Stone of about 10 pounds. This plant was as black as jet and so hard that a knife would hardly penetrate it, in height about that of a Cabbage. Nothing could be more curious than the multitude of its twigs, some of them as fine as an Horse hair and shining much like it, not any appearance resembling leaves. Its growth is in the form of a Cypress tree with its root so firmly connected with the Stone that I may defy a mortal to percieve the least joyning therto. Sponges and Sea Fans or Feathers also—some of these things are extreamly pleasing to the Sight. We have of these fans much broader than the leaf of any Cabbage and of all the variety of Colours, also Sponges in the form of Cups, Tubes, Roses, &cc.

But I must not omit in this place to mention a Tree of Coral Now hanging over the Enterance of our Cave. This Curious plant Came up with our Killick as we were fishing one day and Harry Stowed it in the Yawls bows. It is White as Snow, full of small stars And branching forth much like to the horns of a Stag or Elk. It is of such a Solid consistancy that it rings when struck like a Bell. Toward the Root it is as thick as the small of a Mans leg and in height 5 feet and upwards, weighing at least 50 pounds.

The Remora or Sucking Fish has been so often discribed that I need not mention it unless that I hint we have the Skin of one of those Singular fish stuffed which measures at least 3 feet.

We have a Bird here about the Size of our Starling, black, grey and White. This sweet animal we have given the name of Charmer to. Its daily practice is to repair Every Morn at the rising of ye Sun to the utmost twig of some dead tree and there hold forth its enchanting melody for the space of an hour, never failing to do the same as that Blessed Luminary is sinking in the west. Its notes are so loud and Various that it never cloys. This bird we hold in such esteem that none of our family ever molests it in the least.

We have another much of the same colour and size but with a larger head. This bird is so inveterate against the Eagle that he never percieves him on the wing but he directly mounts after him, Where he so worries him by beating on his head that the Eagle is under the necessity of quiting that quarter. This Bird we call the Little Hero, and nothing is more curious than to see the means the Eagle takes to shun it, now mounting aloft then darting with the greatest rapidity toward the Earth. Neverthless, his Enemy keeps close behind his head, making one continual noise. If chance this sport should begin at a distance from trees, in that case the diversion lasts perhaps a quarter of an hour. And I verily think could this Small bird have a fair chance at the Eagle it would weary it out. It has the Same malice against the Fish Hawk or any bird of prey, and it will sit on the top limb of a tree for hours as on the look out, now and then flying up perpendicularly and return to the same branch.

Chapter 33: Twentieth Year

By this time our young Gentleman Owen, Harry and Rory had made such work of the Pirates pit or reservoir to discover more treasure that they have extended the diameter of the hole to the breadth of 10 feet at least, but as yet all their labours prove of no effect. Yesterday morning Rory came down from the hill to me As I was sitting on our bed and said in his broken English, "No Friends can come over Long Key now. Long smoke, Fire make."

"What, is the Key vanished then in the night?" Said I to him. But he, finding that I did not fairly understand him, went out to Harry directly. I overheard him saying that he saw people; this was pronounced in the Indian tongue. I then call'd Harry in and asked him what Rory would be at. "He says there are people on the Key with a great fire and that they are not our friends."

"Call the White men, then," Said I, and taking my glass away I marched. They were all Soon at my heels. When we got on the Clift we percieved about ten or twelve people round a large fire about 100 Yards from the old well but could percieve no Canoas, boat or Vessel. But that they were Indians we knew as none appear'd to have any covering on the head. Many conjectures we had among us on the affair but neither Harry or Rory would say of a certainty that they were our friends as by many actions they observed, altho at so great a distance, seem to confirm them that they were none of their tribe. "Well," said I, "are you willing to go out and speak them, Lads?"

"Do you think I will not go to God than the Devil sooner?" said he. "It may be they are some of the Sancoodas, and they would soon roast me."

Upon this Old Nunez lifting up his hands say'd, "Le Diabola per los Sancoodas!" and asked if the fire might be put out, shewing signs of dread.

"Who are those you Call Sancoodas?" said I. Nunez then told me they were the same we call'd Moskeetos and that they were the most inveterate Enimies to all Spaniards, and that he was certain, should they come among Us, they would soon put him out of pain. "If that be the case," I replied, "It shall not be said we gave them an invitation," so ordered the fire to be deminished to prevent future trouble.

Neither Harry, Nunez or any of our Indians would venture up the hill again after this. Therfore it fell to Bells lot and mine, and when we took the second observation which was about noon, we saw them all busy At a Dance, as we judged by their actions. But about two hours After, they all retired behind the trees on the South Side, and in a Short time after that we saw them all paddling away South with 4 Canoas. And thus they took their leave of our territories which was What most of our family heartily desired; and what brought them there or whither they were bound we could not conjecture.

After they were gone I asked them what occasion they had to shew so much fear As I had been informed those Indians were in friendship with the English; or perhaps they were not Sancoodas as they thought but Indians of some other Nation. Harry replied he was sure they Were not any of his people; otherwise they would never have came so nigh to our place and not have visited us, saying they must be some other Indians with whome they never walked or heared, and that was full Enough for him. This happened on the last day of July according to my account as I calculate the time.

Some months passed on from this time without any thing worthy our observation, when one day I observed Messmate Bell prostrate on the Green and very busy about somthing or other. I was at that time siting Reading, but finding him still imploy'd I got up and went to satisfy my curiosity. When I came to the place I found him scratching on a kind of flat Stone with his knife. "Can you judge what I am about?" said he.

"Not I, truly. What may it be?"

"Why, you must understand I am trying to shape out the draught of our habitation, but I believe I shall make but a poor piece of work of it without your help."

"Help?" cried I. "How should I assist you as You know I can draw no more than a Horse?"

"Oh, ho, ho!" said he. "Can you draw only as well as a Horse? If you can, come try your hand."

I took the Joak and replied that I percieved he understood much more of the matter than my self, and that we would have it transfer'd to paper when he had done. This he agreed to and in a few days, what by alterations and amendment, he finished it such as it is. And altho Mr. Bell values himself not on any Skill that way, yet as to the general form of the place he is tollerably exact; and this made me hint to him that some day we would make a draught Of our harbour, this being a thing I judged we could better succeed in as we knew all the Bearings and distances full well by long and Frequent observations.

About the middle of December on a Morning as Bell and I were out in the Bay on our plan we had intended, (Viz) that of making a kind of Chart of the Islands and Coast, I observed that our Signal was out at home. This made us lay all thoughts of proceeding further for that time, as we knew not what might have happened in our abscence. Accordingly we put away for our Lagune. When we arrived we were met at the Landing by Owen who informed us that four Friends from overland were come and that the Women were all crying about the Spaniards. What to make of this we knew not, So away we ran up to the House where we found them all huddled togather as in deep council. We knew them all and saluted them in the most friendly manner, but my impatience was so great that I desired Harry would recite over the true Cause of the sad wailing I heard, let it be ever so bad or deplorable.

His translation ran thus: That Gainasunto, one of the Indians, informed them they were sent off by the Old Man at home to give us timely notice that some Spaniards had been to visit them about ten days past, and said they were ordered strictly to enquire among them concerning some English People who were settled somewhere on the Coast and had much Money among them, wherby they Were suspected to be Pirates or come there for no good intent one way or other; and that the Commandant looked to them for information As he had reason to think they were privatly correspondent with them.

I cannot say the News surprized me much as it was what I long expected, but it was not so with my two Friends Bell and Nunez. They seemed to express a Great concern, and how or in what manner to proceed I knew not. The next thing I enquired was if they Could inform me by what means the Spaniards came to discover us, and if their folks had acknowledged their being acquainted with us. They told me that when they found we were discovered they could not but acknowledge the thing as we had people of their town living among us; but that they were ordered to inform me they had always been true Men and that they could not understand by what means we had been discovered unless we had discovered our own selves; and if so, it would then be madness in them to deny it. All this was delivered in so plain and honest a way to me that I could by no means charge them with infidelity, as I judged with reason that The Guarda Costa must have been the sole cause, they having some way suspected us altho we strove so much to decieve them.

I Now asked the Indians if the Spaniards had informed them when they intended to pay us a Visit. They say in about two moons as they learnt from their old folks, and that they were ordered to do us good if we wanted assistance. I thanked them and desired they would inform my kind friends on their return that I was determined to stand or fall by my innocence, let what would happen, as I could not think any People on earth who own'd the title of Christians could be so barbarous as to ill treat a Man in my Circumstance and condition.

The Indians tarried with us but two days and then took leave of us. We promised to send them intelligence by Harry and Rory if matters went well with us or no, if the visit should happen as they expected; but if on the contrary that they did not come, I should nevertheless contrive it so that they should be informed if they were not Disposed to pay us any more visits for a time. They then parted with us, perhaps forever.

Matters are now changed greatly; at this my Once peaceful dwelling a general confusion reigns. But I am determined to stear with my helm a Midships and take fortitude for my Pilot, and I trust by a due resignation to the Divine Will to end my days in peace. But as to how or where, it is now a thing of little or no moment, knowing a Sparrow Cannot fall without the knowledge of God.

To add to my perplexities My two friends Bell and Daddy Nunnez are come to a resolution not to wait the Spaniards arrival, as they declare they have sufficient reasons to the contrary, and are determined on removing to some distance untill time may bring about something more favourable for them. Alas, I must condesend. They propose to seek out some place most Convenient to build them an habitation whither they intend to retire, and to return if things shall prosper well with me. But it is my opinion Nunnez will not survive long as he seems to fall off daily, being become now an aged Man.

I have been with Mr. Bell to see the place he has fixed on for his retreat. It is about half a Mile directly back of our own residence near to a Small pond of water and under a bank shaded with thick trees, where they have clered a small Square for erecting studs which he intends to thatch after the best mode they can, and there to retire with some few of our articles untill such time as the Enemy, as he terms them, have been among us. Thither I have proposed to convey What Moneys we have left, with my Bible and Journal as there are circumstances mentioned in the latter I should be unwilling might come to their Ears. For this purpose We intend to contrive a small strong Box and nail them up in it, then Tar the outside so as to prevent the worms or Ants penetrating it. I purpose digging a small cell in the bank aback of the house and there deposite them.

Notwithstanding all my fortitude, all my resolutions fail me at times; one while I charge myself with so idly spending such a series of years so unprofitable to mankind as I have done, when I could have left this forlorn place at the time the Dutchman so generously invited me and again with Old Mr. Horgan, so that I may justly charge myself as to the choice. But then on the other hand, had I left those to whom I had pledged my faith, to wander I knew not where, or to what unknow events might have come to pass—perhaps to lead a reprobate life among those who would never give themselves concern about the welfare of my Soul, being altogather as wicked as my self—surely then it is far better for me as things are. Or even should the Spaniards chuse to remove me hence to some place where perchance they might permit me to revisit my native country, in that case I cannot see what it could possibly avail me. For a Man who has spent so many years in tranquility and solitary freedom, as I may call it, where he might say all was directed according to his own will and where he lived quite independent,—for such a Man estranged from all the wicked arts and devices of the World to return from a scene of Love, Harmony and affection to joyn a croud of utter Strangers in busy life, poor in a manner and friendless—In such a case what happiness can he expect even in his native land? For my part when cool reflection takes place and Intervals of solid reason come in to my aid, I prefer If I may be suffered to remain and end my life in this blessed retreat among those in whom I know I can with confidence put my trust. And I think Should I ever voluntarily forsake these poor cretures around me, out of a mad whim to explore novelty, I should think my self one of the most abandoned Villains in nature and draw down on my head the Vengance of the holy Author of All creation. But I Will not dwell more on so melancholy a Subject, Knowing it can never enter my heart so to do.

As the Spaniards have been informed of our cash We need not doubt of their coming, were it only to that End and to satisfy their curiosity also, perhaps. And for to make matters run as easy as we can Bell and I have concluded to produce a part of what mony we have by us to present them. This he leaves all to me. My Son Owen is made privy to the manner of my bestowing my Journal so that if things turn not out as I wish he may perhaps find a means one day or other to convey it into the hands of some Subject of Great Britain, to whose care I charge him to deliver it unless Providence may direct his Course that way himself. —Not that I entertain any thoughts of its material use to my fellow Mortals, But it may shew the world the manner I Spent my time in, and what became of the Schooner *Recovery* and poor Lewellin Penrose. But If Providence so order it that I remain where I am unmolested, I shall continue my narrative as long as my strength and materials last.

Now I must lay by my subject as we know not the hour they may heave in sight. I have the faith to think they will not treat me ill when they shall See the state of innocence we live in; nor are we so much at a loss at this day as in time past, being Enabled by Mr. Bells instruction to converse in Spanish so as to be well enough understood. And as to any Question they may put to me I am determined to deliver my story in plain truth as far as reason shall guide me.

Twenty Years had almost ran out since my first landing on this Shore, and having Seen nor heard the least tittle concerning a Visit from the Spaniards, nor indeed from our friends the Indians, we much wondered at it and often form'd various conjectures on that head. At length My Two friends returned to dwell at my Place as usual, yet they would often sleep as it Suited their fancy at their new hut. And as the Old Man frequently retired in the day time to Sleep, Or rather perhaps to ease his aged bones, it so fell Out that Messmate Bell missed him longer than Ordinary, And on going to call him found him Expired and laying on his left side. When he Brought us down the news in the evening we were at first struck with surprize, and the young ones began to set up their pipes as they were but seldom used to Scenes of Death. However, I gave orders that Some should sit by the Corps during the Night, And on the Morrow prepared for the funeral.

Chapter 34: Twenty First Year

We buried old Nunnez In the Grove among the rest of our departed friends in the most decent manner our circumstances Would admit, and began the New year after the Old fashion. Now my friend Norman advised with me that he judged it proper we should put Ourselves out of farther suspence by sending Harry And Rory off on a Visit to our friends to gain some kind of intellegence. I jumpt into his opinion at Once and concluded to put the question to them On the morrow. They both agreed with us that the motion was right and concluded to set off. I told them I thought it best that they should go by themselves and not to take women with them as the thing did require dispatch. And as the Women were at this Day so well used to us they were very placid on the proposal, and Off they went, furnished with what they thought proper for their journey, the next day. We had taken care to council them after the Best manner we could devise before they left us.

About 4 days after the Young men were gone We had a sad casualty happened among us, as thus. In the morning Mr. Bell and Owen sat out on a March after Flamingoes with their Guns; and as They went in a Canoa I desired they would stop as they returned at the Old plantation and bring Some large Callabashes with them as the Girls Wanted some for their use. But how was I struck About two hours after with the sound of a Conck, And that of my friend Normans sounding as I knew fulwell by the manner. "What can this be?" Said I to my Wife. Down we ran to the Lagoon and Into the Indian Canoa I got. But I had not gone far when I saw our boat on the return with Only messmate Norman padling without my Son. Therfore as soon as he turn'd the Point I hail'd him. He made me no answer, only paddled the faster. But when he came up, and Seeing Owen on his back in the boat, I cried out, "What is the matter, Shipmate? Speak, tell me at once!"

"Dont alarm your self," said he. "Your Son has Had the mishap to break his leg."

"O hard fortune!" said I. "Mr. Norman, how shall we get the better of this terrible affair?"

"In the first place," said he, "We must get him home with all speed and do our Best, a Gods name, after."

But when we got to the Landing how to manage I was at a loss, so gave A toot with the Shell. This soon brought down the Women, but when they understood what had fell to my poor son Grief unfein'd burst out and all became a scene of Woe. But as there was not Any time to be lost I sent up to the Kitchen for a board and we laid the poor soul on it as Easy as possible, and in great agony he was Nevertheless. It was the Right leg and about 3 Inches above the Ancle. But for a mear Lad, as I may say, he bore it with resolution beyond all our expectations. It swell'd to a great Degree; and happy for us was it to have a person Of Mr. Bells judgment and skill at such a time. Therfore the whole proceeding was given up to his direction, and we got his Leg fish'd up snugg Or Set, as they say.

Now I [it] happened as they informed me After this manner. As they were running along shore Owen espied a Monkey and they put in to get a shot at it, but as he ran with his piece cocked his leg unfortunately Slipt into a kind of Crabhole and by the force snapt it at once. I fix't his place of durance just within the front of our dwelling, and clapt a small kind of Awning over his head to shade the morning sun from him, so that he Sat and Laid in a sort of State, as it were. And here I must Give messmate Bell all his due. He was ever studying Some kind of amusement or other to pass the time or to Lull his pains, and often has he sate by him during his Confinement a full hour playing on the flute to amuse him, for which he has my sincier thanks unfeigned. And as for Owen there can be no esteem lost between them, nor has he wanted all kind love from the rest as far as their poor powers extended.

Our Lads had been gone above a fortnight when on An Evening as we were all sitting relating former Transactions, and the night fair and clear, all at an instant of time such an explosion went off that gave the whole of us sudden surprize. But my Child, little America, cried, "Look! Look!"—upon which we saw in the Air a number of small globes of blue fire. As they were vanishing one after the other Bell said he has seen such often before; but we all agreed never to have heard so loud a noise attend the same. I had seen of them my self, but never to half the effect of this. However, it sent us all into our dormitories for that night without more ceremony.

After we had turned in a short time My Wife observed to me that she hated those Fire balls very much. On my asking her how So, she told me that she was sure we should have much sickness among us soon, upon which I Laught at her and bid her go to sleep and forget it. "No, no," she said, "All Old men said so"—where she came from, and I should see it "as plain and round As the Moon." And thus talking we fell asleep.

On the morrow came running down the hill one of Our Dogs call'd Sleeper which had gone away with The Lads, and soon after came down the hill Harry And Rory as we thought, but when they drew nigh We found Rory to be missing and a strange Indian In his company. "What news?" said I to Harry with a face of Wonder, being quite impatient. But by this time All had gathered round him so that it was became a Dover Court (all Speakers and no hearers). Now I was surprized Harry did not direct his discourses more to me. On this I call'd, "Brother Harry, where Is Rory, pray, that I dont see him?"

On this he came Up to me and said, "I know you have a great heart

And wont cry if I tell you Rory is dead behind with my people, and a great many more old friends." Upon this I begged him to be brief and give a true and fair relation of all since his departure, and if his Wife knew as yet of the matter. He said no, as yet.

He says they got thither without any thing happening to them in four days and nights, when on their first Entrance they met a woman who told them all were Sick of the flux, as he says, and many dying every day—Among whom Futate for one, and others who had been on visits to our place. That two days after their arrival Rory fell sick and lived but three Days, after which a few Indians came to him And said they would take good care to bury my friend, but as for him he must think to return back again As soon as possible least he should die also, and that They had advised Young Sappash to accompany him. And that when they came to my place to tell their good friends, meaning us, that I should take Sappash and make a husband for Jessy at once, As they were too sick to hear any more mad complaints from women; And to inform me that they had never heard Any thing from the Spaniards since about us.

After my brother had satisfied Mr. Bell and me as to all farther matters I sent for Jessy and when she Came desired she would mind well what I was going to tell her. Upon her saying she would, I began: "You are to know in the first place that your people have thought proper to keep your Husband among them for a great reason they have, and have sent this Young man to be your Husband in his stead. And What do you think of it?" On seeing her struck dumb, as it were, I thought best to cut matters short as I could, And told her the Great One She had heard me talk so much about had been pleas'd to lay Sorateet in the Ground; and as that young man Sappash was Sent by her friends out of their love to her and me, She must not make me angry if she could help it. Off she went, mute as a Fish and weeping, to my spouse for a dish of condolence; and thus the affair remain'd for a day or two, when my wife informed me that Jessy desired her to inform me that she would be ruled as I thought best, but that she hoped Sappash would look to my wife and me and learn to love her as her first husband did. I then sent for Harry and had him inform the young stranger that I intended to Celebrate the wedding on the morrow. Harry was much concern'd for my Owen and asked me if I thought he would ever walk again upright. I told him I hoped so, but Mr. Bell was the Man could tell most on that matter. "Ay, ay," said Bell, "he'el be taking to his Qats ere lang again."

On the following day the ceremony was perform'd And we all spent the time as merry as possible allowing for Jessy's bashfulness on the occasion. The next day Harry requested to know What New name we should give Jessy's Husband. I told him Rory as before. This pleased all round, especially his Wife.

After this my Girl desired me never to say Indians were fools again. "As how?" said I.

She Said, "Did I not tell you Fire balls made sick for my people?" I knew not how to answer her, Therfore contrived to alter the subject. And in regard to my poor Indian friends I must need say the melancholy afflictions they have of late been visited with touches my Heart greatly. But it is of the Lord, and I must hold my peace and wait patiently untill I may hear more favourable tidings of them.

No great matters fell out for a long time After this, and my Son began now to goe on Crutches freely. Mr. Bell observed to me That although he had shewn himself so dextrous as he pretended at the Spliceing of Owens Leg, yet he felt the contrary in his mind, having never assisted at such an Operation but once before.

Soon after this Our poor Children fell Sick of the Flux. This gave a general Alarm to the Whole Community, as we expected it to be of the Same kind with that of our friendly Indians, and My Girl prophisied that we should all die at least of it. This vexed me a little and made me insist that she should talk no more after that sort or I Should be very angry with her. This she dreaded, as I never had words with her at any time in anger. But in about a fortnight they all recovered and Came about again, to my great satisfaction After so dreadful a prospect before us.

Some time after this Mr. Bell proposed an Excursion to the northward by land if it were any Way agreeable to me. I told him that he might take His own pleasure but that in regard to my self I was not

So very forward about it. Yet if Harry chose to go with him they had my full consent, and in the Morning they began preparing for their jaunt. Now while matters Were getting ready I begged Mr. Bell not to venture more than a few miles or so from home, the which he promised Me to observe strictly; and on the day following they Both marched off before we were turned out. They took 2 Dogs with them and my small Spyglass.

In the evening Owen took a whim to go a fishing with Rory down the lagoon. He went away about 4 oclock And while they were abscent I took a walk up ye hill In order to look out, as was my usual custom. I had not Been long there before I descried two Sail in the offing And as I thought by my naked Eye standing right in shore. I eagerly clapt the glass to my eye and plainly percieved It to be really so. Now what to think I knew not, but as They seem'd to stand in rather from a northeast quarter I had doubts in my mind wether they were Spaniards or not. They were both Sloops as I imagined at first, being so far Out; but on one of them gybeing her mainsail She proved to be a Schooner. In a short time after it came up thick in the Horizon and I lost sight of them, when I returned down the hill again and, lighting my pipe, walked down to the landing, waiting with impatience about an hour. I did not throw out my signal for my lads to Return as I knew it to be of non effect; but in a short time after, they came in from fishing and I told Owen What I had seen. "Let us go up again," said he, which we did; but as night was then coming on and the air thick we could percieve no more of them.

No signs of our travellers returning for that night, And I sat smoaking by my Wife full of cogitations untill midnight, when we turned both in. I was up Before the Sun-rise and on the lookout, but not a Sail could I percieve any where along the whole Horizon; And who or what they were remains to this Day an intire secret to us. Yet I must need say I could not refrain from many foolish conjectures at the time.

The next day in the evening arrived our two Adventurers weary enough, and glad we all were to See them safe again returned, And as they came in late and almost famished the Girls got them a good mess, And to sleep they went for the night. The next day Messmate Norman gave us a brief Of their journey, as thus. He says after they had gone About five miles away Northwest, mostly through Woods, they observed the land to rise gradually and at Length came to an open country, and that there they both sat down to refresh themselves, and as they were Eating remarked a tree of a most amazing size but Hollow, and so large within the trunk that he thinks Thirty men could stand within it easily.

"From this tree we took our departure afresh," Says he, "and took our course north with the ground Still rising untill we came to a small Wood of Lofty trees, and at this place Harry mounted one of them in order to take a look out." When he got Down again he said they were then on a very high hill And that the land fell away into a deep Valley full of Woods, but that towards the sea there was a hill of Rocks and a great Lagoon with much water. Upon this intellegence they desended the hill and As they went on found the bones of several Deer, but In all the whole time had seen no living beast. Now they concluded that they were at least 10 miles from home, and began to have thoughts of what was next to be done, when Harry proposed to Ascend another tree, which he did and brought Down word that he judged they were not above 5 miles from the Great Clifts but that they must keep more away toward the Sunrising. And on this they both determined to set off for the place But found Harry's judgment out rather as to the Distance, as it was evening before they could get to the bottom.

Here as being got into a Valley and the Sun far then to the West behind the hills, it became Very gloomy and they had thoughts of making a Large fire for their preservation in the night. But soon after they found the trees to become fewer and could percieve light through between them. This gave them fresh courage and they put on, When in about a Quarter of an hour they found themselves at the Verge of the Wood Where a vast expance opened at once to their View.

Here, he says, Nature became very wild indeed or perhaps an Earthquake might have in former Ages torn or split A Whole Mountain, as there were Massy stones lying at all points of the Compass and of the magnitude of large houses. And in between some of these they concluded to lodge for the night with a good fire round them, and on the morrow began to look Round them, when on getting on one of the high stones they Could see over the mangroves and the low country clear out to Sea which they judged not above 5 miles from them. With this discovery they returned without the least harm to bring us the strang report, as I may call it.

Chapter 35: Twenty Second Year

I had been here on this shore now twentv one years and two months when A Very uncommon event came about, and I shall give it As faithful a narration as possible. On a certain day as Messmate and I were out in the Bay fishing for our pleasure he observed to me that it Was a little odd I expressed no desire to visit his new Northern discovery, as he was pretty sure it could be Easyly done by sea. "Why, as to that part of your speech," said I, "Bell, I have half a mind indeed."

"Well, then," said he, "When shall we go?"

"We go?" I reply'd. "Can that be good policy? Rather Either you or me and Harry is best, as it is so far from our Women."

"Well, then," said he, "you And Harry can go. Let him stand pilot as to the place." I now came to a determination and when we got in told my Brother Harry what I intended. He was glad of the voyage and said he could hit the place exactly. I then told him that he must get one of our boats Ready and all things necessary for our trip.

About two days after, we put dow the lagoon and got the length of Towers Field by 2 oclock in the afternoon, Weather'd Whale Point, and got the whole length of Boom Bay in the evening, where I concluded to stay that night. In the morning we put out to sea to get around a long point and opened a new scene of country. Along this Shore we ran at the rate of about 5 knots an hour. Now Harry concluded we must soon see the clifts from the Sea, but we coasted the shore untill by my judgment Wee were got 8 leagues from our own bay and I had thoughts of returning back, just as we were abrest of a high bluff of land full of high trees and here we Concluded to go on shore and stay for the night, to return In the morning. After we had got on shore and made up a Fire which was toward Evening, Harry said he had a mind to climb a tree which he did and cry'd out that we were Not above a mile from the lagoon for that he saw the Clifts and all quite plain. "Then let us make up a tent for the night," I said, "and in the morning we go in Round the Bluff if the wind stands."

The next morning we got round by sunrise but not a Signe of any Lagoon could I see at all until we had got About a mile farther, when out on a point I observed a few White Poaks standing fishing. "If it be any where," Said I, "it must be there." When we got thither the mouth of a small lagoon shewed itself, and I should not have Given myself the trouble to enter had not Harry espied The tops of the Clifts between the bushes.

We put in and found a narrow pass for the space of a Mile or so, not more than a ships length wide and Very crooked, then it opened into a much larger space And the water was above three fathom deep there. Now Another streight for a short length, and all at once we Opened a lake or pond of Water at least a mile or more Across, surrounded by a large, stoney flat Shore. This Ran back half a Mile or more, then began to rise A most tremendous mass of Rocks, Clifts, and fallen Huge stones. Now as we were viewing this new sight I was prompted to take up my Glass and I had not had It in my hand long before I cried out to Harry that I saw a black man or some wild creture moving Among the Rock stones. This startled Harry and He begged the Glass of me. Now as he was looking he Percieved him move to a clear place, and returning the glass to me said, "It is a strange man, indeed, and Let us be going back directly, Brother, pray!" I told him not to be in a fright, for were it the very Lucifer himself I was determined to speak him if Possible before we returned. "Then," said he, "if you are Not afraid of him I wont nither be afraid, brother."

We then put in to shore and both got out with our Guns and marched directly for the place we saw Him in first, but found that he did not observe us. After we had gone Some distance towards him I sat dow to take a fresh review and then could see Plainly as I thought a Tall Old Negro man with his Head and Beard white as wool, and naked with a staff or club in his hand. We were at this time about halfe A mile from him and found that he did not observe Us as yet. Now all of a suddain we lost sight of him Among the rocks. We then advanced apace but could Not get the least glimpse of him again. Therfore we ran Back to our boat, dreading least we might be deprived Of her before we could reach her.

Soon after we had put off from the shore on our return Harry espied a Smoak Arise among the Rocks and cried, "There is the old Devil now Againe!"

"And there may he be," said I, "and remain. Let us Get out and make home as fast as we can, Harry."

"Brother's afraid!" said he.

"Not I," replied I, "but what would you have done should there have been more of them come And run away with our boat while we had left her?"

"Then we must have gone home by land," said he.

"And so Starve by the way without fire tackling, you blockhead," I answered. But out we got and put away before it for Home as fast as we could high; got home in two days by Hook or Crook after getting aground on Whale Point. Our People rejoyced at the Sight of us and Bell had the Whole relation from me. But I must need confess when the Object first disappeared, my former idle notions of the Yahoos began to return on me strong but I got the better of it when I percieved the Smoak arise from between the rocks.

Mr. Bell said that he was determined he would go If I would permit Rory to go with him, and he would not Return before he spoke to him if he could find him In any reasonable time. "With all my heart," I reply'd. And according about a week after, they sat out by my odd Chart I formed for them. And the following is Mr. Bells Story:

They got there with ease and after waiting A Whole day without getting a sight of any living Soul concluded it to be a mear Visionary affair as No kind of Smoak was to be seen. Yet he was bold Enough to continue there in the boat all night, when Rory awoke him to shew him a smoak early the morrow. Upon this he said he told Rory to bring out the Two Guns and follow him. They made right away for The place where the Smoak arose which was about a Mile from them up among the Rocks. But as they were Got about two thirds on their way and just as they turn'd Round a large high piece of Rock, the Grey dog they had With them gave a long howl; when to his surprize a Tall Black Wretch stood but a short distance from them, as going to turn off to leave them after the best Fashion he could, being but feble in his joynts.

Upon this Messmate hail'd him but he seem'd not for any parly. Upon that they went both up to him And stopt him, wherupon the Old Soul fell down on His knees and began to beg for mercy in Spanish. Mr. Bell told him he need not shew any fear on their Account as they intended him no manner of harm in the least, and asked him how many of them there were In that place, seeing him appear so very ancient. But how greatly was he amazed when the Old man told him he had been there alone longer than he could Remember well. "But would you not rather chuse to End your Days," said Bell, "among people, than so? How do you live? What do you eate? Does any people Ever come to relieve you?"

He answered no, nor had he spoken a word to any man from the time that he first got thither, nor did he want to speak to any man or see any man again for the rest of his days, and then asked Bell where he came from. When being told he replied, "Then go back to the Same place and dont trouble a poor old man Who stands not in need of any help. I have lived Long, Long quiet since I left the faces of the White men. I shall not covet to return among those who live

upon poor Black mens blood. But if I had a mind to return to them
again they could get nothing but dry bones to suck at, Now I am so
old; so, young man, be advised by me And leave me where I am.
May be I shall die Tomorrow."

"And who can you have to bury you?" Said Bell.

"The Crows," said he, and began to move off. But we [they] followed him at a small length of distance untill he got back to his fire
which was between 4 Rocks in a very secret place. When the old man
found they had followed him he turn'd about to them and fixing his
aged Eyes on Mr. Bell Stamped his Staff on the ground, then cried,
"White Man, Trouble me no more. Go! I hate you and all those of
Your colour in the world. I have no more Blood for you to suck. Let
me die quiet by my self."

But messmate did not think to leave him thus without being better
informed of his story And began with him as thus: "Old Fellow, let
me tell you there are thousands of White men in the World far better,
perhaps, than Any it has been your fortune to fall among. So pray,
let us have fair play however on both sides. You are one of the verriest
Old Churles I ever ever met with In all my days. I dare to say had
you spent a year or Two among us at our place your opinion of White
men might take a turn; or you must have been so ill used by the
Whites formerly as to be past all cure of temper.

"The Old man then replied he was now very old and had not the
least desire to be ever more acquainted With us at any rate, for that
it was his oppinion I spake only in favour of my own colour; but if
that what I Wanted to advance was true he could tell Such stories as
would plainly prove his cause was Very just as well as mine, ending
with a disdainful Laugh and uttering, 'White Man good? No, no,
no!' "

Bell thought then he would try what coaxing could do And remarked that it was true—he had observed when in the Islands that the
condition of the poor Black men was Very miserable; and for his part
it was a practice he had not Been concern'd in nor none of his relations that he ever had Knowledge of; nor should he ever give into
the like opinions As he detested making any men slaves whom God

made Free at their birth. Upon this the Old man asked him if He would blame him for chusing to keep himself free. Now finding the Old man to become rather more civil And complying, he took the Opportunity to desire he Would give him some account of his life and how he Came thither, for that he supposed he had gone through Misery enough before he came to that place.

"True, True, man," said the poor old Wretch with a Heavy groan. "You see my head all White and no Friend left to stand by me now at the last hours." At this he stoped short and looking at him stern said, "How did you find me out? You are no Spaniard. I know very well What countryman are you."

"I am a Scotchman," he replied, "but Thats no matter. I will contrive to make your Old heart more Easy before you die if you will but be advised and come with Me to my place. I have a partner who has been for many long Years continually doing good to his fellow cretures, altho he Has been unfortunate enough himself."

"What country Man is he?"

"English," he answered.

"All the same, no better for that," said the old man. "Where do you live? How far off?"

"About thirty miles," Answered Bell, "to the Southward. And if you will goe we will Give your old days rest, and my friends will kindly recieve You if you can leave this forlorn place."

Now the Old man told him that if he would sware to be a true Man, to bring him back to his old place again if he should not like to remain among them, on that condition he would Goe as he said they all live free men togather and did not Keep black people in Slavery.

"All this discourse passed in Spanish but he observed To me that he could speak English once, to, before he Learnt Spanish, having lived long, long with them at Barbadoes and Jamaica. We had spent so much of Our time now that we began to grow hungry," said Bell, And told the Old man that they would set off as the next Day erly in the morning, and then pointed where the boat Lay and took their leave for that time of him.

When the morning came they observed the Old man on his Way to the boat. They Embarqued with him and put out Of the laggoon and arrived without any long delay. But before they came in, Owen came down from the look out and said he thought he heard a Shell blow. This mustered us togather presently and we marched Down to the Landing, when soon after the Conck went Again not far off. But no sooner did they come in and A third object was discovered in the boat, I must confess myself somewhat surprized. Away flew the young fry As fast as legs could carry them. Indeed, I was left alone for my Wife had taken herself off. Now after they had landed We were obliged to assist the old man to rise. The long time he had sat in the boat, not being used to it for years, and his Age togather had quite cramped him but we made a Shift to get him up to my place and there seated him in the shade, my young family peeping from behind the Kitchen and other places. And indeed he cut a most odd Figure as he sat with his hands over his knees and his chin on them.

In the first place, as they had brought him contrary to my expectation, I told Harry to get him a bed made up in the old Shed where Old Nunnez had formerly slept. And after I found the Old soul had risen from his seat and was stumping about a little I walked up to him and asked him in Spanish what Was his name. He said which name, for he had three—One Negro, one English and one Spanish. "O ho, then," said I, "old daddy, you have been among the English, have you?"—for I had recieved what I have before related from Bell, soon after they had landed.

"My name Primus in English, Master," he said. "The Spaniards gave me the name of Diego. But my first name was Qameno (or Quammeno) in Ginny." I asked him then how old he thought he might be. "Indeed, man," said he, "I cant tell you for true but I had a Wife when I came From the Ebo country[1] to Barbadoes." I then bid him try if he could recollect what King there was of the English people At that time. Yes, he said, he knew very well. They said the king at that time was a Woman and a great Warrior, he heard. This

---

1. This area is inland in what is now Angola, at about 11° S. and 14.40° E., lying to the South of the Congo. "Ginny" is Williams' spelling for Guinea.

must mean Queen Ann most certainly; but be it anyhow his appearance shewed him to be very old, 80 at least as we both judged.

"But, Old man," said I, "how comes it about that you have Got such a great hatred against the White man as my friend tells me you have? I should be glad to hear all your story and Then I can be a better judge. It may be you have been a great Rogue when you were young. What say you to this?"

He then said, "The man who brought me here to see you and to hear you talk promised to take me back when I wanted to go, and if you think I am a rogue send me back when you please." I told him he was brought to a place where there was nothing but constant friendship; that I was then the Master of the place, and if he thought good of it he was as Welcom to stay as he could desire himself; and that I should be glad he would give me the whole Story of his life on the Morrow. Then he came and took hold of my hands and said, "I believe you have learnt to be a good man since you have come to live at this poor place of woods and stones like my place, and, Master, I will tell you all what I can think on in my mind if I live til tomorrow." Thus we dropt it As I did not chuse to trouble him too much.

I was surprized that a man of his years should not be Bald. His head was as large as a thrumb Mop[2] by the quantity of White Wool on it, and a most copious white beard. This joyn'd to a black skin give him intirely a new appearance to us. Quammino had been a very stout man in his younger days, At least six feet high but stooped much by reason of age.

The next morning the Old man coming to visit me, I desired him to make himself free and tell me all his Story as he could remember. He then sat down by me and Began as follows: "I remember they put me on board a Ship One morning along with three more. The ship was full of Black people before I came there. My wife was there too, but I did not know it then when I first came on board Untill she espied me out. We were all made fast down in the Hold. And when we had been out about ten days at Sea my Wife, having liberty to go

2. A thrumb mop (used on shipboard) is made of bits or ends of rope yarn.

into the Cabbin, found out that There was much Knives there in
boxes and told it to us Privatly. Upon this the men agreed if they
could get at the Knives to kill all the Whites and go back to our
country Again."

I asked him if he did not think it a very wicked And barbarous
undertaking. On this he replied not at all, As they then thought, not
knowing what ever became of All their country folks the ships took
away, for that it Was evident they never came back again. Therfore it
was Nothing but right to kill those who would kill them. After she
had convey'd about 5 knives among them which they hacked against
each other in the dark to make saws of which they intended to cut
off their shackkles with, singing All the time they were at work that
the Whitemen should not hear the noise, The Scheem was discovered by a little Negro of the Cabbin who had observed her to steal
away the knives at times, and he informed the mate, and it was all
blown.

"Then," said he, "they took my Wife and tied her up to the mast of
The Ship by her arms and whipped her sadly to make her confess
Which of the Blacks set her on the busines, but she would not Confess. Then the Captain ordered them to whip her more, but I was
down below and could not se it. Still she would not say Anything
about the men of the secret. Upon this the Captain told them to whip
her worse than ever, and they did whip her Dead and threw her into
the sea, and two of the men after that were whipped; and had they
known the Woman to be my Wife they would have whipped me
dead, also," said he. "I suppose From that hour I have never loved
White men since."

I could not help feeling for the poor old soul when he had given
me his first cause of resentment, but I did not chuse to Interrupt his
story. After this had happened and they came To Barbadoes he was
sold and bought by a fisherman, who Treated him so heartily at his
first coming home to the House that he burnt his Back with a hot
Iron. This he Was told by other Negros was to mark him as his own.

"My Master was a Molatto Man, and any good people Would think
as he was part Black himself he would love the poor Slaves more than

the White people did." But he was as hard hearted As any Devil in the whole Island, and he had not been with him A Year before he got a most severe whiping only because he had not comprehended him right in a trife [trifle] for want of understanding English enough.

"After I had been with him some years and did all The service for my Master in my power, yet I got several times Whipt for his own humour, as it were, or just when the Devil put It in his head. For as sure as any white people happened to have Words with him in trade, then Poor Negro men must stand Clear at home. But I got from his hard hands on the account of a Young Negro Girl who lived about 4 miles off from the Bridgtown, my sweetheart. I had leave to go and see her on A Sunday, and staying at the dance too late did not go home All night; and in the morning, knowing that I should have been out with the boat, was afraid to return as I expected the whip. Soon after a Negro call'd Joe came for me and I went Home. My master ordered me to be tied up and I got 30 lashes. This I could have born with quietness, but he was not content with that but swore I should be branded on the cheek for a Runaway." And that was true. "Se here," said he, shewing the place. "I then told him he might kill me if he pleased for I would live no longer with him. He told me I might get a new master And be dam'd, for that he did not care who had me if he had his Money again.

"I knew one Mr. Freeman from Jamaica who liked me and he bought me from my Master and took me to Jamaica with him, but he died of a Feaver soon after and I was sold again. My new master lived on the north side of the Island and he, knowing that I had been a Fisherman, kept me for that purpose so that my life was spent mostly by or on the Water. I lived with this Man several years, and had a Wife belonging to the same estate by my old masters consent. We had had two Children, when once on a day as I was Sitting under the rocks on the seabeach near a point of Land, all at once Three Men jumped upon me and said, 'Vamus! Vamus!' I stood amazed finding them to be three Spaniards, and go I must. When they took me round the Point there lay a small Piccaroon sloop onboard of Which I was ordered, where ther were more of my colour they had plundered like myself. I was not grieved at my new Change but for my Wife and dear children.

"I knew I was but a Slave still, but when I thought on my Wife and poor children I never expected more to see, then I hated the Whites More than ever. They took me to St. Jago da Cuba and there I Was bought by a Rich old Gentleman, and he, finding that I had Followed Fishing, gave orders that I should have the same Employment under him. My Old master never ordered me to be Whipt as I took great care now I had got among new people to Do all I could for the best. Now one day my Master, after I Could talk Spanish a little, asked me if I had not left a Wife And children behind me at Jamaica. I said yes, but that they were no more for me now. 'Never mind that, Diego,' said he. 'You shall Have another if you want one. We have girls enough.' I thanked Him and I thought to give my heart a little new comfort I Would look out for a new Wife as I was sure I should never se Benneba again. My Master liked me better every day and Made me overseer of all the Negros who had anything to Do about boats, and I lived happier then than for many years Before.

"At last one day as we were at work on an old canoa to patch her up, master sent for me to come to him under a Great tree where he was sitting and Said to me, 'Diego, do You know Old Marias daughter, the Molatto Girl Isabella?' 'Yes, master,' said I. 'Very well, and she likes you, I find by Report.' 'I hope so, Sir,' said I. 'Then you have my consent,' Said he.

"But O, Man, that brought trouble enough on me. About 6 months after I had my new Wife my Young Master Came home from the Havannah where he had been a good while About Business for Master, and behaved very ill natured to me. I Wondered at it as he used to like me much before he went away. But one day my Wife when she was alone with me Told me she wondered what ailed young Master. He hated her, she was sure, he call'd her such bad names when he thought Nobody heard him. 'May be,' said I to her, 'he wanted you for himself.' She did not know it, she replied. But soon after this she began to grow sick, and an Old Man of my colour told me he was sure she was poisoned and would never have A Child but that she would look like it as long as she lived. However, in about 2 Years she died, and soon after her an Old Negro Woman when she was dying sent privatly for me And begged forgiving as her Young master had employ'd her to do it. But I had no power of revenging myself for I had better thoughts than to Murder at this time, so kept My mind to myself untill time should bring me revenge.

"And after about a Year when all seem'd to be blown over My Old Master, seeing me striving so hard at work, began To laugh and Said, 'Why, Diego, I think you have bad luck in Wives. Have you got any woman?' I answered him no sir, nor did I ever intend to have another, for I could speak freer to him than any of the rest. 'Why so?' said he. I said his God gave me three Wives but Whitemen took them all from me, and I was Resolved they should never take another. 'How was it,' said he, 'Diego?' I then told him concerning my other Wives, but 'Hold, hold! Diego,' he cried when I told him the last was Poisoned. 'Say you she was poisoned? If you find out who did the thing you shall have full satisfaction done.'

" 'Ah, master,' Said I, 'she is dead and gone home.''Who did it?' 'But one is alive now Concern'd.' 'Tell me who that is,' said he with a fierce look. Upon that I went down on my knees and begged he would let me keep it a secret as long as I lived. 'You have been well used by me, Diego,' said he, 'and can trust me with your secrets, I hope.' I did not know what to say now for he left me quickly in ill will, As I thought. And I grew very sorrowful on the occasion, but soon after there came two Negros and told me I must come to the Stock house. I threw down the Net I was at work on and Went with them, was laid on my back with my head in a hole, And left there for two days.

"The third, Master sent for me up to the house. As soon as I came in he said, 'Well, Diego, you see I dont like for Blacks to be too free with me. I know how to be angry some-times, and if you dont tell me now who is was concern'd in the affair of Poisoning Isabella you shall be shott without delay and Sent after her.' Down I went on my knees again and say'd, 'My Good master, if I tell you it is all the same to poor Diego. Young Master Hernan will kill me when he comes

home again from Veracruze, because he made old Quasheba Poison
my wife.' Master when he heard this told me to go back to My work
again, and went into another room. Master took no more notice of
me; But the white men about the house Said I was got into a bad condition and would come to be Hanged, they supposed. This threw
me into sorrow of heart; And as they did not expect Young Master
home under about 2 Months I came to a resolution of leaving them all
and flying I did not care where, for now I hated all Whitemen as
much as possible for me to hate them.

"And It happen'd soon after that Master ordered me to collect several things for to be sent away to a Country house he had About 5
leagues to windward where he was to have Much company to meet
him. I let no man know what was In my heart, but put every thing on
board that I looked on I should want for use, and with another Negro
call'd Mingo put off for the place. When we got thither I bid an old
Negro who lived there to collect yams and many Other kinds of
things for to goe with the boats return. Then on the Next morning
I went down to the boat erly And shoved her off, hoist'd sail, and
stood directly out on a Wind untill Evening when the Land Wind
came off and Carried me clear of the coast, so that by morning I was
got so far out that I had almost lost sight of the shore. In about 5 days
I fell in with the place Mr. Bell found me at, and there I have lived
by my self from that time. And there I expected to die if you or
somebody else had not found me out at last."

Quammino having finish'd he [his] odd Story, I asked him how
long he thought he had live at that Place. "Moons enough," he said.
Now as he had not kept any kind of Reckoning of his time I could
form no other way to Estimate it but by the age he was at the time
of his flight, Which by his account I supposed to be about forty-five
or Not much over or under; and at the time Messmate first Discovered him he thinks him to be about 70 odd perhaps. Yet notwithstanding his age the old fellow seems active Enough at fishing matters
and very strong except his stooping.

I have since asked him how he lived and provided for him Self.
His answer was by Catching fish and Eating Yams and Other Roots

and fruits. I asked him how he obtain'd them At that Barren place where he lived. From whath [what] he first brought in his boat, he told me, for that there was Good ground enough back of the Clift; and as to his way of Sleeping and other things he would shew me if I would Goe some day thither with him. Upon this I asked him If he had a desire to return again. Just as I pleased, he said—it was all one to him. What was an Old man good for when he was past labour? "But could you willingly Go and leave company to remain there alone again?" He said he would rather that I should please my self As to that. "Then," said I, "here are young ones enough to Feed you, old man. You shall do no more than what your fancy leads you to at any time."

I had lived there almost Twenty two years when I fell Ill of a Violent Sun headach, as Messmate Norman calls it, and I would not wish my greatest Enemy to be worse afflicted than I have been for some time past. The nature of this disorder is Such that the pain comes on as the Sun rises, so that the time of Meridian drives the person quite lighheaded and so great is the throbbings that the stomach becomes quite sick and casts. Messmate Norman had a remedy of a kind of large leaves Bound round the head, which has wrought a cure.

Chapter 36: Twenty Third Year

Some few months after my head Ach had left me I took a fancy of visiting the old mans former dwelling place, and he seem'd much pleased with my proposal; and accordingly I told Messmate Norman of my Intention. I proposed that My Son should bear us Company as he longed so much for a ramble. Accordingly In a few days off we went, the Old man, Owen and my self. I need not be particular as to our voyage except that we found a fine piece of Ambergrease directly of Towers Field on the strand. When we came in to the Lagoon the poor Old man hove a heavy sigh and said, "There is my hole, Master. Trouble never touched me at that place untill I Saw A White mans face again. Then trouble came back to me, for I thought no less but that I should be forced away Against my will, and that made me so cross to Mr. Bell. For I could not think there were such White men as I have found you to be in the World."

"Now," said I, "yonder Is the spot where I first saw you, Old man, when I was here."

"Ay, but that was not the place where I used to sleep," said he. "Now if you pleas we will get the boat up to the head of the bay and I will show you my Cannoa where she lays. I believe you would hardly find her out," said he, "unless You were directed how to find her."

When we got thither there opened another inlet which I had not seen before, it being intirely land locked from my sight; and on our Enterance we came up to some of the fallen Clift stones. And in a place formed by the fall of the Stones into a kind of sharp Archway overgrown with poppanack bush there lay his Cannoa quite hid from the rays of ye Sun. This boat Quammino told me he had made himself, and I gave him credit for what he told me. Nor was she of the Worst shape I had ever seen; she was small, about nine foot Long and suited his purpose well enough. This put me on asking Him what became of the boat he arrived in at that place. "Oh," sd. he, "she lays sunk a little way out yonder, quite rotten now. Now we will go to my old lodging," said he, and away wee went Over divers rocks and broken paths untill a large grove of Small trees appear'd before us. "That is the place," said he. "I Set all that to grow my self."

When we got there, "Now," said he, "Please to follow me," and we entered among the trees when we Soon began to desend among Rocks to a considerable depth Untill we came to a kind of level wall'd up on each side by the Accidental fall of the Clift. This place may be about the Size of a large Cabbin. This he had covered over with limbs of Small trees and thatch and made a very good place of. After we had seen his bed he asked us to walk and see his cook Room. This was not above twenty yards from his bed chamber And consisted of only a large shelving place among the rocks. From that we marched to his storeroom. This indeed was much More furnished than the other. Here was to be seen Several articles Such as Fishing nets, old darts, paddles and A Number of other things and some remains of his old sail. I observed several kinds of old Spanish tools but quite Worn out with frequent use. "I have one place more to shew you," said he, "but I did not make it my place to live by because I could not look out from it." So after we had been to dinner He lead us round the south side of the hill and shewed us A Very large opening in the Clift. "Here," said he, "Men have lived in old times, I believe, or used to come to it At times, for there is marks that fires have been made many times and there is a pond of fresh water below In the Vally, where I found an old path and burnt Sticks in abundance with several things cut with knives And marked."

I told him I did not doubt but that it was Well known to the Pirates formerly, as well as my place. After this he shewed us where his Yamms and plantains Grew and where his usual fishing ground was. These he said he generally struck with small darts or caught and killed by night with an Old Cutless and torch wood, and that he never had tasted hardly of any kind of Flesh meat from his first arrival at that place.

Soon after this Quammino lead me into the Clift pass, and I did not just then take notice that Owen did not follow us. As such places in many respects had a resemblance to our own home it was not a curiosity to him, but he had clambered up the Rocks to get an eminence to explore the country more at large. Soon after we were in I heard a Voice as from my son just As we came under an opening above our heads. This caused to me some wonder at first, when looking up to my surprize I Beheld my Owen standing on an high precepiece over our heads And saying he saw a sail in the Offing. "Bon voyage," said old Quammino. "Let them go their way. We are content without their company."

This put me on asking him if he had not seen vessels now and then. Yes, he said, he had seen them several times; that once in the night he had seen one on fire, as he thought. "Ay," said I, "that is a long time now Since we had the same sight, daddy, at our place. You must have Been a great length of time here," said I. He told me he knew not how long, but that he judged he had been by himself almost As long as he had lived among people, and I doubted it not. Or not many years short of it.

There being a large Stone on the ground behind us, "Come," said I, "Quam, let us sit down and take a pipe togather, for never was I in this place before, nor did you ever expect to see me here, much less to conduct me hither." Then filling, I took out my tackle to strike a light. As I was doing this I said, "Daddy, what a Great pitty it is that you have never been made a Christian Of, as you seem to me to Shew sufficient judgment and can Reason on things very well."

"What good would that have done to me?" said he. "Would it have made White men love me the better? No! No! Dont they Curse and Dam each other, fight, cheat And kill one the other? Black men cannot do any thing Worse than what White men do. They go to Churches and Tell God they will never do any harm to any people, and the same day come out and Kill, Cheat and say lies again. They say Black men should be whiped to make them Good slaves. How can they expect Blacks to be good and No Christians when they who say they are Christians Are worse than we who know not the books of Gods as they do? Young men learn to be wicked in our Country As well as any where els, and when they are brought among the Whites they learn to do their Wickedness also."—That the Whites did not care for the Blacks more than For the use they were of to rid them of hard labour; otherwise they Might all go to the Devil who was their father, as they said.

Then he asked me if I could tell who was Cain Devil for that the Whites said the Negroes were all his Children, and how could they pretend to know who was their father beter than themselves. That for his opinion he thought the same God made them all, Black and White. Did I not see many other kind of things Differ in colour on the outside, but the same within?" "Mind," said he, "if you look at the inside where the heart is you can find no difference between the White and Black. I can Remember on a time my master had a White Horse died in Jamaica and the Negros skin'd him; and when I lived With my Master at St. Jago he had a black horse died and When he was skinned the colour was the same as the white one. But the White men when they go about to do good always Keep it from the Blacks for fear they should learn if ever they do any. But I cant think they do much, because they Go to confess often and remain still as wicked as before. They often say, 'Curse your colour' to poor Blackmen When they have been about blacker works themselves."

All this time I sat silently puffing, for indeed I had Little to answer in behalf of my own colour, but told him that I believed him a much better man than many Thousands who call'd themselves Christians.

After Owen joyn'd us we arose and return'd to the old mans Bed chamber, as I may call it, and there made our supper After the best sort we could, and lay down on his palmetto bed place all three togather for that night. In the morning I asked Quam if he did not find it very doleful to be So much alone at first. He said yes, but that he soon became used to it as it was his chief desire so to be; but That there was one affair surprized him much especially At the first when he had been there about a year, as he took it—(Viz) a loud noise as it were a body of men Giving a great Huzza, and that he heard it above Twenty times in the course of his being there but never Above one Huzza at a time, that it sounded sometimes from one quarter and then another. I told him that It [I] judged it to proceed from the Wind in that large Cave.

In the morning we prepared for our return to my old Habitation, but just as we had proceeded about halfway out A Musket was discharged to seaward of us. This gave us all three the alarm. But as I had braved so many dangers I could Not give way to terror in the least nor was Old Quam much Disturbed at the novelty. So we concluded to push out without the least fear or dread, but it was not so with Owen. He was really frighted as being so seldom used to strange faces. When we got out I observed a Vessel at an anchor about halfe a mile to the north of us. Presently Owen pointed To three men sitting on the beach not far from us. "Shall I hail them?" said I, "Or shall we take no heed of them?"

"Do what you please," he replied. Upon this I determined to Speak them and put to shore. Then I jumped out and Walked on the beach untill I got within about 40 Yards When I hail'd in Spanish. They all got on their legs and Returned an answer, on which I advanced up to them. They Were all three Elderly men and Spaniards who belonged to that Schooner, they said, and had been looking for a Watering place. I told them I would shew them a good place for their purpose if that they were bound down the coast. They told me they were. I then enquired from whence they Came. Campechy,[1] they said, and their Skippers name Was Joachim Valdes. They asked me to go on board with them when their boat came on shore. I thanked them And made a signal for my companions to come up to us, which in a short time they did.

Now when they Observed the different complexions of my comrades One of the men asked me of what country I was, as he knew by my speach that I was neither Spanish or Portugues. I candidly acknowledged myself to be An English Man at once, as I judged it most proper At that time rather than to be found in any falshood scituated as we then were. Poor Owen Stood motionless before them and Old Quammino kept his silence, fearing perhaps they were from St. Jago de Cuba and might recollect him. But to put him out of fear I told him they were of Campeachy.

Now while we were sitting all togather on the Sand, All at once one of the Spaniards as I took him to be, the same person who had discovered to me that he Knew me to be no Spaniard, Said to old Quammino, "Faith and Soul, Old Trojan! Sure you wont say you Are A Spaniard to, will you? For by H-ns [heavens] you look As tho you were born in the days of Fin MacCoul."[2] I was greatly struck at hearing this Man speak to him thus in English, and he as much when the

1. Campeche in Yucatán.
2. Semi-mythical Irish hero, the subject of Ossian's poems. He was possibly a third-century warrior.

Old man Answered him in English again. "Oh, Booba, Booba, boo!" Cry'd he, "We are All English togather I find now. And pray what is your name, my honny? Are you any Thing of a Seaman," said he, "and what brought you here, Joy, among this spotted clan?"

I told him my Story was Rather to long for the present but that my name it was Penrose if that was of any signification. "Sure," said he, "may it be Welly then was your name? Ever Welly Penrose, atall?"

"Who can you be," cried I, "that ever knew Lewellin Penrose who has been so many years lost from his Country?—unless you mean Another of my name."

"How never," said he, "did you or Did you not once belong to the *Flying Oxford*?"[3] Certain, I told him I had. "And don't you remember me, then, now—the man that was washed Overboard and washed in Board again in a gale of Wind off the Bay of Biscay?"

I said I well remembered the circumstance but had forgot the persons name except it was Tady. "Oh, Thats right, child! Tady Lort, thats my name, joy. But what keeps you among these Dung coloured like Thieves?"

"Old shipmate," said I, "as I find you have once been, many changes have I gone through since that Day; and to make short of the matter now as I see Your boat is coming on shore, you are to know That Lad is my Son and never knew what a Thief means."

"Oh, Blood! Welly, I ask your pardon, Young Lad. My good fellow, gives us your daddle," said he, and shook Owen so heartily by the hand that he made him stare again. "Ah, Messmate Welly," said he, "I knew you were no Spaniard by the true English brogue on your Tongue. Agrah, my dear!"

The Spanish boat being now arrived, they asked me on board with them, and I told Owen to come alongside the Schooner with our boat also, so off we went to her. When we got on board Messmate Tady took me Aft to the Captain and told him he had found a Countryman on shoar who would shew them a watering place. Capt. Valdes re-

3. A fifty-gun ship named the *Oxford* was built in Bristol in 1674, and was twice rebuilt at Deptford and Portsmouth.

cieved me kindly and asked me many odd Questions concerning my manner of aboad and living. After I had informed him of the circumstances of my life he was pleased to Say it became every man to treat me with all Civillity as perhaps God had place me there to administer relief to distress'd Seamen, and that he was glad to hear I was so well resigned to my uncommon way of life. Sent a boy down for a flask of Augua dienta and Drank to me. I told him as it was what I was seldom Accustomed to I would rather decline it. Upon this he Laughed heartily and observed to me that English and Dutch men never flinched the glass, he thought, and I must not plead any excuse. Upon that I drank It off.

He then gave order for them to run up the Cable and we stood down along the shore, keeping a good Offing as I told him there were many Shoals on the Coast. But as the wind fail'd us in the afternoon we Let go the anchor of the Whale Point and there remain'd for the night as I did not care to charge my self with the Risk of the Schooner by any means. I now thought I would send off Owen and the old man to inform them At home what had fell out in our abscence.

Erly on the morrow, the wind coming up at East, we Streatched off and in a short time came abrest the Point of Long Key where we came too again, when I went on shore with them and shewed them the place. Then I asked the Captain to come on shore with me And see my family and place of residence, as I Expected my friend off with our boat shortly. About noon Mr. Bell and Owen came off to us from our place and saluted the Captain.

Captain Valdes did us the favour to go on shore With us in the evening. When we got into our own Lagoon Owen took up the Conk shell and blew a blast. Harry answered it directly from the shore. The Capt. observing it asked the reason. I told him it was Our stated custom, that we all had our particular ways of Sounding so that when a strange Indian sounded we Were always ready to recieve him or them when they Came to visit us. When we came to land all our whole Congregation flockt down to view the stranger. Signior Valdes on seing so many courtsies and bows from my brown crew stood amazed, And turning to me Asked which was my Wife. I shewed him my Lady and our Children and introduced Mr. Harry as my Brother in law. Mr. Bell entertain'd the Captain the Best way he could for he was obliged to take the Office on himself as speaking Spanish flewently.

In the Mean time Harry and Rory went off after some Crayfish and the Women provided Yams and other Matters as I directed them. While this was doing, the Capt., Bell and my self walked all round our Habitation, shewed him our burying ground and that of Old Nunez, his countryman, also. But Owen Out of his Simple honest good nature asked me to Shew the Captain the place where we had found All our treasure. Now as he asked me in English It was happily lost on the Captain, and by Bells Giving him a check it soon stopt his gabb.

After Supper the Captain asked us if we had not A desire to revisit our country again. I made him the following answer, that as for myself I was well Content to End my days where I was in peace and Quiet as I had been on the Spot for so great a length of time. And Messmate Norman said the Same, observing that he should prefer my company before that of all Men, as he had thoroughly proved me and knew my ways, saying we had all we wanted. Kings could have no more in human life.

I proposed my own bed for the Captain to sleep in for the night, and we all turned in about Eleven oclock. On the morrow I went off with the Captain to the Long Key and there renewed my discourse with my Old fellow Sailor, Tady Lort. He no sooner espied me than he gave me this reception: "Oh, the Devil from me! Are ye there, Welly? Sure and Ime glad to see you again with all hearts. I have been telling my shipmates all about you and where I know'd you first. Faith, and thats a long, long time since. This is the last turn and we shall soon abord, my Soul, and then we'el have a small drop of the Crater together for ould acquaintance sake, honey."

I thanked My old Shipmate and went on board with the Captain, And about half an hour after, the boat came along side With the Water. The Captain proposed to take his Leave of us that afternoon or Early the next day, when Tady came aft and making his leg to the Captain Asked me if I would not take a parting drop of Grog With him before I left the Schooner, altho he was But a poor foremast man; and perhaps I might have more money than he now, yet he hoped I would not forget Old times.

"Forget?" said I, "No. For the honour of Old Ireland If it shall prove the last Grog I shall ever drink of more I'le drink with thee, my Old Boy, altho I am not used to drink spirituos liquors."

"Wel, Well, then, enough said. Shall I call you Capt. Penrose?" said he. "I suppose You trade in some craft or other by this time. Come, here is merry madness to all Misers, Mr. Penrose!" said he. I recieved the Calabash from his hand and drank to all True hearts and Sound bottoms. But while I was Drinking, "Ads flesh, man!" said he, "do you never send home to the ould Country atall? Give me a letter and I'le be Bound to deliver it at Surinam safe on board some Dutchman bound home, and that you may be as sure of as that the Devils in Ireland, I'le be Bale for that," said he. I return'd him thanks and promised that if They did not sail before the next day I would send one off.

Just at these words a lad at Masthead cried, "Vela! Vela!" This I knew meant a Sail, and he pointed her to be in the offing with his hand. Directly orders Was given to hoist a Saint Andrews Jack or what our Seaman call a Ragged Staff. This was no sooner done than the word passed forward to run up the Anchor. On this I went aft to the Captain to take my leave. He told me it was a Sloop which Sail'd in company With them and he would stand out to joyn them as She was bound to Surinam with them but had parted company in thick weather about 7 days ago. I bid Owen Jump into our boat and had but just time to shake hands with C. Valdes when they filled and Stood out to sea, Lort waving his red cap and crying, "Long life to you, Welly, Long life, my Soul!"

We Waited among the Reefs striking fish for some time to observe their motions. At last we saw them Speak each other and both stand away South, when we return'd home to our place of abode. We lived on after the old sort without any thing new happening untill the year ran out, and by my own Account I had been here now full twenty three Years and better.

Chapter 37: Twenty Fourth Year

Messmate Bell Observed to me on a day as he and I were out in the Bay togather Concerning my Son Owen, saying had I not remarked a sort of change in the behaviour of him of late? I answered that I had not, except that he grew more sedate, I thought, than before but that I supposed was owing to his time of life, being now grown almost a man. "What age may he be," said Mr. Bell, "at this time?"

"About eighteen," Said I, "or therabout. What causes this curiosity?" said I to him.

"Because I think, Messmate, the sooner you can Obtain him a Wife it may be the better for him As well as your self, and indeed the whole of us, For there is not a soul among us but truly regards him."

"As to that matter, Messmate," I replied, "you need Not doubt but that I could easily obtain a Wife for Owen among our friends, and they would be proud enough to provide him one or even give him the preferrence of any Indian Girl belonging to their whole tribe."

On this Bell began to laugh and said, "I find you are Quite Ignorante of the whole matter, Mr. Penrose; for That your Son is in love already nothing was ever more Certain, to my sorrow."

"To your Sorrow in love already? My friend, what mean you, for Gods sake?" cried I in a commotion. "Not with your wife, I hope!"

"No, no, no, Messmate. No, a far different Object, I can assure you, One fairer than she by many degrees. No, no, pray don't Give your self the least uneasiness that Owen would Once attempt the Virtue of my dame. His Amours are of a more refined taste, I can assure you."

"Upon my Soul, Bell, you stagger my understanding," said I. "Come to the Point at once, friend."

"Well, dont be startled, then. What Think you of the Virgin Mary?"

"Oh, pray, Bell, give over. You cannot be in ernest now, I am sure, or the Boy is of A certainty loosing his senses unless it be in a Spiritual Way; and, poor fellow, he has never recieved edification to work such eager love in his breast, I am sure."

"No, No," said Bell, "it is all Carnal, you need not doubt. But to put you out of pain, dont you remember what a Beautiful Picture of the Virgin and Child he saw on board of Captain Valdes vessel? Tis that has set his heart so on fire, as you may remember to have heard him speak frequently about it. And, indeed, you And I have been the innocent cause of All Owens sad malady by our extolling the beauty of our own fair Country women, and the frequent repetitions of their charms in the songs he has learnt. So that I Judge it a hard trial to bring his stomach to come to digest one of our Mahogany coloured beauties for Some length of time at least. But when he finds that You are acquainted with the affair he May be brought to some degree of reason and think More reasonably of the thing, as I am sure he can not think of Obtaining any object of that cast in this forlorn part of the World."

When Bell had made an end, "Let me alone to find Out a method of cure," said I. So the subject dropt for that time and we returned home with our game.

Some time after this on a day when Harry and Owen were Standing togather Bell observed that Owen was the tallest of the two. "Ay," said Harry, "Owen big enough for a Wife now. But he wont never have one here among our trees and rocks."

This made me laugh. "And pray where is She to come from, then?" said I. "And who made you so wise, Harry?"

"Oh, I Know," said he, "if one ship would come here with some of the fine White and Red women of your country, he knows You would not begrudge to give some of the Gold and silver We have yonder hid in the hole for one of them to be a Wife for him, for I know he loves them quite madly."

"What say you, Owen?" said I to him. "Are you so mad to Desire a thing cannot be obtain'd? Pray, cannot one Of our friends Daughters serve your turn as a Wife as they have done for Mr. Bell and your Father before you?" But they were not so White and Red, he said, Nor would I or Bell have had any like his Mother had we had our own choice in our own country. "You silly Blockhead, where did you gather all these Whims?" I said. "How can you be such a fool to fall in Love with what your Eyes never saw?"

He replied, did He not se the mark of one of my Sort of Women on Board of the Captains Vessel? I answered, true, that Was the mark of one who was much finer that [than] many Thousands; but could he think one of our country Women would ever condecend to marry such a black Fellow as he was?

"Why, then," said he, "did you and Mr. Norman marry black people yourselves?" I said the reason was plain—we knew that where we were No other Wives could be had, and therfore we were Content to have such as God ordain'd for us, and that It became him best to think after ye same way, and not to aim to touch the clouds with his fingers, Notwithstanding they lower so much at this time.—For the Sky was at the time overcast very much and it threatened to come up thick and dirty from the South East. This was about five in the Evening when it began to freshen Up smartly so that it soon banished all matrimonial thoughts out of our minds, And we began to collect all our light gear And stow it away the best we could.

About the shutting in of night the Rain came on attended With such tremendous Lightnings and Thunder that the Like we never had heard in our lives. Add to this, Job the Boy about Eleven years of age had got little Somer with him dow the lagoon in the Canoa, and what to think or Do in that case none could tell, as it blew so strong none Could keep their legs by this time. Yet Harry would insist, as he saw what a taking my Wife was in, to endevour to go to seek them; but while we were all in this distress The poor boy Job came in with the child safe and sound to our great surprize. I asked him how far off they had Been. Not far, he said, but that on their return he could not keep the Canoa clear of the Mangroves so that He and Little Somer were forced to take the water And Swim to the landing, a task fit for few except Indians. The Storm continued the best part of the Night.

About five in the morning I turned out to se what devastation had happened and soon had the sad scene of desolation open to my view. As for our Kitchen, that was flat to the ground, I mean all the weightiest parts; for as to the thatch and lighter Materials, they were all blown as far as the clift would suffer them. Not a Goat, Dog or Fowl was to be seen. I then took a Shell and gave a blast. This brought forth All our family one by one, and I was well pleased to find all well. Bell observed had it been in a cold Climate in all probability most of us had died, as the Rain penetrated but through every place Except my Cavern. We soon found several of our Poultry dead and the poor old Mackaw also.

In a few days after, old Quamino shewed signs that he would not continue long among us, and on A Morning Harry came in to me and inform'd that the old man was departed in ye night, and that he went off quite easy without groaning in the least. The truth is he certainly died of Old Age unless the last Tempest had hastened him rather sooner, as perhaps it Was the case, for he wanted no kind of indulgence or care While he live among us. However, he lived long enough to be at least convinced that all White men were not of the like turn of thinking as to the poor Africans.

After Quaminos funeral was over, which we conducted after Our usual mode, we began to fall on repairing with all the Expedition possible as to what was most needful; but Harry, Owen and Rory did the chief of the business. And after all things were tollerably reinstated again Messmate proposed to take a trip out to Explore the coast, for we had not been Abroad above six weeks. According, we got all ready and Stood out for our Grouper Ground which was about two or three miles from the mouth of the lagoon. Now it happened as I was sitting with the glass in my Hand I discried away to the North a Wreck as I judged. I gave the Glass into Bells hand to look and he was Of the opinion also, but it was so far to northward that We could but just make it. We continued at our killick fishing for about two hours and then returned home, Intending to send the lads thither on the morrow.

It was not untill the third day that Owen, Job and Rory sat off on the discovery, well provided with All nesesaries for the trip. And as

Owen was to be skipper I gave him strict charge that if it did prove a wreck and any people were saved, In that Case to inform them that they might have all the Assistance from us lay in our power, let them be of what nation soever, if he could but understand them; and if not, to bring us notice forthwith how matters lay. With this charge, off they went and we saw them full well out, from the hill.

On the third day in the morning they returned And Owen gave the following account of the Voyage. He reported that it had been a Vessel of three masts But that the Main one was gone down low, as he termed it, but that she lay a great way out on a sunken reef And was very low down in the water, quite in the sand; But that there was nothing to be found except some of the sails cloth and an Oar which was stuck up on end On the Shore right abreast of her with a Bottle made fast to it which they had got with them, But that They saw no people either dead or alive, only a Vast Smoak at a great distance along Shore more to the Northward. I sent down for the Bottle and when It was brought up Mr. Bell undertook to examine Its contents. When he had gotten out the stopper there Was within it a small note to this effect in Spanish: "The Polaccre[1] *Isabella* shipwreck'd on this coast August 29 anno 1769. Andreas Lopez Capitain. Nine drowned and seven including the Captain left this coast in their boat on the 31st for the North." So that she was lost in that dismal night I have mentioned above, but if She had guns or fired any We could not know as the wind was so strong and she Also too far away for us to hear.

In a short time after, Bell and Owen with Rory Paid a fresh visit to her and brought home with them all the Sail cloth that was left, and It came In a good time as we wanted Sails for our boats Very much, but, God wat! not at the expense of any poor unfortunate people whatever. Some of her Rigging also they got, which was of good use to us. Bell says she appear'd to him to have been a good stout Vessel almost new, as he conjectured by some of her things, Especially her blocks, burthened about 200 tons. A Saint was painted on her Stern in a white dress.

---

1. Polacre: a three-masted vessel found chiefly in the Mediterranean area.

We had nothing of moment from this time Untill about 5 months after when the Indians came On a Visit, or rather deputed to enquire how matters Went among us. We were not a little surprized to find out how they learnt the way as they were all 5 Strangers and had never been here before. But Rory inform'd us that they had travelled by the Ttrees and the Sun as he interpreted it, and by sleeps. Harry well remember'd two of them and told me Their names were Atory and Manabo. I desired to be informed from them how it came that they had Neglected us so long a time. They gave for answer that their Old men thought it not proper to send so soon after the great sickness had been among them, least we being fresh, it should break out anew among Us; and that they were bid to tell us that now we Were grown men in our place and had all we wanted, We could the better live without them than in the Days of our first coming hither.

I then bid Harry to inform them that I should be glad they would think Mr. Bell and Myself their friends In every respect equal with all those who had been here before them. They then observed they had been Informed I had a custom to mark down the names Of all my good friends on stones but that I had not Done so for them. Upon this Harry went and got Four stones and gave them to me, then he gave me the name of each Indian one by one, as first Atory, Manabo, Rabaito and Pannee; and when they Were all inscribed they were placed among the rest.

After this ceremony we entertain'd them after our old fashion. They tarried with us a whole Week and in a Very friendly manner invited Harry and Owen to go Home with them on their return. But Owen declined the going, saying he had been there once before and that he had much rather go to Jamaica I [if] he could but Ever get the chance. N.B. This he spake in English And I was glad it so happened; otherwise their backs had Certainly been up on account of his disdainful Speech, but they parted in good friendship with us all. And when they were gone I concluded to have a Serious conversation with Master Owen, for now I Began to think on the matter in a more serious light. But after what way to treat it I was as yet A Stranger, therfore determined in my mind to hold A conferrance with Messmate Bell as to the point In hand—that to obtain the booby a White Wife as We were scituated was next to impossible and then what White Girl could be procured so indelicate as for to contaminate with an Indian? And even this could not be obtain'd but by sending him off with the Next Spaniard should by chance touch here, which When that might happen God only knew. And then Again, should he make any such proposals to any Spanish Girl he must first be baptized a Catholick And that would never go down with me.

Some time after, Mr. Bell and I being abroad in the Woods, he observed to me that he took notice I was not so cheerful as usual. I told him Owen Gave me much uneasyness on account of the strange humours he gave himself of late. In regard to that, he knew was quite out of my power or any one else as we were scituated, he knew. "Oh, let the whole be to me and I shall take a course with him that shall succeed, I'le warrant you."

"You will do me A very kind deed, my good friend," I answered, "if you Succeed, for truly I am too proud to let him se how much concern it gives me. Yet I love him as becomes a Father, but not to madness, my dear friend. Perhaps were he where White Women are to be got at, What money I could give him might induce Some giddy Girl to think him fair enough for A time. But such connexions are of short duration."

After this I heard no more of the matter for Some months, and Owen seem'd to appear rather More sprightly than he used to be. But it chanced to Come about on the carpit among the women one Day when Bells wife said she hoped soon to se Owen, now He was come back from Jamaica, Married to one Of her own sort of Woman. "How so?" said I.

"Oh, ask my Man and he will tell you all about it," said she. I Was now quite impatient to have a talk with Bell And asked my Girl what she knew of the matter, but She said she knew no more than that Mr. Bell had Quite cured Owen of White Red women, as she Understood it, And if I asked Owen, to be sure he Would confess the matter. But I rather chose to have It from Bell the first convenient opportunity.

Soon after, Messmate and I being down a stricking togather, I asked him how the affair between him And Owen went on. "Oh, Swimmingly," said he. "He is as Much off now as on before. You remember the time Owen and I made a match after the Flamingoes? Twas then when I had him alone with me from All the rest. I began with observing that 'Harry said you wished much to be in Jamaica, for there you Could soon obtain a White Red Girl for a Wife,' but that he was much mistaken in that point. 'As how?' he said. I told him the Women in Jamaica were all White, Yellow, or as Black as old Quamino was; that it was in England where we came from these Charming White Red Girls lived. But there was One great secret I could tell him which, when he knew, he would not be so mad after my country Women. That raised his curiosity at once and he Desired to know. 'Well, then, Owen,' said I, it is a thing you would never pass by, I am sure. It is this —Should any Girl be so mad as to marry you, a Black Man, the other Girls would poison her soon out of Madness that she should disgrace herself so much Because it is what the White Women never do at all, And perhaps poison you after if they could but once Get the opportunity.' Upon my saying these last words He hung down his head with his face to the ground and said not one word for the space of two or three Minutes, when breaking silence as from a trance, 'My own colour for me,' said he, 'Master Bell. There Is enough of them would have me for love of my dear Father and Mother. I shall try to love one of them And make my self as easy as I can. I need not to go Out on the great Water to look for a Wife to get Poisoned, for then I should certainly kill the one Who did it, and I should not like to do such things.' 'O ho, my lad,' said I, 'they would hang you for that Up to a Tree and leave your flesh for the Eagles to Devour.' "

"Well, say no more, good Norman. I dont Want to talk any more upon the matter, and I find he is quite Gone off his old humour, by Harry's account."

About this time, I think it was, we had a shock of an Earthquake which lasted full half a minute and about Midnight. It was attended with a noise like that of a cart Shooting rubbish; and my Wife complain'd of a sickness at her Stomach caused by it. What was very remarkable, All the Ducks, Geese and fowls began to make a great

Noise in their different ways, but on a new alarm of a much greater kind they all became silent. And at that time came in Messmate Bell and Owen; they call'd to us to know how it went with us. I got Up and asked them what had happened, when they Said they knew not unless the old dead Ceder tree had fallen down by the Shock of the Earthquake, And on going to the place they found it so. It had fallen thwart our way up the Hill or lookout and Broke down another which stood opposite of a less size. This kept us all awake for the rest of the night; and On the morrow the lads fell too on cutting away All its branches to clear the road up the hill and to chop It in sunder for a pass.

While they were about this work Bell and I went on the look, but such swarms of Butterflys Of a new sort were to be seen all though the woods that it was Surprizing to behold. These flies were not large; they were of A Pale Red, and disappear'd in less than a Week so that not A flie was to be seen. Our Indians said it proved there Would be great heat for the time was coming. This was as I think about March.

While we were thinking one day on Various circumstances of our lives and how lonely we dwelt Sequstered from the society of Eurpeans, out of the knowledge Of all trade and what the busy world were about, our Young Boys came down out of breath from the Hill and told us that all the Sea was full of Great Fish fighting. This took the curiosity of the whole family, and soon the whole of us were on the Hill. We found it as the Boys reported. We saw a number of Grampuss's[2] sporting and throwing Up water to a great height; and while we were viewing them Messmate Started a notion that suppose we should go out And try to catch one of them, It would yield us a fine large Parcell of Oil for our burning. I could not help laughing At the proposal, asking him how he would proceed on his Whimsical project.

"Have we not got a good length of stuff," Said he, "from the Polacre wreck will serve us for line? And you know we have a good harpoon. What say you, Harry, Are you for a trial?"

"If Brother is willing," said he, So Nothing would appeace them but

2. Grampus: a small but fierce cetacean, also called killer whale.

out they would go, and Owen one of the formost to be sure. But here I chose to interfere and said he should not go, But that Rory Might go with them, but that Owen should absolutely Remain at home with me. To work they all three Went and got ready soon and were off in less than an Hour. I cannot say but I thought it one of the most Presumptive undertakings Bell ever took in hand, but His will was for it and the Lads were full as willing for the sport as he for the proffit. But little did I imagine what dire effects the curst undertaking Would work in the end. Oh, what may not man prevent Would he give himself five minutes cool reflection. But Bell was an older man than myself and as I thought needed not my precaution. How short Sighted are the young and heedless! Owen became quite Chapfallen on being denied going, and retired to his hutt.

Mean time I kept a constant look out after them and Saw the boat at length out beyond the Bay in full pursuit after them. By this time it was become evening And I kept my station untill I could see no longer, nor could I for my life devise what was become of them. I came then down from the hill, concluding they had given them Chase round the Long Key to the Southward.

When night had closed in I gave order that none should Go to sleep but make up a large fire and watch for their return. Owen said I need not fear, they would be Back in the morning. "Well, Get me my Pipe," I said, "and We will sit here untill Sleep sends us to bed for I am By no means that way disposed at present." I sat musing And smoking untill fair day light, then with fresh ardour Mounted the hill with Owen by my side but could not see the least sign of any Canoa, nor was there a fish left on the Coast. What to think or imagine we knew not, but that somthing extraordinary had happened I greatly dreaded.

About nine oclock Job came running down and said he saw two People with the Glass from the hill. Up I ran and Owen after me, when out on the Long Key I saw two of them Plain enough but no boat. We waited with impatience to se them put off, but after two hours longer patience we had the grief to see them both sit down as no way concern'd at all. I then left the Children on the hill to keep a Good lookout. While I was standing with the Women about me, little

Somer camd down, and told us the men were both Gone into the Sea to swim over to the other side the bay. I claspt my two hands togather and followed the child Up the hill, and by the help of the Glass plainly saw them swim for the opposite shore.

On this I bad Owen to run down and get the other Canoa ready and off He and I went with all speed, leaving the whole Family roaring and bellowing. We paddled away as fast as we could lay hands to the paddles, and in about two hours landed opposite the place they swam for. There we waited with eager desires untill they landed. I seated myself on the Beach and in a melancholy Mood looked on them as they drew towards the shore; but As to describe the condition of my poor heart at that time Is beyond my power. When they got ground I sent Owen Down to meet them for I could not go myself, being certain that somthing of a sad consiquence had fallen out.

They soon joyned me and with all the tokens of unfeigned Grief the two poor naked Indians related their dismal Story, while I sat looking at the earth with my Head On my knees and arms claspt round my legs, Owen with his Arms claspt togather round his neck which was a Custom with him when any thing extraordinary happened and was relating. This is what they declared to us as the true circumstances of their misfortunes.

That when they got out and about halfe a mile from the end of the Long Key A large Fish came bogueing[3] Athwart them and Harry got the dart in order to Strike him but Mr. Bell insisted that he would have the Dart and staff out of his hands, and that he gave it Up to him as he knew I would have it so. That then Mr. Bell advanced forward and sent the dart right Into the fish nigh the tail. The fish on that flew to the Southward with great speed and they were forced to heave out all the rope they had, with a large piece of Wood fastened to the other end. They told me that they never saw Norman in such high spirits before, And that they followed the fish to about a miles distance where they saw him rise again. They came up with the log of wood and haled in several fathoms of it, intending to cut it off least the fish should

3. To bogue, or to bog: to sink, submerge, or entangle.

carry it all away with him out of their reach again; and while they were doing this Mr. Norman said to Harry, "We will get as much of it as we can while he is So still."

He had no sooner spake when the fish gave a Sudden commotion and with one Stroke of his tail he Struck athawart the Canoa such a violent sweep that They were all beat in to the sea. That for his part it was Some time before he could draw his breath so as to have Power to look round him. He soon discovered Rorys head at About a boats length from him, but that they could not Find Mr. Bell, altho he could swim so well, so that they were certain the fish must have killed him with his tail When the Canoa was split. For that she was split from one end to the Other, and one of the ends quite through so that she was of no more use to them, on which they were obliged to swim for the Key back again.

"Say no more," cried I, "you have told enough already. When you are Rested take me back again home. I have heard enough this day to last me months." Soon after this we all four put away home In silence, not a soul speaking untill we got to our landing. We were soon surrounded by the whole family, and on my requesting Owen and Harry that they would not trouble me untill I sent for them a general howl began. I walked up to my cave with arms folded and there threw myself at my length on my bed.

Soon after this my wife came in to me weeping, and as I refused to Speak she began after the following manner with pushing me: "Penoly, dont you be mad sorry. You cant break great Canoas Like great Fishes. You wont go away from me and the children Like Norman did because you know you cant kill them very Well, or else you would have let Owen go with them. I did love Norman, Penoly, indeed, but not so much as you do, because he was foolish mad to take away himself from his Wife to Go catch what he could not catch, because it was to strong for all Men. The Great fish has eat him up now down his belly for it. You must not kill me and the Children because he would go, for You know I did not send him. So, then, get up and Eate fish With me, and we will love you as long as we have days."

"Full well do I know," Said I to her, "that the Man was well Esteem'd among them all, and I loved him as a Brother. Can I then refrain from paying due respects to his memory? After I have subdued my grief a little I will Eate with thee. Untill I give liberty then to be visited I pray keep them all away, as I have some thoughts In my mind which Must be composed before I shall again be myself." Upon that She arose and left me to my cogitations to go and Condole with Janet, as I supposed.

And I fell into a Serious rumination. What, thought I, have I to say or think that these things are not as they are permitted by the Great Author of nature, and for causes I know not or wherfore. Shall I then pine thus because my friend has been removed from me quick, as I may say, and before I had even reflected that such a time would Surely happen to us, as it does to all friends after one way or other. I need not launch out in his praise. He was lent to me For a few years. I loved him, it was return'd, he is call'd as my Dear Somer was, and I am left. But why I am spared or for how long is a profound secret, as it is to What end. Let me be resigned, then. For wherever I am scituated on this Glob of Earth is equal to Him who created me; and Sure am I if I live according to the divine ordinances He will enable me to bear up against all sudden alarms and Casualties, let them come when they will....

Chapter 38: Twenty Fifth Year

It is now several months since my Sinecer friend died, from which time I have not put pen to paper untill now, being May of my Twenty fifth year, having rather Indulged my melancholy humour to much and finding Nothing worthy recording, the time passing on in a sort of Sameness day by day. But I shall remark that Bell's Wife has determined never to have another husband any more while She lives, as she says, and indeed she seems to Be resolved theron as my Wife thinks, too.

My Son Owen has been gone with Harry on a Visit Among our Indian neighbours above two months On the great business of Getting him a Wife, for his Passion for European Women has subsided a considerable time past. So that I am at this present time of writing In a scituation almost as forlorn as I was twenty years ago as to my own colour.

I must not forget to Observe that Rory the other day found a Young Faun in the back Woods and brought it home to my wife. She insists on rearing of it altho I am not much for it. Yet we have seen no Tigers now for years. Nor do I think they frequent our Quarter, altho our Woods are grown almost as ample as ever. But it May be the constant fires and frequent chopping in the Wood may have caused them to abandon these parts. And indeed their abscence is the best company, As we have Goats breeding among us frequently.

Chapter 39: Twenty Sixth Year

August 20. My Son Has been now returned about a month and has brought With him a Young Indian Girl, By name Bashada. She is the Grandaughter of Old Komaloot and not above fifteen Years of Age, altho so tall that she measures at least above Five feet four inches; so that if he could not obtain one of the fair Ladies of his Fathers country he has made it up In length of person as to one of his own sort. But she seems to be of an agreeable temper and Person, so that I am at Ease on that score—were it not for the misery I undergo As to the agony of my limbs, being so much tormented at times that Sleep is a stranger to my nights. Nor can I but Seldom hold a pen or any other light thing in my hand, such A tremor attends me almost constantly. Yet I can Strike Fish or do other laborious work as easy as heretofore. And what adds to my sorrow is that I fear I shall soon be past the power of writing unless my disease should abate, Which I little expect from the nature of disorder which Is Fish Poison; and I am sufficiently confirmed in it As none tasted of it except my Girl America and myself, She being touched with the like simptoms but being young May outgrow it. As for my Part, I can take but little joy or comfort nowadays, but if my disorder continues to gain Ground my days cannot be many more either here or any Where else in this World. . . .

October 30. It is impossible for me to carry on my poor Account any farther, being entirely helpless of my right hand And almost of my other, So that what may be wrote from this Date must be carried on by my Son as I shall direct him, Or otherwise by My Brother Harry as they have both learnt to Write tollerably enough. I find my memory much impair'd Also at times by my disorder, yet my Girl America seems to Have but small simptoms of the poison left about her. How many Times have I feasted on Red Snappers before, quite clear Of all danger. But Death has his Agents planted in every place Both by Sea and Land, and when the Grand Summons comes We must be gone, sooner or later as the Lord wills it. Therfore Let me be content. Let me be dumb and patiently bear my pain, As I know that I shall be as surely relieved as that I began first to Exist. There must be a last time for every Mortal Man. . . .

[*The Journal*
Continued by Owen]

My Dear Father has been so bad in all his joints for above Six months that we have been forced to feed him like a Child. But he is now getting better fast, for the pains begin to leave him. This came about by the good help of some of our friends Who have been here of late as they know many kinds of Roots good for several disorders. But my father has lost much of The feeling in his limbs and cannot speak plain enough At times for us to understand his meaning. . . .

Chapter 40: Twenty Seventh Year

July 21. I had a Son Born and we carried him into the Cave to my Father And Mother. My Father would have the Child in his lap And asked me What name we intended for it. I said he Should call it what he liked best, but that I should like To have him named Lewellin if he pleased. "Call him so," Said he, "Son, but yet I think one is enough of the Name Unless more fortunate in regard to his passage through this Vale of Tears."

About the middle of September as My Uncle and I were Out in the Bay fishing Two Ships hove in sight in the East Quarter. But as my Father was now become quite past all his Curiosity or care for such things we let them pass to the Southward without stirring from our business or giving our selves Any concern about them, but only told him of them when we Got home. "I dont think, Owen," said he, "that I shall ever See another Sail with my Eyes Unless it should happen that I may be carried up to the Hill by some of you should another Appear before I die. And, Indeed, Owen," said he, "I cannot think the day of my death very far off if any stress may be put on Dreams.

"I Dreamed that I was become a very ancient man And that I lived alone at the Old Plantation, and as I was Walking along the strand by the Whale Point I thought I saw two Men going on before me. At last they stopped As tho they halted untill I came up, which I did soon After, and to my surprize found them to be my two Old Companions Somer and Bell. I thought they Were overjoyed at my joyning them and told me there Was a Ship waiting for them at Boom Bay bound For Europe, and that if she did not Sail that day they Would make interest with the Captain to give me My Passage—on which they were gone from me in an Instant and I was left alone. It awoke me."

About three Weeks after On a Morning early came young Somer and call'd me to come with him for that he was Sent by my Father to fetch me, and his own Father directly Would die if I did not make haste to come. I soon judged what My Brother would be at and ran directly thither, where was Harry my Uncle and most of the rest got before me, which Grieved me, fearing he would think I neglected him. But He turned his Eye on me and said, "Owen, come by my side," Which I did and sat down by him on the right. He then call'd to Uncle Harry and he came and seated himself on the left. "Now," said he, "give me your hands and I have a few words to Say to you both."

He then began: "Remember what I am Going to deliver to you. Love that Woman at my feet now on her knees, my Children, and yourselves. I shall not See another Sun arise. Lay me by Your Mother Luta. Preserve my Journal and with care deliver it into the Hands of the first European or White Man shall chance to touch on the Coast; and pray, and pay him to deliver It safe if possible among my Country men."

We promised Truly to observe all his desires and we went out for we Could not refrain our Grief. About Sun set Mother sent For me in, and said she believed my Father was gone to England, wherupon I told them to call in the whole family, And when my Uncle came in he said it was certainly true. And altho my father in his lifetime had used all means in his power to wean the whole family of the Savage customs, Yet directly such a scene of Madness and outragious sorrow Began that the whole place eccho'd by reason of the cry. The Poor Dogs howled at a great rate; and I wished that Very day would make an end of me also, when I saw how my Dear Uncle ran about tearing his hair and Beating his breast, the Womens hair strewed about at a most sad rate, the Children skreeming and throwing about brands of fire. All was madness and distraction and it continued on the Whole night.

In the morning my Uncle came to me and Said, "Owen, come let us be Men. We must put our troubles Out of our sight. My Brother

MR. PENROSE

said, 'Lay me by Luta,' We will do so, and then you shall be as he was among us. But we will Let your Mother have it all her way because we must love her as he charged us before he died."

The next day after our hearts had wearied with throbing I told my Uncle that we gave all up to his direction as he knew Best, having lived longest with my father, and he said he would do the best in his power. He shewed Rory how to make the Grave, And the Body of my Father was done up in some old cloth we Had yet left among us. Then my Uncle ordered that he and Rory would carry the body and that I should walk with his Wife, The rest to follow after; and thus we proceeded to the Grave. When we got there they laid it down by the side and My Uncle Told us he would do as he had learnt of my Father, and that we All knew how and must say the same. He then begain the Belief and we ended with the Lords Prayer all togather.

My Uncle advised with me that we ought to let our countrymen know of my fathers death, and as Rory seem'd to have no longer A desire to remain with us we took the opportunity to send the News by him over land. He took his leave of us about a Week after and returned home.

About three months after, came two Canoas of our folks to Visit us. We entertain'd them after the old way my father Had been used to treat them. We were asked wether we Concluded to break up or remain as we were. But we Had resolved to continue to live after my fathers manner before they came, and that was the answer they recieved.

Chapter 41: Twenty Eighth Year

We had not seen one sail for a long time, but about August as Job was on the Hill he discovered a fleet of above twenty vessels all Standing to the Southward. I got the glass, but they were So far out that I could not make much of them and we Lost sight of them towards Evening....

———

Mr. Paul Taylors Account of the Journal

"Being Mate of a large Brigg, one Captain Smith Commander, and laying at the Havannah anno 1776, It chanced that we lay nigh to a Spanish Sloop late From the Main, and as the mate of her happened to Get a little acquainted with me by my speaking the Spanish tongue, He on a day asked me on board to Spend an hour or two, that he had something to shew me. According, the next day being Sunday and He Only being on board except an Old Negro fellow, I went on board to have a little chatt with him.

"We had not been long together before he unlocked a Ceder Chest and got out a bundle of old Papers and Bid me look at them, saying they were English. After I had looked over a few leaves I asked him how it came into his hands. He told me he had it from two Indians who spoke good English, and that one of them Told him in Spanish it was wrote by his Father Who had lived and died there, and that they would 'Give me money enough if I would sware to give it Into the hands of some good English man As soon as I could after we had took in what water we wanted. They brought me above fifty Pieces of Eight, And I swore by the Holy Cross to deliver the Papers. Now as you are the first English man I have met with, If you will take it in charge You shall have It. Otherwise I shall take it on shore and deliver it to some other, and if not, to the Governor.'

"I told him He might depend that for my countrymans sake I Would put it in the best road for information I could possible, upon which he deliver'd me the Journal And I offered him an acknowledgement of a Doubloon. But he refused the taking it from me, saying He should think himself a Thief so to do; and I have preserved it through many dangers.

"You will find when You come to Read it many curious accounts of things which I Know to be matters of fact, altho I never knew any thing of ye Man. During the time I was out of employ at Charlestown I took it into My head to Coppy it all out and send it You, as you live at this Time in London. I think it may be of some Service to you, and if So shall be proud of the little kindness I can render for the former services you have shewn me.

"If you do not get it soon Published I shall dispose of the Original at Philadelphia Or New York, but not before I hear from you. N.B. You must Remember John Waters who formerly sail'd with Capt. Dean. It is he who has wrote it all out just as the Author spelt it, for I desired him so to do and he has been as carful as possible.

"May 2d 1783——New York."

Afterword: Penrose in the Twenty-First Century

WILLIAM WILLIAMS, Painter, at Rembrandt's Head, in Batteaux-street,
Undertakes painting in general, viz. *History, Portraiture, landskip,* sign
painting, lettering, gilding, and strewing smalt. N. B. He cleans, repairs,
and varnishes, any old pictures of value, and teaches the art of drawing.
Those ladies or gentlemen who may be pleased to employ him, may
depend on care and dispatch. [emphasis added]

William Williams was at the height of his artistic career in 1769 when
this advertisement appeared in *The New-York Gazette and the Weekly
Mercury.*[1] Newly arrived from Philadelphia, where he had conducted
his business of "painting in general" for twenty years, Williams had
completed numerous paintings, including three full-length portraits for
David Hall, Benjamin Franklin's printing partner. During a temporary
relocation to the British West Indies, he had produced dozens more
paintings. And in Philadelphia, he had also established himself as the
first professional scene painter in the history of American theater while
supplementing his income by painting and ornamenting vessels for the
prosperous shipbuilders Thomas and James Penrose. There, too, he had
instructed the young Benjamin West, whose fame as an artist would far
surpass his own. Williams's colonial contemporaries would have recognized most of these activities–yet he made his most remarkable contri-

bution as the author of *Mr. Penrose: The Journal of Penrose, Seaman*, a novel that would remain practically unknown for nearly two centuries. A medley in words of Williams's favored genres in oil–*History, Portraiture*, and *"Landskip"* (landscape)–*Mr. Penrose* is the story of a British castaway, an innocent who becomes "accustom'd to all Vice except Murder and Theft" (302) but ultimately finds redemption among the Amerindians of Nicaragua's Mosquito Coast.[2] The narrative is replete with ecological and anthropological interest, rife with adventure, and enriched by the narrator's reflections on racial equality, religious freedom, and the autonomy of the individual in a world threatened by coercive forms of rule. Though seldom recognized as such, it also appears to be the first novel to be written in what would become the United States.

The late David Howard Dickason, who initially recovered Williams's novel, argued that *Mr. Penrose* contains the first critique of American slavery in book-length American fiction and the first sympathetic treatment in American fiction of Native Americans.[3] In addition, Dickason argued, Williams was a pioneer in the art of nature writing who made important contributions to the use of realism and humor in American fiction. To this impressive list of historical and literary firsts, I would add that *Mr. Penrose* includes the first felicitous portrayals of interracial marriage and the first interpolated slave narrative in the history of the American novel, together with some of the most sustained and thoughtful treatments of racial justice, religious tolerance, and human rights to appear in American literature before Melville's *Typee: or, A Peep at Polynesian Life* (1846), with which it shares a similar ethic, aesthetic, and eclecticism. Yet the initial publication of Williams's original novel was a landmark achievement that, ironically, passed almost unnoticed. Like Williams in the late eighteenth century, Dickason in the late 1960s was ahead of his time in recognizing the centrality of *Mr. Penrose* to themes and ideas that have shaped American history, literature, and culture from the contact period onward.

Apparently composed more than a decade earlier than William Hill Brown's *The Power of Sympathy* (1789), the text customarily regarded as the first American novel, *Mr. Penrose* offers a rewarding starting point for the study of American fiction.[4] In contrast to Brown's conventional cautionary tale of a woman who is seduced and abandoned, *Mr. Penrose* is deeply embedded in an originary New World tradition of quests that begin with captivity and exile and end with transformation and redemption—a tradition reaching back to Álvar Núñez Cabeza de Vaca's *Relación* (1543) and extending into the twenty-first century. Unpublished in the author's lifetime, *Mr. Penrose* first appeared in print in the early nineteenth century, but only in bowdlerized editions. Not until 1969, when Indiana University Press released the current edition, was the novel published in its original form. Even then, however, acceptance of the novel into the canon of American literature seems to have been hampered by the nationalist, exceptionalist model of literary history that defined the field for most of the twentieth century. As a novel set in Nicaragua and written by a colonial Briton of Welsh heritage who was born (or at least christened) and raised in England, lived in the Middle Atlantic and British Caribbean colonies for nearly thirty years, remained loyal to his native country, and returned to England at the outbreak of the Revolutionary War, *Mr. Penrose* held a tenuous position within this circumscribed theoretical landscape. Beginning in the late twentieth century, however, the study of American literature shifted toward transnational paradigms acknowledging the broad transatlantic context of European, African, and American literatures as well as the intersecting histories and shared cultural heritage of hemispheric colonialism and indigeneity. At the same time, emerging interdisciplinary fields such as environmental, oceanic, and diasporic studies have influenced recent scholarship. To all of these approaches, *Mr. Penrose* is well suited because of its deep engagement with transnational histories, cultures, landscapes, and seascapes.[5]

William Williams was far more than a colorful figure in Franklin's Philadelphia. As the eminent historian James Thomas Flexner noted, "the activities of this forgotten genius spread across almost every branch of American culture."[6] And as the writer who initiated the conversation on empire, race, and the environment in American fiction, Williams deserves a wide audience. Taking his intriguing *Self-Portrait* (frontispiece) as a focal point and visual cue, I seek to situate Williams and his novel within the critical landscapes of the new American Studies.

As this afterword emphasizes, *Mr. Penrose*, like the artistic repertoire Williams advertised in the *New-York Gazette*, embraces multiple generic modes, which, as narrative constructions, unfold simultaneously and chronologically within a single textual frame. The following sections illustrate to readers of *Mr. Penrose* that in this novel *history* cannot be reduced to "context," *portraiture* defies the fixity of static representation, and *landscape* refuses to lie tranquilly in the background.

(1)

History

I have looked at the portrait so often that I find it one of the most interesting I have ever seen. I see a strangeness written in many lineaments—the exact character of which I cannot describe; and it is the more strange on that account: sensible, shrewd, inquisitive, patient, unimpassioned—as one cognizant of other men's doings and thoughts—uncommunicative of his own.

In an article in *Blackwood's Edinburgh Magazine*, John Eagles, a Victorian gentleman who had known Williams many years earlier, contemplates Williams's enigmatic *Self-Portrait*. This portrait has perplexed and fascinated many others who, like Eagles, have tried to account for it. Not least among its mysteries are questions of date: when did Williams paint it, and how old was he at the time? Recent art historians have argued that it depicts Williams in his prime, clad in the velvet cap and silken gown characteristic of gentlemen-artists of the mid-eighteenth century. To Eagles, however, Williams appeared to be attired in the "Alms-House dress" he recalled from childhood, although, he pondered, "he looks not so old in the picture as I remember him." Williams's famous student Benjamin West was similarly flummoxed by Williams's history, volunteering information about his life and the time he may have spent shipwrecked in the Caribbean that doesn't add up. Their confusion is not surprising: William Williams, whose very name carries in it a sense of doubleness, readily re-invents himself, both in paint and in words.

In his novel this re-invention appears as a believable but decidedly fictive version of Williams in the character of a man he names Lewellin Penrose.[7]

Like the *Self-Portrait, Mr. Penrose* invites rumination on time, temporality, and the intricacies of chronology. It not only conveys readers through Penrose's adventures; it also leads them into the tangled, partially unwritten histories of Europe, Africa, and the Americas. Like many other eighteenth-century novels–including the early American potboilers *The Power of Sympathy*, Susanna Rowson's *Charlotte Temple* (1791), Hannah Webster Foster's *The Coquette* (1797), and Royall Tyler's *The Algerine Captive* (1797)–*Mr. Penrose* presents itself as unvarnished life story, a mode Williams substantiates with precise references to actual locations, dates, historic events, even the names of ships and their commanders, most of which have been authenticated.[8] Such details lend texture and verisimilitude to the expansive geopolitical canvas of the eighteenth-century Atlantic World. At the same time this historical realism also highlights the text's examination of the intersecting histories of colonialism, mercantile capitalism, slavery, empire, and warfare that bound together the New World and the Old.

The action begins in Wales in September, 1744, when the nineteen-year-old Penrose runs away from home in order to follow the sea. With twenty-six colonies in British America–the thirteen that would rebel in 1776 and thirteen others that did not–England, in the middle of the eighteenth century, was heavily invested in a lively maritime economy that kept people (slave and free), raw materials, and manufactured goods in constant circulation. Arriving in the port city of Bristol, Penrose is quickly absorbed into the contending, mutually sustaining networks of transoceanic commerce and imperial militarism.

"It was now War-time" (38), Penrose announces, making it clear that the story of his life and adventures will involve momentous affairs of society and state. Penrose refers elliptically here to the conflict retrospectively dubbed the War of Jenkins' Ear, which erupted in 1739 over the breakdown of a trade agreement between Spain and Britain. According to this agreement, Britain was entitled to supply an unlimited number of slaves and up to 500 tons of goods per year to the tightly controlled markets of the Spanish colonies. Ostensibly beginning as a skirmish over Britain's alleged piracy in the West Indies, the War of Jenkins' Ear peaked with the British capture of Portobello, Panama (1739) and eventually bled into the War of the Austrian Succession (1744–1748), the third of four imperial wars that would also be fought in–and over–North America.[9]

Warfare quickly intrudes upon Penrose's life. After sailing on commercial voyages to London and Cork, Ireland, he signs on with a privateer, and then, while spending his "prize money" on shore, is "pressed" into the Navy–that is, captured by agents of the Crown, locked up, conducted to a ship, and forced into military service. He then "shift[s] from one [ship] to another . . . going under different names" until he manages to escape (42). Embarking on a West Indian trader bound for the sugar-rich island of Jamaica (a hub in the Atlantic slave trade), Penrose soon finds himself once more a pawn in the European wars for control of the seas and dominion over the New World. Off the coast of Cuba, his ship, having received its "full lading in" (43), is attacked and defeated by a Spanish Man-of-War. Penrose and his compatriots are imprisoned in the Cuban stronghold of Havana, where, forced into labor, they witness North American vessels routinely supplying their enemy with staples by sailing in under "Flags of truce" (45). After some six weeks in Havana, Penrose and his countrymen are released on a prisoner exchange. Destitute in the Bahamas, a now hardened and embittered Penrose, bent on retaliation, throws in his lot with a crew of pirates and embarks with them on a continuous "round of Gunning, Fishing, drinking, fighting, and uproar" (52).

Penrose's maritime career ends abruptly following an unsuccessful attempt to spear a tortoise from the ship's canoe. "Much the worse for liquor" (52), he falls asleep in the canoe only to awaken alone and adrift off the coast of the Spanish-controlled mainland (or "Spanish Main"). Although, in response to the war with Spain, Britain sought to tighten its control of the region, the stretch of the Mosquito Coast (or, to the British, the Mosquito Shore) where Penrose alights is so remote from European and Amerindian routes alike that years pass before he has any significant human interaction. And yet even in this isolated location,

Penrose is acutely aware that this land has a historical past (native as well as European)–"I am not the first of Mankind who have visited this place" (59), he reflects–as well as a continuing role in the ongoing drama of empire. As Penrose, from his secluded vantage point, observes an increasing number of passing ships and makes intermittent contact with European seafarers, Williams, through Penrose, begins to "face east from Indian country" and "look out at Europe from the imperial frontier" as current historians Daniel Richter and Mary Louise Pratt recommend.[10] In his journal, spanning the course of three decades, Penrose registers the impact of imperialism, slavery, militant Christianity, and international trade on the indigenous people whose land and labor European colonizers so highly prized.

Although the Caribbean coast of Nicaragua, where most of *Mr. Penrose* takes place, remained free of direct European control throughout the colonial period, beginning in the sixteenth century numerous Europeans attempted to exploit its human and nonhuman resources. By the time Penrose arrives on Central America's Atlantic coast, despite Spain's official ban on the Indian slave trade, "the Caribbean islands, and the heavily populated central American mainland region between Mexico and Panama" had become "a vast catchment area" for this nominally illegal slave trade.[11] True to the region's history, Penrose and the indigenous people he encounters live in constant fear of enslavement. When his Indian allies ask him to shelter a youth who has escaped from a Spanish mine, for example, we realize that Penrose's dread of forced labor is founded on more than the "Black Legend" of past atrocities.

In *Mr. Penrose* Williams evokes an uneasy balance of power among Spanish, English, and indigenous people that is deeply rooted in the history of the Mosquito Coast. Despite armed expeditions in the sixteenth century and politically motivated missionary campaigns in the seventeenth century, Spain's efforts to control the region failed, owing at least in part to the diffuse and relatively egalitarian social structure of the indigenous cultures. More productive in their relationship with Mosquito Coast Indians were English, Dutch, and French pirates, who, in the 1660s established "social, commercial, and military ties" with tribes inhabiting the region near Cabo Gracias a Dios (well north of Penrose's hideaway). Beginning in the seventeenth century, notes the cultural anthropologist Baron Pineda, these Indians "adopted a common set of political and economic strategies that entailed cooperation with the English and hostility to Spanish and Indians from the interior." As a result, "identification with English symbols, be they language, commodities, or 'customs,' had long been associated with prestige among all groups on the Mosquito Coast." It is little wonder then that Penrose would "[take] care to style [himself] an English man," or "Englese" (101).[12]

When he discovers that the Indians he meets have "a traffick with the Spaniards" (87), therefore, Penrose asks that they not reveal his presence, since his "nation was ever at war with them" (116). These words turn out to be more accurate than the castaway could know. In his thirteenth year of exile, Penrose observes "many large boats out on the Waters . . . all standing to the East" and concludes "that it was a Squadron of King's ships . . . belonging to Spain probably" (227). A short time later, he learns that Spain "had but just then concluded a peace with the English, for there had been another war since that he . . . [was] concerned in" (294).

As a young man in England, Penrose had been swept into a European war centered half a world away in the Americas. Now, exiled in the Americas at the very crossroads of British and Spanish imperial ambitions, he appears to be wholly sheltered from this geopolitical strife. For unknown to Penrose, this lately concluded war is the Seven Years War (1756–1763), the last of the European imperial wars to be fought in North America. Ironically, this war, which had enormous consequences for the subsequent fortunes of Europe's New World empires, is passed over entirely in Mr. Penrose. Penrose simply doesn't know that it was going on, and so his journal makes no mention of it. The amity between him and an elderly Spaniard who had fought, like Penrose, in the War of Jenkins' Ear and is subsequently "elected one of our society" (291) underscores the novel's dominant message of tolerance and peace. At the same time, readers with the benefit of historical hindsight cannot escape the knowledge that the consequences of distant wars would have profound and often devastating effects on the lands and people over which they were fought.

Yet the Atlantic World Mr. *Penrose* depicts is not merely an arena for battling European empires. As a mariner, Williams would likely have worked alongside African seamen; moreover, during the period he spent painting in the West Indies, he lived within a society composed of a vast (up to 90%) black majority ruled by a tiny white minority with whom he did not sympathize.[13] His novel is clearly embedded within this African Atlantic milieu as well. Mr. *Penrose* includes, or alludes to, numerous minor characters identified as African, black, or "mulatto": the Jamaican William Bass; his friend Bell's first wife; Rodrigo, a sailor whose wife purchased his freedom; a biracial pirate appointed (or rather, slain) to guard a cache of treasure (from the grave); and crew members of a Spanish Coast Guard from Cartagena (Colombia) described as "a Medly of Mortals composed of all the dips or casts from the Spaniard down to the Indian and Negro" (326).[14]

More pointed than these passing references is Penrose's speculation that a sixteen-foot shark attained its "prodigious" size by "follow[ing] some ship from the coast of Africa after the dead Slaves, was caught by one of those Ships and had been let go again or made his escape" (280). The suggestion of the shark's "escape" is particularly relevant in light of the fact that the Mosquito Coast was a well-known haven for fugitive slaves, or maroons, many of whom became integrated into Mosquito society through marriage.[15] The Sancoodas, or Mosquitos, a tribe with which Penrose's friends are at war (and "the most inveterate Enimies to all Spaniards" [329]), figure prominently in the second volume of *The Interesting Narrative of the Life of Olaudah Equiano* (1789). In this text, a Mosquito leader harbors the escaped Equiano at a period coinciding with the final installments of Penrose's journal.[16] These references lend both historical legitimacy and urgency to the interpolated narrative of the fugitive slave Quammino, who ultimately finds ease and community among Penrose's extended family (343).

Finally, the very language of Mr. *Penrose* savors of the cultural watershed of the Black Atlantic. In an analysis of lexical and grammatical data in Williams's novel, the linguist John Holm identifies numerous "features characteristic of European languages in intense contact with African languages." This verbal hybridity makes Mr. *Penrose* a prototype for the rich linguistic "un-Englishness" (to borrow Holm's expression) that later writers such as Walt Whitman and Mark Twain would strive to emulate and promote as vital features of American speech and writing.[17]

(2)

Portraiture

During his lifetime and for the better part of two centuries thereafter, William Williams was known primarily for his contributions as a painter, not as a writer. By his own count, while living in the Mid-Atlantic and Caribbean colonies he completed more than 240 paintings, many of them commissioned by wealthy clients. Although only a fraction of his paintings survive, his *Self-Portrait* exhibits a level of artistry and technical skill that distinguishes him among his contemporaries. Seated at his easel, palette in one hand, paintbrush poised in the other, and a sketch on the wall behind him, the "self" this portrait projects is every inch an artist. And yet x-ray photographs of Williams's brushwork reveal that portions of the canvas have been "over-painted," obscuring a deeper layer of portraiture. Before the subject held a palette, he had held a book; and before he wielded his brush, he appears to have gripped a pen.[18] Like the literary sleuthing of Dickason, the "scholar adventurer" whose rediscovery of *Mr. Penrose* began with a footnote in an art history text, radiographic analysis has revealed the writer behind the painter.[19]

Benjamin West, who rose to prominence as a founder and second president of the Royal Academy of Art, credited Williams, his boyhood mentor, with launching his career. Many years later, West partially repaid the debt when he engaged an elderly, indigent Williams to pose as a model for one of the toiling sailors in his massive historical panorama *The Battle of La Hogue* (c. 1775–1780). West's portrayal of a shirtless, battle-weary old salt hoisting a fallen mate into a lifeboat provides a fitting companion piece to Williams's *Self-Portrait*. Together, these eighteenth-century masterpieces–Williams's only known likenesses–reveal multiple facets of this intriguing subject: Williams the creative genius whose work lies at the very fountainhead of American art and fiction, and Williams the man of action whose adventurous seafaring past inspired and shaped *Mr. Penrose*.

Williams's artistic sensibility is abundantly evident in the numerous verbal portraits and self-portraits Penrose presents to the reader. His attention to sartorial details, for example, allows us to trace the protagonist's transformation from naïve landlubber with an eye to the sea, proudly sporting a jaunty new Scotch bonnet, to ragged, sun-scorched castaway wearing little more than tattered trousers. Later we see him transformed again from seasoned islander outfitted in his "best attire"–straw "Sambraro" adorned "with two fine Maccaw feathers," "Tigers skin" jacket ("hair side out"), and hatchet, bow and arrows, and machete all secured by "a belt of bass rope" (144)–to "counterfeit Spaniard" complete with cross at his breast, crucifix tattooed onto his hand, a clean-shaven face, and hair "platt[ed] . . . behind after the Spanish mode" (278–280).

Williams's skill in verbal portraiture reveals an exceptional ear for language as well as a painter's eye for visual details. In the figure of Penrose, Williams departs from eighteenth-century decorum by presenting an "Illiterate" working-class colonial–a "poor Jack Tar" (218, 227), writing chiefly for his "Brother Tars" (267)–as narrator. His speech, down-to-earth and colloquial, will seem refreshingly up-to-date to modern readers despite the archaic spellings: in Penrose's parlance, clothes are "dudds" (49), and in their absence a person might be described as "stript . . . to his buff" (251) or "in his birthday suit" (84). Penrose shows his friends "where to turn in for the night" (85); when he's in a quandary, he's in "a fine pickkle" (119); and when "tigres" (wildcats) run away they "turn tail" (122). Although written as a journal, *Mr. Penrose* is surprisingly dialogic, and in the verbal exchanges that punctuate the novel, we hear other colloquialisms, such as "knock it off" (172) and "Shew me the money" (212), along with humorous, and sometimes ribald, jibes. In one memorable exchange, when his Dutch "Messmate" airs his racist objections to consorting with Amerindian girls, Penrose slyly assures him that "he need never to stand in any great dread of being ravished by any of them either a Wake or in his Sleep" (174–175).

Williams's gift for representing natural, unaffected speech "by ear" appears, too, in Penrose's rendering of his interlocutors' distinctive idioms, which span a range of pidgin languages and Creole dialects. Most prominently appear the Dutchman Somer, with his crisp Teutonic consonants (one can practically *hear* him say "plows out his pranes" [158] and "you ben choakin? [joking]" [191]), and Norman Bell, a long-time resident of Venezuela whose Scottish brogue regains its "burr" as he becomes established in Penrose's community. The most intriguing use of spoken language, however, occurs among the indigenous characters. Rather than attempting to "translate" the Indians' speech into British English, whether idiomatic or stylized, Penrose records their words precisely as he remembers them. These indigenous voices, in dialogue with Penrose, illustrate a cultural reciprocity or transculturation that is seldom clearly conveyed in early Anglo-American literature. Through its multilingual heteroglossia, *Mr. Penrose* thus rewrites the myth of unilateral European influence acting upon receptive colonial subjects. As Holm's groundbreaking linguistic analysis reveals, "Penrose was not only teaching the Indians his English, he was also learning theirs."[20]

Despite its linguistic authenticity, however, readers will likely find Williams's indigenous characters less fully realized than are their European counterparts. Still, the novel is careful to reject the Eurocentrism that constructed the apparent opacity of non-European societies as a cultural void. Instead, Penrose acknowledges his own deficiency with respect to indigenous languages and traditions. For instance, he explains, "in regard to Indian informations, Spelling their names, and the like I do not affirm them to be exact as a Man must be born among them before he shall be able to give a true pronunciation or be able to coppy their Ideas and manner of conveying sentiments" (167). As this example illustrates, Williams does not claim for his protagonist a privileged "insider's" perspective.

Nor does he subject Amerindians to a colonizing gaze in order to portray them as passive victims of "inevitable" Europeanizing "progress." Indeed, on numerous occasions he actually inverts the imperialist dynamics. An unwitting Penrose learns that he has been under surveillance by Indians; and in Penrose's community a "Dover Court," described as "all Speakers and no hearers" (337), suffers by contrast with an orderly delegation of Indians, among whom a single designated speaker mediates while the others respond "in one short word as one voice" (244). He also shows Penrose adapting gradually to Indian ways, even as he teaches them to read and introduces them to the Bible. More subtly and

more remarkably, Williams does not invariably present European ways
of knowing as normative, naturalized, or absolute. Following a period
of instability in his relations with the Indians, for example, a discomfit-
ed Penrose confesses that he has "no liquor to treat them with now in
store"; in reply, the Indian delegate is philosophical, "answer[ing] that
all things decayed in time except the Sun, Moon and Stars, so that he
wondered not at it in the least" (277). In this exchange, Penrose does
not come off as masterful. Instead, here and elsewhere, his incomplete
knowledge of Mosquito Coast languages and cultures proves a source of
tension, humor, and occasional volatility in the novel's plot.

   To survive as a British castaway on the Mosquito Coast, Penrose considers it necessary to establish authority as well as to exercise diplomacy. When he becomes acquainted with two young Indians, brother and
sister, he is careful not only to "gain their regard" but also to "carr[y]
[him]self so as that they should regard [him] as a kind of superior" (88).
Although Penrose has no desire to subjugate the Indians, he does claim
a position of unquestioned leadership among the small group of Indians who choose to reside with him. His perceived need for control becomes most urgent, however, when he welcomes into his community its
first European member aside from himself. Regarding the Dutch sailor
Somer as possibly less "tractable" than his Amerindian friends, Penrose
urges him to accept his "advice in all respects," as knowing the Indians
better (162). One of these Indian "ways" involves the role of marriage
as a crucial tool of diplomacy on the Mosquito Coast. Through marriage, Penrose becomes a "White Brother in blood and flesh" to the
Indians (274), and soon comes to "look upon Harry," an Indian, as his
"new Brother" (92), "a part of [him]self" (255). When a conflict arises in
Penrose's relationship with the Indians, marriage provides the solution,
and when a recently widowed woman considers leaving Penrose's community, the Indians fear that the peace between them has been broken
and death permitted to vanquish life.

   Although indigenous women are not individuated as clearly as their
male counterparts, they compare favorably with the few English women
who appear in the novel's early pages. These English women are either
sentimentalized (as is Penrose's mother), identified as "brutes" (prosti-

tutes), or portrayed simultaneously as pathetic victim of male violence and licentious object of male lust (as is the waifish wife of the Bristol landlord). Troubling too is Penrose's inability to imagine any white woman who would be "so indelicate as for to contaminate with an Indian" (371), which, like the depiction of the landlord's abused and faithless wife, signals a decided failure of marriage as an instrument of harmony. Taken together, these images bespeak a gender ideology in which sexual purity, racial purity, and sexual violence are implicated in the imbricated projects of commodification, conquest, and exploitation.[21]

The stark contrast between the depiction of women in the European and Mesoamerican sections of Mr. Penrose is one indication of the gradual and uneven but ultimately radical transformation Penrose experiences over the thirty-odd years of the narrative. This transformation appears most clearly in his response to the constructed categories of "savagery" and "civilization." Although Penrose fears that if he returned to Europe, his children, remaining in America, would grow up "savages," he unequivocally challenges not only the "barbarous stories . . . related of [the Natives]"; he also sharply criticizes the actions of Europeans (especially, but not exclusively, the Spanish), urging readers to "let us first enquire who were the agressors." As he confidently attests, "I have resided so long among them that I know the error to fall on the Christian side" (130). Ultimately, his indictment of European aggression impinges on the entire imperialist project, not sparing the conventional Christian defense of imperialism as a civilizing force. Contemplating a separation from his Indian friends, Penrose reflects:

Here I was to part, perhaps never more to meet, with some of the most disinterested mortals, a people who out of common humanity had done the utmost in their way to be the generous relievers of my wants, had come so many leagues without any expectation of reward. And this I blush to own was not done by Europian Christians but by men we are pleased to call brute Savages. So I may with justice remark, where is the advantage they have gained by the Spaniards' discovery of this New World? Have they not done all evils among them, destroying and Enslaving under colour of Exchanging one Idol for another, while they committed such crimes among them which ought really to point them out as the most infamous and inhumane Savages on earth? I say, had not those poor cretures been in a much better state so to have remain'd untill God should have been pleased to have brought about their Redemption in or by some more Apostolical means? (116–117)

As his extended "family" of fugitives, exiles, their wives, and their children increases, Penrose comes to embrace a providential worldview in which "the poor Savages, our sincier friends" inspire a decidedly ecumenical "Model of Christian Charity" (to repurpose John Winthrop's phrase), one which Penrose and his mates strive to emulate by "reliev[ing] the Distressed" (216)–regardless of nation and race–whom Providence sends their way.

Although Mr. Penrose has clear affinities with eighteenth-century autobiographies and travelogues, it resonates even more profoundly with castaway fiction (called Robinsonades, named for Robinson Crusoe) and its nonfiction analog: survival literature. Described by Mary Louise Pratt as "first-person stories of shipwrecks, castaways, mutinies, abandonments, and (the special inland version) captivities," seventeenth- and eighteenth-century survival literature, Pratt explains, "furnished a 'safe' context for staging alternate, relativizing, and taboo configurations of intercultural contact: Europeans enslaved by non-Europeans, Europeans assimilating to non-European societies, and Europeans cofounding new transracial social orders." In exercising the artistic license of fiction, Williams departs from the generic conventions of survival literature in one crucial respect: he rejects the denouement of the marooned or captive character's return to European society, and Penrose chooses to make the Mosquito Coast his permanent home. In contrast, as Pratt elaborates, "The context of survival literature was 'safe' for transgressive plots, since the very existence of a text presupposed the imperially correct outcome: the survivor survived, and sought reintegration into the home society. The tale was always told from the viewpoint of the European who returned."[22] To be sure, Mr. Penrose is inescapably implicated in the ideology it critiques, and aspects of it clearly participate in the familiar imperialist fantasy of a New World Eden presided over by superior Europeans. And yet there is this key difference–the fantasy that Mr. Penrose develops rejects expansionist tactics and challenges imperialist assumptions. If vestiges of an assumed, unexamined European/British/ white supremacy remain, they are very tenuous. Instead, the novel depicts a multiracial, multiethnic political sanctuary in which Manoluvy, or "a general amity and concord," prevails and "The Killing Spirit" (311) has no place.[23]

(3)

Landscape

As an artist with a professional interest in theater, Williams displayed a flair for dramatic scenery. In *Imaginary Landscape* (1772), a particularly lavish and fanciful painting, Williams conjures a whimsical turret guarding a frothy bay as a fleet speeds by with the wind in its sails. His portraits, too, feature striking or picturesque backdrops, ranging from seascapes and bucolic meadows to villages and formal gardens. Even the *Self-Portrait*, set indoors in the confined space of the artist's studio, incorporates landscape. In the background, the careful viewer can just discern the hazy outlines of a sketched scene affixed to the studio wall: a leafy pastoral in which an animal grazes placidly in the foreground. A far cry from the tumultuous seascapes and lush tropical scenes depicted in *Mr. Penrose*, this picture-within-a-picture nevertheless draws our attention to the regenerative power of the New World landscape in Williams's novel.[24]

Mr. Penrose depicts terrain unlike anything extant Williams portrayed on canvas. (Late in life Williams began a "picture . . . on the subject of Penrose," but this work has not surfaced.) If he adhered to European models for his paintings, for his strikingly original fictional landscapes he drew on first-hand knowledge of the New World. Where previous writing about American nature tends toward the general, Williams prefers the specific and precise. Barbara Harrell Carson accurately remarks that Williams presents details of the natural world "not as factual tidbits interrupting the fictional flow, but as integral components of the literary work, contributing to the development of the novel's plot, characters, and themes."[25]

Like many contemporaneous writers, including J. Hector St. Jean de Crèvecoeur, William Bartram, and Thomas Jefferson, Penrose is fascinated by unusual specimens of plant and animal life. He explains that he has an "inquisitive inclination, having from a Child ever taking much delight in prying into the works and wonders of Nature" (267). This interest was by no means unusual in the period in which Williams was writing. The publication of Carl Linnaeus's *The System of Nature* (1735) catalyzed a radical transformation in the way Europeans conceived of—and wrote about—the lands they colonized. The Linnaean method of claiming and analyzing the natural world, according to which plants and animals were "subsum[ed] and reassembl[ed] . . . in a finite, totalizing order of European making," contributed to what Pratt identifies as an emerging "planetary consciousness." Although it is not difficult to extrapolate from *Mr. Penrose* this kind of precise, scientific "systematizing of nature" (as did a pirated, heavily annotated German edition of *Mr. Penrose*, titled *Der neue Robinson, oder, Tagebuch Llewellin Penroses, eines Matrosen* [1817]), Williams resolutely resists the trend to classify, label, and possess. More than its rejection of the dominant scientific discourse, however, what separates Penrose from this "European knowledge-building project" is his tendency to move seamlessly between the close study of nature and philosophical reflection. Although more often than not, Penrose simply observes and describes what he sees, taking the contemplation of nature as a worthwhile end in itself, he also draws insights about humanity from nonhuman life, much as Thoreau would do decades later.[26]

In place of the planetary consciousness Pratt describes, with its "rationalizing, extractive, dissociative understanding," Penrose advances an awareness of place that is both intensified and elevated by his belief in Providence. He muses, "Oh! how often have I been soothed in this Solitude when the divine Works of Nature have insensibly drawn me into deep contemplation" (169). Like another keen eighteenth-century observer of nature, Jonathan Edwards, Penrose finds that his empirical investigation of nature strengthens and even proves his faith. A finch-like bird whose purple and green plumage provides perfect, ever-changing camouflage amid the variegated fruit of its arboreal roost prompts him to exclaim, "How manyfold are the Wonders of our Divine Creator when our Eyes behold these things" (316). Commenting on this kind of narrative "shift from the physical to the cosmic," Carson observes that in *Mr. Penrose* "nature, humanity, and the divine are brought into dizzying intersection."[27]

But the landscapes and seascapes in *Mr. Penrose* are not simply "nature." They are also geographic, political, economic, and ecologic. In Pratt's reading, the eighteenth-century planetary consciousness paralleled European efforts to map interior continental spaces. She explains, "The systematic surface mapping of the globe correlates with an expanding search for commercially exploitable resources, markets, and lands to colonize." More recently, the historical geographer Karl H. Offen has argued that the "spatial practices" of Amerindians–including their political alliances, warfare, trading practices, and diplomatic efforts–contributed substantively to colonial maps of the Mosquito Coast. While Spanish maps emphasized the threat of Mosquito power to Spanish interests, English maps reinforced Britain's strategic alliances with the Mosquito people by emphasizing their sovereignty. Offen explains: "British cartographic strategies common in North America that possessively transformed place-names, or justified settlement by referring to lands as empty or Indians as 'savages,' were entirely absent in Mosquitia." These two complementary perspectives on eighteenth-century cartography–the colonizers' mapping of colonial space and the "mapping back" of colonized peoples–provide valuable templates for thinking about European and indigenous space and the complexity of geographical representation in *Mr. Penrose*.[28]

The effort to map continental interiors was preceded, as Pratt notes, by "navigational mapping [which] is linked with the search for trade routes." This link is borne out in the early chapters of *Mr. Penrose*, in which Penrose scrupulously records longitude, latitude, depths, dates, and other navigational details as he traverses the seas in vessels bearing commercial cargo or protecting British commerce. Even after many years on land, Penrose conceives the idea of "draughting" (mapping) the harbor near his "Castle," since he knows "all the Bearings and distances full well by long and Frequent observations" (330). Similarly, the oceanography of *Mr. Penrose* is inscribed by an intricate network of transatlantic and hemispheric trade routes. Even as a castaway Penrose benefits from the fruits of exchange: although he avoids trading directly with Europeans, he does make exceptions, as when he purchases the "prize" library of a Jamaican planter from the Irish captain of a Spanish privateer. He also acquires a wealth of European-manufactured items in the form of flotsam that washes up from wrecked ships. In addition, his Indian friends bring him goats, chickens, ducks, and geese, implicitly acquired through trade with Europeans and gradually absorbed into an evolving creole ecology.[29]

For all its attention to navigation and trade, however, Penrose's journal opposes rather than endorses the imperialist interests associated with these activities. Both his Amerindian alliance and his recounting of the escaped slave's narrative reflect an awareness of environmental knowledge as a tool of resistance. In addition, his attention to ocean-going traffic exposes the confluence of military (or paramilitary) and commercial interests–both legal and illegal. (As Offen points out, the contraband trade was "an important feature of the Mosquitia until independence."[30]) This relationship comes into focus with the end of the Seven Years' War as the battle for the seas is reconfigured. With Spanish "Guardacostas" from Cartagena patrolling the waters "to prevent contraband trade" (294), while Fair Traders from "Pensilvania, New York, Maryland or New England" cruise the coastline "upon what they call the fair thing" (296), the novel's geopolitical space seems to realign along an invisible hemispheric North-South axis.

In *The Environmental Imagination: Thoreau, Nature Writing, and the Formation of American Culture*, Lawrence Buell defines four characteristics of "environmentally oriented" texts: "the non-human environment is present not merely as a framing device but as a presence that begins to suggest that human history is implicated in natural history"; "the human interest is not understood to be the only legitimate interest"; "human accountability to the environment is part of the text's ethical orientation"; and the text manifests "some sense of the environment as a process rather than as a constant or a given."[31] Readers will have little difficulty locating these characteristics in *Mr. Penrose*, although they might disagree about their application and implications. There is no sense in Williams's novel of the "environmental dissonance" (4)–defined by Pineda as a "nagging" sense of discord "between the abundance of [the] natural environment and the stagnation of the [local] economies"–that would become endemic in the region by the twentieth century. Instead, the novel emphasizes what twenty-first-century readers might term sustainability. Penrose may miss the "onions and garlick" (72) of his native island, but he does not want for the necessities of life. Through hunting, fishing, gathering, and the cultivation of his "plantation"–the latter activity connecting the novel with the domestic and georgic traditions in American nature writing–Penrose, his family, and friends can get what they need and enough extra to protect themselves from shortages, but with no attempt to accrue a surplus for trade or profit. In polar opposition to the Puritan work ethic and the drive for material success valorized in Franklin's *Autobiography*, Penrose pronounces his community "perfectly happy if we could but be content as we wanted for nothing but such things as we could well do without" (196).[32]

From the restless youth swept up in the flurry of European expansion, Penrose achieves his greatest victory by learning to live content in "a little society hid away from all the World" (196). For his part, Penrose has few regrets about the portion of his life spent in exile. Unlike John Winthrop, who conceived of the Godly society of Massachusetts Bay as a "City on a Hill," shining forth like a beacon of hope to the rest of the world, Penrose has no interest in expanding his sphere of influence, evangelizing about his way of life, or attracting converts. Instead, he is fully satisfied to live apart from "life's great hurry" (121). For Penrose, his family, and the voluntary members of his "Elected" society, no greater satisfaction exists than to "[dwell] Sequstered from the society of Europeans, out of the knowledge Of all trade and what the busy world were about" (373).

(4)

Despite its realism, the image Williams presents in the *Self-Portrait* is deceptive. The momentary glimpse of the artist captured on canvas belies the countless hours, invisible to the viewer, that Williams spent composing at his easel, reconceiving and perfecting this idealized self-image. A composite construction, the *Self-Portrait* silently effaces the lapse of time. In contrast, Penrose's journal draws attention to time, segmenting it, articulating it, and marking it out. As a castaway, Penrose becomes preoccupied with time-keeping, adopting alternative methods to record the passage of time: committing important dates to memory, collecting shells to use as counters, marking trees, and ultimately writing in the journal that descends to us today.

Throughout *Mr. Penrose*, Williams offers images and dialogue pointing to parallel systems of comprehending or "reckoning" (60, 158) time. Time functions differently in the early, European sequences and the later Mesoamerican portion of the novel. To Penrose's Indian friends, incidents long ago in the historical past occurred in human or ancestral time, referred to as their "old fathers time" (195); environmental time, as "when the very old trees were but small" (95); or even cosmological time, for example, "when the Moon was a little Star" (95). In contrast, Penrose's journal, by virtue of its very form, seems to contain and control time. Like the Indian Harry, who shakes an hourglass with determination, convinced he can make the sand flow more rapidly, Penrose uses the journal's form to manipulate the narrative passage of time. With entries accruing year by year, the *Journal* seems to accelerate and decelerate time. Extended periods can be telescoped into shorter entries in which "empty" time seems to collapse. Interleaved with these brief sections, Penrose inserts longer, more detailed entries in which time seems to slow down and thicken, allowing narrator and reader alike to linger over passing occurrences or "look inward and reflect" (302). Midway through the journal, the moment at which Penrose, having acquired paper and writing materials (in August 1754), "catches up" with the passage of time marks a pivot between a long retrospective view and a more immediate recording of recent events. Possibly corresponding to the period when Williams began composing *Mr. Penrose*, this narrative transition can be imagined as one "bookend" of the writing process that constitutes the journal's creation.[33]

Coinciding with the final pages of the novel, the other "bookend" is the "transmittal letter" that concludes the volume. A bridge between the fictional story of Penrose and the history of the novel's composition and dissemination, this epistle, signed by "Paul Taylor," contains two dates that are suffused with historical resonance: 1776, the year the completed journal passed into Taylor's hands, and 1783, the year indicated in the dateline of the letter itself. Coinciding with the Declaration of Independence and the Treaty of Paris, respectively, these dates are remarkable for the seven-year gap they frame. Like the Seven Years War, earlier in the novel, the period bracketed by these dates marks a cataclysmic phase in the intersecting histories of Europe and the Americas. Yet on this subject, too, *Mr. Penrose* is, ironically, utterly silent. Despite its post-Revolutionary New York dateline, the letter makes no reference to the rebellion of the thirteen colonies, the long war for independence, or the beginning of the new republic. Nor does it allude to imperialist developments closer to the scene of the novel's action, where Spain, in response to the American Revolution, attempted–but failed–to drive British colonists from the Mosquito Coast. Similarly, the radical geographic decentering of Penrose's account shifts our attention from the metanarrative of Euro-American history and invites us to live vicariously at the very margin of empire.[34]

Like Williams's *Self-Portrait*, with its layered renditions of writer and painter, *Mr. Penrose* is a palimpsest in which readers can explore multiple layers of meaning. It may have seemed an outlier in American literature fifty years ago, but in the new American Studies, with its spatial, temporal, diasporic, and ecocritical turns, this novel could hardly be more central. Readers may wonder what it means to begin the timeline of American fiction with *Mr. Penrose*. What is at stake, after all, in the designation "first American novel"? (How) Does literary history change when this book, and not some other, becomes the point of origin on a timeline that continues up to the present and projects forward into the future? Readers will disagree on the extent to which the novel reproduces the ideologies it simultaneously critiques; the extent to which Penrose's "colony" problematizes his anti-imperialist stance; the degree to which his own benevolent authoritarianism compromises the autonomy of the individuals who comprise this familial, consensual society; and the degree to which its patriarchal hierarchy rests on an assumption of European (or British) and male superiority. Such questions, and the voices that enter into dialogue in response to them, will ensure that *Mr. Penrose* is valued not merely as an enjoyable read (which it is) but as an important book for current and future generations to consider.

SARAH WADSWORTH

NOTES

1. *The New-York Gazette and the Weekly Mercury*, May 8, 1769. Reproduced in Rita Susswein Gottesman, comp., *The Arts and Crafts in New York* (New York: New York Historical Society, 1938), 1:7.
2. In several respects, *Mr. Penrose* resembles Daniel Defoe's *Robinson Crusoe* (1719). For a detailed discussion of this aspect of the novel, see David Howard Dickason, *William Williams: Novelist and Painter of Colonial America, 1727–1791* (Bloomington: Indiana University Press, 1970), 100–114.
3. Although the anonymous *The Female American; or, The Adventures of Unca Eliza Winkfield* (1767) features a half-Indian, half-English heroine, its status as "American" is by no means certain. See *The Female American; or, The Adventures of Unca Eliza Winkfield*, ed. Michelle Burnham (Peterborough, Ont.: Broadview Press, 2001).
4. On the "first American novel," see, for example, Cathy N. Davidson, *Revolution and the Word: The Rise of the Novel in America* (New York: Oxford University Press, 1986; 2004), chap. 5. To Davidson, who places Williams's novel in the nineteenth century (based on the posthumous, heavily revised 1815 edition), *Mr. Penrose* is an example of early American picaresque. See *Revolution and the Word*, 169–170, 171–172. For a more recent transatlantic approach, see Melissa Homestead, "The Beginnings of the American Novel," *The Oxford Handbook of Early American Literature*, ed. Kevin J. Hayes (New York: Oxford University Press, 2008), chap. 23.
5. Recent issues of *PMLA* have explored many of these approaches. See, for example, discussions of hemispheric studies (January 2009), oceanic studies (May 2010), and sustainability (May 2012). On the pitfalls of the nationalist "origins" model, see Ralph Bauer, "Early American Literature and American Literary History at the 'Hemispheric Turn,'" *Early American Literature* 45 (2010): 217–233.
6. James Thomas Flexner, *The History of American Painting. Vol. 1: First Flowers of Our Wilderness* (New York: Dover, 1969), 180.
7. E. P. Richardson, "William Williams–A Dissenting Opinion," *American Art Journal* 4 (1972): 17; John Eagles, "The Beggar's Legacy," *Blackwood's Edinburgh Magazine* 77 (March 1855): 267–268. For more on Williams, West, and the "problem of chronology," see Dickason, *William Williams*, 7–52.

8. Dickason, *William Williams*, 78–99.

9. The inflammatory name of the War of Jenkins' Ear alludes to an earlier incident in which a Spanish officer severed the ear of an English captain in the West Indies whom he suspected of piracy. The War of the Austrian Succession was known as King George's War in the colonies. See Eric Nellis, *An Empire of Regions: A Brief History of Colonial British America* (Toronto: University of Toronto Press, 2010), 201–203 and J. H. Elliott, *Empires of the Atlantic World: Britain and Spain in America, 1492–1830* (New Haven, CT: Yale University Press, 2006), 233.

10. Daniel K. Richter, *Facing East from Indian Country: A Native History of Early America* (Cambridge: Harvard University Press, 2003); Mary Louise Pratt, *Imperial Eyes: Travel Writing and Transculturation* (London: Routledge, 1992; 2008), 35–36. On Spain's efforts to tighten its control, see Baron L. Pineda, *Shipwrecked Identities: Navigating Race on Nicaragua's Mosquito Coast* (New Brunswick, NJ: Rutgers University Press, 2006), 48.

11. Pineda, *Shipwrecked Identities*, 22, 27–29, 46; Elliott, *Empires of the Atlantic World*, 98. Columbus, whose New World adventures ignited the Amerindian slave trade, visited the Mosquito Coast on his fourth voyage (1502). Forty years later, the Dominican friar Bartolomé de las Casas estimated that the Spanish had transported 500,000 Indians to Panama and Peru. Although Spain officially outlawed the Indian slave trade in 1542 (largely in response to Las Casas's *A Short Account of the Destruction of the Indies*), the capture and sale of Amerindian slaves continued through most of the nineteenth century.

12. Pineda, *Shipwrecked Identities*, 36, 53–54. See also Linda A. Newson, *Indian Survival in Colonial Nicaragua* (Norman, OK: University of Oklahoma Press, 1987).

13. Nellis, *Empire of Regions*, xx. See also Andrew Jackson O'Shaughnessy, *An Empire Divided: The American Revolution and the British Caribbean* (Philadelphia: University of Pennsylvania Press, 2000), chap. 1–2.

14. For a relevant discussion of piracy, ethnicity, and "motley crews," see Peter Linebaugh and Marcus Rediker, *The Many-Headed Hydra: Sailors, Slaves, Commoners, and the Hidden History of the Revolutionary Atlantic* (Boston: Beacon Press, 2000), chap. 5–7.

15. According to what Pineda terms the "shipwreck theory,"

> The shipwreck of a slave ship in the area of the Mosquito Keys in the 1640s is presumed to have begun a long-term migratory trend in which escaped slaves of African descent trickled into the Mosquito Coast. This trend ultimately resulted in the rise of the Miskito as a new 'raza mixta' (mixed race) or 'hybrid' Indian group (34).

16. Olaudah Equiano, *The Interesting Narrative of the Life of Olaudah Equiano, Written by Himself*, 2nd ed., ed. Robert J. Allison (Boston: Bedford / St. Martin's, 2007), vol. 2, chap. 11.

17. John Holm, "An 18th-Century Novel from the Miskito Coast: What Was Creolized?" Paper presented to the Meeting of the Society for Pidgin and Creole Linguistics (Accra, Ghana, Aug. 3–5, 2011), 20.

18. The art historian E. P. Richardson speculated, "Perhaps Williams had first wished to be remembered as a writer and on second thought deemed more memorable his career as a painter." See Richardson, *American Paintings and Related Pictures in the Henry Francis du Pont Winterthur Museum* (Charlottesville, VA: University Press of Virginia, 1986), plate 39. To the art historian Susan Rather, the x-ray photographs "[show] him holding what appears to be a book in his left hand while draping his right arm over the back of a chair" (840). See Rather, "Benjamin West's Professional Endgame and the Historical Conundrum of William Williams," *William and Mary Quarterly* 59 (2002): 840, 842n45.

19. The phrase "scholar adventurer" comes from Richard D. Altick, *The Scholar Adventurers* (New York: MacMillan, 1950). For a useful (but dated) survey of Williams's surviving paintings, see Dickason, *William Williams*, 138–180 and 207–217.

20. Holm, "An 18th Century Novel from the Miskito Coast," 20. Holm finds in *Mr. Penrose* "what a creolist can hardly hope for"–"dialogue in the local vernacular that was still undergoing restructuring." Based on close textual analysis, Holm has identified "evidence . . . [to] confirm that the contact [depicted in *Mr. Penrose*] was in fact with the Rama and Miskito of Nicaragua's Caribbean Coast." This evidence "includes words from Rama, Miskito, Spanish and African languages and phrases suggesting convergences with Creole structures" (1). For further information, see John Holm, *The Creole English of Nicaragua's Miskito Coast: Its Sociolinguistic History and a Comparative Study of Its Lexicon and Syntax* (Ph.D. dissertation, University College, University of London, 1978).

21. As Laura Brown has argued, "The female figure, through its simultaneous connections with commodification and trade on the one hand, and violence and difference on the other, plays a central role in the constitution of this mercantile capitalist ideology" (3). See Brown, *Ends of Empire: Women and Ideology in Early Eighteenth-Century English Literature* (Ithaca, NY: Cornell University Press, 1993).

22. Pratt, *Imperial Eyes*, 84–85.

23. Readers of Pratt's *Imperial Eyes* may find elements of what she terms the "anti-conquest" in *Mr. Penrose*. As Pratt relates, however, in anti-conquest narratives, "'cultural harmony through romance' always breaks down," and the "outcomes" follow a predictable pattern: "the lovers are separated, the European is reabsorbed by Europe, and the non-European dies an early death" (95).

24. As Barbara Harrell Carson argues, *Mr. Penrose* demonstrates "the capacity of the natural world of the Americas to stimulate moral and spiritual growth in the attentive observer" and effect "the familiar American transformation: a developing sense of 'psychic at-homeness' in an alien environment." See Barbara Harrell Carson, "'I have heard [. . .] things Grow': Uses of Nature in William

Williams's Colonial Novel," *ISLE: Interdisciplinary Studies in Literature and Environment* 17 (2010): 495, 486.

25. Carson, "'I have heard [. . .] things Grow,'" 20n8, 5. According to J. H. Elliott, Williams's portraiture imitates European models. See *Empires of the Atlantic World*, plate 33. On Williams's "picture . . . on the subject of Penrose," see Dickason, William Williams, 48. Note also the opening of Chapter 16 of *Mr. Penrose*, in which Penrose imagines the scene as an "Ingenious Artist" might depict it.

26. Pratt, *Imperial Eyes*, 35–37.

27. Pratt, *Imperial Eyes*, 38; Carson, "'I have heard [. . .] things Grow,'" 7.

28. Pratt, *Imperial Eyes*, 30; Karl H. Offen, "Creating Mosquitia: Mapping Amerindian Spatial Practices in Eastern Central America, 1629–1779," *Journal of Historical Geography* 33 (2007), 264, 280–281.

29. Pratt, *Imperial Eyes*, 30. I borrow the term "creole ecology" from J. R. McNeill, *Mosquito Empires: Ecology and War in the Greater Caribbean, 1620–1914* (Cambridge: Cambridge University Press, 2010). On the "chain of ecological events" resulting from these new "pressures on the environment," see Carson, "'I have heard [. . .] things Grow,'" 17–18.

30. Offen, "Creating Mosquitia," 266. For relevant discussions of "Indian sagacity" and "topographies of slave knowledge," see Susan Scott Parrish, *American Curiosity: Cultures of Natural History in the Colonial British Atlantic World* (Chapel Hill, NC: University of North Carolina Press, 2006), chap. 6–7.

31. Lawrence Buell, *The Environmental Imagination: Thoreau, Nature Writing, and the Formation of American Culture* (Cambridge, MA: Harvard University Press, 1995), 7–8.

32. See Timothy Sweet, "Projecting Early American Environmental Writing," *American Literary History* 22 (Summer 2010): 425–428 for a relevant discussion of biogeography; on the domestic and georgic traditions, see Annette Kolodny, *The Land Before Her: Fantasy and Experience of the American Frontiers, 1630–1860* (Chapel Hill: University of North Carolina Press, 1984) and Sweet, *American Georgics: Economy and Environment in Early American Literature* (Philadelphia: University of Pennsylvania Press, 2002), respectively.

33. For Dickason's theory of the novel's composition dates, see *William Williams*, 74–75.

34. See Wallace Brown, "The Mosquito Shore and the Bay of Honduras during the Era of the American Revolution," *Belizean Studies* 18 (1990), 43–71. On the long-range consequences of "dislodging the US experience from a central position of normativity" in hemispheric scholarship (226), see Bauer, "Early American Literature," 220–226.

Contributors

WILLIAM WILLIAMS (1727–1791) was a professional painter and land-scape artist who tutored a young Benjamin West. Williams primarily resided in Philadelphia and New York and is thought to have substantially completed *Mr. Penrose* shortly before the Revolutionary War.

DAVID HOWARD DICKASON (1907–1974) was Professor of English at Indiana University and a specialist in American literature. He recovered William Williams's original manuscript, which is now housed at Indiana University's Lilly Library.

SARAH WADSWORTH is Associate Professor of English at Marquette University. A specialist in eighteenth- and nineteenth-century American literature, book history, and children's literature, she is author of *In the Company of Books: Literature and Its "Classes" in Nineteenth-Century America* and (with Wayne A. Wiegand) of *Right Here I See My Own Books: The Woman's Building Library at the World's Columbian Exposition.*